Praise for Alex Barclay's
Darkhouse

'*Darkhouse* is a terrific debut by an exciting new writer' *Independent on Sunday*

'Excellent summer reading . . . Barclay has the confidence to move her story along slowly, and deftly explores the relationships between her characters . . .' *Sunday Telegraph*

'With no-hold, non-stop action moving seamlessly between North Texas, New York and Waterford, Barclay confidently delivers a knockout first novel' *Irish Times*

'This rips along and shows great technique for a debut novel. Take my word for it we will hear more of young Barclay'
Irish Independent

'A great thriller . . . There are loads of twists and turns, it will make your bus journey home fly by!' *B*

Visit www.AuthorTracker.co.uk for exclusive information on your favourite HarperCollins authors.

Alex Barclay

Alex Barclay lives just outside Dublin.
Darkhouse is her debut novel.

ALEX BARCLAY

Darkhouse

HarperCollins*Publishers*

HarperCollins*Publishers*
77–85 Fulham Palace Road,
Hammersmith, London W6 8JB

www.harpercollins.co.uk

This paperback edition 2006
1 3 5 7 9 8 6 4 2

First published in Great Britain by
HarperCollins*Publishers* 2006

James Baldwin quote with the kind permission of
Gloria Smart for the Estate of James Baldwin

ISBN-13 978 0 00 781005 5

Set in Meridien by Palimpsest Book Production Limited,
Polmont, Stirlingshire

Printed in the UK by CPI Bookmarque, Croydon, CR0 4TD

To Brian, my hero

To my parents

'The sea rises, the light fails, lovers cling to each other, and children cling to us. The moment we cease to hold each other, the moment we break faith with one another, the sea engulfs us and the light goes out.'

JAMES ARTHUR BALDWIN

PROLOGUE

New York City

Edgy hands slid across the narrow belt, securing it in place on the tiny eight-year-old waist. Donald Riggs pointed to the small box attached.

'This is like a pager, honey, so the police can find you,' came his lazy drawl.

'Because you're going home now. If your mommy is a good girl. Is your mommy a good girl, Hayley?'

Hayley's mouth moved, but she couldn't speak. She bit down on her lip and looked up at him, beaming innocence. She gave three short nods. He smiled and slowly stroked her dark hair.

The fourth day without her daughter was the final day Elise Gray would have to endure a pain she could barely express. She breathed deeply through anger and rage, guilty that it was caused more by her husband than the stranger who took away her child. Gordon Gray's company had just gone public, making him a very wealthy man and an instant target for kidnap and ransom. The family was insured – but that was all about the money, and she didn't care about the money. Her family was her life and Hayley, her shining light.

Now here she was, parked outside her own apartment at the wheel of her husband's BMW, waiting for this creep to call her on the cell phone he left with the ransom note. Yet it was Gordon who dominated her thoughts. The insurance company had told the couple to vary their routine but, good God, what would Gordon know about varying his routine? This was a man who brewed coffee, made toast, then lined up an apple, a banana and a peach yoghurt – in that order – every morning for breakfast. Every morning. *You stupid man*, thought Elise. *You stupid man and your stupid, stupid, rituals. No wonder someone was waiting outside the apartment for you. Of course you were going to show up, because you show up every day at the same time bringing Hayley home from school. No detours, no stops for candy, just right on time, every time.*

She banged her head on the steering wheel as the cell phone on the seat beside her lit up. As she fumbled to answer it, she realised it was playing *Sesame Street*. He'd actually set the tone to *Sesame Street*, the sick bastard.

'Drive, bitch,' each word slow and deliberate.

'Where am I going?' she asked.

'To get your daughter back, if you've been behavin' yourself.' He hung up.

Elise started the engine, put her foot on the gas and swung gently into the traffic. Her heart was thumping. The wire chafed her back. By calling the police in that first hour, she had set in motion a whole new ending to this ordeal. She just wasn't sure if it was the right ending.

Detective Joe Lucchesi sat in the driver's seat, watching everything, his head barely moving. His dark hair was cut tight, with short slashes of grey at the sides. He questioned again whether Elise Gray was strong enough to wear a wire. He didn't know where the kidnapper would lead her or how she would react if she had to get any closer to him than the other end of a phone. He had barely raised his hand to his face when Danny Markey – his close friend of twenty-five years and partner for five – started talking.

'See, you got the kinda jaw a man can stroke. If I did that, I'd look like an idiot.'

Joe stared at him. Danny was missing a jawline. His small head blended without contour into his skinny neck. Everything about him was pale – his skin, his freckles, his blue eyes. He squinted at Joe.

'What?' he said.

Joe's gaze shifted back to Elise Gray's car. It
started to move. Danny gripped the dashboard.
Joe knew it was because he expected him to pull
right out. Danny had a theory; one of his 'black
and whites', as he called them. 'There are people
in life who check for toilet paper before taking a
crap. And there's the ones who shit straightaway
and find themselves fucked.' Joe was often singled
out. 'You're a checker, Lucchesi. I'm a shitter,' he
would say. So they waited.

'You know Old Nic is getting out next month,'
said Danny. Victor Nicotero was a lifer, a traffic
cop one month shy of retiring. 'You goin' to the
party?'

Joe shook his head, then sucked in a sharp
breath against the pain that pulsed at his temples.
He could see Danny hanging for an answer. He
didn't give him one. He reached into the driver's
door and pulled out a bottle of Advil and a blister
pack of decongestants. He popped two of each,
swallowing them with a mouthful from a blue
energy drink hot from the sun.

'Oh, I forgot,' said Danny, 'your in-laws are in
from Paris that night, right?' He laughed. 'A six-
hour dinner with people you can't understand.'
He laughed again.

Joe pulled out after Elise Gray. Three cars
behind him, a navy blue Crown Vic with FBI
Agents Maller and Holmes followed his lead.

*   *   *

Elise Gray drove aimlessly, searching the sidewalks for Hayley as though she would show up on a corner and jump in. The tinny ringtone broke the silence. She grabbed the phone to her ear.

'Where are you now, Mommy?' His calm voice chilled her.

'2nd Avenue at 63rd Street.'

'Head south and make a left onto the bridge at 59th Street.'

'Left onto the bridge at 59th Street.' Click.

The three cars made their way across the bridge to Northern Boulevard East, everyone's fate in the hands of Donald Riggs. He made his final call.

'Take a left onto Francis Lewis Boulevard, then left onto 29th Avenue. I'll be seein' you. On your own. At the corner of 157th and 29th.'

Elise repeated what he said. Joe and Danny looked at each other.

'Bowne Park,' said Joe.

He dialled the head of the task force, Lieutenant Crane then handed the phone to Danny and nodded for him to talk.

'Looks like the drop-off's Bowne Park. Can you call in some of the guys from the 109?' Danny put the phone on the dash.

Donald Riggs drove smoothly, his eyes moving across the road, the streets, the people. His left hand moved over the rough tangle of scars on his cheek, faded now into skin that was a pale stain on his tanned face. He checked himself in the rear-view mirror, opening his dark eyes wide. He raised a hand to run his fingers through his hair, until he remembered the gel and hairspray that held it rigid and marked by the tracks of a wide-toothed comb. At the back, it stopped dead at his collar, the right side folding over the left. He had a special lady to impress. He had splashed on aftershave from a dark blue bottle and gargled cinnamon mouthwash.

He turned around to check on the girl, lying on the floor in the back of the car and covered by a stinking blanket.

It was four-thirty p.m. and five detectives were sitting in the twentieth Precinct office of Lieutenant Terry Crane as Old Nic shuffled by, patting down his silver hair. *Maybe they're talking about my retirement present*, he thought, narrowing his grey eyes, leaning towards the muffled voices. *If it's a carriage clock, I'll kill them.* A watch he could cope with. Even better, his boy Lucchesi had picked up on his hints and spread the word – Old Nic was planning to write his memoirs and what he needed for that was something he'd never had before: a classy pen, something silver, something he could take out with his good notebook and tell a story with. He put a bony shoulder to the door and his cap slipped on his narrow head. He heard Crane briefing the detectives.

'We've just found out the perp is heading for

Bowne Park in Queens. We still don't have an ID. We got nothing from canvassing the neighbourhood, we got nothing from the scene – the guy jumped out, picked up the girl and drove off at speed, leaving nothing behind. We don't even know what he was driving. This is just from the father who heard the screech from the lobby. We also got nothing from the package the perp dropped back the following day, just a few common fibres from the tape, nothing workable, no prints.'

Old Nic opened the door and stuck his head in. 'Where'd this kidnapping happen?'

'Hey, Nic,' said Crane, '72nd and Central Park West.' With no clues to his retirement present apparent in the office, Old Nic moved on, until a thought came to him and he doubled back.

'This guy is headed for Bowne Park, you gotta figure the area's familiar to him. Maybe he was going that way the day of the kidnapping, so he could have headed east across 42nd Street to the FDR. I used to work at the 17th and if your guy ran a red light, there's a camera at 42nd and 2nd might have given him a Kodak moment. You could check with the D.O.T.'

'Scratch that carriage clock,' Crane said to the group, winking. 'Nice one, Nic. We're on it.' Old Nic raised a hand as he left. 'You just want to hug the guy,' said Crane as he put a call in to the Department of Transportation. Thirty minutes later, he had five hits, three with criminal records. But only one had a prior for attempted kidnapping.

Joe could feel the drugs kick in. A warm cloud of relief moved up his jaw. He opened and closed his mouth. His ears crackled. He breathed through his nose and out slowly through his mouth. Six years ago, everything from his neck up started to go wrong – he got headaches, earaches, pain in his jaw so excruciating that some days it was unbearable to eat or even talk. Strangers didn't react well to a dumb cop.

Hayley Gray was thinking about *Beauty and the Beast*. Everyone thought the Beast was mean and scary, but he was really a nice guy and he gave Belle soup and he played in the snow with her. Maybe the man wasn't all bad. Maybe he'd turn out to be nice too. The car stopped suddenly and she felt cold. She heard her mommy shouting.

'Hayley! Hayley!' Then, 'Where's my daughter? You've got your money. Give me back my daughter, you bastard!'

Her mommy sounded really scared. She'd never heard her shout like that before or say bad words. She was banging on the window. Then the car was moving again, faster this time, and she couldn't hear her mommy any more. Donald Riggs threw open the knapsack, his right hand pulling at the tightly-packed wads.

Danny reached for his radio to run the plates of the brown Chevy Impala that was driving away from Elise Gray: 'North Homicide to Central.' He waited for Central to acknowledge, then gave the number. 'Adam David Larry 4856, A.D.L. 4856.'

Joe was on Citywide One, a two-way channel that linked him to Maller and Holmes and the 109 guys in the park. He spoke quickly and clearly.

'OK, he's got the money, but he hasn't said anything about dropping off the girl. We need to take it easy here. We don't know where he has her. Everyone stand by.'

Danny turned to him and gave his usual line. 'And his voice was restored and there was much rejoicing.'

Halfway down 29th Avenue, Donald Riggs stopped the car, reached back and lifted the blanket.

'Get up and get out of my car.'

Hayley pulled herself onto the seat. 'Thank you,' she said. 'I knew you'd be nice.'

She opened the door, got out and looked around until she could see her mother. Then she ran as fast as her little legs could carry her.

Joe and Danny were behind Riggs now, Agents Maller and Holmes behind them. Danny was holding for the information on the car. Joe was distracted. He had a feeling this was bad; the kind of bad that happens when everything is too easy, when the maniac is so fucked up, it gets scary calm. He looked at Danny.

'Why would the guy give this woman her child back without a scratch?' He shook his head. 'It's too easy.'

He slammed on the brakes and, arm out the window, waved the Crown Vic ahead of him. Agent Maller gave a quick nod and took the right, eyes locked on the car ahead.

Joe turned around and saw the swaying shape of a mother and daughter reunited. Too easy. He got out of the car, grabbing his vibrating cell phone from the dash. He flipped it open. It was Crane.

'We got your perp.'

'Brown Chevy Impala,' said Joe.

'Yup. '85. Riggs, Donald, white male, thirty-four, born in shitsville, Texas, locked up for petty larceny, scams, bad cheques, collared at the scene of a previous kidnapping.' He hesitated.

'And be advised, Lucchesi, he was done for C4 in Nevada in '97. We got ourselves a boom-boom banjo-player.' Joe dropped the phone, his heart pounding.

'I got ESU and hostage negotiation on stand-by,' Crane said to no-one.

Joe began to run. He willed his heart to carry the new pace his legs had taken up.

* * *

Donald Riggs had reached the corner of 154th and 29th. He rocked back and forth in his seat, skinny fingers clenching the wheel, eyes darting around, taking in everything, registering nothing. But something caught his eye. Behind him, a black Ford Taurus pulled into the kerb and a dark blue Crown Vic overtook it. A rare heightened awareness flared inside him. He kept driving, his breath shallow as he slowed to a stop at the next corner. Then a sudden burst of activity drew him in. Two men stepped out of a Con Ed van by the entrance to the park. They walked quickly to the back and pulled open the doors. Two others stepped out. In the rear-view mirror, the dark blue car loomed back into sight, driving alarmingly on the wrong side of the road. Donald Riggs lurched across the passenger side, grabbed the knapsack, pushed open the door and tore out of the car towards the park. By the time Maller and Holmes screeched to a stop seconds later, the four FBI agents in Con Ed uniforms were surrounding an empty car. 'Go, go, go,' roared Maller and all six men ran for the park.

'You used my pager!' says Hayley, amazed, pointing down at the belt around her waist and the black box with its flashing yellow light. Her mother stands up, confused, searching out anyone who can understand what this is, but knowing in her heart the answer. Her pleading eyes stop at Joe.

* * *

'You stupid bitch, you stupid bitch, you stupid bitch . . .' Donald Riggs is running wildly across the park, clutching at his knapsack, concentrating on a small dark object in his hand. He stops, rooted. His eyes widen and deaden as his mind and body shut down. Then a twitching, after-thought of a movement connects the thumb of his right hand to the black button of a detonator.

Elise Gray knows her fate. She makes a final grab for her child, hugging her desperately to her chest. 'I love you, sweetheart, I love you, sweetheart, I love you.' Then a frightening, shockingly loud blast tears through them, the bright light stinging Joe's eyes as he watches, now motionless. Then red and pink and white, splattering grotesquely, as a confetti shower of leaves and splintered bark falls around the place where a mother and daughter, seconds earlier, didn't even make it to goodbye.

Joe was absolutely still, paralysed. He couldn't breathe. He felt a new throbbing pressure in his jaw. His eyes streamed. He slowly sensed warm concrete against his face. He pulled himself up from the pavement. Too many emotions flooded his body. The radio on his belt crackled to life. It was Maller.

'We lost him. He's in the park, heading your way, along by the playground.'

Now one emotion overrode all others: rage.

* * *

'I don't think your mommy was a good girl, Hayley, I don't think your mommy was a good girl,' Riggs was howling, ranting, rocking wildly, bent over, his face contorted. He clawed desperately at the inside pocket of his coat. Joe burst through the trees, suddenly faced with this deranged display, but ready, his Glock 9mm drawn.

'Put your hands where I can see them.'

He couldn't remember his name. Riggs looked up; his arm jerked free, swinging wildly to his right and back again, as Joe pumped six bullets into his chest. Riggs fell backwards, landing to stare sightless at the sky, arms outstretched, palms open. Joe walked over, looking for a weapon he knew did not exist.

But something did lie in Riggs' upturned palm – a maroon and gold pin: a hawk, wings aloft, beak pointing earthwards. He had been gripping it so tightly, it had pierced his palm.

Ely State Prison, Nevada, two days later

'Shut up, you fuckin' freak. Shut your fuckin' ass. I got National Geographic in my fuckin' ears twenty-four/seven, you sick son of a bitch. Who gives a shit about your fuckin' birds, Pukey Dukey? Who gives a fuckin' shit?'

Duke Rawlins lay face down on the bottom bunk of his eight by ten cell. Every muscle in his long, wiry body tensed.

'Don't call me that.' His face was set into a frown, his lips pale and full. He rubbed his head, disturbing the dirty blond hair that grew long at the back, but was cut short above his chill blue eyes.

'Call you what?' said Kane. 'Pukey Dukey?'

Duke hated group. They made him say shit that was nobody's business. He couldn't believe this asshole, Kane, knew what the kids used to call him in school.

'This hawk has that wing span, this hawk ripped a jack rabbit a new asshole, this hawk is alpha, this hawk is beta, and this little hawk goes wee, wee, wee, all the way home to you, you sick son of a bitch.'

Duke leapt from his bunk, sliding his arm from under the pillow, pulling out a pared-down, sharpened spike of Plexiglas. He jabbed it towards Kane, who jerked his head back hard against the wall. He jabbed again and again, slicing the air close enough to Kane's face to let him know he meant it.

The warden's voice stopped him.

'Lookin' to book yourself a one-way ticket to Carson City, Rawlins?' Carson City was where Ely's death row inmates took their last breath.

Duke spun around as he unlocked the door and pushed into the cell. The warden smoothed on a surgical glove and calmly took the weapon from a man he knew was too smart to screw up this close to his release.

'Thought you might like to read this, Rawlins,' he said, holding up a printout from the *New York Times* website.

Duke walked slowly towards the warden and stopped. The pockmarked face of Donald Riggs jumped right at him. KIDNAP ENDS IN FATAL EXPLOSION. Mother and daughter dead. Kidnapper fatally wounded. Duke went white. He reached out for the paper, pulling it from the warden's hand as his legs slid from under him and he slumped on to the floor. 'Not Donnie, not Donnie, not Donnie,' he screamed over and over in his head. Before he passed out, his body suddenly heaved and he threw up all over the floor, spraying the warden's shoes and pants.

Kane jumped down from his bed, kicking Duke in the gut because he could. His laugh was deep and satisfied. 'Pukey fuckin' Dukey. Man, this is quality viewing.'

'Get back to your business, Kane,' said the warden as he turned his back on the stinking cell.

ONE

Waterford, Ireland, one year later

Danaher's is the oldest bar in the south east; stone-floored, wooden and dim. Salvaged timber from unlucky ships stretches in beams under the low ceiling, making shelves for rusty tankards and tangled green fishing nets. Fires live and die in the wide stone hearth. The mensroom is called the jacks and the jacks is outside: two stalls, one with no door. 'And we haven't had a shite stolen yet,' Ed Danaher liked to say when anyone complained.

Joe Lucchesi was undergoing an interrogation at the bar.

'Have you ever said 'Freeze, motherfucker?' asked Hugh, pushing his glasses up his nose. Hugh was tall and gangly, bowing his head as he talked, always ready to walk through a low doorway. His black hair was pulled into a frizzy

ponytail and his long fingers tucked back the
stray strands.

His friend, Ray, rolled his eyes.

'Or anything you say or do can be held against
you in a court of law?' said Hugh.

Joe laughed.

'Or found peanut shells in someone's trousers?'

'That's *CSI*, you fuckwit,' said Ray. 'Don't mind
him. Seriously, though, have you ever planted
evidence?'

They all laughed. Joe couldn't remember a
night when he had gone for a drink without being
asked about his old job. Even his friends still
pumped him for information.

'You guys need to get out more,' he said.

'Come on, nothing happens in this kip,' said
Hugh.

A kip in Ireland was a dive in America, but to
Joe, Mountcannon was far from a dive. It was a
charming fishing village that had been his home
for the past six months, thanks to his wife, Anna.
Concerned for their marriage, their son, Shaun,
and the family sanity, she had brought them here
to save what she loved. Anna wanted him to quit
after his last case, but he didn't, so they agreed
he would vest out for a year – temporary
retirement that gave him nine months to decide
whether or not he'd go back.

He didn't know then where that year would
take him. Anna was a freelance interior designer

and pitched an idea to *Vogue Living* to renovate an old building, bought by the magazine and shot in stages. The building she chose was Shore's Rock, a deserted weather-beaten lighthouse on the edge of a cliff outside Mountcannon, the village she had fallen in love with when she was seventeen.

When they got there, Joe understood how she felt. But he needed his New York fix. He would go to the local store and pick up *USA Today* or USA Two Days Ago. He'd say to Danny Markey, 'If anything big happens back home, call me a couple days later, so I'll know what you're talking about.' In New York, Ireland was Sunday afternoons and WFUV 90.7, *Forty Shades of Green* and *Galway Shawls*. But in an isolated lighthouse near a small village, the real Ireland was not all sentimental ballads . . . and it was far from simple practicalities. He could score a great pint and find a friend in any of Mountcannon's three bars, but try renting a movie, ordering in or finding an ATM. For most people, Ed Danaher played banker and barman, always happy to refill his till with the cash he had just handed out.

Joe stood up, slid some notes across the bar and said goodbye to the two men. He made his way home in fifteen minutes, enjoying the turn of the last bend when the stark, freshly painted white of the lighthouse would rise up from the dark. He pushed open the gate and walked the hundred metres along the lane to the front door.

The site was sloping, carved into the cliff side, and made up of an almost jumbled collection of buildings, dating back to the eighteen-hundreds and added to over the years until it was finally deserted in the late sixties. There were three separate two-storey buildings, two of which could be used as living spaces. The first held the hallway, the kitchen, the living room and the den on the ground floor, and the main bedroom, guest bedroom and bathroom on the first floor. The second building was like a huge basement to the first, set lower into the cliff – a darker small-windowed space. The first storey was Shaun's bedroom and the lower storey, a wine cellar. The third building was the round tower of the light-house, a separate structure to the rear of the main house. From the outside, it looked complete, but it was what lay inside that was the biggest challenge. Higher up on the site, above the house, a large shed had been transformed into a fully kitted-out workshop that Joe was still learning to use. He had made some of what Anna called the cruder furniture in the house, but she said it like a compliment, so that was good enough for him.

By the end of the year, she wanted the house to be modern and comfortable, with as many of the original features as she could keep. She was in the right part of the country for that, with carpenters, ironmongers and builders easy to find, but she learned quickly not to be as exacting in her timings as she would have been in New York. And the usual enticement of a mention in *Vogue* was hardly likely to stir these guys. But even in six months, they had helped to transform the unfulfilled potential of the dank, crumbling rooms and battered exteriors. When the family had first walked into Shore's Rock, it was as if everything had been deserted in a hurry, like some great tragedy had swept old keepers away. It stank of the sea, of damp, of rotting timber. It looked hopeless to Joe and Shaun, but Anna called it perfect dereliction.

Now all the exterior brickwork had been repainted. In the house, underfloor heating had been installed and interior walls and floorboards whitewashed. Simple white wooden furniture with modern touches added minimal decoration to the rooms. Shaun's bedroom was the first to be finished, but only after a satellite dish was installed. Anna had had to do something to stop the spread of his sixteen-year-old angst. For him, the culture shock had been intense, because he was young and his world was so small. He couldn't bear the isolation that for Anna was heaven, removed as she was from the same old faces at the same old press launches and gallery openings, transported now to another era. In Mountcannon, you knew your neighbours, you left your car unlocked and no street was unsafe.

Joe slid into bed beside Anna. 'Assume the

position,' he whispered. She smiled, half asleep, and turned her back to him as he wrapped his arm around her waist and pulled her tiny body towards him. He pressed kisses into the back of her head and fell asleep to the sound of the sea crashing against the rocks.

'Full Irish?' asked Joe, smiling. He was dressed only in jeans, standing over the stove, pointing a greasy spatula at Anna.

'No, no!' she laughed. 'I don't know how they do this every morning. Bacon, eggs, sausages, black pudding, white pudding . . .' She shook her head and walked barefoot across the floor to the cupboard. She stood on tiptoes to reach the top shelf.

'Makes a man out of you,' said Joe.

'Makes a fat man out of you,' said Anna.

'Everyone is fat to a French woman,' said Joe.

'Every American, maybe.'

'That's gotta hurt,' said Shaun, sliding into his chair at the table, stretching his legs wide at either side. 'Bring it on, Dad. I am proud to fly the American flag this morning.' He grabbed his knife and fork and smiled his father's crooked smile. The Lucchesi genes overrode the Briaudes', but what made Shaun so striking was that against the dark hair and sallow skin of his father shone the pale green eyes of his mother.

'Thank you, son,' said Joe.

'But it wouldn't do you any harm to put a shirt on,' said Shaun.

'You're just jealous. And I always fry topless,' said Joe. 'So I don't stink after.'

He dished the food out onto two plates and breathed in dramatically.

'Your mother does not know what she's missing.'

'I do,' said Anna, nodding at Joe's belly. He slapped it.

'One day of crunches, it's gone,' he said. She made a face. He was right. He had always been in shape.

'C'mon, honey,' he said. 'How am I ever going to compete with a woman who shops in the children's department?' She smiled. He pulled a white long-sleeved T-shirt over his head and walked over to the kettle. He took the cafetière down from a shelf beside it, then poured in boiling water and shook it up the sides. When the glass was hot, he threw out the water and tipped four scoops of Kenyan grounds into the bottom. He filled it with water to the edge of the chrome rim. He rinsed the plunger in boiling water and put it on top, twisting it so the opening to the spout was blocked. After four minutes, he plunged gently, watching the grains being pushed slowly to the base of the jug. He rotated the top of the plunger so the grate was lined up with the spout and the coffee would pour. Joe could never watch anyone else make coffee.

'Your father rang last night,' said Anna suddenly. Shaun's eyes widened, but he knew when to stay quiet.

'Sure he did,' said Joe, carrying the coffee to the table.

'He did. He's getting married.'

Joe stared at her. 'You're shitting me.'

'Watch your language. And I'm serious. How could I make that up? He wants you to go over.'

'Jesus Christ. Is it Pam?'

'Of course it's Pam. You're dreadful.'

'Well, you wouldn't know with that guy.'

'He's unbelievable,' said Shaun.

'Yup,' said Joe. 'Roll in the family so you'll look normal to your new husband or wife. "See? My kids are here for my wedding. They're pretty cool. I'm not an axe murderer."'

'Well . . .'

'Well, nothing.'

'Uh, Mom,' said Shaun. 'I hate to change the subject, but do you have any baby photos of me? I mean, did you bring any to Ireland?'

'You know, you would think I wouldn't bother,' said Anna, 'but they were so cute I put a few in my diary. Hold on.'

She brought her diary from the bedroom and pulled three photos from an envelope in the back.

'Look at you,' she said. She held up the first photo, a two-year-old Shaun in the bath, his face smiling through a halo of foam. Then one of him at four, in camouflage gear, holding a plastic rifle. In the third, he was blowing out five candles on a cake shaped like a beetle.

'That cake was a nightmare,' she said. 'Your father hovering over me the whole time, making sure it was anatomically correct.'

'That cake was awesome,' said Shaun. 'But I'll go with the GI shot. Cute, but politically incorrect. Like me. The secret bug life might be a bit much.'

'What's it for?' asked Anna.

'Our school website,' said Shaun. 'St Declan's is actually getting a site. We have this computer teacher, Mr Russell, who was in some massive software firm in the nineties, but burnt out and went into teaching. Anyway, he's cool. He wants every kid in fifth year to have something posted on the site with a biography. So we all have to bring in photos, kind of like before and afters. From geek to chic.'

Anna laughed. 'Well, there's nothing geeky about my little clean-cut army boy,' she said looking at the photo. 'Maybe you could be the chic to geek guy,' she said, eyeing his jeans.

'Mom, you don't know the meaning of geek.'

'Well, what is it, then? Boys in sloppy jeans with shirts down to their knees?'

'No. That's someone cool. A geek is a nerd. Think of Dad.'

She hit him with her diary. Joe laughed. Shaun

finished his breakfast, grabbed his school bag and ran.

'See you at the show tonight,' he called and the door slammed behind him.

Anna turned to Joe and pointed at him. 'Call your father.'

'OK, I'll call my fazzer,' he said. Her English was almost perfect, but 'ths' still got the better of her. She gave him a look.

'You're so exotic, Annabel,' he said, lingering on the 'l'. She gave him another look.

Sam Tallon stood in the service room on the second level of the lighthouse, shaking his head. He was a short man with a doughy chubbiness.

'My God, this brings back memories,' he said. 'The keeper would be sitting at this desk, filling out his reports . . .' He stopped and pointed. 'You'll have to get a scraper to the paint on the treads of that ladder.' Sam was Anna's restoration expert, a former engineer with the Commissioners of Irish Lights. He was sixty-eight years old and she had just made him walk up a narrow spiral staircase.

'Right,' he said and grabbed on, heaving himself up the rungs of a second ladder, then pushing through a cast iron trap door into the lantern house. His laugh echoed down to her. When she climbed up, he let out a whistle.

'You've got a job on your hands here.'

'I thought so,' said Anna, looking around at the cracked, rusty walls.

'You'll have to strip that right back,' said Sam. 'There's layers and layers of enamel there. It'll be rock hard.'

At the centre of the room was a pedestal holding a vat of mercury that supported the five-ton weight of the lighthouse lens. Only its base could be seen from the lantern house – most of it filled the gallery above. Sam checked the gauge at the side of the vat.

'Well, the mercury level has dropped a small bit. So the rollers underneath the lens are probably taking a little more weight than they're supposed to. But it's not a big problem, especially if the light's not going to be on all the time.'

'I'm just hoping I'll be able to light it at all.'

'Ah, you should be fine,' said Sam. 'I'd say they'll make you agree to light it only at a certain time and to have the beam travel inland.'

Anna held her breath as Sam studied the base of the lens, checking the clockwork mechanism that rotated it.

'I don't believe it,' said Sam eventually. 'I think it's all right. After nearly forty years. We'll need to get the weights moving, but I think you're in luck.'

'Thank God,' said Anna.

'A mantle, like the wick of a candle, burns inside that,' he said, back to the lens. 'If you didn't have a mantle, there'd be no light. And it's only a little silk thing you could fit in your pocket.' He chuckled. 'Anyway, the prisms in the lens refract the light, the lens rotates and there you have your lovely lighthouse beam.' Sam climbed the ladder inside the lens, breaking cobwebs as he went.

'It's filthy,' he said. 'You'll have to get at this later, probably after you strip the walls. And you'll need to get your hands on some new mantles, by the way – 55mm.'

They moved back down through the lighthouse and out through the old doors.

'You'll need to replace them too,' said Sam.

'They're on their way,' said Anna. He was impressed.

'Now, what I'll do,' said Sam, 'is clean the rollers and check the pressure in the kerosene pumps. I'll leave you to clean the lens and the brass.' He smiled.

'OK,' said Anna.

'Then we can give it a run-through, see if it's all still in working order,' said Sam.

'Maybe not right away,' she said. 'I'll let you know when's a good time.'

'No problem at all.'

The last ripples of conversation died and the audience turned to the stage. Haunting music filled the room. Katie Lawson stepped forward and began to sing. Shaun smiled. Here was his beautiful girlfriend, stunning the audience into silence with the sweetest voice he'd ever heard. She had changed his life. He had come to Ireland reluctantly, miserably, desperately missing baseball, cable, twenty-four-hour everything. And then came Katie. On the first day in his new school, she was all he saw. She was bent forward on her desk, slapping it with her fist, bursting with her contagious, singsong laugh. Then she sat back, pushing her dark hair off her face and wiping tears from her eyes. Shaun's heart flipped as he walked towards her. She had the cutest smile and it lit up her whole face. She was all natural; glowing skin, fresh cheeks, sparkling brown eyes. Once they locked onto his, he was gone.

Katie left the stage to sit beside him, her head bowed, embarrassed by the applause.

'Wow,' Shaun whispered to her. 'You were amazing. You blew everyone away.'

Katie blushed. 'No, I didn't,' she said, shaking her head.

'Shut up,' said Shaun. 'You rocked.'

Ali Danaher, Katie's best friend, came next, with a poem she had written herself. Shaun was smiling before she even started because he knew it would be black and heavy, like her clothes and her eye shadow. Ali had dry bottle-blond hair and if she pulled her sleeves up too high, skinny razor marks on her arms – for effect. She never admitted she came from a happy comfortable home, because her art would suffer. She finished the poem solemnly:

"... rotten core
Seeping through, finally breaking the ivory surface
A tarnished history
No longer hidden, too late to hide."

Shaun and Katie cheered over the parents' polite applause. Ed Danaher rolled his eyes at his wife, but was the last one to stop clapping.

When it was over, Shaun took Katie's hand and guided her through the hall.

Joe kissed Anna goodbye and left with Ed for Danaher's. She turned away, still smiling, and saw Petey Grant, the school caretaker, loping towards her. Petey had sallow skin and dark brown hair cut tight before it started to curl. Under thick eyebrows, his almond-shaped eyes were a soft blue and rarely made contact with anyone else's. When he spoke, he leaned to one side, holding his big hands in front of him, moving his slender fingers in and out as if he was about to catch or pass a basketball.

'Hello, Mrs Lucchesi. Nice to see you tonight. Did you enjoy the performance? I thought it was excellent. Katie is a lovely singer. She's also a pretty girl. I heard her practising the other day.'

He blushed. 'Is Mr Lucchesi here? I wouldn't mind dropping into his workshop tomorrow if that's OK. Is he doing anything tomorrow? I have a day off. I wouldn't mind helping him on that table he's making.'

Petey liked to reveal every thought that came into his head. He'd had learning difficulties since he was a child and the kids in school were split between those who gave him a hard time and those who defended him fiercely. Anna adored him. He was polite, enthusiastic, sensitive and charmingly innocent for a twenty-five-year-old. From early on, Petey had found a friend in Joe and someone who shared his interest in lighthouses. Although, for Petey, it was his specialist subject and the only thing he would talk about if he could get away with it. When Joe was working on furniture for the house, Petey would come in, lean back against the worktop and talk for hours about the history of Irish lighthouses.

'You're welcome at the house any time, Petey,' said Anna.

'Thanks very much, Mrs Lucchesi. That would be great.'

He hesitated, never knowing quite when a conversation was over.

The keys to Seascapes were heavy in Shaun's pocket. His job was to mow the lawns and carry out repairs at the holiday homes, but now it was

September and most of the houses were vacant. His plan was to slip away with Katie to one of them later that night. She had told her mother she was going to his house, he had told his he was going to hers. Martha Lawson was a tough woman to get around, but she trusted her daughter.

'There seems to be a bit of a mix-up about tonight,' said Martha as she approached the pair. 'I was just talking to Mrs Lucchesi and she says you're coming to our house.'

Shit thought Shaun.

'I thought we were watching *Aliens* tonight,' said Katie.

'No,' said Shaun. 'Playstation at my house.'

'Well, I'm leaving now, so I'll give you a lift,' said Martha.

'Shit,' Katie mouthed at Shaun.

Anna stayed for another two hours, tidying up after the performance with some of the other 'sucker moms' as Joe called them. It was midnight by the time she left. She walked along by the church, lost in her thoughts.

'Well, if it isn't the beautiful Anna.' The tone was all wrong.

She held her breath, then turned around. She was stunned at how John Miller now looked. The glazed eyes, the mottled red face and the unsteady legs she could put down to drunkenness, but everything else came as a shock: his hair, greying and greasy, his skin, puffy, his shirt straining across his stomach. He swayed in front of her.

'I know I look like shit,' he said, his arms outstretched.

'No, you don't,' Anna said quietly. 'Not at all.'

'Fuck off! You're French. You're fucking perfect.'

She didn't know what to say.

'So, it's Anna Lucheesy now or so I've heard. Very nice.'

'Lu-caze-y,' she said, trying to smile.

'So, you married your cop then? Lucky guy. Lucky, lucky guy.' He grinned. 'Any chance of a fuck?'

'Jesus Christ, John!' she said, looking around. 'What are you saying?'

'That I want a fuck.'

'And where is your wife?'

'Still in Australia. Kicked me out. Hah! Can you fucking believe it? I'm back here living with Mother. Psycho up on the hill. About to take over managing the orchard. The one thing I swore I'd never do.'

'I'm sorry, John.' She turned to walk away.

'You're a great girl. A gorgeous girl,' he called after her.

She kept walking. Her hands were shaking, her face burning.

Suddenly he was behind her again, grabbing

her, forcing her up against the wall, his breath smelling of onions and alcohol, his clothes reeking of fish. There was a shiny smear on his chin and crusty white corners to his mouth. She pushed his heaving drunkenness away.

'John, go home and sober up.'

'You were always a tough bitch, Anna . . . you little ride.' She stared at him, searching his face, but she found no trace of the John she used to love.

TWO

Stinger's Creek, North Central Texas, 1978

'He won't bite you, Duke. It's not his beak you gotta be worried about. It's his claws. His claws're his weapon. 'Bout sixteen pounds' worth of pressure he can use to tear through your skinny little arm.' Duke looked up at his Uncle Bill, worried. Bill was smiling.

'Solomon won't hurt you. You're givin' him food. He knows who his friends are. And if he laid a claw on you, I'd shoot him dead.'

'Don't you dare shoot him, Uncle Bill. Don't you dare.'

Bill chuckled, ruffling Duke's hair. He turned to the Harris' Hawk perched on his hand, untied the leather straps that tethered him and with an outward sweep of his arm, released the bird upwards. They watched him land gently on a cottonwood tree high above them.

'How 'bout you, Donnie? You wanna try it? I think Duke here's a little scared.'

Duke's eyes narrowed to a slit, his face hot with anger. He flew past his uncle and went straight for his best friend, Donnie, charging him to the ground.

'Duke Rawlins is never scared,' he hissed.

'Jeez, Duke. Take it easy, fella. Take it easy. You OK, Donnie?'

'Sure am, sir.'

Duke got up and dusted down his jeans, putting his hand out for the leather glove. Bill handed it to him, pulling a piece of raw meat from the satchel that hung at his side. He pressed the meat between the thumb and forefinger of the glove and went through the routine.

'Stretch out your left arm, there, the one with the glove, and aim that shoulder at him. Then call him and wait for him to land.'

Solomon swooped down and landed on Duke's hand, pulling with his beak at the meat until it gave way.

'Now show him your open palm, so he don't think you got nothin' in it that he can eat.' Duke held out a shaky hand to the bird.

'Now catch a hold of the leather straps on his legs and slip them through your fingers, make sure he won't get away.'

Duke fumbled with the straps and Solomon flapped his wings, but stayed where he was until he was secured.

'Well done, Duke. Let him go now, just like I showed you.' Solomon flew again.

Bill walked over to the bow perch nearby where his second Harris' Hawk was tied.

'Come on, Sheba, now it's your turn.' He released the second bird, who landed high on another cottonwood, flicking her head from side to side.

Bill was eyeing both hawks. 'Always checkin' out what's goin' on,' he said. 'Always watchin', waitin'.'

Suddenly Solomon dived from his perch, swooping low, parting Duke and Donnie. A second flap of wings and Sheba was gone, in determined flight behind him. Bill moved after the hawks, calling to the boys to follow.

'They've seen somethin'. You can tell by the way they're flyin'.'

They arrived at an open patch of dry ground and saw a lone Bobwhite quail.

'That's what they have their eye on,' said Bill. 'That's their quarry – whatever they're lookin' to kill. Like another word for prey.'

Solomon flew in low and just as he reached the quail, it scrambled desperately towards the scraggy borders of scrub along a row of mesquite trees. Then it stopped suddenly. Solomon overshot his target, too late to change his course and was forced to land high in one of the trees ahead. But Sheba had been moving along perpendicular to the quail and before it could react, she was on it, puncturing its flesh. Solomon was down an instant later, securing the quail by its head, both hawks savaging their quarry.

'Like Jekyll and Hyde,' said Bill. 'One minute they're on top of the world lookin' down on creation, next minute they're tearin' that creation apart. And helpin' each other to do it.' Bill nodded, proud.

Wanda Rawlins used to be the star attraction at the Amazon. Drunken, toothless men who had never been out of state swore she was better than any of those Broadway bitches, but were just glad she stayed in a backwater like Stinger's Creek to dance for them. Ten years later, when her breasts went south, the most she had to offer was a port in a storm. Ten dollars got you a hand job, twenty dollars covered straight sex, no funny business and for twenty-five dollars, her mouth was all yours. Everything was free for acid; you could stay the weekend if you had coke. And two minutes over one weekend was all it took for one of her loyal fans to create the burden of little Duke, now eight years old, but making her feel like a hundred.

The first time Duke walked in on his mother, he was four years old and he thought she was being strangled. Then he realised she was being strangled, but she didn't seem to mind. A huge naked man was kneeling behind her, thrusting

into her, his thick arm leaning on the wall above
her head, the other fiercely gripping a pink silk
scarf, twisted and pulled tight around her neck.
Her face was crimson, her eyes glazed, her lids
heavy. The man looked up at Duke, leering drunk-
enly, blissfully, continuing what he paid good
money for. Duke turned around and walked out.
His mother came into the kitchen minutes later,
naked under her faded bathrobe. She threw Duke
a look. 'What?' she snapped as she moved to the
work-top. Then 'Scram!' right in his ear as she
walked by with her coffee. Duke jumped with an
innocence that disappeared forever when her next
john came to call.

Westley Ames was a squat, rheumy-eyed,
sniffly man, with an apologetic hunch. He had a
mousey wife who lay down from the start to be
walked over and who bore him three watery
daughters. For years, he fought a battle inside, too
weak to ever act out the sick fantasies that
consumed him.

He picked his way slowly around the debris in
Wanda Rawlins' yard, a half-gram of coke in a
neat folded square of paper in his suit pocket.
'Howdy, Westley,' said Wanda, leaning against the
doorway, her free hand arced across her brow
against the sun. She had been a pretty teenager,
tanned and curvy, with a sweet smile that wrinkled the bridge of her upturned nose. Now her
body was pale skin stretched across thin bones,

her face sharp cheeks and empty blue eyes. Her scrawny legs curved backwards and rocked against the sides of her scuffed white ankle boots.

This was Westley's second visit and this time he was here for the weekend. After the last encounter, Wanda thought she may just find herself bored to death before Monday came.

In a burst of head-to-toe red and blue, four-year-old Duke came running out from the side of the house. 'Well, who do we have here?' said Westley, his urges swelling in his chest. 'You must be Superman! Aren't you the handsomest little fella?' He smiled. Duke stared up at him and moved behind his mother's leg. Westley looked at Wanda and the panic dancing in her eyes. Then he focused on her dilated pupils. He turned back to Duke. 'Let me talk to your mama a while.'

Wanda Rawlins was alone in the kitchen, radio blaring, singing along to Tony Orlando and Dawn. Beside the unfolded square of paper on the counter top, she bent low to take in her treasured lines, choosing to ignore the raw, agonising screams from the bedroom.

Two weeks later, when Duke was walking through the schoolyard, he saw the stooped form of Westley Ames at the front gate, a startling silhouette against the bright sun. He began to shake violently. His stomach flipped, then lurched and he threw up all over his trainers.

'Hah! Pukey Dukey!' said Ashley Ames as she skipped past him and ran ahead, jumping into her daddy's arms.

Duke walked back from his Uncle Bill's with a smile on his face. He had never seen the hawks before, let alone held them. He loved hanging out with Uncle Bill. No-one got hurt at Uncle Bill's house. Except that poor quail. Bam! Bam! Dead! He could think of a few people he'd like to do that to. And as he turned the corner up to his house, one of them was standing there, waiting for him, combing back his thin brown hair with taut fingers. He was in his early thirties with a soft, boyish face. He took everything in, his blue eyes sliding back and forth across the yard behind black lenses. Everything else was still. His hands were firm on his hips, his feet rooted in polished black shoes, his shirt and pants neat and close-fitting. Duke stopped and cocked his head to one side to watch him. He shivered. This guy was a total freak.

Duke called him Boo-hoo – during his first visits, he always tried to stop his tears. Only the name remained. The tears had dried up long ago.

THREE

Anna was sitting on the sofa with a book on Irish lighthouses open on her lap; almost two thousand miles of coastline and eighty major lighthouses to guard them. She turned to Joe.

'You know, the motto of the Commissioners of Irish Lights is *in salutem omnium*, for the safety of all. It's funny, I look at our little lighthouse and I feel safe. I can't imagine how intense it feels when you're out at sea in a storm, thrown up on massive waves and your whole life depends on that flashing light.'

'You've gotta admire those keepers.'

'Sam has some great stories. Some of the keepers used to play poker with the locals and used Morse code to tap out their hands.' The phone rang and she jumped up to take it in the kitchen.

'Oh hi, Chloe,' she said. She listened for a minute and then she was pacing, stretching the yellow cord across the room. Joe followed her in. He saw her frown.

'No. I need someone who's not going to come over here and get traditional. Greg's work on Iceland was three Björks by an igloo. Not good enough. I was thinking of this Irish guy, Brendan—'

She rolled her eyes up to Joe at the interruption.

'No, no, listen! I've seen his work, it is completely different. And he'll avoid all those terrible clichés. I've made a few calls and apparently he's amazing—'

She stopped again.

'I didn't say I wanted Irish models! We'll use American or French girls, that's fine. But this is an interiors spread, Chloe. They should not be the focus.'

She held the phone away from her ear, then brought it back when Chloe stopped.

'OK, OK. I'll call him, get him to send you his book and the spread I saw in the Irish magazine. Then you make your informed decision.' She hung up.

Joe looked at her, amazed. Miles away from the office, she was still secure enough to stamp her feet.

'What's for lunch then?' he said, teasing.

'Chloe is so stupid,' said Anna as she walked to the fridge. 'Meatball sandwiches with barbecue sauce.'

He squeezed her tightly, wrapping his arms around her from behind. 'I love your balls.'

She laughed in spite of herself. '*Tragique*. Oh, by the way, the doors should be here today,' she said.

'If they were still together and Jim Morrison wasn't dead.'

Anna simply shook her head.

'Come on, you love the bad ones,' said Joe.

She stared at him. '*Quel curieux caractère*.' He recognised the quote, from the French version of *Toy Story*. In the English version it was 'You sad, strange little man.'

After lunch, Ray's van bumped up the stony drive. Anna waved him towards the lighthouse. He took a left and drove down the sloping grass as close as he could get to the steps. He got out and threw his hands up in the air.

'What am I supposed to do now?' he shouted to her.

She jogged over to the bottom of the steps.

'I'll need to call in back-up,' she said, laughing.

'Love that cop speak.'

'Can I have a look?' she said, nodding at the van.

'You can indeed,' said Ray. He opened the back doors and lifted a layer of green tarpaulin.

'Oh my God,' she said, her hand to her mouth. 'They're beautiful!'

'They're wooden doors,' said Ray.

'No, no. They're beautiful. You did an amazing job.'

'Thank you. I had the picture of the old lighthouse doors pinned to my board the whole time.'

'They're magnifique,' she said.

'They could almost be magnificent,' he said.

'Stop that!' she laughed. 'You're always making fun of me.'

'I always used to make fun of the girls I fancied in school,' he said, winking.

'You flirting with my wife again?' said Joe, coming up beside them. 'I'm pushing forty here, Ray – thirty-year-old charmers worry me.' Ray was the same height as Anna, but looked shorter because he was so broad. His dark eyebrows and constantly furrowed brow could make him look either incredibly sensitive or just plain stupid. He was neither.

'The doors are great,' said Joe, running his hand over the wood.

'Don't. I'll get a swelled head,' said Ray. 'OK, now how're we going to get these down? Where's this back-up of yours, Anna?'

'I'll get Hugh.'

Anna disappeared to drag Hugh away from his tea and tabloids. Between the four of them, they hefted the doors to the lighthouse and secured them onto their hinges. Anna bolted them shut.

'Wow,' she said. 'I am thrilled. I am so grateful.'

Ray raised an eyebrow.

'Not that grateful, pal,' said Joe, putting a firm hand on his shoulder.

'To be honest,' said Ray, 'I'm hanging out for the models who'll be draping themselves over me for the photo shoot. I'll be the "bit of rough". Might wear an Aran jumper and tuck my jeans into my boots for the occasion.'

'Anything else you need?' asked Hugh.

'No, no, thanks for your help,' she said.

'I'm off, too,' said Ray. 'If those doors get unhinged at all, you'll know where they get it from.'

Anna didn't understand. Joe laughed. She turned to him, taking his hand.

'Let me show you my nightmare.' She unlocked the new doors and led him up the winding staircase. They reached the service room and climbed the sloping ladder to the lantern house.

'Look at this,' said Anna, hooking the tip of her finger under one of the cracks in the wall. 'Doesn't move.'

'Paint stripper?' said Joe.

'Not a chance,' she said. 'It's taken years for it to get that way. And because of the temperature in here, it . . .' she moved her hands in and out.

'Got bigger? Smaller?' said Joe.

'No, no, the metal . . .'

'Oh, expanded and contracted.'

'Yes,' she said. 'So I don't know what to do.'

'I could get some of the guys, scrape it off.'

They both shook their heads.

'We'll think of something,' said Joe. 'Do you have to do this part? I mean, the thing doesn't work anyway,' he said, looking at the old mercury pedestal, 'and won't the shoot be really from the outside?' She knew he was half serious.

'I'm not even going to answer that,' she said. And besides, he didn't know her plan.

Shaun dropped his bag on the floor of the small Portakabin he had seen lowered earlier that day onto the concrete at the side of the soccer pitch.

'What the hell kind of locker room is this?' he said.

'Can you see a locker in here anywhere?' said Robert, looking around the empty room. He liked to tease his friend. 'It's called a changing room, Lucky. We change our clothes in here. Even when we think our balls will be frozen off.'

Shaun discovered early on that teasing was called slagging in Ireland and if you weren't getting slagged, there was something wrong.

'Out of the way,' said one of the boys, pushing past him. The rest of the team, miserable in shorts and T-shirts, ran towards the blinding floodlights. The pitch was bald, hard and unseasonably cold. Running in head-to-toe black Nike along the sideline was the coach, Richie Bates. He was twenty-five years old, six foot three and two-hundred-and-ten pounds, every inch of his body carefully toned into hard muscle. His neck was short and thick and the top of his head was Action-Man flat. Richie was a guard, short for garda, singular of gardai, the Irish police force. He worked with a sergeant out of the small sub-station in Mountcannon. After an hour of play, he was still running up and down, roaring.

'Come on, lads! Move it! Move it!'

'It's freezing,' said Robert, jogging after the ball.

'If you run, you'll warm up,' said Richie. Robert rolled his eyes. He had just come on. Everyone around him had hot red faces and white breath. He was still ghostly pale, but knew the slightest effort would turn him to crimson and make his eyes stream. He was not a sportsman. He sweated too much, he breathed too heavily, his hair fell across his face, his legs were dark and hairy, thick and slow. But he could appreciate the irony. He was the sports writer for the school paper.

Shaun had the ball and was heading for goal. He stumbled and landed hard.

'Get up, Lucchesi!' said Richie instantly. Shaun breathed through the anger. Richie blew the whistle. 'Right, lads, that's it. Off you go. Well done.' No-one responded.

Back in the changing room, Billy McMann, a short, skinny twelve-year-old, was hunched shivering in the corner trying to do up his fly, but his fingers were curled and numb from the cold. He caught Shaun's eye and gave a weak smile. Shaun stepped over, quickly zipped up the boy's fly and patted him on the head.

'Thanks,' said Billy, blushing.

'Don't worry about it,' said Shaun.

'Jesus Christ, Billy! Can't even zip up your own pants?' It was Richie, standing, laughing in the doorway.

Shaun stared at him. 'Give the kid a break.'

Billy fumbled with his bag.

'You need to toughen up,' said Richie pointing at him.

'There's nothing wrong with him,' said Shaun. 'His goddamn fingers were freezing.'

'Watch your mouth, Lucchesi,' said Richie. 'Or we won't be calling you Lucky for much longer.' His look challenged the rest of the room.

'You're not in uniform now,' someone shouted from the back.

'You watch yourself, Cunningham,' said Richie. 'Or I'll be waiting outside that off-licence when you're picking up your next six pack.' He left.

A few of the boys groaned. Then Robert said, 'You're still a fag, Lucky.' Everyone laughed.

'Do you need a lift?' Robert asked Shaun.

'Nah,' said Shaun. 'My dad's coming.'

He walked out of the school and stood by the gates, watching all the other parents come and go with their sons. Joe eventually pulled up in the Jeep.

'You're such a loser,' said Shaun through the window. 'I've been standing out here for, like, twenty minutes.'

'I was busy. I'm trying to pack.'

'You forgot.'

'No, I didn't. Just get in, Shaun.'

'What's your hierarchy of things to remember, Dad? Like on a scale of one to ten, where do I come in?'

'Here we go,' said Joe.

'Yeah, well, it's a pain in the ass. You can remember everything for work, but—'

'Drop it,' snapped Joe.

'Jeez, relax, would you? I'm the one who got stood up here. Again.'

'I said drop it,' said Joe, too loud. They drove the rest of the way in silence.

They were just in the door when the phone rang. Joe picked up.

'Come back, all is forgiven,' said Danny Markey.

'Please stop calling me at this number,' said Joe. 'I told you. It's over.'

'Yeah, yeah, I know the drill,' said Danny. 'It's not me, it's you.'

They laughed. Shaun made a face at his father's transformation.

'So things that bad?' asked Joe, ignoring Shaun.

'You've no idea,' said Danny. 'I'm with Aldos Martinez or All Doze – guaranteed to help you sleep or your money back. And if that's not enough, I'm out last night, date with Maria, and my wife calls looking for me. And this rookie on the TS tells her I'm finished hours ago. I go home telling her the hard night I've had and she knees me in the downtown area. I swear to God. What happened to, "He's out on the road, I'll get him to call you." I'm gonna rip the guy's rookie head off next time I see him. He's a retard. Clancy called to fuck with him, pretended he was some pimp looking for his girl Juanita Sophia Marguerita whatever and the guy leaves his desk to go check. I shit you not. Anyway, it's like everywhere I look I'm getting screwed.'

'Wish I was there to offer my support,' said Joe.

'Yeah, yeah, sure,' said Danny. 'So how are those ugly Irish broads?'

'They're doing great,' said Joe. 'Want me to pass on your regards?'

'Sure,' said Danny. 'I'll come over, wrap myself round one of those wide backs.'

'Hey, Shaun isn't doing too badly with his Irish girl.'

'Yeah, but I've seen the pictures. Katie's an exception. Let me tell you, if he ever gets tired of her . . .'

'You're a sick man, Danny. A sick man.'

'True,' said Danny. 'Anyway, I was wondering if you're coming back for your birthday.'

'What are you, a girl?'

'It's a big deal. When I'm old like you I'll want you to make a big deal over me.'

'I don't know what I'm doing for my birthday, Danielle, but maybe we could have a sleepover—'

'You sound like me. A guy tries to do the right thing . . .'

'Look, I don't know what I'm doing for my birthday. But I'm in New York tonight.'

'What?'

'Giulio is getting married tomorrow. Don't ask. I don't know if I'll make it into the city. I'm only there a couple a days.'

'Call me. I'll come to the airport, meet you for a drink or something.'

'Sure.' He saw Anna walk in. 'Danny, I gotta go catch a flight. Here – maybe you should talk to my lovely lady wife about any birthday plans.'

'Hmmm, French accent . . .'

'Jesus Christ. No-one is safe.'

Anna smiled and took the phone from Joe.

'Bonjouuur,' she said. Joe could hear Danny whooping.

The taxi driver guided the red saloon along the winding tree-lined road. One hour ago, he had picked up his first fare of the morning at Shannon airport. He had been talking ever since.

'That's what we need over here – Rudy Giuliani. The guy cleans up a whole place like New York and our politicians can't clean their own back-sides.' He looked in the rear-view mirror. He got no response. He kept talking.

'I ended up in Harlem once, you know. Only white guy there, I swear to God. And I'm from Cork and in Cork, we call everyone "boy". We say "How's it goin', boy?" or "What're you havin', boy?" Well, I tell you one night in Harlem straightened me out fairly quickly. My mate, this big black guy, tells me, "Someone will pull a gun on you here if you call them boy." So I started calling everyone "man" instead. "Hey, man, how's it goin', man?" Now I'm back here and I'm saying "man" and they all think I'm nuts.' He turned back to his passenger. He drove on. 'Right,' he said after two quiet minutes, 'here we are. Will this do? They usually seem to have a few good deals.'

'This is great,' said Duke Rawlins.

Brandon Motors stood on a winding back road, sloping down a field by a red-brick bungalow. New and used cars lined the grass, fluorescent green and pink price tags wedged behind their windscreen. The Car of the Week was mounted on a slanted wooden platform edged with green and gold bunting. The dealer stood beside it, nodding to the car and then to Duke. Duke shook his head.

A white '85 Ford Fiesta van stood out from the shiny rows, battered, dull and cheap. Duke walked around it, looking through the windows, then came back around to the bonnet, leaning on it with both hands. He pushed himself upright.

'You take cash?' he asked.

'I do,' said the dealer.

Duke handed over the money and scribbled a signature on the forms. He sat in the van, reached up and yanked a swinging pine tree from the rear-view mirror. He threw it out the window as he pulled away. After a twenty-minute drive, he stopped at a petrol station and bought a black felt-tip pen and a map. He circled where he needed to go, then traced his finger along the route. He turned the key in the engine and headed for Limerick. On the outskirts of the city, he stopped at a Travelodge, slept and showered.

It was dark by the time he was on the road again, this time on a busy stretch to Tipperary. He was soon caught between two huge sixteen wheelers; he twitched at the wheel, swerving right to find an opening. The line of cars ahead was constant. He pulled back and saw a large sign for a town called Doon. Turning the wheel sharply, he took a last-minute left onto a narrow, winding road. His headlights picked up a black and white sign for Dead River. He crossed its stone bridge and drove through pitch black into the small town. He took a right at the corner onto Doon's main street, a tidy row of houses, shops and pubs. It was eleven-thirty p.m. and deserted. He kept driving, then brought the van to a stop alongside the iron gates to a field. He clung to the steering wheel and breathed deeply. Then he got out to walk back towards town. He wanted a beer. But another opportunity presented itself.

The driveway was long and curved, bordered on each side by tall sycamores. Giulio Lucchesi was waiting for his son in the marble foyer. He was fit, tanned and groomed, his grey hair combed glossy and neat. His navy blazer was crisply cut, his pale blue shirt and beige pants perfectly pressed, his suede loafers brushed.

'Joseph,' he said, clipped and anglicised.

'Dad.' They shook hands.

'You remember Pam,' said Giulio.

'Yeah, hi,' said Joe. 'It's great to see you again. Can't believe he's finally got you to say yes.'

She smiled.

It was no surprise that Giulio Lucchesi's second wife was nothing like his first. Pam was tall, thin and subdued, a Nordic blonde. Maria Lucchesi was dark and fiery.

Giulio stepped back. 'I'll show you to your room.'

'I think I can remember,' said Joe. He took his suitcase and went alone up the stairs to a room he hadn't seen in twelve years. He opened the door on the hotel minimalism that had never welcomed him before and didn't welcome him now. From the age of fourteen to seventeen, he caught a ride with his neighbours to Rye to spend August with his father. And each September his mother would run down the steps of their little Bensonhurst apartment to welcome him back home.

Pam led Joe to a vast cherrywood dining table. She went to the kitchen and came back with three small plates of blackened asparagus in balsamic vinegar.

'Put some parmigiano on that,' said Giulio, pushing a small bowl towards Joe.

'This is good,' said Joe, raising his fork. 'Is Beck supposed to be here? I couldn't get hold of her on her cell phone.' Beck was Joe's name for his older sister, a movie locations manager.

'Rebecca is on set,' said Giulio. 'Quite fittingly, in a lunatic asylum.'

'We're one big let-down,' said Joe to Pam. She looked away.

Giulio ignored him. 'How's Shaun?'

'He's great, settling in—'

'—until he's uprooted in a few months to come back home.'

Joe looked at him. 'Maybe it's in his genes.' He turned to Pam. 'I spent my childhood in Brooklyn, then we all moved when Dad got his job at Louisiana State, then I had to come back to Brooklyn with my mother when they divorced, then split my time between there and Rye when Dad bought the apartment and then this house. I went back to LSU for a few years, then back to New York. And now of course, there's Ireland.'

'Wow,' said Pam. 'That's a lot of moving. You went to the same college as your father? I didn't realise.'

'Briefly,' said Joe. Giulio cleared his throat.

After dinner, they moved into the living room with its thick carpets, ornate white and gold tapestry sofa and heavy velvet drapes. Anna's worst nightmare.

'So, you looking forward to the wedding?' said Joe.

Giulio and Pam exchanged glances.

'We already got married,' said Giulio. 'In Vegas. At the weekend.'

'In Vegas.'

'I know,' said Pam. 'It sounds so tacky. But it was wonderful—'

'Jesus, Dad; you know, I've never actually been invited to a wedding where the bride and groom have gone ahead and married before I got there. This is really something. A real special day for all of us.'

'What's done is done. I'm glad you came all this way,' said Giulio.

'Great,' said Joe. 'Look, goodnight, OK?'

He put down his drink and went to his room. He lay on the bed and flicked on the TV. Later, when he heard his father's bedroom door shut, he got up and went to the kitchen for coffee. He took his mug and wandered down the hallway,

drawn to the study. He looked across the shelves
at books that traced his father's career: texts from
the sixties on general entomology – introductions
and field guides, then agricultural entomology –
tabanids, mosquitoes.

Joe had just turned four when Giulio started
college at Cornell. He was twenty-seven years old
and worked three jobs to pay his way through an
entomology degree. He was the only father in the
neighbourhood who stayed in at the weekends to
study. Joe felt an unfamiliar stab of pride. He forgot
the boy in the garden bouncing a ball off the wall
so he could swing a bat at it.

The rest of the books covered Giulio's final
specialism, titles just as familiar to Joe – *Time of
Death, Decomposition and Identification: An Atlas,
Entomology & Death – A Procedural Guide, Forensic
Entomology: The Utility of Arthropods in Legal
Investigations*, then four copies of *Learning to Tell
The Time: A Guide to Forensic Entomology* by Giulio
Lucchesi. Row after row of books about insects
and forensics. At the bottom of a fallen pile, Joe
recognised the navy binding and yellowed pages
of a thick manuscript that made his heart flip. He
pulled it out and wiped down the cover.

Louisiana State University: '*Entomology and Time
of Death: a field study.*' Three names were printed
beneath. The one that leapt out at him was his
own. It was 1982. He had been nineteen years
old, a sophomore. Because of his father's friend-

ship with Jem Barmoix, LSU's medical entomology professor, Joe had been invited to join the
team for a groundbreaking new research project.

'Regrets?' said Giulio from the doorway. Joe
jumped.

'No, Dad. No.'

'I don't think you appreciate what you had.'

'I don't think you appreciate what I have.'

'But Jem—'

'I know. I know how much the research meant.
But instead of squinting down a microscope all
day, I'm the one who goes out and finds the
fuckers who create the corpses in the first place.
No corpses, no decomposition, no maggot and fly
timeline. But no murderers, no corpses.'

'*Found* the fuckers.'

'What?'

'You said you find the fuckers who commit
murder, but shouldn't you have said *found*? Aren't
you on a break? What are you now, Joseph? Anna
tells me you're a carpenter. How biblical.'

'What the hell is your problem?'

'You could have been an academ—'

'Listen to yourself.' Joe jabbed a finger at his
father. Then he stopped and took a breath. 'You
know something? I'm not gonna bother. We both
know what's going on here. I'm not rising to it,
the same conversation over and over.' He threw
down the paper and walked out of the room.

* * *

Pam made a wasted effort over breakfast. Joe gave short, sharp answers through teeth he had been grinding all night.

'I hate to leave on your wedding day,' he said, getting up from the table and walking out to the bags he had left in the hall. Giulio followed him.

'There's no need to go after one night.'

'I came for your wedding,' said Joe. 'which is now over. Which was over before I got here. Congratulations. Pam is a lovely woman. I'm now going to spend some time with Danny and Gina.'

'As you wish.'

'As I wish. Sure.'

It was dark when Anna went out to close the gate at the end of the lane. She was about to turn back to the house when she saw the tip of a cigarette light up across the road. John Miller raised a hand for her to stop.

'I *definitely* lost last night,' he said, walking towards her with his head hanging, looking at her with sad eyes. He was freshly showered, dressed in a clean but rumpled rugby shirt and jeans.

She looked at him, confused. Then she remembered. The first night they met, twenty-one years earlier, he was celebrating. France had beaten Ireland by one point in a rugby match in Paris. At the start of the night, John was mourning the loss, but by the end of it, he was drunk and jubilant that the Irish had come so close.

'Whiskey doesn't agree with me,' he said, leaning his arms on the gate, staring down, kicking at the loose gravel.

She shook her head and sighed.

'I'm sorry,' he said, looking up. 'I really am.'

'It's fine,' she said and tried to walk away.

'Come on,' he said. 'Please.'

'What do you want me to say? It wasn't a nice introduction after all this time.'

'I wish I hadn't met you last night.'

'And how would you have been if you met me today?'

'I'd be sober and you'd still be beautiful.' There was a familiar sparkle in his eyes.

She couldn't help smiling. 'I better go back,' she said, nodding towards the house. She locked the front door behind her. When she went into the den, Shaun swung around in his chair.

'Check this out, Mom. I'm live.'

She leaned over his shoulder and saw Shaun's smiling face on the screen, beside his G.I. Joe photo.

His name was printed underneath with a list of vital statistics.

'Your favourite movie is *While You Were Sleeping*?' said Anna.

'What?' said Shaun, panicked.

'Gotcha,' said Anna.

Shaun looked at her, deadpan. 'You're such a dork.'

'I know,' she said.

She read that Shaun's favourite food was anything American, his favourite drink was Dr Pepper, his favourite sport was baseball, his favourite place was Florida.

'I see you're becoming a real Irish man,' said Anna, pointing to the screen.

'Ah, but my favourite girl is Irish,' said Shaun. 'That's the difference.'

She scrolled down further and saw question marks in the career section.

'Don't you know what you want to do?' said Anna.

'No,' said Shaun. 'It's like I look at my future and it's blank, you know? Like living on the edge of this cliff, but not being able to see a thing.'

'Have you been watching *Dawson's Creek* again?'

FOUR

Stinger's Creek, North Central Texas, 1979

Flakes of rust flew from the battered white pickup as it lurched from side to side along the twisted road out of Stinger's Creek. It was after midnight and Wanda Rawlins was slumped, disorientated, against the passenger door, her skinny legs splayed under the dashboard. Her face was pale and her white blonde hair with its dark roots lay in damp strands across her cheeks. Duke's eyes flickered open. The sickly smell of pine air freshener flooded his nostrils. He looked up at his mama, his fingers clawing listlessly at her arm. He could see flashes of light across her face and black pools of mascara under her eyes. She was staring out the window. He tried to speak, but his throat was dry and raw from screaming. The only colour on his face was the redness that flared at the centre of his forehead. Slow throbs pulsed through his head and a cold tingling sensation moved in waves down his arms to his fingertips. Darts of pain spiked beneath him and he slowly shifted his tiny frame onto its side, his navy shorts twisting around him. He passed out with the effort.

'I think he moved, I think he moved,' cried Wanda. 'Come on, baby, come on, baby, come back to me,' she began to sob. She clutched his head to her stomach, spilling tears onto his face. She got no response.

'What's happening to him? What's happening to him?' she screamed, shaking Duke's shoulders, too wasted to know any different.

'Calm down, Wanda,' said the driver, 'calm the fuck down or we won't be taking him any further than the end of this road.'

Wanda sat in silence for the rest of the journey, rocking Duke jerkily back and forth, his bare legs dangling over the seat edge.

Ten minutes later, they screeched into a parking lot and came to a stop. Wanda pushed open the door and hauled herself out, pulling Duke with her, taking his limp body in her arms. She staggered through the double doors in front of her into a brightly lit hallway. Duke's eyes opened again, fleetingly. Hospital, he thought.

'What the fuck you doin' bringin' him through the house, you dumb bitch?' hissed Hector Batista, pulling shut his living room door behind him. His accent was thick. 'Told you to bring him around back. Who you think you are?' He glanced down at the vomit on Duke's T-shirt, shook his head and grabbed Wanda's elbow, guiding her roughly out the door she came in. Hector nodded at the driver of the pickup to follow them around.

A fluorescent light pierced the darkness in the filthy room, swinging low over a metal table at the centre. Wanda lay Duke down and began to sob again, spreading herself across her son's body. Hector pulled her aside and reached over to lift the boy's eyelids, shining his light in.

'Pupils OK,' he said. 'What happened to him?' No-one answered.

'You say on the phone he hit his head. Is that all I look for?' said Hector.

'Yeah,' said the driver.

Hector wrung cold water out of a grimy cloth at the sink and turned back to place it on Duke's forehead. His eyes opened.

'Can you remember what happened?' asked Hector.

Duke tried to shake his head.

'You know what day it is?' asked Hector.

'Friday,' whispered Duke.

'Tell me who is your president.'

'He wouldn't—' said Wanda.

'Jimmy Carter,' said Duke, proud.

'He's just fine,' said Hector. 'Little concussion. Wake him up some times during the night, make sure he don't get any worse and keep him away from jumping around for the next weeks. He must rest.'

Duke moved his head slowly to look at his mother. From behind her, the driver of the pickup stepped out. Duke's eyes shot wide in alarm and he opened his mouth to scream. Hector's hand was quick as he clamped it over the little boy's cracked lips. Duke was writhing underneath the pressure, his eyes darting everywhere. He couldn't breathe.

'You stop, I let go,' said Hector, his face two inches from Duke's. He held his hand firm until Duke calmed down, the energy draining from his shuddering body.

Hector leered at the driver. *Los niños pequeños hacen mucho ruido,*' he said.

'No speaky the Spanish,' said the driver.

Hector walked over and whispered to him: 'Little boys make lots of noise.' He laughed.

Duke had curled into a ball on his side and began to cry. He felt the hand of the driver in the small of his back.

'No more boo-hoos, Dukey. No more boo-hoos.'

Duke shivered. All he could remember was Boo-hoo coming into his room. What he couldn't remember was the man's weight bearing down on him, pushing harder each time, slamming his forehead into the wall over and over again, until he crumpled and lay face down, unmoving on his bed.

*   *   *

Wanda Rawlins heard a faint knock on the screen door and pulled it open carefully. Smoke billowed out around her. She flicked her hand at it.

'Mornin', Mrs Rawlins,' said Donnie. 'Duke about?'

'Duke had an accident yesterday, he's resting.'

'What happened?'

'Nothin' much. He had a knock to the head.' She smiled. 'You boys. You sure know how to scare the livin' hell out of a mother.'

'Can I see him?' asked Donnie.

'For a few minutes,' said Wanda, stepping back to let him in.

Donnie walked in to the kitchen and was hit with a smell that caught at the back of his throat. The oven was wide open and a baking tray lay diagonally across the folded-down door. Cracked black circles steamed on the surface. More had fallen to the floor.

'Tray was hot,' laughed Wanda. 'And I didn't quite make it in time,' she said.

'Well, I'm sure they'll taste just fine,' said Donnie.

Wanda laughed out loud. 'And I'm Julia Child.'

Duke lay on his side, covered by a thin sheet. His face was pale and beads of sweat gathered on his forehead.

'Hey,' said Donnie. 'How you doin'?'

Duke tried to talk, but his lips stuck together. He wiped his mouth.

'I'm OK,' he said. 'My throat hurts.'

'How's that?' said Donnie. 'I thought you hit your head.'

'Just does,' said Duke.

'You fall from a tree?'

Duke hesitated. He opened his mouth, then closed it just as quick.

'Yup. What an idiot.'

Wanda slid her thumb under her nose and pushed herself up from the kitchen chair, slipping her feet back into her mules. She picked up the baking tray and went to the doorway of Duke's room.

'Look what I made for you, sweetie,' she laughed, her eyes wide. 'To cheer up my little soldier.' Duke lifted his head to see her. She looked crazy. 'They didn't quite work out,' she explained looking down at the cookies. 'Mama fucked up.' She laughed again.

'I'm talkin' to Donnie,' said Duke.

'Aren't you even gonna thank your mama?' she pouted.

'Thank you, Mama,' he said flatly.

'Aw,' she said, walking over to the bed. She let the tray hang by her side, dropping the cookies onto the floor. She leaned down to look at them and picked something up.

'Found you a chocolate chip!' she said, holding

up a burnt cookie crumb. She put it up to Duke's mouth. He buried his head back into the pillow.

'No!' he said. 'I don't want it.'

'Jeez, Duke, no need to shout. You want this, Donnie?' she said as it crumbled between her fingers. 'Oops!'

Then she held up her hand. 'Shush,' she said, trying to focus. 'Shh.' They heard twigs cracking as someone walked up to the front of the house. A shadow passed over the blind in the bedroom.

'Donnie, you stay right where you are, sweetheart. I have myself a visitor,' said Wanda, smoothing down her hair, leaving black crumbs on the blonde.

She left the room and went to the kitchen. Westley Ames stood at the door.

'Hey, Wanda,' he said. 'Is this a good time?'

'You know, Westley? You shoulda called, but I guess it's OK.'

'I have some excellent produce for you,' he said and she could see his hand flex in his jacket pocket. 'You look mighty interested,' he chuckled.

'Duke's taken a knock, Westley,' she said. 'He's resting.'

Westley's eyes flashed anger and the smile disappeared. He clenched the bag again. Wanda looked up at him.

'Come back tomorrow, Westley,' she said and closed the door. She turned back. 'Or later tonight,' she shouted from the open window.

FIVE

'Surprise!' said Joe, carrying a large box into the kitchen. 'Magic paint stripper. A tip from Danny. It will get through all that crap on the lantern house walls. I hope.' He put it down by the back door. Anna ran towards him and jumped into his arms, wrapping her legs tightly around his waist.

'Hellooo,' she said. 'Welcome home to your wife!'

'This is great,' he said. 'I gotta go away more often.'

She shook her head. 'No, no, no. Never again.' She kissed him all over his face.

'I missed you,' he said. 'Way too much.'

She climbed down. 'How did Giulio take to you leaving early?'

'What could he do? He knew he'd screwed up. He always knows.'

'He's an oddball.'

'I know. And I've got some of his genes.'

'Don't worry. I could never forget that.'

'That's going to take a while,' said Joe, pointing to the paint stripper. 'You have to put it on, cover it with paper, then wait a couple days, see what happens. It's a big job for one little lady.'

'Well, I'll get some of the guys to help, if I can. But I couldn't just hand the whole thing over to anyone.'

'No,' said Joe. 'That would be a disaster.'

She gave him one of her looks. Joe laughed.

'I'm going out to the workshop,' he said. 'Petey's waiting.'

'Already?'

'I know. I can always sleep later.'

He was barely in the door when Petey started. 'Did you ever hear how some lighthouse keepers earned extra money?' he asked, not waiting for an answer. 'They turned to shoemaking, prostitution and distilling. In 1862 . . .' He stopped suddenly.

'What's prostitution?'

'Whoa,' said Joe, searching his face to see if he was kidding. He wasn't. 'Uh, do you know what sex is?'

Petey went red. 'Yeah,' he muttered, his eyes downcast.

'Well, some men pay to have sex with women called prostitutes. That's prostitution. I guess those lighthouse keepers were renting some of their rooms out to these ladies.'

'Oh,' said Petey and moved quickly back to his comfort zone. 'Around Waterford, smugglers used to come ashore with alcohol, candles and building materials and the keepers would store them until they needed to sell them on—'

'Even in smaller lighthouses like this one?' said Joe.

'Yes,' said Petey, 'they would—'

'Petey,' called Anna, waving a ringing mobile phone at him. 'Did you leave this in the house?'

'Thanks a million,' he said, answering the call. When he hung up, he looked traumatised. 'My mother's driving Mae Miller somewhere. She wants company for the trip back. I always have to go stupid places with her.'

'That woman needs to give him more independence,' said Anna when Petey had left. 'She shouldn't be dragging him around all the time like a child.'

It was three p.m. when Duke parked his car and headed down the main street in Tipperary town. As he stared in the window of a hardware shop, a tiny grey terrier trailing a tartan lead bounced over to him and looked up expectantly. Duke paused, then hunkered down to pet him.

'Hey, little fella,' he said, picking him up, holding him against his chest and letting the dog nuzzle him. 'Aren't you a beauty?'

The owner, a young mother, rushed over with a toddler on her hip.

'Thank you so much. He's unbelievable,' she said. 'Nuts.'

'He's a friendly little guy.'

'Don't I know it?' she laughed. 'Thanks again.'

Duke stared after them, then turned and went into the shop. Minutes later, he came out with a yellow and green plastic bag under his arm. He walked further into the town and stopped outside a fast food restaurant. A group of teenagers were inside, slumped on yellow bucket seats screwed to the grimy floor. He looked up at the sign. *American Heroes* was printed between two stars and stripes across a faded blue background. He walked in and a buzzer sounded. The waitress glanced his way, then turned back to her notebook. Her uniform was hospital-scrubs style and strained across her back, twisting into her thick thighs. Her dark hair was scraped into ridges across her skull and ended in a dry ponytail at the base of her neck. Duke watched as one of the boys pulled her notebook down, so he could read what she had just written. He laughed.

'Spell glass, Siobhán,' he said flatly.

'G.L.A.A.S,' she said.

They all laughed.

'G.L.A.S.S.,' he said. 'As in ass.'

'That's just 'cos I was writing too quickly,' she said, blushing. She went back to the counter.

'As in big fat ass,' the boy whispered, loud enough for everyone.

The waitress stopped when she saw Duke. 'Hiya,' she said, awkward and eager. 'I'll be with you in a minute.'

She poured juice for the boy, then squeezed back behind the counter.

'Now. What can I get you?' she said.

'Could I get a beef taco and Coke?' Duke said, smiling as he looked into her eyes. He squinted at her name tag: Siobhán. 'Sy-o-ban? Is that your name?' he asked.

She laughed. 'It's pronounced Shiv-awn,' she said. 'It's Irish.'

He smiled again. 'Savawn? That's not easy to say.'

She disappeared into the back room and Duke sat listening to the anxious conversation behind him.

'That's not your mum,' said one of the boys.

'It *is*,' said one of the girls, ducking her head under the table.

'Even if it was, she wouldn't be able to see in,' he said. 'I'm waving at her right now.'

'Stop it! She'll see!' she pleaded.

'For fuck's sake,' he said, 'you're totally paranoid. There's no point in going on the hop if you're going to be freaking out.'

'Is she gone?'

'Yes, seeing that she was never there in the first place.'

'It's all right for you. I'm on report,' she said, sitting back up. 'Which means,' she continued dramatically, 'I get expelled if I'm caught missing school one more time.'

'Well, I'm missing a major biology exam,' said the boy, 'and unless I have a pretty good story, I'm fucked too. I'll be sent down to the lowest class. With the dopes.'

'I'm only missing double music and a double free class,' smiled the second girl. 'And Mr Nolan can be worked on,' she said. They all laughed.

Siobhán arrived with some fries, desperately trying to involve herself in their conversation. She was quickly back with Duke, her eyes down, rejected again by a cruel, casual remark.

'People are idiots,' said Duke.

She smiled. 'Ah, they're OK,' she said, glancing back over at them.

'You know? You've a really beautiful smile,' he said.

She blushed. 'Yeah, right.'

'You do,' he said. 'Just thought I'd tell you. No big deal.'

She was called away again, but Duke stayed at the counter, talking to her every time she was free. He was the only person there when she closed up the restaurant two hours later, standing with her on the pavement as she snapped the lock on the shutters. When she was finished, she waited anxiously.

'Come with me,' said Duke, holding out his hand. She took it and smiled.

*　*　*

Anna stood outside the lighthouse with Ray, Hugh and Mark, the landscape gardener.

'Here's what we're dealing with, guys,' she said, handing them white masks. 'There are layers of paint on these walls with rust underneath. We need to strip it all back to the bare metal, so we can preserve it and then paint over it properly.'

Mark started to speak.

'Before you say anything, Mark, no, we couldn't just scrape it off.'

He smiled and ran his hand through his wild blond hair.

'I don't even know why I bother,' he said. 'I've absolutely no idea what I'm doing. You should have left me on the lawn.'

'Well, I appreciate this,' she said. 'You've no idea.'

'Many hands and all the rest of it,' he said.

She went on, 'So what you need to do is put this stuff on with a trowel and cover it with this paper. Once we get that done, we can leave it for a few days. It should sweat the old paint off. Then we can see the real damage, see if any of the panels have to be replaced. So that's it. Oh, and cover the floor with newspaper before you start.'

The wind whipped around Mountcannon harbour, rocking boats and tugging at sails. The concrete walkway thirty feet above was deserted except for Katie who stood swaying in the wind, her hands buried in the pockets of her pink hoodie. She turned her back to the boats and looked out to the ocean, lit in flashes by the sweeping beam from the lighthouse on the opposite headland.

'This place still freaks me out,' said Shaun, coming up behind her, pointing at the six-foot wide walkway that had no railing for its entire length. 'I mean, your choice here is flaying your ass on a rusty skip then suffocating to death in a pile of rotting nets or,' he looked down on the other side, 'crashing onto some huge rocks and drowning.'

'It's like – which would you rather die in, a barrel of pus or a barrel of scabs?' said Katie.

'What?' said Shaun.

'It was one of my granddad's favourites,' said Katie. 'I'd probably go for the scabs.'

'Which sounds like a good idea, until they're scratching at the inside of your throat, then you're inhaling them into your lungs . . .'

Katie shook her head. 'Ew.'

Shaun pulled her into his arms, pressing her head against his chest, squeezing her close. She looked up at him and he knew how she felt.

'I still can't believe you asked me out,' she said.

'What? Why? You're a babe. Why wouldn't I ask you out?'

'I am not a babe,' she said, hitting him. 'It's just that you arrived looking like . . . like a big American footballer or something, with your perfect teeth and we all thought that none of us would have a hope. I just think it's weird that here I am.'

'You're crazy. You're really beautiful. You make me laugh, you're smart, you're cute—'

'Aw, that's so nice.'

'It's not nice, it's true.'

He took her hand and they moved against the wind back down the steps. They walked along the harbour, then past the sweaty windows of Danaher's and up a winding road behind a short row of shops. They stood at the sign for Seascapes Holiday Homes.

Straight ahead, was an empty tree-lined dead end. To the left, the road sloped steeply into a second, larger cul-de-sac, where fifteen four-bedroom holiday homes faced out towards the border of trees. Lights were on in three of the houses, each of them close to the entrance. Shaun's boss, Betty Shanley, lived in the first one, but she was out of town for the night. Shaun and Katie took a right, running along the trees and down the slope, glancing around quickly before Shaun slipped the key into the door of the last house, number fifteen, and they both fell into the hallway, laughing.

'I put the heating on earlier,' said Shaun.

'Yeah, I can smell it,' said Katie, wrinkling her nose at the stale air from the storage heaters.

'Would you rather freeze your ass off?' asked Shaun.

'No.'

'Do you feel a bit guilty?' he asked.

'A little bit.'

'Me too. It's just . . . Mrs Shanley. She's been good to me. And to mom, when mom was her nanny or au pair, whatever.'

'I know. But I'm sure our parents did stuff when they were our age.'

'Let's not go there,' said Shaun.

'Yeah. Ew.'

'Are you ready for your surprise?'

'I get a surprise? Cool!'

'Go to the fridge.'

Katie hunched down and pulled open the fridge. In it was a tiny chocolate cake in the shape of a heart, a half bottle of wine and a white rose. She smiled up at him.

'That's the sweetest thing anyone's ever done for me in my whole life,' she said. 'You are adorable!'

'I know it's not original, but what the hell.'

'Shut up. I love everything. I love you.'

Joe sat down at the table with the mail that arrived that morning. He looked down at his plate – spinach ravioli with a side of broccoli. His glass was filled with freshly squeezed orange juice. He leaned back to see his dessert in a bowl by the stove. It was custard with something brown hitting the surface. Stewed prunes.

'Why didn't you just cut to the chase and slap two laxatives down on my plate?'

'Pop a pill,' said Anna. 'Your answer to everything. It's because of those killers you get all blocked up.'

He smiled at her mistake. 'There is nothing wrong with my insides.' He opened a letter from a cut-price phone company, glanced at it and tossed it aside. Anna kept talking.

'Your breath stinks. I know what that means.' She pointed to his abdomen.

He laughed out loud. 'It's too easy to be blunt in a foreign language. How would you like it if I said something nasty to you in French?'

She shrugged. 'All you know is bonjour. And I'm not nasty. I have to look after you, because you are no good.' He loved her quirky phrasing. 'You've been on an aeroplane and you've been wound up by your father. I know your jaw hurts and you've been taking things.'

He started eating the ravioli and then laughed to himself.

'You know, pretty much everything sounds sexy in that accent,' he said.

'You're nuts,' she said.

'What about them?'

'Now you sound like Danny.'

Joe was smiling as he picked up a letter from the bank. He tore it open and frowned.

'Why has four hundred euros gone out of my account? To a furniture store in Dublin.'

'Oh. I went a bit over budget on the bathroom.'

'What?'

'I overspent on the fittings.'

'That's not what I meant. I meant what the hell are you thinking? Again! I presume the magazine isn't going to pay me for this, either.'

'No, but you know this is important to me.'

'Yeah, I do, but I'm not gonna go bankrupt for it. You know what I'm up to now? Two thousand euros on a house I don't even own. "I ran out of money for the bedroom, the living room . . ."'

'It's worth it. I've never had a project like this, something I've done from start to finish. This will change my career.'

'And what if it doesn't?'

'What do you mean what if it doesn't? All along it's been your job, your job . . .'

'Yeah. The one that's kept you and Shaun financially secure for the last eighteen years. What would have happened if I had given up a few years ago to try something new?'

'I would have supported you.'

'With what, for Christ's sake? You do not live in the real world. Regular people have budgets. The magazine has a budget. I have a goddamn budget. But that's no good, right? That's too normal for you, right?'

'That's not true.'

'What you're doing is selfish.'

'In the end, it will work out. I'll be making a lot of money. I'll buy you some nice things.' She tried a smile. Joe ignored it.

'I have everything I want right here, Anna. I'm not always looking for something better.' He finished his meal in silence.

John Miller leaned heavily on the bar, his hand clamped on a pint of Guinness, a glass of straight whisky beside it. Ed Danaher was nodding patiently at him. Usually, he was cranky and brusque. Yet people opened up to him because if they were lucky, he could bark out a useful truth. He rubbed the ends of his black moustache, then pushed up the sleeves of his white shirt.

'Is that so, John?' he was saying. 'That's a dreadful thing altogether. What did you do?'

'I got drunk,' smiled John. 'And I haven't looked back since.'

Ed laughed with him.

'Seriously,' said John. 'I stayed with a friend. But he was a bigger loser than me. The two of us just drank ourselves into oblivion, morning, noon and night. That was when my brother, you know, Emmett, came to get me. Sally had a restraining order against me, I couldn't see the kids.' Tears welled up in his eyes, sorrow quickly shifting to anger. 'I still can't see my own fucking kids.'

Ed had learned to say nothing when the barflies were on their rollercoaster.

'Oh, don't worry,' said John. 'I may be bitter, but I haven't quite twisted yet.' He swayed on his chair, looking around the bar, his elbows against the back of the chair, his movements loose.

Joe arrived in and walked up to the bar.

'Hey, Joe,' said Ed. 'How're things, how's the woman herself?'

'Things are good. Anna's run into a few problems with the lighthouse, but you know her—'

'Now, here's a man,' said John, gesturing wildly, 'who has it all.'

Joe stared at him. John thrust an arm his way.

'John Miller,' he said.

'Joe Lucchesi.'

'I know who you are, all right,' said John, 'Anna's husband. Shaun's father . . .'

'You in local intelligence?' said Joe, smiling briefly.

'Once you're a local, you're in,' said John.

'Really?' said Joe tightly, trying to get Ed's attention again.

'I'm only messin' with you,' said John.

'Sure,' said Joe.

'Don't be gettin' funny on me now,' said John, pushing lightly against Joe's chest.

'Let me get you a drink,' said Joe. 'Ed, a Guinness for me and a Jameson for Mr Miller here.'

'Keep your fucking money,' slurred John. 'Keep your fucking wife and your son and your lighthouse and your perfect—'

'Whoa, buddy . . .' said Joe.

'Do you hear this shit?' said John.

Ed put Joe's pint on the bar and turned to John.

'That's enough now. Maybe you should take a walk out to the jacks, get a bit of air in your lungs.'

John snorted, but got up and left.

'Don't mind him,' said Ed. 'His wife left him, he can't see his kids. They're at the other side of the world, he's pretty cut up about it.'

'No shit,' said Joe. 'But I wasn't the one who changed the locks.' He smiled and headed for the snug. He watched John Miller lose his footing on the stool when he came back from the mensroom. His eyes were buggy and shot off in opposite directions like a fly. Joe was smiling to himself when Ray and Hugh walked in to join him.

'What are you so happy about?' asked Hugh.

'I was just looking at wino-man over there with his bug eyes and it reminded me of this fruit fly experiment. It was for some research on alcoholism, because fruit flies live on fermented fruit and even though they can still go hyper or pass out like we do, they never get addicted.'

'Can people sign up for those experiments?' asked Hugh. 'I'd say they'd give you a rake of pints.'

Frank Deegan sat by the door of Danaher's watching his wife, Nora. Gruff, opinionated, fiercely intelligent Nora. She had a brandy in her hand and an imaginary cigarette between two bony fingers. She was ranting at her friend Kitty about an artist who had hung up on her when she asked him would he show his work at the gallery she was planning for the village.

'The little shit,' she said, then looking at Frank, 'excuse my language. Trying to cultivate this image of himself as some unpredictable genius. When he's just a reasonably talented, broke, borderline-alcoholic, shoeless, dwarf. And – *predictably* – he called me back and said he'd do it. And I know it's because he needs the money. Possibly for sandals and a smock.'

Frank and Kitty laughed. Nora knocked back the last of her drink, her short, blunt strawberry blond hair swishing across her high cheekbones.

'Brandy, sarge,' she said, handing out her glass, winking at her husband.

'Back at the house,' he said. 'Look at the time.' It was eleven-thirty, unstrictly closing time.

Nora glanced at Kitty. 'Sorry,' she said, 'it's never pleasant.'

Frank stood, not quite reaching his slender wife's five feet eight. He ran a hand through his thick grey hair, smoothed down his dark green golf sweater and stretched his arms out by his side. Nora had seen him perform the same routine for forty years. He caught her watching him and he winked.

Ray, Joe and Hugh were leaving at the same time and stopped in front of him.

'Uh-oh,' said Ray, putting an imaginary bull-horn up to his mouth. 'People, step away from your glasses. Please put down your glasses. We are now three point four seconds past closing time. I repeat. Step away from your glasses.'

Frank smiled.

'You need any help clearing the place, sergeant?' said Ray. 'You could cuff a few of these guys. Joe would probably get a kick out of frisking them, wouldn't you?'

Frank and Joe laughed.

Mick Harrington pushed through them on his way out with a large brown paper bag full of bottles.

'Jesus Christ,' said Hugh. 'It's Fr Merrin.'

Mick looked at him. 'You know, the Exorcist. He comes in, he takes away the spirits,' Hugh explained.

Mick gave one of his hearty laughs. 'I've got about twenty pissed Spaniards down at the harbour that I have to keep lubricated,' he explained. 'This is my second bar run of the evening. Their boat's being worked on and they're hanging off it singing shite drinking songs.' He turned to Joe, 'By the way, if Robert is with Shaun, tell him to go home. Someone better keep the wife company.'

'They're out,' said Joe.

'Looks like there'll be a big black mark beside both our names, then,' said Mick.

* * *

Katie stopped and held her head back, squeezing the corners of her eyes. The tears still fell. She started walking again, quickly, desperate to be home in her bed. Suddenly, a set of tail lights came to life in front of her, the car tilted across the ditch. She squinted into the glare and slowed her pace until she was close enough to know something was very wrong.

SIX

Stinger's Creek, North Central Texas, 1980

Mrs Genzel looked out at her fifth grade class. They were bent over a history term paper, arms hooked around their answers. Duke Rawlins sat with his head bowed, his pencil moving furiously. She could see the pages he'd finished, crisp on his desk with the pressure of his strokes. He looked up, searching for something and she wondered what was behind those pale eyes. Then he stopped, suddenly ripping out pages and scrunching them up. He threw one or two on the ground. The rest of the children stared. A giggle broke the silence.

'Shh,' said Mrs Genzel. She turned to Duke, 'Is everything OK?' She spoke softly.

He gave a quick, jerky nod. His mouth was shut tight. The fingers of his left hand were drumming the desk.

'Do you want to start over?' she said.

He shook his head again, slower this time. 'No, ma'am.'

Then he leaned back and squeezed his eyes closed. His chest was heaving.

She studied his expression. 'Could I see you outside, Duke?'

He got up from the desk and walked out the door.

Mrs Genzel tried to look at him, but he kept his head down.

'Things don't seem like they're going too well for you,' she said.

'I'm OK,' he answered.

'What happened back there?'

'Nothin', ma'am.' She waited.

'Stuff,' he added.

'What kind of stuff?'

'Don't know, ma'am.'

'Were the questions too difficult?'

'No,' said Duke. 'I just . . .' He looked away.

He caught her off guard then, lifting his head to stare right at her. Her heart leapt. She was close enough now to see the struggle behind his eyes. Duke saw only kindness in her face, but it flickered quickly and changed to darker images of faces he couldn't trust, of reactions he couldn't predict.

'Nothin',' he said, retreating. 'Couldn't spell somethin'.'

She didn't realise she had been holding her breath until she let it out.

'OK,' she said. 'Come on back inside.'

The office was tidy and homely, cream walls and floral wallpaper, sunflower chair rails and base boards. Children's drawings covered a small bulletin board. Mrs Genzel sat behind her desk, short grey hair cut like a man's around her soft, warm face.

'Mrs Rawlins—'

'Miss,' said Wanda. 'Can't live with 'em . . .' She shifted in the wide chair, withdrawing into it, making her crossed legs and the black scab on her knee the first thing the teacher could see.

'Yes,' said Mrs Genzel. 'Miss Rawlins, I've called you in here today to talk about Duke.'

'That boy'll be the death of me,' said Wanda, blinking slowly, her head loose on her neck.

'He was crying yesterday. He said his dog was dead. Someone had killed his dog.'

'Sparky,' said Wanda. She began scratching hard, her nails travelling up and down her thighs, trailing hot red lines. 'Poor Sparky.'

Mrs Genzel watched her, frowning.

'Is that true?' she asked.

''Fraid it is. I came out in the yard Monday and found the little critter lying there, cold as a witch's tittie – oops!'

'What had happened to him?'

Wanda leaned forward. 'No idea.' She sat back

again, twisting in the chair, leaning on her elbows, raising her body up, then sliding it back down.

'I know Sparky was important to Duke,' said Mrs Genzel. 'He brought a photograph of him to show and tell in third grade, he used to draw pictures of him. He must be very upset.'

'Yup,' said Wanda.

'Is there anything we can do to make this easier for him?' said Mrs Genzel.

'He'll get over it.'

'It's not that simple . . .'

Wanda was already struggling up from the chair. She offered a limp wrist to the teacher.

'Is everything OK for Duke? At home?' said Mrs Genzel.

Wanda kept moving, towards the door.

'I'm on my own, but I look after my boy.'

'Of course you do. I was just . . . concerned.'

Wanda took a dramatic step forward. 'Tsss!' she said, stamping an imaginary branding iron onto her forehead. 'Bad. Mom.'

Mrs Genzel stared at her. Wanda's laugh ended with a small sigh.

'Anyway, I gotta go.'

She left the office and checked her watch. It was late enough to wait for Duke. She slouched at the school gate and lit up a cigarette. She saw Duke trudge out behind the other kids. He walked over and she ruffled his hair, giving him a playful punch on the shoulder.

'That Mrs Genzel sure is an ol' dragon,' she said.

'I like her,' said Duke. He walked home ahead. Wanda finally spoke, reaching out and spinning him by his shoulder towards her.

'Jeez, Duke. I told you! I'm sorry about the damn dog, OK?' She threw down her cigarette end and stamped it out with her boot and a twist of her leg. 'Who'd a thought a few kicks would have sent it to its grave? Yap, yap yap, the damn thing.'

Duke stopped, rigid. He glared through her. All she did was smile.

The tiny mongrel reappeared through the powdery dust. When it settled around him, he flipped again, sending up another cloud. Duke couldn't speak. He just watched. Wanda was waiting for a reaction.

'Honey?' She waited. 'Honey?' Her voice was razor sharp in his head.

'Honey!'

'What?' he said, too loud.

'What do you say?'

Duke's heart was thumping. Sweat trickled down his back. He looked up at Boo-hoo, who stood tall over him, his legs spread, his hands on his hips, nodding and smiling. Then he looked back at the miserable creature skipping about in front of him. It was all so wrong.

'Thank you, sir,' said Duke.

'Whatcha gonna call it?' asked Wanda.

'Fucker,' said Duke. Wanda hit him hard across the side of the head.

'You tell him what you're gonna call that lovely new dog!' she shouted. 'That's a very kind thing someone's done for you, Duke. You need to show some respect.'

'It's OK,' said Boo-hoo. 'He'll know soon enough.' He patted the boy's head and went inside to wait with Wanda.

Duke didn't follow. He picked up the skinny animal, held his wriggling body under his arm and walked to Uncle Bill's house. Bill was standing in a clearing, his arm outstretched after releasing a young hawk.

'That Bounty?' shouted Duke. 'That baby hawk?'

'Yup,' said Bill. 'Just lookin' after her a short while 'til Hank gets back.' He glanced over at the dog. 'Is that yours? A new one already?'

'Mama got him for me.'

'Oh. OK. Well just be careful—'

'I'm not gonna let him go if that's what you mean,' said Duke.

'It's important because—'

He was interrupted by a car pulling up around the front of the house. He handed Duke the leather glove.

'She won't be doin' anything,' he said, nodding

to Bounty. 'I've got the meat in my bag. I'll be back in a minute. We'll start with her then.'

Duke put the dog down and held him between his calves as he slipped on the glove. Then he released his grip and the dog sprung into the clearing, dashing wildly from tree to tree. Bounty's wings shot open. Her head darted from side to side. In a flash, she rose and swooped, fear driving her to an unlikely prey. The dog howled as her talons sank in. Duke's eyes glazed over. He was only dimly aware of noise, flapping wings, frantic blurred activity. He brought his eyes back into focus for the final moments. Then silence.

'What the hell is goin' on here?' said Bill, batting branches away as he ran through the trees by the house. He stopped when he saw the dead dog.

'Did Bounty . . . ?'

Duke nodded. He stared at the blood pooling out from under the body.

'I'm mighty sorry that happened,' Bill said. 'After Sparky an' all. I'm mighty sorry, little fella. The damn bird's a dog-grabber, too young to know any better, got scared, probably—'

'It's all right,' said Duke.

'I shoulda told you the young ones can be like that—'

'You did, Uncle Bill. You told me last week.' He patted the man's big hand.

They stood in silence. Eventually Bill went

inside. He returned with a stack of newspapers and set a slim layer on the dirt to soak up the blood. Then he picked up the lifeless body and laid it across the rest of the stack, folding the pages tightly around it. He heard a sob behind him. He turned and saw tears streaming down Duke's face, shudders cutting through his breath.

Uncle Bill wiped his hands on his overalls, then pulled Duke close, holding him tight as the little boy wept for a dog called Sparky.

SEVEN

Joe could feel the alarm pounding in his chest. His heart beat wildly. He realised it was the phone when Anna reached across him to answer it.

''Allo?' she said. She listened, confused.

'No, Martha. He came in about eleven-thirty on his own. Unless . . . I don't know. Let me go check.' She handed the phone to Joe.

'Hi,' said Joe. He let her talk. 'I've no idea,' he said eventually. 'I'm sure there's—' Anna walked back into the room, shaking her head. Shaun bounded in after her, frowning.

'What?' he asked, looking at both his parents. 'What?'

'She's not here, Martha,' said Joe. 'What time did you leave her?' he asked Shaun.

'About eleven thirty, quarter of twelve,' said Shaun. They all turned to the clock. It was four-thirty a.m.

'Oh my God,' said Shaun, his eyes wide.

'What would you like us to do? Is there anyone we can call?' said Joe into the phone. 'OK,' he said, then put it down. 'Martha's gonna call some of the girls from school.'

'But she wasn't with any of the girls from school,' said Shaun.

'It'll be OK,' said Joe. 'She could have met one of them on the way home. Why didn't you walk her home?' He hesitated. 'Did you have an argument?'

When Shaun saw the concern in his father's eyes he had to look away. There was no way he could tell him what happened tonight. Katie would kill him.

'No, we didn't,' he said. He looked like he was about to cry. 'She just wanted to walk home on her own.'

'Don't worry,' said Joe. 'She'll show up.'

For the past two hours, Frank Deegan had been staring at the ceiling. He had nodded off on the couch earlier, but a phone call had jerked him too wide awake to handle his regular bed time. It had been a hang-up, to make matters worse. He turned to look at Nora, asleep by his side. Raising himself up on one elbow, he lumbered out of bed, pausing to sit on the edge before standing. He tightened his navy pyjama pants and headed for the kitchen. He stopped at the counter, his short fingers hovering over a shiny foil bag of coffee grounds.

Nora had to be different, a coffee addict in a gener-
ation of tea drinkers. She would complain when
she visited friends' houses that they'd use the same
instant coffee that they offered her a year before-
hand, its granules in damp clumps against the side
of the jar. Only the teabags were replaced regu-
larly in most Mountcannon homes.

'Vile,' she would say to Frank, afterwards. 'Vile.'

He looked up at the clock, heard the rumblings
of his ulcer and ignored the call of caffeine.
Instead, he put a small saucepan of milk on the
stove and sat down at the table with the newspaper. He reached for his reading glasses with their
thick magnifying lenses. He'd bought them from
a stand in the pharmacy. Nora loved to poke fun
at him and his super-sized eyes. He reminded her
of something she could never remember.
Sometimes he would look up from his book or
paper just to make her laugh.

As he settled back into the chair, the phone
rang.

'Hello,' he said as if it was ten o'clock in the
morning.

'Frank, it's Martha Lawson. Katie didn't come
home last night.'

'You mean the night before last?' asked Frank.

'No, well, tonight I mean. She should have been
home at midnight.'

'It's five a.m., Martha, the night is still young
for a teenager. Especially at the weekend.' He

rubbed a hand through his hair. 'Was she in one of the discos in town?'

'No,' said Martha. 'She's not allowed. She was in the village with Shaun. She wanted to walk home on her own for some reason and now she hasn't shown up. Oh, hold on, Frank. There's someone at the door.'

'Well, there she is now,' he said, rolling his eyes.

She came back on the line, her voice shaking.

'It was just the Lucchesis,' she said.

'Oh, OK. Well, I'll come over to you, so,' said Frank. 'Sure I'll probably pass Katie by on the drive.'

'Thanks, Frank. I appreciate it.'

Frank took the milk from the stove and reached for the Colombian roast.

Martha Lawson lived with her daughter in a small white bungalow with a large garden – a suburban home on a country road, a ten-minute walk from the harbour, a thirty-minute walk from the Lucchesis. Inside, the house was a blend of different woods, carpets and fabrics; a mahogany dresser with varnished pine coffee table, floral carpet with Aztec print drapes. Every surface was spotless.

Frank sat to Martha's left on a brown sofa, his body turned towards her. She had a plain face, but most of the features that made Katie beautiful. Her eyes were red-rimmed, her eyelashes wet from tears.

'I'm sure Katie is fine,' said Frank. 'I don't know what she's up to, to be honest, but whatever it is, I'm sure she'll have a good explanation when she walks through that door.'

'No, Frank, I really don't think so. Please. I know Katie. It's not like her at all. God knows, she could be dead in a ditch somewhere. You hear about these hit and runs . . .'

'Don't be worrying about things like that,' said Frank gently.

'I'm sorry,' she said. 'This is just, I've never . . .' she trailed off.

'It's OK,' said Frank, patting her hand.

'Shaun called here for Katie at eight,' she said. 'She didn't stick her head in to say goodbye, she just hopped out the hall door to him.' She thought about this for a while. 'I didn't even say goodbye to her,' she cried.

'We don't know anything's happened to her,' said Joe, who had been standing at the fireplace opposite. 'And if we all got up to say goodbye to our kids every time they went out the door, we'd be up and down all day.'

Martha smiled, wiping her nose with a pink tissue.

'Shaun said they had been hanging around the harbour, but she wanted to walk home on her own or something, so he let her.' She glanced over at Anna and Joe. 'She was supposed to be home at midnight.'

'Where *is* Shaun?' asked Frank, frowning.

'He wanted to stay at home,' said Joe. 'And wait by the home phone. He figures she could call him on that because he doesn't get a great signal on his cell.'

Shaun stared at his bedroom wall. His heart was thumping. He moved around, trying different positions to get a signal on his mobile, but he knew nothing would work. He used the portable phone to dial his message minder. There were no new messages. He tried his private line in the bedroom. It rang. He hung up. He checked the answer phone. There were no messages. He picked it up, pushed buttons, turned it over, put it down again. Still no messages.

There was a knock on the door. Martha looked around at everyone. They all stood up at the same time, but left her to answer it. Low muttering came from the hallway. Richie Bates, in his pristine navy uniform, bent his head to get through the door and nodded when he saw Joe and Anna. He was pale, but alert. His hair was still damp from the shower. He turned to Frank.

'Howiya, Frank,' he said sombrely, nodding again.

Martha walked in behind him, disappointed and exhausted.

'Will you have a cup of tea, Richie?' she said.

'I'll get it,' he said.

'You will not,' she said. 'Sit down there.'

She brought him out a plate of plain biscuits and tea in a china cup that looked lost in his big hands.

'Thanks,' he said.

After a long silence, Frank spoke up.

'Sorry to have to ask, but was there anything wrong with Katie?' He pulled out his notebook. The formality of Frank Deegan, out of context, sitting on her sofa as a policeman made her cry.

'What do you mean?' asked Martha.

'Did you have an argument or anything?'

'No, no, everything was fine,' she said defensively.

'Was she fighting with anyone in school?'

'She wouldn't tell me if she was.'

'You know with young girls, they could have been jealous or there could have been something—'

'No. I know a bit of bullying goes on at the school, but she's never been part of it.'

Frank searched for questions that wouldn't alarm Martha at this early stage, but would reassure her that she was being taken seriously.

'I'm trying to think,' said Martha, 'did I do something that annoyed her?'

'Tell me what she did during the day today.'

'She went to school and was home straight-away afterwards. She didn't have any homework, so she went out to meet Shaun. She didn't change out of her uniform. She came home on her own for dinner, then went upstairs and had a shower. She spent a good while getting ready. She had a lot of makeup on, which she normally doesn't. I might have told her that she could have taken some of it off. I think that annoyed her.' She looked up at Frank.

'I wouldn't worry about that,' he said.

'I went into the kitchen then and I presume she took a jacket from the hall, because then she just shouted "See you later," and off she went out to Shaun. I went into the hall after her, but she was gone.' Tears welled in her eyes. 'I don't know why I had to say that about her makeup. She looked beautiful.'

Richie Bates stayed silent throughout the interview, but took notes every time she spoke. The bones in his hand were rigid. Frank wondered if the pen was going to snap.

'Maybe she hated me and I didn't know,' blurted Martha. Everyone looked at her.

'No,' said Anna, rushing to her side. She patted her arm. 'She loved you. We all know that. She's just late home.'

The questions continued until Frank was satisfied he had enough information. But that didn't mean he had any idea where Katie Lawson was.

The cottage, at the end of a damp, mossy lane, was five miles from Mountcannon and had lain

derelict for fifteen years. Wooden boards criss-
crossed the fractured windows, protecting the
place from people less determined than Duke
Rawlins. His hands tore at the rotting frame,
pulling free parts of the brittle timber. Within
minutes he was climbing through the back
window into a dark, cramped kitchen. He breathed
in the stale air, then worked on the rusted door
latch, finally pushing the door open to the breeze.

He moved through the house, shining his torch
over mahogany furniture, ragged net curtains and
religious pictures, crooked on floral walls. The
bedrooms were small and dark, barely lit by the
tiny windows. A tarnished picture frame lay
upturned on a sideboard. A strip along the centre
of the photograph had been bleached white,
where a gap in the boards had let shafts of sunlight
through the window. He picked up the frame and
slid out the photograph, letting it float to the floor.
He reached into his back pocket and pulled out
one to replace it. Uncle Bill stood in a faded XL
denim shirt and jeans, his right arm extended. The
sun was setting behind him and glowed orange,
catching his brown hair and full beard. His left
thumb was hooked into a brown leather belt that
was too tight for his vast stomach. His smile was
broad. Solomon sat on a bow perch next to him,
one foot raised. Sheba was swooping through the
air, poised to land on Bill's gloved hand and collect
her prize.

'Solomon was majestic,' said Duke, holding the photograph to his chest. 'He truly was.' He stretched out his arms and looked into the shadows. 'But Sheba, you are the most beautiful creature I've ever seen.'

Anna pushed aside plates, bottles, cutlery and mugs to add a jug of maple syrup to the breakfast table. Joe looked at the waffles, juice, croissants, bacon, sausage, coffee and tea. 'Whose room will we charge this to?' he asked. Anna laughed and looked to Shaun for a reaction. He had none. Tears were dripping onto his empty plate.

'Do I have to sit here?' he said. 'I feel sick.'

'No, no, you go,' said Anna, tilting his chin up. He looked away, then left the table.

Frank stood quietly in the doorway, smiling at Nora. She never let him down. He knew she would have got out of bed as soon as he left. There was something about her and that navy satin dressing gown that always touched his heart. She hadn't heard him come in. She sat in a corner of the sofa, her legs stretched out and resting on the low table in front of her. One hand was flicking through a book telling her how to de-clutter her life. The other was reaching out for her coffee mug. She missed the handle, but grabbed it back before it rocked off the side. Frank laughed. She jumped.

'You're dreadful,' she said, smiling. She put down the mug and turned around to him.

'Well?' she said, closing the book.

'There's still no sign of her.'

'Really?'

Frank nodded.

'How was Martha?'

'Very upset. God love her, though, she's very innocent. I asked her a few questions, but I think it scared the life out of her . . . and I hadn't even gone near the serious ones.'

'Ah, it's hard for someone like Martha. She's from another era.'

'God knows, Katie could have got fed up with how strict she is and run away to make a point.'

'Maybe. And who knows? Martha's never got over Matt's death, maybe her moping around the house all the time made Katie feel guilty for getting on with her own life.'

'Could be.'

'Or maybe it just suffocated the poor girl.'

'Possibly,' said Frank.

They looked at each other. They knew they were already sounding desperate.

'Either way, we'll know soon enough,' said Nora. 'Good kids like Katie don't last too long away from home. She'll be back before lunch, probably.'

'I feel guilty even saying this, but I called the hospitals and a few of the other stations, but nothing.'

'I don't know whether that's a good or a bad thing,' said Nora.

'Hmm.'

'And what about Shaun?'

'I don't know what's going on there,' said Frank. 'He didn't walk her home even though he was out with her. We're always seeing him walking her home, that funny walk they do, wrapped around each other.'

'I know,' said Nora.

'And he didn't come with Joe and Anna to Martha's.'

'What was he doing?'

'Waiting for her to call him, says Joe.'

'That's a bit odd,' said Nora. 'You'd think he'd want to be around everyone. And surely, if she didn't get hold of him, she would have called her mother, let her know she's all right.'

'I had a chat with him after Martha's,' said Frank, 'and the poor lad definitely seems out of it.'

She studied Frank's face.

'You're worried.'

'Yes I am, actually.' His eyes were tired and sad.

Nora was about to ask another question, but he held up a finger.

'I can't really stop,' he said. 'I'm going to have to talk to some of Katie's friends, maybe have a look around the harbour and the strand and out towards town, see if I can see anything. If she isn't back after that, I suppose I'll have to call it in to Waterford, make it official.'

Shaun walked for a mile past Shore's Rock along the scenic route from the village. He climbed the iron gate into Millers' Orchard and jumped down onto the path. John Miller was hunched in the corner, shovelling leaves into a smoking pile, far enough away not to notice Shaun run along the wall to the opposite side and slide down behind the trunk of an apple tree. He closed his eyes and was still in the same position ten minutes later when footsteps behind him made him jump.

'Hi,' said Ali.

'Hi. What's up?'

She sat down beside him and took out an empty soda can. It was bent forward at the bottom and pierced with nine tiny holes. She pulled some grass out of a plastic bag.

She turned to him. 'Where do you think she's gone?'

She put the grass over the holes and held the opening of the can to her mouth. She held her lighter to the grass and sucked in hard. She tried to pass it to Shaun. He shook his head.

'I don't know,' he said. 'I've spent the whole morning wandering everywhere . . .'

'I went into town to look for her around the shops. Which I know was a bit stupid.'

'It's just not like her to—'

'I know.'

'This was my last resort.'

'Me too.'

Nora and Frank locked eyes when the phone rang. He was sitting at the kitchen table, trying to eat a sandwich. He slowly reached across to answer it.

'Frank, it's Martha. She still isn't back.'

'All right,' he said firmly, looking at his watch. It was twelve o'clock. 'What I think I'm going to have to do now is call Waterford.' Waterford Garda Station was the district station over Mountcannon.

Martha gasped at the other end of the phone. He could barely hear her when she spoke.

'OK. Thanks.'

'So I imagine a Detective Inspector will be out to see you later on this evening. Do you have someone with you, Martha?'

'Yes. My sister, Jean.'

'All right. I'll let you know what's happening.' He put down the phone and dialled Waterford. He was surprised at how his heart had started racing. He never suspected the worst of anyone or any situation, but he was now hit with a fear he tried to tell himself was irrational.

Joe bent down and looked at the four pieces of steak under the grill. The butter had barely melted on them. The Worcestershire sauce wasn't sizzling.

'Get away from there,' said Anna.

'Come on. Steak sandwiches. You never say no.'

'The only problem is that you know none of us are going to eat. And the last thing you need is something to chew.' She tapped the side of her face. He looked under the grill again. She sighed.

'I hope I'm wrong,' said Joe. 'But I think there's something Shaun's not telling us.'

'What? But he would have said something to Frank earlier.'

Joe straightened up, turned off the grill and slid the steaks into the bin.

'I'm not so sure,' he said. 'I think it's something he doesn't want to tell anyone. He wasn't even being put under any pressure and . . . I don't know . . . he looked kinda scared.'

'Worried, probably. I think it was because we took him by surprise, arriving back with Frank like that. I don't think he thought Martha would have called the police that soon.'

'Maybe.'

She stood up. 'I'm making you one of your shakes. You can use a straw. And it will be better than that LV8 energy stuff, full of caffeine.'

'It's pronounced "elevate".'

'I don't care,' she said. 'All I know is anything that comes in bright colours like that is not good for you.'

He rolled his eyes. Anna went to the fridge for the ingredients. She pulled the liquidiser out from the wall and threw in a sliced banana, two scoops of ice-cream, two teaspoons of peanut butter, a spoon of honey and filled the rest up with milk, whizzing it until it was creamy. She put in a straw and handed it to Joe.

The Garda station at Mountcannon was small and neat, with grey floors, cream walls and bulletin boards with posters on awareness of everything from drinking and driving to using machinery near overhead wires. There was no cell; just a main office, Frank Deegan's office, a kitchen and a bathroom. Frank leaned back in his chair, his light blue shirt straining across his armpits. Detective Inspector Myles O'Connor had driven fifteen miles from Waterford city and was sitting on the edge of his desk with a stylus in his hand, punching text into a slim silver PDA. He was the first person Frank had seen who looked comfortable with one.

Every guard had heard about O'Connor – at thirty-six, he was the youngest D.I. in the country and the first in Waterford. Frank couldn't define it, but there was something about O'Connor that didn't say guard.

'Were you on holidays?' asked Frank, noticing his fading tan.

'Yes,' said O'Connor, without looking up. 'What was the name of the girl's boyfriend again?'

'Shaun Lucchesi. Where did you go?'

'Portugal. And did you say she'd been at a nightclub that night?'

'No,' said Frank. 'Out with the boyfriend around the harbour.'

Frank saw that O'Connor's eyes were bloodshot. Every now and then, he would raise his hand to his face as if he was about to rub them, then stop himself before he did. Frank wondered was it from squinting at the small screen. Then he thought maybe he was tired, but he showed no other signs.

'OK, fill me in on the rest of it,' said O'Connor.

Frank went through all the details. O'Connor listened, then took notes when he had finished.

Richie barged in, breaking the silence.

'You've met D.I. O'Connor before,' said Frank. 'Waterford's going to be handling Katie's disappearance from here on in. Superintendent Brady is on his way over.'

Richie flashed O'Connor a quick smile, squeezed his hand, then hovered in front of him, enjoying the six-inch height difference.

O'Connor didn't have the insecurity to make it worthwhile.

'Hello, Richie. Good to see you.' He smiled and held eye contact with him until Richie looked away.

'Right. What's your take on all this?' asked Superintendent Brady as soon as he walked in. He was almost entirely bald, with a narrow band of soft white hair around the base of his skull and a thick white moustache.

Frank opened his mouth to answer.

'Ah, I'd say leave it for now,' said O'Connor. 'She'll turn up later. It was Friday night, she's young—'

'Frank? You know the girl, the family . . .' said Brady.

'She was on her way home,' said Frank. 'It just doesn't ring true that she'd—'

'We've all been on our way home,' said Richie.

'You were there for all that this morning with Martha,' said Frank, annoyed.

He turned back to Brady. 'I've a bad feeling about this,' he said. 'There's not a thing about Katie Lawson would have me believe she'd run away. And, yes, I've known the family for years. I don't think we can ignore this.'

O'Connor sighed. 'In fairness, she's got no money, no passport . . .'

'I think this is fairly serious,' said Frank, nodding.

'OK,' said Brady. 'We'll get a search team in for tomorrow morning if she doesn't show up in the meantime.'

'Will you act as liaison officer with the family, Frank?'

'I'd say Richie would be the man for that.' Frank felt Richie could learn something about handling a delicate situation.

Superintendent Brady nodded at the men.

'I'll leave you to it,' he said. 'We don't all want to land in on the mother and scare the life out of her. I'll see you in the morning.'

'Right,' said O'Connor, turning to Frank, 'I suppose we'll call in to Mrs Lawson.'

'She'll be worn out going through everything over and over,' said Richie.

Both men looked at him.

'Well,' said O'Connor, 'she might be doing it all over again tomorrow with the Chief and Superintendent Brady. You never know what you might miss the first time.'

'What an asshole.' said Richie later.

'Well, you better get used to dealing with him,' said Frank.

'"You never know what you might miss the first time". What a load of shite.'

Frank didn't bother responding. Everything was always shite in Richie's world.

Joe sat at the table thinking about what Shaun could be hiding. His first guess was alcohol and drugs, but it was a half-hearted one. He knew Shaun had smoked dope back home, but he didn't think he still did. And the worst he would do was sneak a beer or two when he went out. All kids did that.

And Katie – she didn't drink or smoke. She was more innocent than the girls Shaun dated in New York. They had a predatory look that wasn't restricted to Shaun. Katie had a twinkle in her eye, but it was more about intelligence and wit than bad behaviour. Was Shaun protecting her from something? Did something happen that made her want to avoid home? Was she making a statement? Was she pregnant? He didn't want to think about it any more. An uncomfortable sensation – almost as physical as the dull ache in his jaw – was rumbling inside him.

O'Connor sat in Martha Lawson's kitchen in a stiff wooden chair that pressed into his spine. The radiator behind him was turned up high. He shifted forward. He had already shaken off his suit jacket and hung it on the chair beside him. He ran through the same gentle line of questioning as Frank had, but quickly moved on.

'Does Katie suffer from depression?' he asked. The question hung in the silence.

'She's sixteen years old!' said Martha. 'Of course she doesn't suffer from depression!'

Frank and O'Connor exchanged glances. Between them, they'd been to the scene of four suicides in the previous five months, all of them teenagers.

'Depression can start even younger than sixteen,' said Frank gently. 'You may not even have realised that's what it is.'

'Was she sleeping a lot?' said O'Connor. 'Emotional? Irritable?'

'Isn't that every teenager for you?' said Martha.

'Do you think she was feeling negative or hopeless? Or could she have been worried about anything?' said O'Connor.

'I wouldn't know,' Martha muttered. 'I don't think she would have told me.' She bowed her head and let the tears fall.

Frank's eyes moved over the family photographs on the sideboard. The biggest one was Katie in her white communion dress, her hands clasped around a prayer book and a white satin bag, her parents standing proudly behind her. In the second, she was dressed in pink trousers, a white top and big white trainers, sitting on a bench laughing with her father.

'Do you think she was badly affected by Matt's death?' asked Frank.

Martha followed his gaze. 'She was devastated. She adored him. But she was young when it happened. She'll always miss him, I know that, but I wouldn't have thought it was something that would trouble her at this stage.'

When she turned away, O'Connor leaned down slowly and turned the dial on the radiator. His face was red and his eyes looked dry. He kept blinking.

'Does she drink or do you think there's a chance she could be involved with drugs?' he asked.

Martha looked back at him, confused. She glanced at Frank for support. His look was apologetic.

'No,' she said firmly. 'No, she does not. She isn't allowed. I don't keep drink in the house. And where would a girl like Katie get her hands on drugs?'

Frank was saddened by her reaction. Did Martha really think she would only get drink from her own house? Or that drugs were hard for a teenager to come by?

'To be honest, I'm getting very nervous about these questions,' she said.

'Don't worry,' said O'Connor. 'For us to do our job properly, we have a list of standard questions that we ask people in a situation like this. We're not judging you or Katie or anyone. I don't know Katie, so I'm trying to get a handle on her. That's all. It will help us to look in the right places for her.' Frank nodded.

'OK,' said Martha.

'Is there anything else we need to know about her that you think would help?'

'She's a wonderful girl.' She started to cry.

Joe jerked awake on the sofa and glanced around the empty living room. He checked his watch. It was five to four. He ran to the kitchen, grabbed a banana, two Fuel It energy tablets and a shiny purple bottle of LV8. He peeled the banana against the steering wheel on his way into the village, but as soon as he opened his mouth, he heard a crunch. He decided instead to pop the Fuel It and sip his drink until he felt the familiar buzz kick in. When he got to the school, he parked outside the playground where a crowd had gathered. He saw Shaun standing alone by the wall. He jogged over.

'You finally made it,' said Shaun.

'Sorry. I fell asleep on the couch.'

'Then you probably forgot all about it.'

'No I didn't. Shaun, I apologise. But you're going to have to stop beating me up about this shit.' He rubbed his face. 'Sorry. I'm too sore to talk right now.'

'Sure you are,' said Shaun.

Joe was about to say something, when someone gave two short claps and everything went quiet.

'We're all here today for Martha Lawson,' said Frank. 'And she'd like me to thank you for your support. You may have seen searches like this on the news. Everyone moves in a straight line across their assigned search area. These lines are also made up of members of the gardai, who will be numbered for easy identification. As most of you know, Katie is five feet six, slim, with shoulder-length dark hair. A photo is being passed around the group. She was last seen wearing a pair of wide denim jeans with the brand name Minx, a pair of pink running shoes, a pink hooded sweatshirt with the word *cutie* written across the front and a white T-shirt. She would possibly have been carrying a pale blue nylon wallet and a silver mobile. During the course of the search, if you think you see any of these items, don't move. Notify the garda closest to you and they will call out their number, blow a whistle and shout "Find". If you hear this, stop immediately, whether you yourself have found anything or not. Do not move again until you hear the word, "Forward". Keep any chat to a minimum, but if you must speak, do it quietly. I don't need to tell you not to leave anything of yourself behind during the search. So keep sweet wrappers, cigarette butts or any other litter in your pocket until you get to a bin. Thank you.'

Shaun went over to Frank, his eyes pleading. Frank shook his head and put a hand on Shaun's shoulder.

'I don't think that would be a good idea,' he said. 'Maybe you should wait at home in case she rings. I bet you'll be the first one she rings.'

'I have my cell phone,' said Shaun.

'That's not a huge amount of use to you, with the coverage once we head out of the village,' said Frank.

'Go home, son,' said Joe, coming up beside him.

'I don't know what you're all so worried about,' said Shaun, his voice rising. 'What do you think we're going to find?'

'Probably nothing at all,' said Frank.

'But it's just best that you're not around,' said Joe. Shaun walked away. Frank turned around to talk to D.I. O'Connor.

Joe took the chance to search his pockets for painkillers. He had nothing. He considered his options. He couldn't walk away in front of all these people. Then he felt someone squeeze his arm. He vaguely recognised one of the elderly women from outside the village. Joe waited for the question. He was more patient than he used to be. The intrusion had amazed him when they first moved.

'How's the young lad?' asked the woman, nodding towards Shaun. Her face looked more accusing than concerned, but he suspected it had set that way years ago. The best he could do was nod through the pain, trying to let her know Shaun was doing OK. She still waited for him to speak.

'Is there any word on the little girl at all?' she asked.

He shook his head and murmured a 'Mm-mm,' his usual refuge at times like this.

The woman tutted in disgust. He had seen it all before.

'I've said a prayer to St Jude,' she said as she walked away. He frowned, irritated. He knew St Jude was the patron saint of lost causes.

He turned back to Frank who reached into his pocket and without looking, handed him some ibuprofen. Joe knocked them back with purple fizzy caffeine.

Frank turned and faced his group, which included Joe. 'Right, we're taking the central part of the village, from Seascapes, around by the shops, back down to the harbour and up again toward Shore's Rock.'

About forty people moved into rows and walked slowly up to the holiday homes. In the bright afternoon, the densely packed trees cast black shadows across the drive. Joe was at the edge of the line and almost fell over a little boy crouched behind a sycamore. His eyes widened when he saw Joe.

'I'm hiding,' he said in a loud whisper. He put a finger up to his lips and pointed towards his parents who were packing up a station wagon in front of one of the houses.

'Oh,' said Joe. 'But that might really scare your mom and dad. I'm sure they'd be real sad if they couldn't find you.' He looked through the trees and noticed a light on in the landing of the last house, the odd glow of a bulb in daylight. There was no car in the drive.

'I don't want to go home,' said the boy sadly.

'That's a real pity,' said Joe. 'I'm gonna go over and say hi to your mom and dad. Do you wanna come?'

The boy shook his head furiously. Joe told the man next in line to him that he had to check something.

He walked up to the couple. 'Don't look now, but your little guy is in the trees right behind me. I've been sworn to secrecy.'

The parents looked at each other and rolled their eyes. 'We'll kill him.'

'Have you been here all weekend?' said Joe.

'Yup,' said the woman. 'But it's still not long enough for Owen.'

'You didn't happen to see anyone in that last house, did you?' asked Joe, pointing.

'No. You actually notice the cars coming in and out here. It's so quiet,' said the man.

'Or you'd see the headlights,' added his wife. 'We've been in every night.' She nodded towards their son.

'OK. Just curious,' said Joe. 'Safe trip. Good luck getting him into the car.'

Joe rejoined the group for the walk through the village towards Shore's Rock. Every now and then, the whistle would blow, everyone would stop and a guard would collect whatever had been found. Then the line would move along again in silence until they reached the gate to the lighthouse.

'It's getting dark,' said Frank. 'And the forest is dark enough as it is, so we're going to have to postpone the rest of this. Thank you all for taking part.'

Richie's group had returned earlier and he was at the station when Frank walked in.

'Did you find anything?' he asked.

'Not a thing,' said Frank. 'Certainly nothing I

think will amount to anything. What about yourself?'

'No,' said Richie. 'Mind you, every scrap of
rubbish that has been dropped anywhere along
the way was pointed out to me. Sweet wrappers
I hadn't seen since I was a kid. Kitty Tynan spiked
a used condom on a stick and waved it in my face.
How far did you get?'

'We stopped at the lighthouse.'

'I can organise a posse to do the forest tomorrow
or whenever.'

'Check with O'Connor, but that sounds good
to me.'

Frank shook his head. 'Poor Katie will probably be back tonight, laughing at all this, morti-
fied that the whole village was traipsing around
looking for her.'

Shaun lay on the sofa in front of the TV, the
remote control in his outstretched arm, speeding
through the channels over and over.

'Were you working this weekend?' said Joe.

'Not since Thursday night. Why?'

'Were any of the houses booked?'

'Just three. For the weekend.'

'Which ones?'

'Why are you asking?'

'You left a light on.'

'What?' Shaun's heart started to pound.

'The one at the end. Unless someone's in it. But

I guess you wouldn't have been working on it unless it's being rented out.'

'There's no-one in it. But I didn't leave the light on.'

'Well, it's on, so somebody did. Is Mrs Shanley still away?'

'Dad, who cares?'

'Would you mind taking a look?'

'I've got other things on my mind right now.'

'I can go.'

'I'll go. It's my job. But there's no light on.'

'I'll take a walk with you.'

'Look, I'm fine. I'll go on my own, OK?'

'I'll come with you.'

'Well, I'm going to have a shower first.'

'That's OK. Let me know when you want to go.'

Shaun rushed to his bedroom, picked up the phone and called Robert.

'Rob, I need you to do me a big favour.'

'No problem.'

'No questions asked. And you can't tell anybody.'

'OK. What?'

'Can you get over here and stand under my window, so I can throw you down something?'

'Okaaay. Why? Is this about Katie? Do you know where she is?'

'No, I don't. It's just I need you to sort something out for me. I'll drop you down the keys to

Seascapes and if you could go in to number fifteen, the one at the end, turn off the light and bring me back the keys.'

'OK. Why?'

'Mrs Shanley's away. I left a light on on Thursday night, the next guests might be charged on the meter. I don't want her giving out to me. I'm too fucked up about Katie to do it myself.'

'That's fair enough.'

'Just don't let my dad see you.'

'What's he got to do with it?'

'You know parents.'

'Yeah. What time?'

'Right now.'

Ray rang the doorbell at the house. Anna eventually came out.

'I didn't want to bother you, but it's just about the lantern house, the rust and stuff. I don't know are you interested in having a look or, you know . . .'

'Just one second,' she said and reached in to grab her jacket.

She jogged across the grass and walked up the lighthouse steps, climbing the ladder into the lantern house. The walls had been completely stripped back to bare metal. Some of it was badly rusted.

'It looks so different,' said Anna. 'Very dark.'

'I know,' said Ray. 'The stuff really worked. It

got all the layers of paint off, no problem. Now we can repaint the whole thing white, brighten it up. But we really need to get rid of a couple of the panels. You can see the rust. So, will I go ahead and replace them?'

'That would be great,' said Anna. 'Thanks so much. I really appreciate all the hard work. Tell Hugh, too. I'm sorry I'm too tired to be more enthusiastic.'

'Weird,' said Joe. 'I could have sworn.' He was in the hall, leaning against the banister looking up at the landing light he knew had been on in the house at the end of the Seascapes cul-de-sac.

'It could have been the sun,' said Shaun. 'You know the way.'

'I'm not buying that,' said Joe. 'I saw it, on.' He walked up the stairs and flicked the light on and off. 'So you definitely haven't been here since Thursday?'

'I was out on Friday, Dad. And that was with Katie. And now she's gone. I was in all last night worrying about her. You saw me. So that's what I'm thinking about. Not about answering stupid questions from you that make no sense. So what if there was a light on?' He opened the front door. 'C'mon, Dad, this is retarded.'

Petey was pushing his mop awkwardly back and forth along the floor of the canteen, his first job every Monday morning. Frank came up behind him.

'Hello, Petey. I just have a few questions for you if you have a minute. I'm doing the rounds.'

Frank saw the fear in Petey's eyes when he noticed the clipboard with his name and details across the top of a questionnaire.

'It's about Katie Lawson.'

Petey flushed and stared at the ground. He rocked the handle of the mop back and forth.

'I heard she's gone missing,' said Petey. He shook his head. 'It's awful.'

'Yes,' said Frank. He waited. 'What do you know about Katie?'

'That she goes out with Shaun Lucchesi and she's in the school here.'

'Yes, well the last time she was seen was on Friday night just gone. You didn't see her or anything on Friday night, did you?'

'No,' said Petey, looking down and blushing. 'I was at home. I don't really go out.'

Frank felt a surge of pity.

'Look at me,' he said. 'Was your mother with you in the house?'

'No. She was out at bridge. Then she came back home very late with her friend, Mrs Miller. She stayed the night at our house.'

'What were you doing when they were out?'

'Watching TV. Watching Discovery. An amazing programme. About the Fastnet race disaster of

1979. Between August 13 and August 15, a force eleven—'

'Petey, tell me about Katie. Did you like her at all?' Frank struggled to get eye contact with him.

'She was a nice girl. I got on well with her.' Petey turned his head away and blinked back tears. Frank patted him on the back. Petey flinched.

'It's OK,' said Frank. 'Thanks for your help. We'll get back to you if we need to.' He stopped around the corner to write a note across the bottom of the page.

Richie stood stiffly on the stage, his legs spread, his arms folded across his chest. He looked out on the small group of teenagers that made up the secondary school. Frank slipped in the side door.

'Good morning, everyone,' said Richie. One of the boys from the football team stifled a laugh, then followed it with a loud cough. Anger flickered briefly across Richie's face.

There was a part of Frank that thought Richie would be more respected because he was younger, closer to the kids' ages. But another part of him understood how he wasn't. Richie had never been able to strike a balance between authority and severity.

'I came in today to talk to you all about Katie Lawson,' Richie continued. 'As you know, Katie is a fifth year student here. She went missing last

Friday night and we haven't heard from her since.'

Nervous energy ran through the crowd. They looked around for a reaction from Shaun, but he had been excused for the day.

'So if any of you know anything,' said Richie, 'anything at all, however insignificant or irrelevant it may seem, please talk to myself or Frank.' He nodded towards the wall where Frank stood. Some of the students smiled over at him. A few waved. Richie paused, then went on. 'As well as some detectives from Waterford, we'll be calling to houses around the area over the coming day or two, so you can catch us then as well. And, of course, anything you tell us will be treated in the strictest confidence. Thank you.'

Joe was standing in Tynan's buying *USA Today* when a stack of *Evening Herald*s landed on the floor beside him. For a moment, he was confused by the familiarity of the face under the front page headline. NO CLUES IN SEARCH FOR MISSING TEENAGER. He broke the binding and slid out the second copy. Kitty Tynan wouldn't take any money for it. 'They don't waste their time, do they?' she said. 'They even have a photo of the search. I didn't even know they were there.'

'Yeah, I saw the guy,' said Joe. 'And a journalist asking questions. Some people talked to him.'

'But it's never the ones closest to the families,' said Kitty.

'Never is,' said Joe.

Joe went to a bench by the harbour and read the article about the tragic disappearance of schoolgirl Katie Lawson and the concern of anonymous neighbours.

Anna stood in the kitchen at the chopping board, with a pile of sliced onions in front of her. She had stopped to watch the sun set.

Joe walked in, frowning, pressing his jaws with his thumb and middle finger. Then he used both hands to massage the area above his eyebrows.

Anna turned around. 'Not again.'

He nodded and pulled open the medicine drawer.

'That can't be right,' said Anna, pointing to the decongestants. 'No-one takes those for that long.'

He shrugged, then knocked back the decongestants with two prescription painkillers and a glass of water. He tapped his watch and pointed towards the sitting room. He lay down on the sofa and waited for the effects to hit. The pain had intensified in the last year. He had seen doctors in New York that between them had diagnosed sinusitis, earache and the standard stress they threw out when they read his job description. One young doctor suggested yoga. Joe would have laughed out loud if he thought his jaw wouldn't shatter. He was happy to walk away with a script for painkillers. Anna was putting him under pressure to see a specialist in Dublin, but he hadn't got around to it and he used the breaks from the pain to slip into denial.

After half an hour, he walked back into the kitchen. 'I forgot to say to you – what the hell is wrong with that guy, Miller?'

'John Miller?' said Anna, throwing the onions into a hot pan.

'Yeah, the alco.' He slid his lower jaw back and forth.

'Why do you ask?' she said, going back to the window.

'He was saying some weird shit to me in Danaher's the other night.'

'Like what?' she said, slicing into a red pepper.

'He was giving me a hard time, saying stuff about you. Have you met him or something?' Anna looked at him.

'He's John,' she said patiently. 'I told you. The John I went out with when I was here the first time?'

'Oh,' said Joe. 'What happened there?'

'I left for New York, he ended up in Australia,' said Anna. 'You were grinding your teeth during the night, by the way. I tried to wake you up, but you just turned over and kept going.'

'How long were you and this Miller guy together?'

'Eight months.'

'Oh. Must have been pretty intense.'

Anna said nothing. She kept chopping.

'So was it you who drove him to drink? My baby break his heart?' asked Joe, standing behind her, wrapping his arms around her, kissing the back of her neck.

Anna smiled.

'I don't think so, somehow,' she said.

'Could have,' said Joe, teasing.

'Can you bring up a Merlot?' she said.

'Sure,' he said, walking out the door and down to the cellar.

Anna put down the knife, closed her eyes and breathed out.

EIGHT

Stinger's Creek, North Central Texas, 1981

Geoff Riggs lay on his back on the sticky carpet, his right arm bent high above his head. A grey T-shirt rode up his chest, exposing his pale, hairy stomach. Donnie rushed in as he had done so many times before, shaking his satchel from his shoulder, sliding it down his arm to the floor. He fell on his knees beside his father and put his ear to his heart. Then he pushed up each of his eyelids with his thumbs. He never knew what he was looking for when he did this, never knew what would be a dangerous thing to see. He rolled his father onto his side, then stood up and scanned the room. The TV was on mute. He took the remote control and turned the volume up loud. Then he threw it on the sofa, quickly grabbed his satchel and went back out into the porch. Geoff came to, his right arm dead, his neck rigid. He twisted it slowly, then brought his arm down to his side.

'Hey,' said Donnie, sticking his head in the door.

'Didn't hear you come in,' Geoff snarled, rolling onto his back.

'That's 'cos you got the TV up too loud,' said Donnie, switching it off. 'Can I fix you somethin'?'

'Sandwich,' said Geoff. 'Beef.'

Duke sat by the treehouse door, watching a spider crawl up the frame. He held out his hand and let it move across his palm, guiding it down onto the floor where it skittered across into a dark corner.

'You there?' called Donnie from below.

'Come up,' said Duke. 'Where were you?'

'At the store. Where were you?'

'Uncle Bill's. A friend of his was taking pictures of the hawks. What's in the shoe box?'

Donnie knelt in front of him. His eyes darted left and right.

'Look what I found in the bottom of Daddy's closet,' he whispered, taking off the lid. The box was filled with small packages.

'Blackpowder,' he said.

Duke's eyes went wide.

'Don't worry!' said Donnie. 'I know what I'm doin'.'

'What *are* you doin'?'

'Lightin' it on fire. What do you think?'

'Here? Why don't we blow somethin' up proper?'

'We will, later. I just wanna see this first.'

He squatted down and motioned for Duke to stay back. He put a capful of the powder on the floor and struck a match. He turned his head away and closed his eyes, reaching out to put the flame to the powder. It flashed instantly. He roared. His hands, arms and one side of his face and neck were black. His eyes were huge. Part of his T-shirt gaped across his chest. Duke started to laugh. Donnie laughed with him, but it hurt. Neither of them noticed the pile of comic books on fire behind them until it was too late.

'Holy shit!' said Donnie. 'My treehouse!' They looked around the small room for something to stamp out the fire, but they had nothing. The flames crackled and spread quickly across the dry timber.

'Let's get outta here,' said Duke, 'before the ladder goes up.' They scrambled through the door and skipped most of the rungs, jumping free from the heat. They stepped back to watch the treehouse burn. The flames shone in their eyes. They stood transfixed until it finally collapsed, leaving burning embers and tiny wisps floating around their heads.

'Well, shit,' said Donnie. 'I can't go home to Daddy like this. And he spent ages buildin' that. He's gonna kill me.'

'No he won't. It was an accident,' said Duke. Donnie looked at him.

'We'll go to my house,' said Duke. 'At least you can wash up some.'

When they got there, Wanda was asleep on the couch. The bathroom was a mess. Underwear and filthy towels covered the floor. Donnie filled up the sink and grabbed a bar of soap and a face cloth. As he scrubbed away the black residue, he looked into the mirror. Tears sprang up in his eyes.

'Oh shit, Duke. Oh, shit, oh shit.'

Duke jumped up from the edge of the bath. 'What? What?'

He looked at Donnie and through the black he could see angry red skin with white blisters, some of them torn open by the cloth. They both looked down at Donnie's arms. He started to scrub at them too, ripping at more blisters.

'Oh, shit,' said Duke. 'I'm gettin' Mama.'

'Wait,' said Donnie. 'We need to get our story straight.'

Wanda tried to have a conversation with Geoff Riggs. Her hair was tousled behind, backcombed over a dark greasy patch. She wore a vest top with no bra on underneath. Her hips swayed in her cut-off jeans.

'Can you believe it?' she was saying.

'No, I can not,' slurred Geoff. 'Unbelievable.'

His hands were in his pockets and he rocked back and forth on his heels over the edge of the bottom step.

'Unbelievable.'

'Doctor says they're first and second degree,' said Wanda. 'Might scar his face and arms in places . . .' Donnie looked horrified.

'Oh, sorry, Donnie, I shouldn't have said anything,' she said. 'I'm sure you'll be just fine.'

'Let me tell you, if I find those high school brats, I'll take my rifle to them.'

Donnie shot a look at Duke.

'Goin' around, preying on young boys like that,' added Wanda.

'I know,' said Geoff, trying to settle his eyes on Donnie. 'Coulda been burnt alive up there.' He turned back to Wanda.

'Mighty kind of you to bring him home,' he said.

'No trouble at all,' said Wanda, shaking her head too much.

'Think we should call the police?' he asked on his way back up the steps.

'No!' said Duke. Everyone looked at him. He hesitated. 'The Lord will, uh . . . sinners will be, uh, will pay for their sins.'

Donnie snickered.

'Well, how's about that?' said Geoff. 'Raisin' yourself a minister, there.' He chuckled. Wanda gave a loud hollow laugh.

NINE

The coffee shop was filled with the smell of bacon and eggs. D.I. O'Connor sat opposite Frank Deegan, his PDA open on the table in front of him. A young waitress came over to take their order, smiling nervously at them, hovering before she walked away.

'You'd want to be careful,' said Frank, 'or you'll have the whole parish listening in.'

'It's always the way,' said O'Connor. He looked up. 'How do you think Richie's getting on? I mean, it's plunging him in at the deep end really. One minute, parking tickets, pickpockets and checkpoints. Next minute, this.'

'Not much different to any of us, really,' said Frank. 'I don't know. Richie's grand. He's a serious lad for his age, a bit uptight, that's all. He's working hard though. I think he'll surprise us.'

'Fair enough,' said O'Connor. 'He's very . . . intense.'

'I think I know why,' said Frank. 'I don't know the whole story, but a young friend of his, Justin Dwyer, drowned when he was about eight or nine. Richie was there at the time. Apparently, he had an awful time trying to save him, but . . .' He shook his head. 'Richie's a lad that will do something about Katie. I think the guilt over that little guy has stayed with him for years. He won't want to feel that again.'

O'Connor nodded. 'I've been having a think about Katie's interests and whether or not they've got anything do with this.' He read from a list on the small screen of the PDA: hanging out with her friends, reading, movies, singing, music, computer games.

'Friends? Well, we have their statements. Reading? I think it's safe to say there's nothing untoward there. Movies? She could have gone in to Waterford to see something, but it would have been too late that time of the night. OK. Singing or music. Could there have been an audition on somewhere she would have gone to that her mother wouldn't have allowed? One of those pop star things? Maybe someone promised her something, a career . . .'

'She wouldn't have fallen for anything like that.'

'What if it was someone she knew?'

'I still don't think so. Who?'

'Anyone. Someone's brother, cousin, friend . . .'

'She sang in a folk group in mass,' said Frank patiently. 'And in school concerts. She wasn't Tina Turner.' He leaned back in his seat and stretched his arms behind his head.

The waitress reappeared, setting mugs and teapots carefully down in front of them.

'Thanks,' said O'Connor. He pressed at the corners of his eyes, blinking slowly.

'What about the Internet?' he said, pouring each of them a cup of tea. 'Could she have come in contact with someone online? Maybe gone to meet them?'

Frank shook his head.

O'Connor shrugged his shoulders. 'She's sixteen, it's easy for a girl like that to be flattered.'

'Maybe. If she wasn't a pretty, intelligent, happy girl with a handsome young boyfriend.'

'But some girls might like the mystery—'

'Not Katie.'

'I'm thinking out loud here. I'm not really expecting you to answer all my questions. I know you're familiar with these kids, but I doubt they're going to be keeping you up to speed.'

'They don't have to. It's obvious what they're like. I've known them for years.'

'I'm running some things by you, that's all.'

'Look, you can talk to some of her friends yourself – Ali Danaher and Robert Harrington would be the main two – but they'll probably tell you the same thing. What you see is what you get with Katie.'

'Well, what I'm left with is drugs, pregnancy . . .'

Frank was shaking his head again. 'Unfortunately, what I'm left with is something a lot worse than that. It's been two weeks . . .'

O'Connor sat quietly, then picked up his PDA again and ran his stylus down the screen.

'So you still think suicide—'

'Is not and never should have been a possibility,' said Frank. 'I've been surprised by suicides in my day, but I'd stake my own life on it that she would never do a thing like that. Katie Lawson did not do something to herself. I'm afraid something was done to her.'

Shaun was staring into space. Robert was in front of the television playing Spiderman. Anna stuck her head in the door and shouted. 'I'm going to Martha's.'

'Damn that web slinging,' said Robert. Without even looking, Shaun knew his friend was whipping the controller from side to side.

'You know that doesn't help,' said Shaun. 'The flailing.'

'Shut it,' said Robert. 'I've been on this level eight times. Eight.'

'Give it to me,' said Shaun, taking the controller. 'You have to do this.'

Web fluid shot from Spiderman's wrists, carrying him from building to building. Then he twisted mid-air until he picked up the extra energy that floated between two skyscrapers.

'Doesn't help me,' said Robert. 'I have no idea what you just did.' Shaun threw the instruction manual at him and kept playing.

Ali Danaher was surprised by her brief flicker of panic as she led D.I. O'Connor into the living room. She sat on the sofa. He was swallowed into a battered armchair beside her and left sitting lower down. She held back a smile.

'I know you've been asked a lot of questions already,' said O'Connor, pulling himself forward to the edge of the seat, 'but I just want to get a few things clearer in my head. I'm trying to get a sense of Katie. What kind of person is she?'

'She's a sweetheart.'

'Really?'

'Yes. One of those rare babes-who-don't-know-it. And she has a huge brain . . . which makes me wonder.'

'What?'

'Well, why she's gone.'

'Any theories?'

'No. But I can't wait to find out.' She gave a wry smile.

'Was she impulsive?'

'Sometimes, but never rash, if that's what you're getting at.'

'Would you call her an extrovert?'

'Ish. I mean, she wasn't shy, but she wasn't in-your-face either.'

'Would she be likely to talk to people she didn't know?'

'I'm the one who talks to randomers. And she'll talk to whoever I end up talking to.'

'Is this in Mountcannon?'

'There *are* no strangers in Mountcannon. I'm talking about when we go into town.'

'Is Katie gullible?'

'Are intelligent people usually gullible?'

'Does she go online?'

'Yes. Not a lot, though.'

'What kind of sites?'

'Bomb-making, usually.'

O'Connor waited patiently.

'Music downloads, horoscopes, school stuff, entertainment, cinema listings,' said Ali.

'Does she go into chatrooms?'

'Ew. Freaksville. No.'

'Are you sure?'

'Well, I'm not with her every minute of the day, but I seriously doubt it. She's too busy hanging out with her alive and well friends.' She pointed to herself. 'Ohhh, I get it,' she said, 'you think she's run off with one of those creepy old guys.' She laughed. 'Ew. No way.'

'Was Katie flirtatious?'

'Eh, have you seen her boyfriend?'

'I presume you mean she was faithful to him.'

'He's not my type, but yeah, I think it's safe to say most normal girls would be perfectly happy to stick with Lucky.'

'Was she easily flattered?'

'No. She can't stand compliments.'

'Was she depressed?'

'No. Where are you going with all this?'

'I'm just asking you a few questions.'

He looked down at his notebook.

'Right. As a publican's daughter, you would have access to . . . ?'

Ali looked at him. 'Dirty glasses?'

O'Connor stared at her. 'I was thinking more along the lines of alcohol.'

She rolled her eyes. 'Duh.'

'Come on. This isn't going to take long.'

'Look, that's what I do in the bar – wash glasses. I take them off the tables, I pour out the slops, I inhale the manky stench of stale beer, I load the glasses into the dishwasher, I turn it on, I wipe the counters, I wait for the glasses to be finished, I open the dishwasher, steam my zits, unload the glasses and stack them on the shelves. Yup, I can see the link between that and Katie going missing. I handle beer glasses. Isn't it the Looking Glass you're thinking of? Maybe she went through there.'

'You're not very helpful for someone whose best friend has disappeared.'

'That's because she'll be back.'

'What do you know that makes you so sure of that?'

'It's not what I know, it's who I know. I know Katie and she just isn't the type to go off and not come back.'

'Hmm. You smoke dope, isn't that right?'

Ali's eyes shot wide. 'Uh, what?'

'You heard me. Isn't that right?'

'I presume that means you know that's right.'

'Yes, we do. Did Katie?'

'No.' She laughed. 'No way.'

'Are you sure?'

'Eh, yeah. She's my best friend. I think I'd know.'

'Has she ever asked you for drugs?'

'Lots of times. I'm a known dealer. In Feminax.'

'Please can you take this seriously?'

'Fine, OK. Katie would never do drugs.'

'Did she approve of you doing drugs?'

'What kind of a question is that? We are sixteen. We are friends. We don't approve or disapprove of what each other does.'

'No,' said O'Connor patiently. 'I just wanted to know how she felt about drugs.'

'Look. I've told Frank all this stuff already. This has nothing to do with drugs,' said Ali. 'Nothing. She's neutral on the subject, OK? She doesn't feel anything about drugs. Drugs play no part in her life, no part in her disappearance. I smoke dope the odd time. I'm not a junkie, Katie isn't messed up in the wrong crowd, she isn't in a warehouse somewhere unloading a shipment of coke. We're just two girls from a tiny village, one of whom smokes a spliff every now and then, neither of whom has ever dealt with anyone dodgier than, than . . . See? I can't even think of anyone dodgy we've ever come into contact with. Jesus. What does that say about our sheltered little lives?'

'It's a nice way to be.'

'Don't tell me – the world is a horrible place and we're lucky—'

'Yes, actually. You are lucky. It can be pretty grim out there.'

'Well, it can be pretty uneventful "in here". Thank God for Katie causing a bit of a stir.'

'So you think she's done all this for the attention?'

'Oh, for the love of Mike.' She rolled her eyes dramatically. 'You must have scored ten out of ten in literal interpretation class.'

He looked at her.

She held up her hand. 'And before you say it, I know there was no literal interpretation class.'

Anna put her cup gently back on its saucer and turned to Martha. 'I remember running away once,' she said. 'I packed a little bag, left a note for my parents and took the bus into Paris. I sat crying to my friend in McDonalds. Then she told me her mother hit her and her brothers. And I realised I was crazy. My parents loved me, I had a wonderful home, I just wanted to test it all, spread my wings. I wanted to grab a piece of independence, but really when I found it, I wanted to go right back home.'

Martha smiled and squeezed Anna's hand.

'I'm sure that's all this is, Martha. A young girl trying to have independence. She knows you love her, she knows she has a good home. But she's sixteen, she thinks she's ready for it all. But she'll know soon enough that she's not.'

'Thanks,' said Martha. 'I hope so.' She folded and unfolded a tissue. 'I know I was strict with Katie. I've been going over all the things I stopped her from doing like sleeping over in friends' houses, staying out late or going out with boys. I gave in, of course, when she met Shaun. Katie didn't know, but I had seen them together once on their way home from school and I knew straightaway I'd have no hope of tearing them apart.'

Anna smiled.

'I'd understand if she ran away because of something like that, if I'd stopped her from seeing Shaun. But, this? I don't know what's going on.' Martha paused. 'Are you sure he doesn't know anything?'

'Of course,' said Anna. 'He would tell us. He's devastated. He would say something.'

'I know,' said Martha. 'I'm sorry. I had to . . .'

'It's OK.'

Martha smiled again, then went into the kitchen to make more tea.

Anna sat back on the sofa and breathed in deeply. There was nothing about Katie to make her believe she'd ever run away. She wasn't the type of girl who looked for her next hit of adventure, she was content enough not to want to escape.

The phone rang. Martha dropped the tray with the teapot, splashing hot tea up her legs. She ignored it and ran for the phone. Anna could hear her speaking slowly.

'No. Definitely jeans, Frank. Those wide ones. Yes, the rest is right, yes.'

She hung up and came back into the living room, deflated.

'Someone saw a girl in a pink hoodie, hitching the Sunday after, but she had track pants on and they wanted to check if I could have got it wrong, what she was wearing.' She sat down. 'I suppose I don't mind them calling for things like that, but it's just, you know, every time the phone rings, I nearly have a heart attack.'

Anna looked down at the splashes on Martha's legs.

'Oh, I'm fine,' said Martha. 'You know, my mother used to be able to put her hands into boiling water to take the eggs out. And she'd stick her hand under the grill to get the sausages. Strong women in my family.'

Suddenly she started to cry. Anna brought her a tissue and sat on the edge of the armchair. She laid her hand gently on Martha's shoulder.

'It's funny how you don't know people,' said Martha, wiping her nose. 'Have you met John Miller yet? He used to be in my class. He was a lovely lad, sweet, charming. Would do anything for you. Anyway, I went away to London after school, came back several years later and I heard he had moved to Australia. Now I hear his wife kicked him out . . . because he beat her. And it was his mother who told me, whispered it like a confession in the supermarket. I had known Mae Miller all my life as a very private woman. She never spoke about her business. Then she starts telling me, a casual acquaintance, about something that personal?' She shook her head. 'So you never know with people. Anyone can surprise you.'

Shame pulsed through Anna. That she could have been so intimate with a man who went on to beat women repulsed her. A long-buried image of him pinning her hands above her head flashed into her mind. It repulsed her, because in it, she could see the smile across her face.

'Ohmygod,' said Ali, running down the stairs into Shaun's bedroom. 'Katie owes me big time.'

'Why?' said Shaun.

'For a totally puckering experience. That guy in charge, the D.I.? Came to my house for a chat.

Which was fine. Then he goes, "I know you smoke dope." I nearly puked.'

'Wow. What did you say?'

'I'm, like, fair enough. But it's not like I've run out of veins or something, I'm shooting into my groin in a phone booth. Jesus.'

Shaun shook his head. 'Man, that's unreal.'

'I think they thought Katie was involved in some sort of shady gangland stuff. Bizarre. I'd laugh if I wasn't so shitting it. He was asking about online freaks as well.' She shook her head. 'I mean, it's an arboretum.'

'What?' said Robert.

'Of wrong trees they're barking up.' She threw herself on the sofa and groaned. 'Where are you, Katie, you bad, bad, girl?'

Joe knocked lightly on the door and came down the stairs.

'Who's winning?' he asked.

'Everyone except Rob,' said Shaun.

'Hi, Mr Lucchesi,' said Ali, smiling wide. She leaned up on her elbows.

'Hi, Ali. Like the hair.'

'Blue-black,' she said.

Joe sat down on the edge of the bed. 'So how you all doing?' he said.

'Not bad,' said Robert. 'It's been really hard on everyone.' He made a face towards Shaun. 'We're all a bit in shock. We don't know what Katie's up to.'

Shaun put down the controls and left the room.

'God,' said Robert. 'I didn't mean to—'

'Don't worry,' said Joe. 'It's not your fault.' Then, 'So where were you guys that night, when Katie . . .'

Ali spoke first. 'I hate to say it, but I was at home doing my homework. On a Friday night.' She shook her head.

'Robert?' said Joe.

'Uh, at the harbour.'

'Oh. With Katie and Shaun.'

'No. Just with the others, Kevin and Finn. I think we were, like, down near the lifeboat launch and Katie and Shaun were up the other end.'

'Right. And you didn't see them leave—'

'See who leave?' said Shaun, standing in the doorway with a bag of tortillas.

'You and Katie. That night,' said Robert quickly.

'Just thinking out loud,' said Joe.

'Interrogating out loud,' Shaun muttered.

Joe stood up. Something caught his eye.

'What's that scratch on your hand, there, Robert?'

Robert blushed. 'Aw, football. I'm crap. I crashed into the goalpost.'

Joe nodded. Anger flashed in Shaun's eyes.

'We're trying to play a game here, Dad.' When

Joe didn't move, Shaun snarled an 'OK?'

'Sure,' said Joe, getting up to leave.

Duke Rawlins wandered around the small roadside grocer's, picking up products, reading the
labels and putting them back down again. Two
teenage girls watched him from behind the
counter. He walked up to them.

'Ladies. What d'y'all like eatin' over here?'

They glanced at each other and giggled. 'What
do you mean?' said one of them.

'You know, like, what would you recommend?
What's your favourite dinner?'

'Oh,' they said at the same time. 'Pasta.'

'Both of you?'

'Yeah. Everyone likes pasta. I'll get you the nice
ones,' said the other.

She walked over to the freezer, took out two
bags of tomato and garlic penne.

'Here. Catch,' she said, throwing one to him.
He missed.

'Sorry,' she said, giggling, walking over and
handing him the second.

He put them on the counter. 'And two bottles
of Coke,' he said. 'And a bottle of red wine.'

'Are you going to tell her you cooked it all
yourself?'

He laughed.

'Aw, shit,' he said suddenly. 'I don't have a
cooker.'

The girls exchanged glances. 'Bizarre,' said one of them. 'Well, you can give them a blast in that microwave over there and I'll wrap them in foil for you after.'

'Thanks,' he said.

'But you do know, your cover will be blown,' she said.

He smiled.

O'Connor stood in Frank's office with his hands in his pockets staring out at the harbour.

'Ali Danaher,' he said.

'Ah,' said Frank.

'I tell you, it wasn't like that in my day,' said O'Connor, turning around and smiling. Frank noticed his eyes looked clear for the first time. O'Connor shook his head. 'There'd have been serious trouble if I spoke to an adult like that.'

'Did you have an eye infection?' asked Frank.

'What?' said O'Connor. 'Oh. The red eyes? No. Contacts. She's a bit of a smart arse, Ali, isn't she? Anyway, she blew everything out of the water. Reckons no to drink, drugs, the Internet possibility, no to everything.'

'I tried to tell you,' said Frank. 'There's no point trying to fit modern theories to an old-fashioned girl like Katie. I suppose like me wearing contacts,' he said, holding up his magnifying glasses.

* * *

Joe focused on the wrinkled tourist map of Mountcannon spread out in front of him. It showed the harbour, the church, the bars, two restaurants and the coffee shop, along with the scenic coastal drive past the lighthouse and two other roads out of the village, one a dead end, the other leading to Waterford. With a black pen, he marked the harbour and Katie's house. Ignoring the scenic coastal drive, which would have brought Katie further away from home, he concentrated on the two other roads – the Upper Road and Church Road, both of which curved around to be connected by the straight Manor Road to form an uneven semi-circle. He wrote notes along the narrow white borders and stuffed the map into the inside pocket of his jacket. He took his car and parked it outside the school, walking the short distance to the T-junction at the edge of the village. Left would take him to Katie's house, up the hill, along her regular route home. Right could also take him there, a longer walk down Church Road towards Mariner's Strand and the Waterford Road. If, however, she took a left at the church, she would walk until she met the Upper Road, then take a left to her house.

Joe chose the first route, scanning the ground as he walked, taking everything in. He rounded the bend that brought him to the Grants' house where Petey lived with his mother. Then he moved on towards Katie's. He turned around before he reached the house and walked back to the T. This time he went the other way, taking a right down the steep and narrow footpath at the top of Church Road. He was protected from a sharp drop to Mariner's Strand by a low crooked wall. He looked down at the water, slate grey, rolling diagonally towards the narrow shore in shallow waves. He looked left, across the road to the old stone church and its quaint, cluttered cemetery. Then he stopped, knowing at that moment exactly what he needed to find.

O'Connor came out from the small kitchen in the station with two mugs of coffee. He put one on Frank's desk and walked back over to the window.

He took a mouthful of coffee. 'I'm just wondering, Frank, could you be too close to all these kids?'

'What?'

'Obviously,' he said, turning around, 'your input is a great help, because you know the area, the people involved etc. But do you think your judgment could be clouded at all?'

'No,' said Frank, quietly preserving his dignity.

The iron gate to the cemetery was held closed with a loose length of dirty tow-rope. Joe pulled at it until it gave way. Every footstep crunched across the gravel as he moved along the rows between graves, then silence as he walked up the grassy slope to a modest, well-kept plot.

MATTHEW LAWSON 1952–1997,
BELOVED HUSBAND TO MARTHA,
DEVOTED FATHER TO KATIE

And on the grave was a dead white rose.

Frank stood up to let O'Connor know it was time to leave. There was a charge in the room that he didn't have the energy to take on. He understood what O'Connor said would have crossed anyone's mind in the same situation. He was just surprised he felt the need to say it out loud.

As Joe walked back through the village, his relief at finding evidence of Katie's route was overtaken by dread. What if the rose on the grave was not about her father? Maybe it was a statement. Her father was dead, she was planning . . . Joe shook his head. No-one was safe from the depths of his negativity.

O'Connor sat in his car and watched Frank cross the road to Danaher's, his head bowed, his hands in his pockets. O'Connor knew he had probably lived up to whatever Frank was expecting from the youngest D.I. in the country. But he tried to convince himself he had said what he had to say.

Joe slid onto the bench beside Frank, opening the map of Mountcannon on the table in Danaher's.

'OK,' he said. 'Here's where they were in the village. And here are the possible routes out of town from there.' Frank frowned.

Richie came back from the mensroom.

'Is this guy serious? What is this?'

'Richie,' said Frank.

'I'm just looking at where Katie could have gone that Friday night,' said Joe.

'Why?' asked Richie.

'Because I think I know.'

'You know nothing,' said Richie. 'First of all, flip over that map and look at the date on the back. 1984. That map is ancient. Half the things—'

'I've drawn in or crossed out accordingly,' said Joe. Richie glanced down at the map, then did a double-take at the neat print in block caps at the edges of the page. He shot Joe a bemused look.

'Either way, none of this has anything to do with you,' he said. 'We're having a private meeting here. Do you mind?'

'If you'll just look for a second. You think she went this way—'

'The only reason you know anything about what we think is because you're friends with Martha Lawson. What she does or doesn't say to you is none of my business. What *is* my business is you thinking that all this makes you part of the investigation. So you used to be a detective in New York. I used to work in a bar. But you don't see me pulling pints in here, do you?'

'Richie, a young girl is missing,' said Joe.

'Yes, your son's girlfriend, I know that. So you should be grateful that every part of the investigation will follow procedure.'

'I just want to help out here . . .'

'You arrogant Yanks think you can save the world,' said Richie.

TEN

Stinger's Creek, North Central Texas, 1982

'I think my baby's gonna kick some butt, today,' said Wanda. 'The first Rawlins family jock.' Duke rolled his eyes.

Wanda climbed out of the pickup and smoothed the legs of her wrinkled jeans down to her yellow high heels. She looked at her son, dressed from the waist down in his football gear.

'You look real cute, honey,' she said.

He shrugged and pulled the rest of his gear from the floor of the cab. He slid the shoulder pads and jersey over his head.

'Cougars. Number fifty-eight,' said Wanda. It was the first time she'd seen it. 'What do you have to do, then? What did I pay my thirty dollars for?'

'I throw the ball back between my legs and make sure the nose guard from the other team doesn't tackle the quarterback.'

'Well, that's wonderful, honey. I'll be lookin' out for you,' she said, pointing at his chest.

Duke's eyes wandered past her to another family, dressed for church, the father standing behind his son, pressing strong hands on to his shoulders, smiling.

'Honey, look at all the pretty little cheerleaders!' said Wanda.

In a corner of the parking lot, a group of teenage girls in dark blue shorts and cropped tops stamped with a white cougar stood in a circle, practising their cheers. Beside them, a slim blonde stood on one leg, while she pulled the other behind her until it almost touched her shoulder. Others were jumping or doing splits, their faces set in wide, static smiles. Duke turned to his mother with the same eerie grin. Wanda frowned.

'Stop that, honey,' she said, smacking his arm.

Two men stood in a cloud of cigarette smoke by the entrance to the stadium, laughing loud and hard.

'Or Wanda Blowjob?'

'Wanda Cum-in-my-Face?'

'All I get from Gloria is Wanda Be Held.' They hooted. One slapped the other's back. They stopped laughing when Duke walked between them, pushing a small, firm hand into each man's stomach and continuing into the stadium.

'Hey, buddies,' he spat.

The men looked at each other.

'Twelve years old,' said one, shaking his head.

'A genuine son of a bitch.'

Duke went to the weigh-in area, then sat with his mother and Geoff Riggs for the last few minutes of the PeeWee game. Donnie jogged off the field, his face red and shiny. His hair was limp with sweat.

'You shoulda seen him out there today,' said Geoff. 'Ran his skinny little legs off catchin' that ball.' Geoff rubbed a thick hand across his shaved head, showing the sweat patches on his tank top, letting loose a blast of foul air.

Wanda leaned away. 'Good for you, Donnie,' she said. 'The Midget hero.'

'Donnie's in the PeeWees,' said Duke. 'I'm Midgets.'

Wanda smiled at Geoff. 'Duke's gonna score a touchdown today, aren't you, baby?'

Duke rolled his eyes. 'Yeah, Mom . . . if I turn into a quarterback.' Donnie laughed.

'We gotta go,' said Geoff. 'Good luck, Duke.'

'Thanks.'

Duke grabbed his helmet and left his mother alone in the stands. Five rows in front of her, separated by an aisle, groups of parents chatted and laughed, pointing out their kids on the sidelines. Wanda focused on her feet, rubbing the dull pink marks that scarred them. She tilted her ankles and examined the fresh red scabs at her heels.

Reaching down, she hooked a nail under the hard, dry flesh and picked one free. Crystal Buchanan walked by her, stiff blonde hair, painted like a stewardess, with a flask of coffee and two plastic cups hanging from her little finger. She sat down beside her.

'Hi Wanda,' she said, smiling. 'Duke playing today?'

Wanda looked at her, curious. 'I know you're a good Catholic . . .' she said.

Crystal's smile froze.

' . . . but I'm not your Mary Goddamn Magdalene.'

'I was trying to be nice,' said Crystal.

'Nope. Not buyin' it,' said Wanda, staring straight ahead. 'You were lookin' to rescue the downtrodden. Old folks, handicapped babies and whores. Crystal Buchanan, our Lord and Saviour.'

Crystal stood to leave. 'You're truly beyond help.'

'Well, that's Crystal clear,' said Wanda. 'Oh – and say hi to Mr Buchanan.' Wanda had never met Mr Buchanan, but she liked the way she could make a good woman flinch.

She turned back to the field, watching as the Braves' centre started play. He snapped the ball to the quarterback, then blocked the nose guard pushing towards him. The quarterback sprinted, but was tackled to the ground by a chunky defender and the ball popped loose. The referee blew the whistle. The game continued with players piling onto the ball, untangling, piling, untangling.

At half-time, Wanda looked at the scoreboard. The Cougars were in the lead by one point. She watched as Duke straddled his legs and bent over the ball. The players lined up on either side of him. 'On hut two!' yelled the quarterback. 'Blue! Red! Hut! Hut!' Duke snapped the ball between his legs. In seconds, the nose guard had pushed him aside and tackled the quarterback. The quarterback fumbled the ball and the nose guard recovered it. Everybody dived. The whistle blew. The quarterback turned to Duke. 'Good job . . . you fuckin' retard.' But Duke's eyes were on the retreating back of the nose guard as he jogged to the huddle. Duke moved quickly behind him, leading with his helmet, charging low into his kidneys.

'Go, Dukey!' yelled Wanda before she realised her mistake. Parents craned their necks to stare at her.

The boy collapsed onto the field, crying out through the stunned silence. His mother was on her feet, running towards him. The whistle blew and a yellow flag sailed through the air and landed at Duke's feet.

'Out!' roared the referee. 'You're ejected. Go.' He pointed the way.

Duke stared at him, then jogged off. He passed his coach who stabbed a finger towards him. 'Get outta that uniform! Go sit in the stands.'

The mother of the nose guard pushed onto the field to her son.

Duke's coach ran over to the referee.

'I don't want to hear it,' said the referee, holding up his hand.

The coach's voice was low. 'What can I say, Mike? I agree with you.'

'That's good to know,' said Mike. 'The kid's fucking nuts. Spearing a kid for—'

'I know that, for Christ's sake. You shoulda seen him in practice. Didn't get the whole no-contact thing.'

They both looked toward the stands and saw Wanda stagger through the row, pushing Duke ahead of her.

'Poor bastard,' said the coach.

ELEVEN

'I heard a scream,' said Mae Miller.

Frank waited. 'Did we not get a statement from you already?' he said.

'You didn't. I was away until now, didn't hear a thing about this 'til I got back. As a member of Neighbourhood Watch – your wife's on the committee, of course – I'm well aware of the importance of keeping an eye out for suspicious activity and reporting it immediately, in this case, as soon as I got back.'

Mae Miller was eighty-six years old, slender and poised in an expensive maroon wool suit with a mandarin collar. She wore tan tights and black patent court shoes. Frank didn't know much about makeup, but he wasn't sure about her red lipstick. Mae Miller had taught primary school in Mountcannon for over forty years. Between the ages of four and twelve, most village children had sat in her classroom, in fear.

'It was Friday night,' she said, settling into a chair beside the door and sliding off green leather gloves. 'Myself and Mrs Grant, Petey's mother, had been playing bridge in a friend's house in Annestown. I knew my son John was going to be home late that night, so I was staying with the Grants for company. They live, as you know, at the corner of that road that leads down to the missing girl, Katie Lawson's house, where she lives with her mother, Martha Lawson. Her father, Matthew Lawson, of course, passed on several years ago. 1997 if I remember rightly. He was a fine man.' Frank nodded patiently.

'Anyway, I was up having a cup of tea in my room,' she continued. 'The guest room at the front of the house that overlooks the street.'

'Did you look out?' said Frank, moving her along. 'When you heard the scream.'

'I did,' she said, nodding. 'And I saw two people, walking down the road from the village towards the house.'

'Men, women?'

'A man and a woman, well, youngish, I would say, not too old. He was taller.' She gave a short nod.

'Did you recognise either of them?' said Frank.

'They looked familiar, but I can't say for sure if the girl was young Katie.'

'How were the couple acting?'

'Like they hadn't a care in the world.'

'But the scream?'

'Yes, that was after I had seen them out the window.'

'Oh. I thought that's what made you look out.'

'No. I was looking out the window anyway. I turned to my tea, heard a scream and looked back. Then they were gone.'

She hesitated. 'It could have been that Lucchesi boy I saw.' She paused and leaned forward. 'Do you remember his mother from years ago?'

Frank shook his head. 'We weren't here at that stage.'

'Skirts up to her backside. I never saw a stitch of respectable clothing on her. It broke my heart that my John would have anything to do with the girl. I wouldn't have her under my roof.'

He let her talk on, but she had no more details to give. When she got up to leave, he reached out to shake her hand, but she pulled him into an embrace. She pressed hard against his thighs. He let go politely, giving her arms a gentle squeeze, turning her towards the exit.

'Mother of God,' he said, when he closed the door behind her.

Sam Tallon liked to work early in the morning when everyone else was sleeping. He went straight to the lighthouse and was about to unlock the door when he realised it was already open. He climbed the steps, stopping for breath halfway.

When he reached the lantern house, Anna was already there, picking up damp newspapers from the floor.

'I couldn't sleep,' she said when she saw the look on his face.

'Ah, sure four hours is about all you need, if you ask me,' he said. 'I'll get started on checking everything. We can find out fairly quickly whether or not this old lady can be fired up.'

Joe picked up a length of timber from a stack by the workbench. He secured it with two clamps and stood staring at it. From the top shelf, he chose a plane and started to work along one of the edges, shaving away thin slivers. Then he unclamped the wood and threw it back on the pile. He jumped when he saw a figure standing in the doorway.

'Martha,' he said. 'You scared the hell out of me. How are you?'

'I was wondering if you could help, Joe,' she said. 'With Katie. You've got experience in these things.'

'Yes,' said Joe. 'But—'

'What do you think happened?' she asked.

'Honestly, Martha, I don't know. I don't have all the facts.'

'You were there for all those questions too. I've filled you in over the last few weeks. You know as much as I know, which is as much as the guards know.'

'They may have more information than they're letting on,' he said.

She looked down.

'You don't think she ran away, do you?' she asked.

'She could have,' said Joe. 'If you're here because of my experience, I'll tell you one thing I've learned and that's keep an open mind. Especially with a teenager. You don't know what's coming next. I've no idea what's going through Shaun's head sometimes.'

'Is there anything you can do, can you see if the guards will let you help them?'

He smiled. 'I'm afraid there's nothing I can do on that score. It's just not the way it works. What do they think happened? Where do they think she went that night?'

'It doesn't make sense. It seems like they believe she's run away. But they won't tell me why they think she'd do that. Their theory is that she left Shaun at the harbour, walked up through the village, took a left to go home and then it all gets a bit vague. I think they haven't a notion.'

'Well, I guess I can ask a few questions,' said Joe, 'see if there's anything that doesn't seem right. But it's not like I'm on the job back home with all my regular resources.'

She nodded sadly.

'Look, maybe if you keep me up to date on anything new the police tell you, that would help.'

'All right,' she said. She looked him right in the eyes. 'What if she's dead?'

He didn't miss a beat. 'Remember that open mind,' he said, squeezing her arm.

She nodded. 'I think she is dead.' She hurried from the workshop without looking back. He wondered, not for the first time, why people felt they could tell him things he knew they'd never tell another soul.

Betty Shanley was walking out of Tynan's when she saw Shaun across the street. She waved him over.

'Sorry, sweetheart, I know you're on your lunch break, but I just wanted to let you know; we have guests coming to one of the houses for the weekend. Would you mind getting it organised?'

'Sure, Mrs Shanley,' he said. 'For Friday?'

'Yes. You could go in after school, though. They're not arriving 'til about ten.' She gave him a quick hug. 'I hope you're OK,' she said. 'You poor divil.'

'Thanks,' he said, walking away. 'Oh, which house is it?'

'Fifteen,' she said. His heart lurched.

Joe sat in the den with his PowerBook in front of him.

'Hi,' said Anna, sticking her head in.

'This case is a goddamn nightmare,' said Joe. He tapped his fingers on the keys.

'What case?' said Anna.

He looked away. 'Shit. I meant Katie.'

'Case?'

'Sorry, you know what I'm saying. It's just, you know, not being in the loop—'

'I don't like where you're going.'

'Look, I'm close to this, I know the players, it's just I need to know everything if I was to—'

'Whoa,' said Anna. 'You're on a break, detective.'

'Come on,' said Joe. 'Who would you trust more?'

'You don't know what the guards are doing,' she said. 'They could be, as you would say, "sitting on their perp" right now. Oh my God,' she said. 'Listen to me. I just assumed someone did something to her, that someone's—' Tears welled in her eyes.

'Aw, honey,' said Joe. 'Come over here.'

'I don't know which is worse,' said Anna. 'That someone's got her somewhere or that she's . . . I mean . . .'

'I know, I know. That's why I want to help.'

'You're serious,' she said, wiping away her tears.

'No shit, I'm serious. Our son's girlfriend has disappeared. He's a wreck.' He looked down. 'And Martha asked me to help.'

'Ah. I see,' said Anna. 'You have someone's blessing.'

He said nothing.

'Do you mind?' she said, reaching across him, using the track pad to click on the Stickies icon at the bottom of the screen. Over thirty yellow, green and blue computerised Post-Its opened in front of her. She smiled and shook her head.

'Wow.'

Each note had a reference to Katie's disappearance and comments underneath. Joe moved her hand away and pulled down the screen.

Shaun breathed in when he saw what was inside the fridge. Tiny cake crumbs. He pushed down on them with his finger and they stuck. He swept the rest of them into his palm and stood, his hand suspended over the sink, wondering if he would be jinxing something by throwing them away. He tipped his hand over and turned on the tap, watching the crumbs float, then swirl over the drain, then disappear. He walked around the house into every room, checking everything he was supposed to check, accidentally doing his job. He went into the master bedroom. His heart thundered in his chest. He lay on the bed with the pillow over his face. He sat up. The room was so empty. He opened and closed the wardrobes. He fixed the bed. He cried. He went downstairs. He turned on the heating. He lay the welcome note on the table. He locked the door. He left the keys under the mat and walked home.

*   *   *

Joe jogged into the station and asked Richie if he could speak with Frank.

'I suppose so,' said Richie. 'Frank,' he shouted. 'Mr Lucchesi is here to see you.' His smile was wide and fake.

'Well, both of you can hear this, actually,' said Joe.

Frank came out to the counter.

'It's about what I was trying to tell you that time in Danaher's. Shaun gave Katie a white rose on the Friday she disappeared and I found it on her father's grave. So I think she went down Church Road and stopped at the graveyard on the way. It's still there. You can go check.'

'That's all well and good, but we've got a witness who says otherwise.' Frank told him briefly about Mae Miller.

'Oh,' said Joe, confused. 'Well, I'm sorry to have . . . it must have been another rose . . . maybe Martha . . .' He turned away, then nodded back at them. 'Thanks for hearing me out.'

Anna called into the lighthouse. Sam was finishing up, arranging a set of spanners into a tidy yellow toolbox. He wiped his hands on an oily cloth and smiled.

'I have good news for you,' he said. 'I didn't have to do much. There were a few kerosene leaks and I had to replace the buckets in the air pumps.'

Anna had been expecting bad news.

'What I'm saying is, I couldn't find anything to stop you lighting the light.'

She hugged him tight and patted his back. 'Thank you so much, Sam.'

'Oh, there's one more thing,' he said. 'This!' He pulled out a small pink and cream silk mantle.

'Wow! Thank you again.' She took it from him and held it in her palm. 'It's not what I expected at all. It's so light. It looks like something my grandmother would crochet.'

'Good things come in small parcels,' said Sam, winking at her.

Joe closed the front door behind him and walked along the hallway, obsessing about Frank and Richie and Mae Miller. He felt like the guy in school who puts up his hand to answer every question, but always gives the wrong answer. He needed to go back to the start. As he walked, he realised he was slowing down. Then something made him stop – a strange and vague hope. He hovered at Shaun's bedroom door. Part of him ached at what he was about to do, but the rest was on auto-pilot. He pulled the door open and walked down the stairs. He moved around the room, touching as little as he had to. Anything he did pick up, he imagined it glowing like Luminol as soon as Shaun walked back in. The bed was made and a movie magazine lay on top of it. The only poster on the wall was Scarface. There were no photos of models or actresses in the room – Shaun had taken them down when he started going out with Katie. Joe didn't expect he'd ever put them back up. He stood by the open wardrobe, taking in the boxes stacked on the top shelf. They had small black and white prints of trainers on the front, but they were overflowing with photos, concert tickets and small plastic toys. Joe reached up and pulled out a Magic 8 Ball. He shook it. He didn't hear the creak from upstairs.

'What the hell are you doing?' shouted Shaun from the doorway.

Joe turned around slowly. 'Uh . . .'

Shaun ran down the stairs and grabbed the ball from his hand.

'That's mine.'

'I was just . . .'

'What?' said Shaun. 'Spying?'

'No!' said Joe. 'No. I . . .'

'You're full of shit.'

'Watch your language.'

Shaun snorted. 'This is not about my language. This is about you invading my privacy. You wouldn't search a lowlife crackhead's house without a warrant . . . what were you looking for?'

'I don't know. Something that would help. I want to help. You want to know what happened to Katie, don't you?'

'Damn right I do,' snapped Shaun. 'But if the answer was in my bedroom, I think I might have found it by now. And what the hell was that about with Robert? Do you think we're all stupid? *"What's that scratch on your hand?"* Do you think he didn't know what you meant? You're screwed up, Dad. All you can see is the bad in people. Even in your own son. Even when you've quit your stupid job. That's really sad.'

The chair was damp against Duke's back. His lids were heavy and his head lolled backwards and forwards. Somewhere outside, he heard a cry from the trees. His eyes shot open. He gripped the arms of the chair and raised himself up slowly. He moved towards the back door and stepped into the garden. In the next field, he saw two backpackers, laughing, helping each other over a stile. There was a long trail of flattened, yellow grass behind them. Duke bristled. He walked around the front of the house and down the road to where it started. A small hand-painted sign showed a stickman walking. The arrow pointed towards the backpackers. He reached out and rocked the sign back and forth until it came free. He flung it into the undergrowth, turned around and strode back to the van. He sat inside and drove until he saw the sea.

With one hand on her coffee mug and the other holding a coaster carefully underneath, Nora Deegan burrowed into the vast armchair.

'He knows his coffee. I'll give him that,' she said, bending to inhale the rich steam.

'Joe?'

'Yes. This is another Colombian blend. I could sit here smelling it all night.'

'It was nice of him to bring it back for you,' said Frank.

'Yes. It's a coffee thing, though. Coffee drinkers are the smokers of the beverage world.'

Frank chuckled.

'I'm serious,' she said. 'We're becoming pariahs. "Oh my God, I'd be up all night if I drank as much coffee as you" or "Do you not worry about what it's doing to your insides?" or "No, no. Decaf for me". There are more chemicals in decaf—'

'Some of us have no choice,' said Frank, making a sad face.

'I'm not talking about you, pet,' she said. 'I'm talking about people who haven't a thing wrong with themselves cutting coffee out of their diet. Madness.'

'What are you going to watch?' he asked, nodding at the TV.

'I'm watching,' she said, putting on half glasses and raising a folded newspaper to her face, *Pompeii's Final Hours*. It's history night.'

'Grand. I'm heading down to Danaher's to meet Richie, run over a few things in the case.'

'You'll be sick of the sight of each other by the end of all this,' she said.

'Hmm,' said Frank.

* * *

Joe sat down at the kitchen table. His nerves were still jangled. What kind of father had he turned out to be? He remembered when he worked in Sex Crimes how Anna had arrived into the station one day with Shaun. Joe hadn't seen her for five days. He had been asleep upstairs on a sofa in the lounge when the call came through from the desk. He was exhausted after his shift, but he was staying back to work on a case. On the floor beside him was a file, topped with a glossy colour photo of a four-year-old Hispanic boy in pale blue pyjamas covered in little red aeroplanes. He was laughing, his upper body tilted, his arms held out like he was gliding. Joe still remembered his name. Luis Vicario. He had been lured to a house by a young prostitute hired by the owner, a filthy over-weight trucker who had just moved into the neighbourhood. He had told her Luis was his son and his wife never gave him access. The prosti-tute promised Luis a ride in a real aeroplane, led him into the house, then left. His tiny body was found three hours later. He was barely breathing. An ambulance rushed him to hospital where he was intubated, his wounds were treated as best they could, his arms were stuck with needles and he was hooked up to a life support machine. Joe visited his family every week for three months until their son lost his fight. The neighbour had fled. The prostitute saw the story on the news and came forward. She was waiting in an interview room for Joe. He got up and ran downstairs to Anna who, without a word, pushed six-year-old Shaun towards him and said, 'This is your son, Shaun.' Joe found it hard to look at him, but he bent down and hugged him, patting his back, all the time staring at Anna. She had tears in her eyes. After a minute, he stood up. Anna took Shaun's hand and turned around. 'Au revoir,' she called to Joe as she left. He knew that didn't just mean goodbye. It meant 'until the next time we see each other'. But he'd rather have her mad at him than try to explain.

This year in Ireland had started out as the best he'd ever had with Shaun. He didn't want anything to happen that would take that away. But the worst part about Shaun disturbing him earlier was the realisation that he *was* thinking the worst when he went into his room. He had approached those boxes with his heart thumping in his chest. Grabbing the Magic 8 Ball was just to touch something familiar and cosy. Now he was plagued with feelings of dread.

And why was Mae Miller like a stuck CD in his head? He barely knew her, but he wondered if her evidence could be taken at face value or did she have something to hide or someone to protect. One name came to mind. He needed to get out. He went to the Jeep and drove to the Grants' house. It was just before eleven-thirty, the time Katie would have been walking home. He sensed something was wrong as soon as he got out. There were three other houses close by, yet no-one else had heard a sound. Frank would have backed up his story with as many witnesses as he could. Joe's footsteps alone had already stirred up one barking dog. Another, a yappy little terrier, was pressing his face against the bars of a gate. Joe looked around at the ground floor windows. Lights were on in two of them. The third was in darkness, but when he moved closer he could see a glow at the back of the house. It was not too late for Mrs Grant's neighbours to have been awake.

He rang the doorbell at the first house. A woman in a bright blouse and polyester pants answered. She blushed when she saw Joe.

'Hello, Mr Lucchesi,' she said. 'How are you?'

'Hi,' said Joe. 'I'm doing OK. I'm . . . I was just wondering were you here that Friday night, the sixth, when Katie disappeared.'

'The poor divil.' She shook her head. 'I was,' she said. 'It was my little fella's birthday. I was cleaning up after the party 'til all hours.'

'Like, midnight?'

'God, no. Well after two o'clock.'

'Did you hear anything at all?'

'No. Not a thing.'

'Would you have had the vacuum cleaner on?'

'I would have if the damn yoke was fixed. I was on my hands and knees picking popcorn out of the carpet. Have the lads got you in to help with the investigation?' she asked, her eyes sparkling.

'No, no,' said Joe. 'It doesn't really work that way. Just curious, that's all. Did you see anything that night?'

'No. I hadn't time to bless myself, let alone look out the window.'

'OK,' said Joe. 'Thanks.' He moved on to the second house and a third, before driving back to Danaher's.

The forest at Shore's Rock was utterly still, the silence broken only by Mick Harrington's footsteps and the heavy breath of his dog, Juno. A mile from the Lucchesi's house, through a dense network of shrubs and briars, Mick picked his way along a path towards the edge of the cliff, the same path he had trampled on and off for over thirty years, to a ledge that jutted out over the sea where he sat to take in one of his favourite views. Juno trotted slowly ahead on tired legs. Suddenly he let out a piercing yelp, then barked and barked until Mick scrambled over to him, taking him gently by the head, holding his ears tight, crouching to look into his eyes.

'What is it, boy? What has my old boy barking like a madman?' Mick's gaze moved past the dog and stopped dead. He staggered back, groping for Juno's lead, struggling to snap it back onto his collar. He broke into a run back through the forest, hauling Juno behind him until he eventually picked him up and carried him back to the car in clumsy strides.

Frank stayed calmly finishing his pint as Joe arrived in and sat down beside him, but Richie was almost up out of his seat in protest. He opened his mouth, but his words were drowned out as the door to Danaher's crashed open. Mick Harrington scanned the bar. His eyes locked with Frank's. Frank stood up, drawn across the room to him.

'Jesus Christ,' said Mick, his voice low. He held back tears. 'I was out for a walk. In . . . up at the forest. I saw . . . I thought . . . I didn't know what it was.' His breath caught. 'I think it's . . . was Katie.'

TWELVE

Stinger's Creek, North Central Texas, 1983

Duke knocked on the screen door and walked back down the steps to look through the window. He could see the light from the television shine across the smooth bald head.

'Mr Riggs?' he called out. 'Mr Riggs?'

Geoff Riggs turned his head slowly and waved Duke back to the house. He lumbered out of his armchair and walked to the front door, throwing it open. Today was a happy drinking day.

'Hey, Mr Riggs. Donnie around?' said Duke.

'Thought he was with you down at the creek.'

'Oh, sure,' said Duke slowly. 'I was supposed to meet him there. Sorry to get you up.'

'Don't worry. Need the exercise, son,' he said, waving the remote control at him.

Duke walked down the path and through the trees. He called out, but got no reply. He finally found Donnie lying under a cottonwood by the creek, legs pulled to his chest, skinny feet sticking out of his tight navy jeans. He was asleep.

'Hey, buddy,' said Duke, bending down, pulling gently at his foot.

Donnie woke up slowly, rolling onto his back, rubbing at the dust that stuck to his cheek.

'Didn't you make it home last night?' asked Duke.

'I made it home,' said Donnie. 'And Daddy'd done lock me out again. No amount of knockin' on the screen door shifted him from that chair, six pack happy at his feet. Looked around at me, too. "Go on, now, boy," he says, like I'm some dog.' He laughed, shaking his head.

'Least you don't live at my house,' said Duke.

'Your mom's all right,' said Donnie.

'My mom's all wrong,' said Duke. He sat beside him with his back against the tree and uncurled a book he had pulled from his pocket.

'No,' said Donnie, standing up. 'No readin'. Let's do somethin',' he said.

'Shut up. This is different. It's cool. Uncle Bill gave it to me.'

He held it up without looking at Donnie, then flicked through it until he found what he was looking for.

'Listen to this,' he said, reading slowly, jerkily. '"In mythology, the hawk is believed to have special powers, possessing great knowledge, qualities of pride, nobility, courage and wisdom," something I can't read, "and truth. It is considered lucky to see a hawk first thing in the morning."'

'Your Uncle Bill must be the luckiest man alive,' said Donnie.

Duke continued reading. '"If you hear the cry of a hawk, it is a sign that you should open yourself up to a message, to . . ."' he stopped and finished solemnly, '". . . beware." Spooky or what?'

'Spooky,' said Donnie. 'But I still want to do somethin'.' He began wriggling out of his T-shirt. The early morning sun was hot on his face. Duke looked up at him. Donnie was patting his swollen stomach, his back arched. He pulled off the rest of his clothes and shouted, 'Last one in is a dead man,' before running towards the misty water. Duke watched his naked brown body go. Shivers ran cold up his spine. He didn't like the way it felt. He didn't follow him.

The water looked warm as Donnie jumped in. He surfaced, waving with both hands. He slid under again then came up, pulling himself with the rope that hung from their favourite tree. He climbed to the top, swung, then plunged back into the water. When he was finished, he ran back to shiver in the shade.

'Shoulda come in,' he said. 'It was cool. Hey, whatcha wanna do after school?'

'I dunno,' said Duke, looking up. 'Jeez, would you put some clothes on, for Christ's sake?'

Wanda Rawlins sped through Stinger's Creek in the pickup with a cold can of soda pressed between her thighs. She smoked like a man, the cigarette clamped between her thumb and forefinger, each pull long and deep. She slammed on the brakes when she saw the lonely figure at the side of the road. She reversed in a zig-zag.

'Hey, Dukey!' she said. 'You wanna ride home?'

He shrugged.

'Hey, hey. Look at me. What's the matter?'

'Nothin'.'

'Nothin',' she mocked. 'What is it?'

'Aw, I was supposed to meet Donnie is all. No big deal.'

'Hop in,' she said. 'I'll take you wherever.'

'Just leave me at the store.'

'Well, that's not very far, is it?'

'Then I'll walk.'

'Oh, hop in for cryin' out loud.'

She leaned into him as she drove, turning her head towards him when she had something to say. He stared ahead and kept a hand lightly on the steering wheel.

Donnie stirred his milkshake with a stripey green and white straw.

'You're funny,' said Linda Willard, pushing his arm.

'So're you,' said Donnie.

Linda poked at her fries, using her free hand to tuck her shiny red hair behind her ear.

'So what kinda music do you like?' she said.

'Dunno,' said Donnie. 'Don't have a stereo or nothin'. Don't even have a radio. My daddy has the TV on all day . . .' He shrugged.

'So what do you do? I mean, apart from hangin' out with Pukey Dukey?'

'Aw, he hates bein' called that,' said Donnie. 'That was all Ashley Ames's fault. I like Duke. We get along just fine.'

Duke watched their smiling faces through the diner window, then frowned and turned for home.

Two hours later, Linda Willard was riding her red bicycle out of town when she saw Duke Rawlins waving to her from the roadside.

'Linda,' he called. 'Come over here a minute, will ya?'

'Sure,' said Linda, putting her foot to the ground to stop. 'My brakes are shot,' she said, smiling.

'Donnie told me all about you,' said Duke.

'He did?' She blushed.

'Yeah,' said Duke. 'Know what he said?'

'What?' said Linda, leaning over the handlebars, her eyes bright.

'He said that you and him were down by the creek the other day and that you—'

Duke leaned over and whispered the last part slowly into her ear. Her eyes went wide. It was disgusting. She didn't even know anyone could do that. All she knew was that she never wanted to lay eyes on Donnie Riggs again.

THIRTEEN

'That's it,' said Frank as Richie leaned his hand against a tree, his head bowed, a string of saliva hanging from his lip. He spat it away and waited until the nausea passed. But he heaved again and vomited for the third time. He wiped away the water streaming from his eyes. Four feet away lay the bloated body of Katie Lawson, naked from the waist down. Only her face and legs were fully exposed, the skin a grotesque greenish black and covered with large blisters. Her upper half was hidden under a mess of soil and leaves, her pink hoodie turned a filthy brown. Apart from her clothes, she was recognisable only by her long dark hair, which was fanned out above her and had already begun to detach from her head. Her features were completely distorted, her skin slipping away from the bone.

'That could be animals, maggots; God knows what injuries are under there,' said Frank. 'You know, I would have thought she'd just been out for a walk, maybe fallen and banged her head, but for the . . .' he nodded towards her jeans and underpants, twisted and discarded at her feet, a pink trainer still caught at one end.

'It's a terrible business,' said Dr Cabot, the local GP, edging backwards, holding a blue and white checked handkerchief over his mouth. His job was done, the strange task of confirming the death of the decomposed. Frank made the sign of the cross. 'You'd have to believe in the soul at a time like this,' he said, his voice catching, 'because a body like that – well, that's just not little Katie.'

Joe sat in Danaher's beside Mick Harrington as the shaken man brought his second glass of whisky to his lips. He watched Mick's chest rise and fall. Ed asked nothing when he brought over the drinks. Joe wanted to run. He didn't want to be polite and wait for Mick's shock to ease, he wanted, bizarrely, to get to the most important crime scene he would never see. But he sat in silence. He had too much time to think what could have happened to Katie. For a moment, he imagined her like an angel, lying on her back in a white robe, a small smile on her peaceful face. Then a flood of darker images swept that away and filled his mind with all the evil he'd ever seen. He thought of the woods, her lifeless body hanging by a rope from the limb of a tree. He thought of her face, damaged and broken, her eyes opaque and staring. Then she was wrapped in plastic or buried or posed . . . He looked around the bar and wished that he was anyone else but who he was – a person who had lost forever the chance to view the world as good.

Frank held out his hand and felt the beginnings of misty rain.

'We need to get the body covered straightaway,' he said. 'Have you got anything?'

'Just the couple of rain jackets in the car,' said Richie.

'Run,' said Frank, reaching back to unzip the stiff, folded hood from the collar of his dark green anorak. He pulled the cords tight and tied them under his chin. It was the last thing he did before standing utterly still, staring ahead, his feet rooted to the ground. Every movement he made could compromise the scene. He had failed to protect Katie Lawson once before, he wasn't about the make the same mistake again.

As Richie pulled the jackets from the boot of the car, he was lit from behind by a pair of headlights speeding his way. He spun around as the car crunched to a stop in the gravel. D.I. O'Connor got out with a black notebook in his hand, followed by Superintendent Brady. O'Connor motioned for Richie to turn the blinding beam of his torch away from them.

'It's definitely her,' said Brady.

'Yes,' said Richie. 'It's getting wet. I need to cover her up.'

'We've brought the white tent,' said O'Connor. 'Grab it there. But take one of those jackets for yourself.'

Richie ran for O'Connor's car. He took the tent from the boot and jogged back towards the trees. The men followed, shining a torch ahead of them through the trees. They arrived at the scene, nodded at Frank, then took a brief look at the body before they set up the tent.

'We'll need to put a call in to the Technical Bureau,' said Brady.

The Garda Technical Bureau, based at the Phoenix Park in Dublin, never opened earlier than nine a.m., regardless of what foul crime was uncovered during the night. In eight and a half hours, someone there would pick up a message from the machine about a suspicious death in Waterford and a team would be gathered together. The State Pathologist, who could at that stage have heard about the body on the news, would then get a call from the Technical Bureau to come to the scene.

Brady looked at Frank. 'Let's get this preserved.'

'Richie, you stay here,' said O'Connor. 'Frank, myself and Superintendent Brady will talk to Martha Lawson, before anyone else gets to her.'

Frank did a double-take at O'Connor's rimless glasses.

'OK,' said O'Connor, handing Richie the black notebook. He pulled a pen from the pocket of his padded blue jacket and handed it to him. 'Write down every single person who comes to this scene, starting with all of us. Obviously, don't disturb anything, be careful where you're walking or standing. Or breathing. We absolutely cannot put a foot wrong here, I don't need to tell you.'

Richie nodded, but there was panic in his eyes. O'Connor hesitated, then let it go.

Mick Harrington made it home into the arms of his wife and sobbed like he had never sobbed before. Robert stood at the top of the stairs watching him, thinking something had happened to his granddad, until he saw how both his parents turned and looked up at him.

Joe Lucchesi slipped gently in the front door at Shore's Rock and shook his head slowly when Anna walked towards him. He grabbed her and they clung to each other. Then they held hands and walked down the stairs to Shaun's bedroom.

Martha Lawson howled until her throat went dry, collapsing onto the floor of the hallway, her hands over her ears, repeating the word 'no' over and over again in short, wrenching bursts. Frank,

O'Connor and Brady hadn't even spoken and had to step around her to make their way into the house. Frank was visibly shaken by her reaction. He bent down and reached his arm around her shoulder, half-hugging, half-dragging her up from the floor into the living room and on to the sofa.

'Get some tea, someone,' he said. O'Connor looked at Brady, then took a step towards the kitchen.

'I don't want tea,' Martha shouted. She threw her hand to her mouth. 'Oh God, I'm sorry,' she said. 'I'm so sorry. Where is she? Where did you find her?'

'In the forest,' said Brady quietly. 'By Shore's Rock.'

'What?' she said. 'But did you not look there already?'

'Yes, we did,' said O'Connor. 'But maybe not quite that far in. It's very hard to get into.'

'Obviously not that hard,' she shouted, 'if Katie got in.' She let the thought hang there. 'Oh my God,' she said suddenly. 'What was she doing there? What happened to her? Did she fall? Did—'

'We don't know yet,' said Brady gently. 'The State Pathologist—'

'—Dr Lara McClatchie will carry out a post-mortem on the body later today,' finished Martha. 'I know the rest of that sentence,' she sobbed. 'I hear it on the news. And I think, "Jesus, Mary and Joseph, that poor family" and now, look at

this! I'm the poor family. I'm the poor family.'
Suddenly she jumped up from the sofa and bolted
into the hall, grabbing one of Katie's jackets from
the coat stand. She yanked open the front door
and staggered into the night. 'I have to go to her,'
she said desperately. The men were stunned, but
O'Connor managed to rush after her. He didn't
need to. Martha was kneeling face down in her
garden, hugging Katie's jacket to her, the drizzling
rain falling gently onto her nightdress.

From nine the following morning, people from
the village started to make the trip to the forest,
parking their cars where the road had been
blocked off and walking as close as they could get
to the activity further up the hill. O'Connor had
assigned one of the more sombre young guards
from Waterford to stand at the cordon, accepting
whatever bunches of flowers and teddy bears they
wanted to lay near the scene. Once the collection
had built up, cameramen and photographers
edged forward to get the best shot.

Richie stood with his back to the station door,
rubbing his face furiously. He had stayed with the
body most of the night until he was relieved by
a guard from Waterford. He turned when he heard
footsteps behind him and saw a brunette standing
in the doorway. He was taken aback by her height;
she was at least six foot. He instinctively looked

at her feet. She was wearing flats – khaki trainers with black stripes. He looked back at her face. She was outdoors attractive, with a healthy sallow complexion, thick eyebrows, full lips and no makeup. Her hair was pulled back into a high ponytail.

'We're not really open,' said Richie. 'But if it's an emergency—'

She frowned. 'Hmm. I think it's gone beyond an emergency,' she said, her accent West Brit. 'I'm here about the suspicious—'

Frank had been trying to move out from behind the counter, but was too slow.

'Sorry about that,' he said, nodding towards Richie. 'Good morning, Dr McClatchie. I'm Frank Deegan, the sergeant here.' He shook her hand, then turned to Richie, 'This is the State Pathologist. This is Garda Richie Bates.'

Richie blushed. 'I've—'

'Only ever seen me on TV. I don't look the same in real life apparently.' She smiled.

'Uh, yeah.'

'Don't worry,' she said.

'You're very welcome, if that's the right way of putting it,' said Frank. 'Let me bring you up to the scene.'

'Please, call me Lara.'

Frank guided her outside, past her old black Citroën and into the Ford Focus. He filled her in on the drive. Two news vans had arrived since he had left earlier, their reporters and cameramen loitering outside. Frank drove past and pulled up behind the Technical Bureau van. The first thing they were hit with when they stepped out of the car was the smell of vomit.

'Someone always throws up at the scene,' said Lara. One of the forensic scientists sidled up to her.

'Actually, that was Alan,' he said, referring to one of his colleagues, 'it had nothing to do with the body. He was just on the piss last night.'

She stifled a laugh, then glanced past him into the van. 'Can I get my gear?'

'Sure.'

Over her black trousers and jacket, she pulled on the standard issue XL white suit, which was great for her height, but she'd never want to hit the full width, like some of the chunkier guards. Next came the shoe covers, then gloves and finally she pulled up the hood on the suit to stop her hair getting caught in the branches on the walk through.

'Do you have a bag somewhere?' asked Frank.

'No,' she said, 'just this little plastic one in case I need to take anything.' She held it up. 'My job is done at the morgue, really.'

They walked up to the blue and white crime scene tape. The guard there wrote down her name, Frank's name and the time.

'Who are these other people?' she asked, looking around her.

The guard pointed to each one distractedly.
'They're a couple of the guys down from the
Waterford squad, that's, uh . . . actually, that guy's
my cousin, he works with the paper.' Lara stared
at him. Frank led her to the body along the path
mapped out with tape, then went straight back to
talk to the guard at the entrance.

Close to the body, another guard was pointing
to a footprint while someone called out, 'That's
fresh. It's the Mountcannon guard's print. When
himself and the sergeant got here. I wouldn't
worry about it. They said there were none at the
scene already.'

'Hello, Alan,' said Lara to the forensics guy.
'How was last night?'

'Don't talk to me,' he said.

She looked around. 'This is dreadful.'

'The crime? Or the fuckwits – excuse my
language – stomping around the scene?' He looked
calm, but she knew better.

'Both,' she said.

Alan nodded past her. 'Your man over there's
a journalist, by the way, and he's got a little
camera. So remember not to smile.'

She twinkled her brown eyes at him. 'That's
my crime scene smile. Only for the initiated. It's
like your measured fury. So no-one on the news
looks at you and thinks: "suspect"; no-one looks
at me and thinks "silly woman doing man's job."'

Frank watched as Dr McClatchie crouched

down beside the body, then stood up and walked slowly around it. Everyone watched her as if after each move, there was a chance she would turn around and say, 'Right, everyone. The killer is, and you'll find him—'

The fact they all knew for definite that there was a killer was not a shock, just another depressing reality for them to face. Frank knew most of the men there had never seen a dead body before. The only bodies he had seen were suicides, the most recent one a fifteen-year-old boy who hanged himself in a neighbour's barn. Frank had found him – seconds after the boy's mother had.

Part of him wanted to stop the whole world from revolving, but more urgently, to stop what was playing out in front of him. The violation of Katie's privacy was almost unbearable. But he knew that the real violation had happened weeks ago. This part was something that made sense, that had to happen, that was done for the benefit of the victim.

People shuffled back from the body as Dr McClatchie moved in closer. Two forensic scientists hunkered down beside her. The photographer followed. Piece by piece, they removed the branches and leaves that covered Katie's torso, stopping to photograph and video each new layer. After two hours, the body was fully revealed and they all stood up stiffly and stepped back.

Frank watched as bags were tied around the

head, hands and feet of the body which was then zipped into a plastic sheath and carried away on a stretcher.

'Any ideas as to cause of death?' said O'Connor, walking over to Dr McClatchie.

'That, I'll tell you *after* I carry out the post-mortem.' She looked around. 'Can someone give me a lift back to my car?'

Duke leaned against the van. The man parked in front of him sat with the window open, listening to the frenzied commentary of a Gaelic football match.

'Come on to fuck, Din, you can get the result later,' shouted his friend.

Duke watched them walk towards the entrance to Dromlin woods, bows held low by their side. A large woman in an orange jacket was sitting at a picnic table, a pile of papers in front of her. She smiled at them and handed them pens. When they finished writing, they nodded and she pointed the way. Duke waited. More men arrived and went through the same routine. Some groups walked right through.

'Hi,' he said to the woman. 'Din's gone in ahead with my bow. Can you give me a quick run-through of what's happenin'?'

'Fourteen by two 3D big game,' she said. 'There's a good twenty of you so far. You're a friend of Din's?'

'From the United States,' said Duke, smiling.

'He's a great man for the GAA,' said the woman.

'Sure is,' said Duke. He had no idea what she meant. He filled out a form and walked into the woods. Groups of archers stood by the trees, adjusting their bows. A man in a waxed jacket was putting up danger signs in the distance.

'They should have had them up hours ago,' said one man. 'We haven't even got the place to ourselves. They're lettin' in any Tom, Dick and Harry and we'll have to wait at some of those targets for them to pass. It'll take ages.'

'I'm in no rush,' said a second man, adjusting his compound bow. 'I'm going for a slash.' He lay down the bow beside his friend, who was too distracted by the signs to notice Duke grab, quickly and quietly, first the quiver, then the cool, smooth wood of the compound bow. In seconds he appeared through a clearing in the trees, within metres of the van. He put the equipment in the back, then sped away, briefly on the wrong side of the road.

The post-mortem room in Waterford Regional Hospital was the same size as a school classroom, with steel units running the length of one wall. Frank and O'Connor stood awkwardly by the sink, with masks dangling from their hands. Lara glanced over. It was like a Western, each one waiting for the other to draw. She was dressed in blue theatre scrubs, a long-sleeved green paper

gown to her ankles and a green plastic apron. She
didn't wear a mask. She pulled on latex gloves,
rubbed in a scented hand cream, then pulled on
another pair of gloves. The men were watching
her intensely.

'I don't mind the smell,' she explained, 'I just
don't want it on my hands when I'm eating my
lunch. So I double bag.' She turned and walked
towards Katie's body, laid out on one of the two
stainless steel tables in the room, beside a tray of
instruments. The men followed her, but stood at
a distance. O'Connor was the first by a fraction
of a second to put on his mask. Out of nowhere,
the deep voice of Johnny Cash filled the room.
Lara had slipped four CDs into the stereo on
shuffle through two bluegrass compilations, a
Hank Williams and a Johnny Cash.

'I go through phases,' she said to the surprised
men. 'Never thought I'd hit country, though.'

Then she barely spoke a word, as they watched
her and a technician, a photographer, a ballistics
and a fingerprint expert go to work.

'Hmm, what have we here?' she said, holding
up a small dark fragment she had plucked from
a head wound. The ballistics guy held open a
plastic bag, she dropped it in and turned back to
the body. 'Here's more,' she said, removing a
second and a third piece.

O'Connor stepped forward. 'What do you think
it is?'

'No idea,' she said. 'And I probably never will until I'm sitting in court giving my evidence.' She looked up at the men. 'You're the ones who get all the news back from the lab. No-one tells me anything.' She walked around O'Connor and he stood back beside Frank, where they shifted on their feet until finally, four hours later, Lara pulled off her gloves and led the men over to the sink. Superintendent Brady had just arrived and been let in by the guard standing outside the door. He flinched at the smell, covered his mouth with his hand and crossed the room towards them. He seemed to look around for the source of the music.

'The man in black himself,' he said.

Lara nodded and smiled.

'OK,' she said. The three men huddled in front of her. She looked down at them and they edged back. 'There is evidence of blunt force trauma to the head. She's been struck several times, obviously with something heavy. There is also evidence of strangulation, damage to the larynx, fracture of the Adam's apple. There's been maggot activity on the scalp wound. When flies come to a corpse – which they would probably have done within hours – they look for the juiciest places to lay their eggs: this includes all the orifices, eyes, nostrils, ears, mouth, penis, vagina, anus. But, if there are wounds, that's where they'll head first. Excuse the pun. This explains what I was saying about the scalp. There was also evidence of maggot activity around the arms and hands, which could indicate the presence of defensive injuries.'

'So, the cause of death?' asked Brady.

'I would say she was strangled and was then beaten about the head. When you're strangled you don't die instantly. She may have lain there gurgling which could have alarmed her attacker, who may have grabbed whatever was close by to finish the job. In this case, there were jagged marks, so I would say a rock.'

'And time of death?' said Brady.

'It's hard to say. The closest I could say based on the condition of the body is that it is consistent with the time of her disappearance.'

D.I. O'Connor was frowning.

'I'm afraid I can't be more specific than that,' she said. 'Time of death would be much more accurate if the body was found within days, but when weeks are involved, it becomes much more difficult.'

'So, this guy could have held her somewhere, then killed her at a later stage?'

'If you're asking me whether or not the body was moved, I would say nothing points to it, but after that, it's down to whatever trace evidence is found.'

'What about sexual assault?' said Brady.

'I would say there's circumstantial evidence,' said Lara, 'based on the fact that her underclothing and jeans were removed. Obviously, that would be highly suggestive of an attempted sexual assault but, I can't commit to anything more definite.'

'Why not?' asked Frank gently.

'What happens in decomposition is the genital area becomes very swollen . . .' The men all dropped eye contact with her. She continued, '. . . and you can get rupture of the tissue in that area, which has happened in this case. It muddies the waters. Our only hope is the results from the vaginal and anal swabs. If the attacker used a condom, we have nothing.'

'What about the scene? The top half of her body covered up like that?' said O'Connor.

'I work with what I see from a body. Anything else, you can call in a profiler.' She smiled.

'That is something I never want to hear again as long as I live,' said Joe, stroking Anna's face as she lay on the couch. She knew what he meant – the strangled scream from Shaun's throat. They had stayed with him all night until he eventually fell asleep. He hadn't come upstairs since then. Joe kept stroking until Anna's eyes grew heavy and her breathing slowed. He kissed her warm forehead, then let her head rest gently onto a cushion. He grabbed a torch from a drawer by the front door, slipped out quietly and headed for the forest.

Oran Butler sat on the sofa with his feet up on the coffee table. He was scooping baked beans into his mouth from the plate he held under his chin. Richie came out from the kitchen.

'You're fucking gross, Butler,' he said. 'The place is a mess. Would you not just . . .'

Oran held up a hand to silence him. 'I'm wrecked. Don't start.'

They had both trained as guards together and now shared a flat on the Waterford Road a ten-minute drive from the village. Oran was one of six guards who worked in the Drug Unit out of Waterford city.

'What's the story with work?' said Richie.

'Ah, same old, same old. Trying to track down the usual. Friday week will be a big one. A raid on the Healy Carpet Warehouse in the Carroll Industrial Estate, surprise the fuckers. O'Connor's wetting himself. This could be his big moment.'

He leaned down and pulled open a can of beer, raising it in a toast. He looked at Richie's glass. 'Mineral water. Sad enough.'

'Shut up, coppernob,' said Richie.

'Original *and* observant,' said Oran. 'Call me freckle face while you're at it.'

He drank from his can, shaking it at Richie and smiling.

Joe could have driven further up the hill and crossed through to where the body was found, but he didn't want to miss anything. The light from the torch was weak; a pale, hazy glow that barely lit his way. He had to raise his knees high over the thick briars and imagined that whoever had brought Katie here would have had a struggle, whether she had been alive or dead. Fifteen minutes later he found the tattered remains of blue and white garda tape flapping from a tree and, twenty metres away, another length trailing from the base of a trunk. He looked around carefully, shining the faded light across the ground, picking up the place where the body had clearly lain. He walked slowly towards it, then stepped backwards and crouched down, setting the torch beside him. He reached inside his jacket and pulled out a pen, using it to lift some of the leaves that were scattered on the forest floor. He stopped to examine something closer, taking it gently between his thumb and forefinger, bringing it in front of the light. It was a dull reddish brown, a papery 5mm-long cylinder that tapered at one end and was broken away at the other. He knew what it was, but he wasn't quite sure what it meant.

FOURTEEN

Stinger's Creek, North Central Texas, 1984

'Out of sight, out of mind!' laughed Uncle Bill
when he saw Duke standing on the back porch
looking for him. Duke tried to follow the voice.

'I'm up here!' Bill gave him a broad wave.

'You got me,' said Duke, smiling. 'New camo
clothes?'

'Yes, sir,' said Bill. 'Last gear was faded near
white. Can't have those deer pickin' me out like
a fool. And I've got myself a new Baker tree stand,'
he said, patting the side. 'High and mighty,' he
laughed. 'They won't know what hit 'em.'

'You got plans?' asked Duke.

'Yup. Couple weeks' time I'm drivin' down to
Uvalde for the opening day of deer season.'

He climbed down and slapped Duke's back.

'Need to make sure everythin' is in fine workin'
order before I set out. How's your mama?'

Duke knew Bill didn't get along with his mama.

'Mama's OK. She's . . . she's OK.'

'Good to hear,' said Bill, his head bent to study his bow.

'Think you could teach me how to shoot?'

Bill looked up.

'Are you serious, son?'

'Sure am, sir,' said Duke. 'Am I old enough?'

'Long as you can listen, hold a bow and be safe.'

Duke saluted him.

'OK, then. Let's start with how you're gonna hold the bow. This here's a compound bow. A beauty. More power, less effort. Now, we need to find out which hand you'll use to hold the bow and which—'

'I write with this hand,' said Duke, holding up his right hand.

'Doesn't much matter,' said Bill. 'It's all in the eyes.' He pointed with two fingers.

'Which one of your eyes is the dominant one.'

Duke shook his head.

'OK. Do this,' said Bill. 'Pick out some object in the distance.'

'That old garbage can?' said Duke.

'Perfect. Now point at it, then close your left eye. OK? Then close your right eye. Now when you close one of those eyes, your finger seems to shift to one side. Which is it for you, Duke?'

'My right eye,' said Duke.

'Then you're right-eye dominant, just like your Uncle Bill.'

'What does that mean?' asked Duke.

'Means you hold the bow in your left hand and pull the bowstring with your right. Now,' he said, putting a hand on Duke's shoulder and turning him towards the trees. 'Stand up straight, feet apart. You comfortable?'

'Yes, sir.'

'OK. Now hold this.' He handed Duke the bow, laughing as the boy rocked forward with the weight.

'Heavy, isn't it?' said Bill. Duke smiled.

'You'd probably use somethin' a little lighter,' said Bill. 'Anyhow, next thing you do is nock the arrow, meanin' you put this part here on the bowstring where you see this.' He took the bow from Duke and pushed the nock back onto the bowstring. 'The shaft rests here.' He pointed to a notch on the bow. 'You're probably better off watchin' for the rest of this.'

'OK,' said Duke, disappointed.

'What?' said Bill. 'You think I'm crazy, lettin' a boy loose with a dangerous weapon?' He smiled. 'Now, put your pointin' finger on the bowstring above the arrow and your next two fingers below, but don't touch the nock. Relax the back of your hand and pull back just a tiny bit.'

He brought the bow up slightly, gripping it between his thumb and index finger, nodding towards Duke to watch how he held it.

'Now stretch out that bow arm and raise up your drawin' arm, keepin' that elbow high. Then pull your arm back until your drawin' hand is against your jaw, keepin' your body still all the while. Now move the sight pin over the centre of your target. I'm aimin' for the steel bear over by that tree. Line everything up, the string, the bow and the sight pin, keepin' it all on the vertical. You got this?'

'Yes,' said Duke, frustrated by the interruption. 'Do it! Shoot!' He hopped from foot to foot.

'Hold your horses,' said Bill through clenched teeth, keeping his jaw rigid.

'And release,' he said. The arrow flew straight, reaching its target, springing gently from side to side on impact.

'Cool,' said Duke. Bill hooked an arm around his shoulders and hugged the boy to his side.

'You wanna try?'

'Yes, sir!' said Duke, beaming.

'What you need to remember at all times is the target,' said Bill. 'Be steady and focus. Think about that target, watch that target, every step of the way. Never lose sight of it.'

The bow rocked Duke again, but he moved until he steadied his weight, keeping his legs wide. Bill stood behind him and smiled as Duke struggled to bring the bow to shoulder height.

'This is all gonna happen a bit faster for me, Uncle Bill, 'cos I ain't gonna be able to hold the bow too long.'

Bill laughed loud, a friendly booming laugh. Then he watched, amazed, as Duke followed every step. The arrow stopped short of its target, but only because the weight of the bow tilted Duke forward at the last second. Duke kicked the earth. 'Damn,' he said, twisting on his feet. 'Damn.'

'Don't be so hard on yourself, son. Only thing wrong with that was the weight of that bow. Once I get you one of your own, I think you'll be doin' just fine.'

'Get me one of my own?' asked Duke.

'Sure. I'll get you a bow, long as you can promise me you'll work hard at school, show up every day, don't be swimmin' around that creek when you should be sittin' in class.'

Duke smiled. 'Busted,' said Bill. 'Now, get along. I've got some shootin' to do.'

FIFTEEN

Anna was alone on the sofa, lying on her back, rigid, when her eyes suddenly shot open. Her mouth was clamped shut and she couldn't move. Eventually, she was able to lift her hand to the centre of her chest where she felt a pool of sweat soak into her T-shirt. Her heart thumped. Vague, broken images flashed through her mind, then slowed until she could see their true terror. Her heart beat faster. She knew what it was – sleep paralysis. It gripped her like this at stressful times, usually in the middle of the night when she never wanted to look at the clock in case time would root her in the moment until morning. She would turn to Joe and wonder if she'd ever wake him and let him know about the intense paranoia that followed each episode. But she didn't like to wake him. So she would stay staring at the ceiling until her breathing slowed, then turn on her side, reach over him, lay her arm on top of his and pull herself close, kissing his shoulders, his back, closing her eyes and willing herself to sleep away the fear. This time with Katie and Shaun and everything else that weighed her down, she felt she was losing her grip. She couldn't live with it all. Since she heard Katie had been murdered, her mind was taking horrifying turns and the paranoia seemed frighteningly real. She walked into the bedroom. Joe was lying on the bed with his arms stretched behind his head.

'There's something I need to tell you,' she said. 'I don't think it's relevant to anything, but it might be and I don't want to take that risk.'

'What? Relevant to what?' asked Joe.

'It's about John Miller,' said Anna.

Joe frowned.

'I wasn't just with him for eight months when I was in college,' she said.

'I don't care how long you were with him.'

'It's not how long, it's when,' said Anna.

'I don't understand,' said Joe.

'I was with him again, when I came back here . . .'

Joe slowly realised what she was saying.

'That time we were engaged?' he asked, sitting up.

'Yes,' said Anna. Her eyes filled up with tears. 'Yes. For the two weeks I was here. I don't know why.'

'Why?' he asked.

'I don't know why,' she repeated. 'He was there and—'

'I was miles away and you didn't give a damn,' Joe finished, his voice rising.

'No. It wasn't like that. I just, what can I say? It was a long time ago—'

'Why are you telling me this now?' But Joe knew how emotional traumas impacted on people and made them purge their souls. Dark secrets came out in dark moments.

'I don't know,' said Anna. 'Maybe . . . I don't know.'

'I can't believe I'm hearing this.' He shook his head. 'Has he done something?'

'He's been weird. He pushed me up against a wall. He asked me to have sex with him. Then he was talking to you that time in the bar . . .'

'He asked you to have sex with him?' Joe was on his feet, furious.

'Yes.'

'Well, what did you say to that?'

'No! What do you think I said?'

'I don't know. Yes, maybe?'

'It was a long time ago, what happened,' she said again, her voice louder.

'Great. Well then it doesn't matter. Hey, I slept with someone, but it was five years ago, so let's all just keep going on as normal,' said Joe.

'Did you?' said Anna, fear in her eyes.

'Oh, for crying out loud – no, I did not! My

point is it doesn't matter *when* you are unfaithful, it matters that you were and that you lied and that there was some schmuck who married you anyway, without having all the facts. Do you think that's fair? Do you think that's a good basis—'

'Do you regret marrying me?' asked Anna.

'Don't you dare try and turn this around. You know what the answer to that is. But I'm not going to let this go. I have been faithful to you for twenty years, Anna. And not a lot of cops can say that to their wives. We have pros flashing their tits at us, exotic dancers who'd do anything to beat a drugs rap, women who get off on the goddamn uniform, for Christ's sake.'

'Good for you!' shouted Anna, jumping up from the bed. 'Good for you! Thank you! You didn't sleep with some whore!'

'Oh, I think I did,' he said.

She stared at him. 'You bastard.' He grabbed her arm as she strode past. She jerked it away and kept going.

D.I. O'Connor stood at the top of the room in front of Frank Deegan and the thirty guards working on the case out of Waterford station.

'Right, lads. Listen up. Here's what we've got so far on Katie Lawson: time of death is consistent with the time of her disappearance, but she could have been held somewhere for days before her murder – putrefaction makes the estimate more difficult, as you all know. We also should consider the possibility that she was killed elsewhere and her body was left at that spot for a particular reason. Cause of death was blunt force trauma to the head, caused possibly by a rock and preceded by strangulation. We can't rule out or in sexual assault, but the removal of clothing from her lower half would be suggestive thereof. Little was found at the scene that particularly grabbed us as significant, but trace evidence taken from the body has been sent to the lab, including fragments from a foreign object found in the skull. The results will be provided when received. For now, we are continuing to review our original questionnaires, follow up on vehicles that may have been seen in the area, root out further witnesses – we'll be getting help from the media on that – and in the meantime, we're looking at the boyfriend, Shaun Lucchesi. We know that his father, Joe Lucchesi, a detective from New York and on whose land the body was found, visited the scene late last night and possibly removed evidence that may have been overlooked during our initial search . . .'

The stereo filled the Jeep with a loungey Gainsbourg track. Joe slammed it off and sped away from the house in silence, with no idea where he was going. He was sick and panicked with anger over something he could do nothing

about, an overwhelming anger that he knew
would leave the situation exactly the same in the
end. Anna had cheated on him. Unbearable
thoughts and images crawled into his mind. He
knew he had felt just a little smug when marriages
were falling apart all around him and he could go
home to his beautiful wife and know that they
were different. Now they were just the same as
everyone else: delusional, betrayed, angry, guilty,
scarred. Gripping the steering wheel tighter, he
drove faster and faster until he knew he needed
to pull over. He found himself at the end of the
lane that led to Millers' Orchard. He reclined his
seat, leaned back against the headrest and closed
his eyes, opening them quickly when he heard a
hacking cough from the other side of the road.
He turned his head slowly to see John Miller
standing there, tapping a cigarette on the back of
a box. He tried to picture him eighteen years ago
when Anna, with her engagement ring on her
finger, had risked those two weeks. She was
young, just twenty-one, but Joe thought she had
known what she wanted when she said yes to
him so quickly. When she was going to Ireland,
he had brought her to the airport and cried in a
stall in the mensroom when she left. For John
Miller. Joe watched him light his cigarette like a
pro. John was tall and broad and over the years
had packed an extra forty pounds over his old
rugby build. Joe could only see what was there

now – a pathetic man in sagging grey pants, crumpled shirt and cheap shoes. And this almost hurt him even more.

Katie wouldn't have stood a chance against a man that size, even one who was out of shape. His weight alone was enough. John Miller was a bitter man. He couldn't have Anna, so he had gone for someone close to her, a young girl almost the same age as Anna was when he had first met her. Miller only had to go a mile down the road and he could watch the traffic in and out of Shore's Rock. Katie would have no reason not to trust him. She probably would have felt sorry for the guy.

Joe waited for him to turn back, then he started the engine and drove away.

Anna ran out of the house into the laneway when she heard the horn beep. Ray climbed out of the van and moved around to the back doors.

'Hi, Ray,' said Anna. 'Well done.'

'No problem,' he said. 'I've actually got all three of the steel panels with me. I can slot them right in to where we cut out the rusty bits.'

'That's fantastic,' she said. 'Would you mind bringing them down to the lighthouse?'

'No problem. I've got the kerosene tanks as well, if Sam gives it the all clear.' He stared at the ground. 'Are you OK? You look . . .'

'I'm fine,' she said. 'It's just, this evening . . .'

'I know,' said Ray. 'It's awful. It's so hard to believe . . .' He slapped the side of the van. 'Anyway, I'll get started on all this. Hopefully it won't take too long. And, sure, I'll see you at the funeral home.'

'It's funny,' said Anna. 'I think when it's a child who dies, people want every chance to say goodbye. So they do all the parts: go for prayers to the funeral home, then on to the removal service, then again the next morning for the funeral. It's a good thing, I think.'

Joe's Jeep pulled up behind them and he walked past quickly, grunting a hello at Ray.

He went straight for the phone in the den, flicking open an 01 phonebook for Dublin to find a number for Trinity College.

'Hello, Zoology department?'

'Hi, I was wondering if I could speak with an entomologist?' asked Joe.

'That would be Neal Columb, but he's in class at the moment.'

'Could I leave a message for him to call me?'

When he got off the phone, he checked his watch and looked in on Shaun before taking a shower and getting dressed. He was standing in the bathroom, his foot on the toilet lid, rubbing the corner of a white towel over his black leather shoes when Anna walked in.

'Oh, for God's sake,' she snapped. 'There are cloths under the sink.' He looked up at her.

Tears welled in her eyes. 'I don't know how he's going to get through this.'

'With us,' said Joe. His voice was tight.

'I'm so sorry,' she said.

'Shh.'

Frank stood with O'Connor by the gates to the funeral home. O'Connor wore the same rimless glasses he was wearing the night Katie's body was discovered. Frank noticed his eyes were clear for the first time.

'What happened to your contacts?' he said.

'I got rid of them,' said O'Connor. 'Did you know ninety percent of the crimes our boys are dealing with are alcohol-related public order offences? It's out of hand. That's what's keeping them busy. And the public's going mad. People are ringing in to radio stations moaning about the drinking going on, but no-one is actually stopping their kids going out and doing it. No-one thinks their own kids are part of the problem. It's un-believable. Paul Woods dropped a child home the other night who was too drunk to make it out of the car, let alone walk up the drive. He had to go and get the mother, who didn't believe him until she eventually came out and saw the girl lying there, fifteen years of age, passed out, wearing a mini up to her arse that her mother didn't even recognise. Meanwhile, what these people don't realise is the huge problem we've got with drugs.

A problem my men can't deal with because they're too busy cleaning puke out the back of their cars. Yet there's a very organised gang of criminals pumping drugs around the city and beyond.'

'Really,' said Frank flatly.

'Last month, for example,' he went on, 'we came close to our first even small break in months with this one particular crowd. We'd been hanging around, watching a youth club disco every Saturday for a couple of weeks before then. Next thing, a van pulls up and two young lads go up to it. We approached it, casually, but the van flew out of there like a bat out of hell. Of course the lads would say nothing, but the story was all over the town the next day, parents calling the station, as if this was the first time this guy had ever shown up. One of the papers ran a front page story. So the pressure is on. I can't add to that a nutter on the loose, going around taking young girls.'

'We're doing everything we can,' said Frank. 'We're out there taking statements, we'll be going over old statements after this—' He stopped as he saw Richie approach.

'Late night last night from what I heard,' said O'Connor, smiling.

Oran loved arriving in to work with wild drinking stories.

'Yeah,' muttered Richie, flashing a brief smile. 'But at least I don't have a hangover to show for it.'

'Good man, yourself,' said O'Connor, throwing his eyes up at Frank.

Joe watched Shaun walk over to the side door of the funeral home. He was six inches taller than most of his friends and looked strangely mature beside them in his new black suit. They were all trying desperately to cope with their grief, but everyone looked too stunned to talk.

Joe's gaze moved to the guards standing by the gate. He wondered what the dynamic was between them. The D.I. from Waterford was deep in a one-way conversation with Frank, who was giving polite nods every few minutes. Richie looked uncomfortable beside the two older men. They had turned their bodies away from him, subconsciously, but enough that he was visibly excluded. Frank was in the middle in more ways than one. He seemed pleased to have a break from Richie, just not with a man who made him cock his head at an awkward angle to create some space. Only O'Connor was watching everyone who came in and out of the funeral home.

'What do *you* think?' said Anna, putting her hand on his arm. He pulled it away and shook his head at her. 'I was just saying we could have some of the kids over at the weekend to help them . . .' Joe made a face that said no. He hadn't looked her in the eye since that morning. The Irish had an expression for when something was unpleasant or grating: 'going through you'. Everything Anna did or said was going through him. He was allowing her by his side today for the benefit of Shaun . . . and maybe the neighbours, if he was being honest. And maybe to spite John Miller. Images of Miller and Anna flashed into his mind again. He wondered whether he should care that it all happened almost twenty years ago, but he knew that the love he had for Anna made him care. He shivered. He could feel her looking up at him. His head ached. The pain down both jaws felt mechanical, a constant, driving beat. He continued staring ahead.

Martha Lawson sat before the coffin of her only child as the plaintive chant rose and fell in the crowded funeral home.

'Hail Mary full of grace, the Lord is with Thee, blessed art Thou . . .' Elderly women ground rosary beads through their fingers, their heads bowed, their prayers confident. Groups of confused teenagers in grey school uniforms muttered the parts they knew, strangely comforted by the ritual, but wondering if any of it really worked. Every now and then their eyes wandered up to the oak coffin at the front of the room, closed in depressing finality. These were children used to an open coffin, grasping the hands of the dead, kissing the cold marble foreheads of grandparents or elderly relatives. Never a sixteen-year-old.

Martha Lawson leaned awkwardly against her sister, Jean, the life sucked from her face, her eyes dark and blank. She was a devout Catholic, considering every word of the rosary she was saying, because she believed – in God, in prayer, in human goodness. No killer would strip her of her faith. But she didn't understand. She didn't know why she was sitting here for the second time in eight years, chief mourner again, first losing her husband to cancer and now her daughter to a murderer. She stared at the coffin, unable to accept that Katie's brutalised body lay inside. Her little baby, the lid shut on her beautiful girl. When the prayers ended, everyone moved onto the street where a hearse was waiting to take the coffin the short drive to the church.

Fr Flynn, the elderly parish priest, swept through the service. His words were hollow and weary, delivered too often. He hadn't learned that with each funeral came fresh grief and sorrow. People began to shift in their seats. Martha was thinking about the following day, when her cousin, Michael, was flying in from Rome to deliver mass. He always found the right words.

For an hour after the short service, a steady stream of sympathisers moved up the aisle towards Martha. 'Sorry for your troubles,' they muttered, shaking her hand, working their way along the short row.

* * *

Tall wooden stakes burned in a line on the grass outside the lighthouse. Brendan, the photographer employed by *Vogue*, stood in front of them holding out a light meter. Shaun muttered something and kept walking into the house. Joe looked at Anna.

'There was nothing I could do,' she said. 'He was hired weeks ago.'

'I know that,' said Joe.

'I'll be down there for the evening,' she said.

The sun shone the next morning through the icy cold, offering nothing more than a talking point for awkward mourners. They moved into the small stone church at the edge of the village, filling it, then crowding into the side aisles. The bell rang, the congregation stood and Fr Michael appeared with two altar boys walking behind him. He tapped the microphone.

'Please be seated.' He looked up, then spoke softly. 'When Katie was three years old, I taught her two words from a *Reader's Digest* list. One was empathy and the other was encourage. The next day I asked her what was the word for when you understood what is happening to someone else. She looked up at me and frowned. She couldn't remember. I said nothing. I simply waited, no hints. Then she reached out her little hand and gave me a smack on the arm and said, "Encourage me, Michael!"

'Today, in the face of this terribly tragedy, yes, we can empathise with the family and friends of Katie Lawson. But more importantly, we can encourage. We can encourage people in their faith to be strong for each other, to be strong for Katie. It's what she would want. I know that the songs chosen here today by her boyfriend, Shaun and by her school friends, are positive songs, songs of hope and support and, as I said, encouragement.' He nodded to the small group on the balcony and Katie's tearful replacement whose shaking voice struggled through her first solo.

Fr Michael spoke again. 'We are united here today for many reasons: in our love for Katie, in our support of Martha and the Lawson family, Shaun, in our faith, in hope, but also because not one of us can understand why this happened. How a sixteen-year-old girl who was full of life, who had so much to give, indeed, who gave so much to everyone, could be taken away from us so suddenly. What hatred would lie in someone's heart to make them commit such an act of cruelty and violence?' He stopped.

The only sound to be heard through the silence was the journalists at the back, scribbling on spiral notebooks.

'We may never know,' he continued. Several people looked instinctively towards Frank Deegan and Richie Bates. 'But what we do know is that we can't let hatred take hold of our hearts.

Because hatred will make us suffer. Our hearts should be love, filled with goodness as Katie's heart was.'

Joe was the tallest of the pallbearers, stooped now to accommodate the five other men, arms over shoulders to carry the light coffin. The crowd, led by Martha, shuffled behind them. They moved through the cemetery, forced to stand along the borders of other graves, all eyes drawn to the two foot wide, six foot deep trench and the coffin that lay beside it.

Shaun found himself standing closest to the grave. He couldn't connect the person he loved to what was happening at that moment. It suddenly struck him that her body was now in that box. She was physically inches away from him, but she was dead and in a box. He wondered what she looked like; did she fill it or was she tiny and lost in the satin pleats? He started to sob uncontrollably.

Anyone who managed to hold it together at the mass broke down in the stark reality of a coffin being lowered irretrievably into the ground and a boy's shaking hand as he tossed a single white rose onto the polished lid.

After the burial, most of the mourners moved to the Lawson house. Neighbours had been preparing food and drinks since early morning. Anna was passing through the hall when she saw

John Miller slip away from the long queue for the bathroom and push his way into the back garden. She was disgusted at what he was about to do, but at least she was the only one who saw him leave. When he came out from behind the shed, she was waiting for him.

'What's going on with you, John?' she spat. 'What have you done with your life?'

'Jesus, I was just taking a piss,' he said, smiling around at no-one.

His fly was undone. She nodded at it, fuming. He winked at her.

'You need help,' she said. He looked like he was about to say something, but he turned and walked away, weaving a crooked path back to the house.

Richie and Frank were huddled in a corner of the hallway, cups of tea and sandwiches in their hands.

'Sorry to interrupt you,' said Joe, 'but—'

'We're not interested at this stage,' said Frank, without looking up.

Joe was taken aback. 'But—'

'No, give us a laugh,' said Richie. 'What's your latest theory?'

Joe stood in front of them with his map and felt pathetic. But he knew he was right about this.

'He's got his map,' said Richie.

'Look,' said Joe. 'Let me get this over with.'

When Joe finished his theory about Mae Miller, Richie spoke:

'How do you know none of the other neighbours heard anything?'

'Because I asked them,' said Joe, knowing where this was going.

'Stay out of it!' snapped Richie, raising then quickly lowering his voice. 'What's to say Katie didn't visit the graveyard, then walk back on her usual route past Mae Miller's and oh – what was that again – end up buried in your back fucking garden?'

Frank winced.

'That forest is like public land, you son of a bitch,' said Joe. 'And what you're saying about where she went just does not make sense. And you know it, you stubborn little shit.'

Richie was fuming. Frank stepped in. 'Well, whatever happened,' he said, calmly, 'she went past the Grants' and Mae Miller heard a scream.'

Joe shook his head and walked away.

Frank turned to Richie. 'You need to relax.'

'What do you mean, relax?'

'You're as defensive as . . . as I don't know what. That's not the right way to carry on in a job like this. I'll be gone next year and I don't want things stirred up around the village in my last few months.'

'I'm not being rude, but yeah, you'll be gone. I'll still be here. My career is my life and I don't want any unsolveds marking it. The Lucchesis are fucking blow-ins. That man or his son – or both of them – look dodgy as fuck from where I'm standing.'

'Where you're standing, Richie, is at a funeral. Remember that and get a grip on yourself.' He took a sip out of his tea. 'If Joe Lucchesi is "dodgy" as you say, we still have to go about our job properly. And I'll tell you one thing, I'd rather have an unsolved case than a wrongful conviction on my conscience. This is an investigation out of Waterford, anyway. Your future career is not going to be based on whether or not—'

'But—'

'Listen to me. You don't listen. What matters in the long run is how you handle yourself and other people. You need to be patient. You can't bully and push your way through. Remember, just by the job you're doing, you're starting off on the wrong foot with most people. There isn't as much respect as there was in my day. When I was training in Templemore, one of the detectives said "If you walk down the street putting tickets on every car as you go, the whole town thinks you're a bastard. If you walk down the street and don't put a ticket on any car, the whole town thinks you're a bastard."'

'So we're bastards,' said Richie. 'End of story.'

'No, it's not. It's up to us to try and make people see we're not.'

'Could you be bothered, though?'

'I have been bothered and I'm proud of that,' said Frank.

Anna crept down the stairs into Shaun's bedroom. He lay on the bed in oversized jeans and a baseball shirt, his feet hanging over the end. He was asleep, his cheek red from the heat. His arm was stretched out on the pillow in the same pose she'd seen ever since he was a child. He was still a child, she thought. Tears slid down her cheeks. Shaun's eyes opened slowly and he rolled onto his back. Anna saw it all happen in his face, that dreadful awakening when all the world seems so right and in seconds is all so wrong. His face fell. He sat up against the headboard, drew his knees to his chest and wept. Anna's heart lurched. She walked over to the bed, sat beside him and pulled him into her arms. He broke down, every sob cutting through her. She rocked him back and forth, but said nothing. There was nothing she could say. A beautiful sixteen-year-old girl doesn't belong in heaven, there was no happy release, there was no joyous, spiritual lesson to learn from this.

'I love you,' she simply whispered into his damp hair. 'We love you, sweetheart.'

After a while, the sobbing slowed down and he said, 'I don't get it. I don't get it. Why would . . . ? Why would anyone? She's so perfect, she—' He wept again and for two hours Anna held him in her arms, stroking his hair, until he finally drifted off again and she lay his head gently onto the pillow.

She went into her bedroom and broke down herself as she pulled off her shirt, wet from his tears.

It was almost midnight and Danaher's was still packed with people who had been there since the funeral or who had followed on after Martha's house.

'Good luck,' said Ray as Joe left his bar stool for the outdoor toilet. It was only when he stood up that he felt the impact of the alcohol on his empty stomach. All he'd had that day was one sour milkshake he'd made himself in the morning, six painkillers, two LV8s and three pints.

The stall with the door was taken, so he walked into the other one, unzipping his fly, waiting for his body to relax. He rocked gently on his heels.

'Guess I bagged the private one,' he heard from the next stall.

'I guess you did,' said Joe, still waiting for something to happen.

'You know, you could always . . .'

Joe prepared, as you do with a stranger, to laugh politely at whatever gag was about to be made.

'. . . wait and come in here if you need to pinch one off. I'll keep the seat warm.'

Joe felt trapped into following through on the

polite laugh. His lower body was following through on nothing.

Then silence. He could hear scratching against the wood of the stall door. Then, 'You're not havin' much luck in there, are you?' The voice sounded closer, like it was coming from higher up the thin partition wall and muffled, like the cheek was pressed against it. Joe froze. Then he heard the door beside him creak open, scraping against the cement floor.

'Top o' the morning to you,' came the voice.

Back in the bar, Ray heard the start-up screech and boom of Danaher's tannoy system.

'Could the owner of car registration number 92W 16573, please get out in that car park and get the damn thing out of the way,' said Ed.

'Jesus, you don't have to eat the microphone,' shouted Ray.

'Shut up, you pup,' said Ed into the microphone again. Ray got up, pulling his car keys out of his pocket.

'And it's your car,' laughed Ed as Ray walked out the door.

'Nice hair,' said Ray to the man standing outside by his car. His hair was blond, short and spiked at the top, poker straight and long at the back.

'This your car?' said the man. 'Then move it.'

'Where's the fire?' said Ray, getting into his car. 'And will your hairdresser be at the stake?'

'Move your fuckin' car,' said the man, shifting from one foot to the other, his hands buried in his pockets, his head bowed.

Ray reversed out of his spot, leaving the van in front of it free to move.

'Whoa, we're halfway the-ere, oh-oh, livin' on a pray-er,' Ray sang on his way back towards the bar.

Suddenly a hand grabbed his shoulder from behind and spun him around. The two men hovered in front of each other, neither one committing. Ray took a step forward, but was pushed back hard. He made an awkward grab for the man's jacket to steady himself, but it was too late. The man jumped into his van and sped out of the car park. Ray sat up, bewildered. Then something caught his eye. A small golden flash against the black tarmac.

Joe was back at the bar with a fresh pint.

'What happened to you?' asked Joe when he saw Ray.

'Some fucking wacko in the car park. American, of course. Total weirdo. Mullet, check shirt, skin-tight jeans, big boots. Good lookin' guy, but definitely nuts. Gave me a few digs for slagging his hair . . .'

'Not the hair slagging. No! No! Help!' said Hugh, raising his hands in faux terror.

'I thought I was great,' said Ray. 'Anyway, look

what he left behind. A bit of gay jewellery.' He threw something onto the bar. Joe looked down and in an instant his chest felt like it would explode. He couldn't speak. Everything slowed down. This was something he couldn't understand. He looked again. He tried to work out how this was happening. In seconds, several theories came and went in his mind, none of them right. He grabbed the tiny object and ran for the door, knowing he was too late. He stopped in the doorway under the bare porch bulb and held it up to the light. He saw the familiar outline, the gold and maroon, the wings, the feathers, the hawk in flight, its pointed beak holding the tiniest specks of green paint scratched from the single stall door.

Joe rushed home and stood outside to catch his breath before he put his key in the door. The house was quiet. He went into the kitchen and saw Shaun sitting at the table, staring at the fridge through swollen eyes. A yellow taxi-cab magnet held a photo of him and Katie taken during the summer, his tanned face pressed up against her pale one. Their heads were tilted back and his face was screwed up trying to kiss her cheek. Joe walked over to him and put a hand gently on his shoulder. Shaun released the breath he had been holding in, got up and left the room.

Joe went into the den, sat at the desk and picked

up the phone, punching in Danny's direct line. He hung up halfway through. He turned on the computer, clicked on Safari and the Google home-page filled the screen. He typed in three words: hawk, pin, flight. He got hits on the Wright Brothers and Kitty Hawk, Black Hawks and pilot pins. He tried again, going for the literal: maroon, gold, hawk, pin. He saw sites on spotted hawks, maroon orioles and gold buffalo pins. He went more generic with Texas, hawk, pin, but just got hits for wrestling.com, a lapel pin website and a Texas Hawk Watches site. He wasn't going to go further than the first page, but he clicked again on a wildlife site by a man called Larry: larryloveswildlife.com. *Larryneedstogetalife.com*, thought Joe. Two colour photos gradually loaded onto the screen, the first showing four men who looked to be in their early fifties, wearing tree-patterned camouflage gear with cameras and binoculars hanging around their necks. He read the caption.

Me, Dick, Bobby and Jimmy, Nueces County, Texas where we spotted the first Golden Eagle of the season (yup, you read that right!)

Good for you, thought Joe. He scrolled down to the second image, the same four men from the waist up.

Me, Dick, Bobby and Jimmy pinned down (ha! ha!). Seriously, we picked up these limited edition pins at a stall on the day for just $10!!

Joe's heart thumped as he looked closely at the pins. He studied the faces of the men. They would all be – he checked the year – in their late 60s by now.

'What are you doing at this time of the morning?' asked Anna, walking over to him.

'Research,' said Joe, batting his hand behind him to keep her back.

'OK,' she said. 'But . . . it's been horrible today.' She spoke softly. 'Do you want to come to bed?'

'I'm sorry,' he said. 'No.'

She closed the door gently behind her. John Miller flashed into Joe's mind. Then he remembered being seven years old, hearing his mother's raised voice boom against the floorboards of his room.

'What do you think I do here all day, hah?'

'You tell me!' shouted his father.

'You tell me,' snorted Maria. 'I bring up our children. I cook for our children, for you. I clean for our children, for you . . . that's what I do all day, every day. But what do you do, Giulio?'

'I am building a future for our children.'

'What future?' said Maria, her voice pitched high. 'You think this is a future? Parents who never see each other from the start of the week to the end of the week? You're not the man I want my son to be.' Everything had gone silent. Then he could hear his mother's soft footsteps on the stairs, then along the hall to his bedroom. She pushed open the door quietly and slipped into the bed beside him and hugged him close. He could feel her tears on his hair.

He turned back to the screen. Apart from Larry and his wildlife buddies, at least two other people got their hands on those pins and kept them almost twenty years. Donald Riggs would have only been a boy. Why would the same pin be in his hand when he died? Who left the pin outside the bar? He picked up the phone again and followed through this time.

'Two things, Danny,' he said. 'I need you to pull Donald Riggs' file.'

Silence.

'The guy, Bowne Park, the explosion . . .'

'I know who he is,' said Danny. 'I'm just wondering why you're asking.'

'I just need his known associates, back in Texas,' said Joe. 'If he had any.'

'Sure,' said Danny. 'I can do that. But from what I remember, the guy wasn't in much trouble before he, you know—'

'Humour me,' said Joe. 'And, uh, would you mind checking the evidence bag for that gold pin, the hawk.'

'The fact that you're even trying to make that request sound casual says a lot about you,' said Danny. 'What's going on here?'

'I'll tell you when I know myself,' said Joe. 'Listen, take care.' He put the phone down and sat in the darkness before he walked out and upstairs towards the guest bedroom. He was pushing open the door when Anna came out into the hall, hope flickering across her face. He stopped. She was so beautiful, so sexy in everything she did, even now, drawing her hand through her dark, tangled hair. His stomach heaved at the thought of another man touching her. She saw it in his eyes. And the hope died. Joe walked into the strange room and closed the door behind him.

SIXTEEN

Corpus Christi, Texas, 1985

A red banner flapped between two wooden poles at the entrance to Hazel Bazemore County Park: 'Welcome to Wildlife'.

'Sounds like a porno,' said Duke under his breath.

'Yeah,' said Donnie.

'What you boys whisperin' about?' said Uncle Bill.

'Nothin',' said Duke. He looked around. 'This place looks great.'

'I think you're gonna like it,' said Bill, slapping down notes at the booth. 'You'll get to see pretty much anythin' Texas has to offer in the way of wildlife.'

Children were running around, laughing and shouting, pulling their parents in different directions. A giant furry chipmunk and owl were waving and handing out green balloons. Crammed onto every stall were books, toys or information on Texas wildlife. A photographer in a cream-coloured vest pushed through the crowd.

'Picture, anyone? Take your picture, anyone?'

Four men in what looked like army fatigues, stood like war reporters with their binoculars, cameras and bags strapped across their bodies.

'Go on, then,' said one of them. 'Might as well get one of all of us together. Today is a special day, we saw ourselves a few hundred different birds.'

The photographer stepped back and framed his shot. One click and the moment was preserved.

'Would you like a picture, boys?' said Uncle Bill.

'Nah.' Donnie ran his hand over his spotty jaw.

'Nah,' said Duke.

'Well, maybe we can commemorate our big day some other way,' said Uncle Bill.

'Look,' said Donnie, pointing to a small stall.

'I'll leave you boys to it,' said Bill. 'Here's a few dollars.'

An elderly woman stood shuffling a handful of black rubber rings like they were playing cards. In three rows, like steps behind her, small prizes were mounted on upturned mugs. She looked at the two boys.

'All you gotta do is hook one of these rings over them and it's yours!'

'We know that,' said Duke.

'One dollar, five rings.'

Duke handed her two dollars. He looked across the rows and saw a silver digital watch with a flashing red face. He pointed at it.

'That's mine,' he said to Donnie. The woman chuckled. Duke stared at her as he raised his right hand.

'Like skimmin' stones,' he said, turning to Donnie. 'Simple.' He focused on the watch, flicked his wrist and the ring landed high, bouncing off the step above. Duke shuffled his feet and steadied his hip against the counter. The rings flew again and again until he had no more left. He was furious.

'This game's rigged,' he said.

'You watch your mouth, boy,' said the old woman.

He began to raise his knee up on the counter to climb over. She stepped wide and stood in front of him, her hand poised to hold back his chest. His arm flew up and he hit her hard on the palm, jerking her hand back.

'Fuckin' bitch,' he said. 'Don't you fuckin' touch me.' He walked away. Donnie followed.

'It's three o'clock, boys,' said Bill. He put his hand on their shoulders and pointed to a low dais where a tall, thin man dressed in beige was straightening a triangular sign on a wooden table.

'Cool,' said Duke and Donnie. They walked over to join the crowd gathered in front.

The man tapped a narrow microphone and began to speak.

'Afternoon, everyone. The name's Len and I'm here to talk to you today about the Harris' Hawk, one of the most popular falconry birds in North America.' Bill nodded at Duke.

'First things first,' said Len. 'The Harris' Hawk's official title is *Parabuteo Unicinctus*, part of the family Accipitidae. It's a buteo, a soaring hawk, found in the wild from Arizona through Mexico right the way down to Chile and Argentina. It's a medium-sized hawk, typically weighing in between 1.25, 2.5 pounds. The female is larger and more powerful than the male.

'Now, on to the fun stuff. Wolves with wings.' He looked around the crowd. 'Anyone know what I mean by that?' Duke knew. His eyes were bright.

'What I mean,' said Len, 'is the Harris' Hawk hunts co-operatively, like a wolf, like a lion. It is exceptionally rare for a bird of prey. Two, three or even more Harris' Hawks will work together to capture their quarry. They attack with military precision. This is not a free-for-all. They know what they're doing. First they will thoroughly sweep the area to locate their quarry. After that, there are many ways the combined force of the hawks can pursue it. An example is that one bird will flush it out – whether it's a jack rabbit, a rodent, a lizard

– and then will take turns with the other to, very cleverly, chase that prey until it's weakened, exhausted and ready to be killed. The creature doesn't stand a chance. The Harris' Hawks' talons can grip, crush and kill instantly and they won't release until the prey has stopped moving. Remember this is a bird designed for hunting. It can spot a mouse in motion a mile away. It has a third eyelid that is drawn over the eye when flying at speed to protect it from injury or – once its feet touch the prey – to protect it from a thrashing victim. Its talons are immensely powerful. If you could create the ultimate commando, what would he be? He would be focused. He would be intelligent. He would be accurate. The Harris' Hawk is all of these things. But where your commando would be happy under cover of darkness, the Harris' Hawk hunts in daylight. His night vision is no better than ours.' Duke's attention was fixed on the skinny, hunched man and the controlled hand gestures he used to make his points.

'Yes, the Harris' Hawk is a pretty impressive killing machine. And yet it's hard to find a bird that looks more elegant and graceful in flight.' He smiled. 'But,' he said, drawing out the word, changing his face to serious, 'it pains me to hear those falconers out there who can only talk about the number of kills their bird has made.' Duke was distracted, staring past him, focused on something in the distance. 'That's not what falconry is

all about,' continued Len. 'Killing for the Harris'
Hawk or any bird of prey is about survival. And
we all do what we have to do to survive.' Uncle
Bill stayed for the rest of the talk, but Duke was
on his feet, dragging Donnie away.

'Wasn't that amazing?' said Duke.

'Sure was,' said Donnie.

'Aren't they awesome? The way they work like
that?'

'Yeah, a real team.'

'We could be like that.'

'We're a team, Duke, ain't we?'

'But can you imagine what we could do?'

'Like what? Kill varmin?' Donnie laughed.

'No. You know, get what we want, work as a
team to get what we want.'

'What do you want?'

'I dunno. Maybe, I dunno. What do you want?'

'That girl over there,' laughed Donnie. 'Check
her out.' He pointed to a girl in a short blue skirt
with a tight yellow T-shirt.

'Well, you know if that's what you wanted and
for some reason you couldn't get it, we could help
each other get what the other one wants. Say if
I wanted somethin' else, like . . .'

'Like what?'

'I don't know. I'll think about it. But whatever
it was, we could do it together.'

'Like when I roll my dad over when he's drunk
and you pick out his wallet?'

'Well kinda, yeah. You'd never be able to do that on your own. 'Member the first time we saw them? When they went for that quail? I'll never forget that as long as I live.'

'It's just what they do though, isn't it, to survive?' said Donnie.

'Survivin' is bullshit. I've done all my survivin'. It's time to go out and just get.'

Uncle Bill studied the plastic tray on the table in front of him. It held three rows of pins, each separated into four small compartments.

Uncle Bill picked one up. Duke and Donnie walked over and leaned in to look at it.

'That there a Harris'?' said Bill, squinting at the pin in the sunlight.

'Sure is,' said the old man selling. 'Rare, so it'll cost ya. Not many manufacturers gettin' that far into the breeds. Only a couple left, made by one of the locals.'

'How much are they?'

'Ten dollars.'

'Well, I'm afraid all's I got is a twenty,' said Bill, taking out his wallet and winking at the boys. He put the notes on the table. 'So I'm gonna have to take two.' The man reached out across the rows. 'No, no,' said Bill. He pointed. 'The maroon and gold.'

Duke and Donnie sat cross-legged in the dark by

the creek, a flashlight by their sides. Donnie held out his palm. The small pin shone.

'Close your fist,' said Duke. Then he reached his hand around it and crushed it hard until the flesh was pierced and his friend cried out.

'Now do it to me,' said Duke, clutching his own pin. Donnie wrapped his hand around and squeezed until Duke nodded. They opened their fists and saw the same three cuts where the bird's beak and wings had penetrated. They pulled the pins free and clasped each other's bloodied right hands.

'Loyal to the end,' said Duke.

'Loyal to the end,' said Donnie.

SEVENTEEN

Joe watched Anna from the doorway. She was standing in the living room in front of a large rectangle wrapped in layers of brown paper and leaning against the back of the sofa. She put her knee on one of the cushions and started ripping off the paper, revealing each time more of a deep-framed acrylic painting – white with a thick slash of teal down the right-hand side, roughly edged and textured. When she was finished, she stood back and smiled, then jumped as Joe came up behind her. He grabbed a piece of packaging that hung from a corner.

'The Hobson Gallery,' he said. He picked up the invoice before Anna could get to it and held it up high in front of him. He read it and shook his head.

'Please tell me I will not be billed three hundred and seventy five euros for this.'

She looked up at him. 'You will.'

'For Christ's sake!'

'I ordered it weeks ago, before anything. Brendan is coming again to take shots. I need one big piece—'

'I need. I need,' he mimicked.

'You're not creative,' she said angrily. 'You don't understand any of this.' She gestured towards the painting, the furniture, the perfect white floor-boards.

'I understand what you do. I love what you do,' he said calmly. 'I love how you're so deter-mined – just don't be so determined to ruin us financially.' He walked away. 'And actually, I think the painting is great,' he called back.

Shaun saw the group of boys as he turned the corner, but he quickly pulled back behind the wall when he heard his name. Three of them were talking.

'It's fucking nuts in the States though.'

'I know. We should be lucky he didn't come in here in a trenchcoat and blow us all to shit.'

'Oh, for fuck's sake, grow up. Those guys were total losers.'

'Well, who knows? He could be nuts behind it all. It's always the quiet ones.'

'But he's not even quiet! He's just normal.'

'Exactly. What I'm saying is it's always the ones you least suspect.'

'That would make you bottom of the list.'

'Ha. Ha.'

'Combats, shaved head, knows the scripts of
Full Metal Jacket, Good Morning Vietnam and *Black
Hawk Down* off by heart. Has seen *Platoon* twenty-
five times.' He made an alarm sound.

'Well no-one's come knocking on my door to
take me in.'

'No-one's come knocking on Shaun's either,
you fuckwit. It's so embarrassing, though.
Apparently his dad's going around asking people
questions, doing a Jessica Fletcher on it.'

'Jessica Fletcher.'

'Anyway, people are getting fairly pissed off.
Richie's going apeshit. People are saying things to
Lucky's dad, then not saying stuff to Richie or else
they're just getting fed up saying the same things
over and over again. And maybe the guy should be
looking a lot closer to home. Mr Lucchesi, I mean.'

'There's no way Lucky had anything to do with
this.'

'We'll see.'

'You sound like my mother.'

'We'll see.'

'Shut up.'

'Lucky, though. Could his nickname *be* any
more ironic?'

Shaun turned back and walked home.

'I hate to have to do this again,' said Frank, trying
to smile at Martha. 'But you never know what
you might find that would help.'

'It doesn't feel right,' said Martha. 'She was so private.' She pushed open the door to Katie's bedroom. It was a wet, grey morning and the room was dark. They both looked up, drawn by the fluorescent stars on the ceiling. Martha turned on the light and the glow disappeared. She sat down on the bed, a tissue up to her nose, thinking: *that's all I seem to have been doing for weeks, sitting, rubbing my nose raw.*

'Oh, I'm sorry, Frank,' she said, getting up quickly, 'I'm dreaming.' She closed the door gently behind her.

Frank looked around. The room was a little girl's doing its best to be a teenager's. The wallpaper was pink and girly, but a strip had been torn away for notes to be scribbled on it. The quilt was floral and faded, but the lamp by the bed was simple and modern. Her wardrobe should have been brown, but had been sanded and repainted white with a bright pink border. There were no teddies or dolls anywhere. He walked towards the mirror. A piece of ribbon stretched across the top with tiny clips attached to hold photos. He didn't see Katie's face in any of them. He saw Ali and a few other girls from around the village, he saw Shaun and he saw a tiny little girl at the zoo, holding a man's hand and looking up at him, smiling. He looked closer and realised it was Katie and her father, taken a few years before he died.

A box on the dressing table was filled with hair

pins, scrunchies, makeup and cheap jewellery. He turned around and pulled open the doors of the wardrobe, running his fingers across the clothes. He bent down and saw piles of old shoes and two old tennis rackets. Then he saw an envelope, from an oversized greeting card, stuck into the side. He pulled it free from its slot in the wood and laid it on the bed. The big card was a birthday card, signed by several girls, love hearts and circles dotting the 'i's. The messages were all innocent. He reached his hand to the bottom of the envelope and pulled out more cards and letters from her girlfriends and from Shaun, birthday cards stretching back to her childhood and a few Valentine's cards. One of them, in a soft pink envelope had a teddy on the front, holding a flower. He opened it. 'Roses are Red, Violets are Blue, Sugar is Sweet and So are You.' It was a child's writing. A big question mark filled the left-hand side. Frank was surprised anyone would write such a clichéd poem. But how old was the card? He flipped the envelope over. It was post-marked the previous year. Why would a child be sending Katie a Valentine's card? Or was it someone trying to appear like a child? But that didn't make sense. He flicked through the rest of the cards, had one last look around the room and walked down the narrow stairs to the living room. Martha got up expectantly.

'Well?' she said.

He waved the card at her. 'Do you know where this came from?' he asked.

She took it from him and smiled. 'Aw,' she said, tears welling in her eyes. 'I can't believe she kept this. It was from Petey Grant, bless him. She thought it was so sweet. It gave her a bit of a boost at the time, even though she knew there was nothing really to it. That's why she showed it to me. She'd never have showed me the others she got. I remember she laughed that he'd bother putting a question mark on it, because his handwriting was so recognisable. He used to pin notes on the boards in school to let them know if the floors were wet or a classroom had to be closed for cleaning.' She stopped.

'Anyway, I'm rabbiting on here. Do you need this?' she held up the card.

'No, you can hang on to that,' said Frank.

D.I. O'Connor parked his car in the lane and walked up to the Lucchesis' door, admiring the view as he went. Joe took his time answering.

'You've done a wonderful job on the light-house,' said O'Connor.

'That's my wife.'

'I've always had a fondness for it.'

'Yeah. It's a great place.'

Joe nodded and waited.

'As I'm sure you know, I'm Detective Inspector Myles O'Connor from Waterford and I'm heading the Katie Lawson investigation.'

'Yeah, I know. Come in.'

They stood in the hallway.

'This is about your involvement. I'm going to have to ask you to . . .'

Joe knew O'Connor was hoping to avoid finishing the sentence.

'To?' he said.

'To stay out of things. I've never been in this situation before with a person going around to people's doors asking them questions, arriving unannounced at the station and telling our men what to do—'

'I thought I was helping out. The information I was giving was based on my experience—'

'Let's just cut to the chase here. You obviously think we're not doing our job right, that we're some quiet village with a sleepy force . . .'

Joe said nothing.

'Do you honestly think an investigation into the death of a teenage girl is something every single one of my men is not putting their whole heart into? Things are done differently around here. Don't mistake a measured approach for a leisurely one. We're not all Flash Harrys speeding around the streets chasing down "perps".'

'Neither am I.'

'Well that's two misconceptions out of the way, then.'

'I guess so.'

Joe looked past O'Connor.

'Right, well, I won't keep you. But I want you to know that we're doing OK without your help.'

He went to walk away, then turned back.

'We don't have guns or VICAP or HOLMES or a Ten Most Wanted list, but then we don't have tens of thousands of murders a year. We have around fifty.'

Joe shrugged.

'Don't get me wrong,' said O'Connor, 'we make our mistakes, but so does the NYPD, so does every police force in the world. But any time I've been on a trip to New York, I've never charged into a precinct—'

'Come on. Katie was my son's—'

'Then you're probably one of the last people—'

'Would you stand by if it was you and do nothing?'

'I would leave it to the professionals—'

'Am I not a professional?'

'You're an amateur over here. And you're compromising our investigation. There are people in Mountcannon who think you're consulting on this and that's really starting to bother me. I'm asking you – formally now – to keep out of it. Unfortunately, you have a connection to the victim and for that, you and your family have my sympathies. But the brief interview we carried out with you at the beginning of all this is where your input should have ended.'

* * *

Richie was making coffee when Frank arrived back from Martha Lawson's.

'Did you find anything?' he asked.

'Nothing unusual,' said Frank. 'The only thing is, Petey Grant again. I found a Valentine's card in Katie's room from him. I know he's a harmless divil, but maybe the rejection upset him or if she didn't take him seriously . . . I don't know.'

'Why don't I have a chat with him?' said Richie. 'You've talked to him already. You're off this afternoon. I can fit him in then, save you the hassle.'

'I don't know,' said Frank. He paused. 'That's it! The documentary. He said he was in that night watching something on the Fastnet disaster. What theme would you call that?'

'What do you mean?'

'Discovery Channel.'

'Don't have it,' said Richie.

'Well, their nights are usually themed: superstructures, crime, whatever. Friday night is history night. Nora was watching . . . anyway, it doesn't matter. I can't see a programme on Fastnet fitting in there. It's always history history, nothing that recent. Wouldn't the Fastnet race be sport or shipping or something?'

'I'll check it out with Petey, honestly.'

'You'd need to go easy on a lad like Petey Grant, Richie. Can you do that?'

'No problem.'

* * *

Ray leaned against the ladder in the lantern house with two tins of white and green paint on the floor beside him. The walls were smooth for the first time in years, transformed when they were stripped back and the panels were replaced.

'Right,' said Anna. 'Do you know what you're doing with the colours and everything?'

'I think so. White on the walls, green on the ceiling and green on all the accent bits, like the ladder.'

'Perfect,' she said. 'I'll leave you to it.'

Richie stood before the small mirror in the station. He rubbed his finger down each temple, over lumps that ran like tiny beads under the surface. He softened hard wax in his palms and worked it carefully through his hair. His eyes lingered on the muscles that filled his shirt. He went to a gym in Waterford seven days a week – unlike the guys he trained with in Templemore. Some of them never worked out. They had beer guts in their early twenties that they never bothered to lose.

'OK, Petey, what have you got for me?' he muttered as he walked out the door. He drove to the school in the squad car, rather than taking the short walk.

Students were let out early on Wednesdays and he found Petey Grant in a quiet classroom, washing a blackboard. The whole school seemed deserted.

'Howiya,' said Richie.

Petey looked confused. He took a step back.

'Hi Richie,' he said. 'Are you well?'

'Yes,' said Richie. 'How's it going?'

'Fine, I'm just doing a bit of work on the black-boards.'

'Look, Petey, would you mind coming in to the station to answer a few more questions?'

Petey's eyes widened.

'Why?'

'Because,' said Richie, knowing that Petey wouldn't argue with him.

'OK,' said Petey, 'I'll get my coat.' He walked down the corridor and into the staff room where he picked up his jacket. He felt sick.

'I'm being arrested,' he said to Paula, one of the teachers staying back late.

'What?' she said.

'Richie is taking me to the station,' he said. 'I think I'm in big trouble. Bye!' He rushed out of the building into the squad car, about to sit in the front with Richie.

'Get in the back,' Richie said roughly.

Petey was trembling when he got inside and stayed that way for the whole agonising drive through the village.

'It's me,' said Danny. 'Your gold and maroon pin is here, hasn't been checked out, nothing. And I got your big long list of known associates. You got a pen ready? Duke Rawlins.'

Joe waited. 'That's it?'

'Yup. Donald Riggs, Mr Popularity. Student most likely to be shot in a park.'

'Rawlins. Name sounds familiar. Anything on him?'

'Nothing major. Spent eight years in Ely, Nevada. Stuck some guy with a knife in a parking lot. Your average bar-room brawl plus.'

'That's it?'

'Yup.'

'No rape, no murder?'

'Don't sound so disappointed.'

'Anything else?'

'No, just that it was the warden in the prison who kindly provided us with the link. He put a call into Crane after the Riggs murder, Crane scrawled a note at the bottom of the file. The guy's writing . . . anyway, no-one paid any attention to it. Why would they? Riggs was dead. So I call the warden, nice guy. Seems Rawlins was mouthing off about Riggs to his cell mate. The cell mate gets into an altercation and bargains with the warden to avoid solitary. Tells him Rawlins' pal Riggs was planning to kidnap some kid so a pile of cash would be waiting for him when he got out of prison.'

'When did he get out?' asked Joe.

'Rawlins? Uh, July. Two months ago. Why?'

'Jesus Christ, Danny. I think the wacko's after me.'

'Why in the hell? The guy slashed someone with a knife and was a good little boy in the slammer. Doesn't sound like a psycho to me. You think maybe he's got Irish roots or something?'

'This is fucking serious. He could have killed Katie.'

'That's what this is about? You think this Rawlins guy did this?'

'I don't know,' said Joe.

'Does someone go from drunken brawler to transatlantic psycho, that's the question.'

'Do we want to know the answer?' said Joe.

'How the fuck would he know you're in Ireland?'

'I don't know,' said Joe.

'Who else knows you're there?' said Danny.

'Friends, family, the job . . .'

'Yeah and none of them's gonna tell anyone where to find you. What, you think he followed you to the airport?'

There was an edge to his voice.

'The cab driver who brought us to the airport could have said something, I dunno. One of the neighbours, someone came sniffing around . . .'

'Joe, you sound nuts.'

'How long have you known me, Danny?'

'Too long.'

'Right. And in general how often do I screw up?'

'Yeah, but you're on vacation now. I've never

solved a fucking crime in my life sitting by the pool at the condo.'

'Come on,' said Joe.

'Look, people just don't give up that kind of information. People are suspicious these days, they want to know why someone's asking. Hold on a second, I got a call coming through.'

Joe waited on the line.

'That TS guy is a total retard,' said Danny. 'The call was for MacKenna, I get stuck talking to his ma—' Danny stopped. 'Holy shit,' he said. 'Hold on.' After two minutes, Joe hung up. Just as he walked away, the phone rang again.

'A couple weeks ago,' said Danny, straight to the point, 'a Lieutenant Wade called here from the nineteenth, looking for you. The call was diverted and the bad news is that our boy on the TS has never heard of you, calls out to one of the guys who shouts back you're in Ireland. And we know there's no Wade in the nineteenth. And we know there's a gimp on the TS.'

Joe said nothing. His heart was thumping.

'Jesus Christ,' he said. 'He told him Ireland? But that's it, right? Nothing else?'

'That's it, so he's not even gonna know where you are in Ireland. If we're assuming that's the guy who made the call.'

Joe shook his head. 'We *are* assuming that. And I don't know. Ireland's a small country.'

'It's not that small.'

'How many people live in Ireland, Danny?'

'I dunno, twelve million?'

'Four. And over a million of them live in Dublin. Which leaves under three million spread across the whole country. Believe me, that's small. Look, leave it with me. I'll see what I come up with.' He was about to hang up, when he stopped. 'Uh, Danny? You think you could call that nice warden, get to Rawlins' cell mate, talk to him, see what he knows?' Danny grunted. As soon as Joe put down the phone, he went to the den. He took a box from the back of a row of books and pulled out his dupe – a copy of his shield. It was illegal, but most officers had one. Losing the original meant losing ten vacation days, so when he was on the job, Joe would leave his shield at home in the safe and carry his dupe. This time, there was no original. He had to hand it over when he vested out. He felt a surge of something like jealousy. He flipped open his wallet and looked at his ID card, stamped in red with the one word that changed everything: retired.

O'Connor sat in front of a pile of folders and prepared himself to pick apart every single word of what he was about to read. As usual, each job in the investigation – chasing phone records, interviewing the person who found the body, calling in medical records – had been written on a triplicate form and assigned by the 'book men' to a detective. The blue top copy was glued into the

left-hand page of the jobs book, with a note opposite saying who took the job and what the outcome
was. The other copies were filed in the folders in
front of him: Statements, Witnesses, Suspects . . .
He looked at the stack and pulled out the one
marked Statements. Top of the pile and four pages
long was Shaun Lucchesi's. He could think of three
men over the previous five years who had
murdered their girlfriends and walked free. If the
gut instinct of every guard working their cases
could have been admitted as evidence, three men
would have been locked away for a very long
time. O'Connor's gut instinct was not telling him
that Shaun Lucchesi was a killer, but it *was* telling
him he was a liar.

Joe almost ignored the phone when it rang on
the desk beside him.

'Hi, Mr Lucchesi. It's Paula here from the school
. . . Shaun's history teacher. I can't get hold of
Petey Grant's mother, so I thought I'd call you.
He's just told me he's been arrested by Richie Bates
and he's going down to the station.'

'What?' said Joe. 'Are you sure?'

'Well, no. You know Petey.'

'I'll go down and check it out. Thanks for the
call.'

Richie and Petey sat in the station at opposite sides
of the desk.

'Why have you arrested me?' asked Petey.

Richie laughed at him. 'You're not being arrested, you're . . .' he held up his fingers to make quotes, '"helping us with our enquiries." I mean, we don't have any evidence . . . yet. So,' he went on, deliberately friendly, 'obviously you're here because of Katie.'

'Oh,' said Petey.

'Did you fancy her?' said Richie bluntly. He was tapping his fingers loudly on the wooden surface.

Petey blushed. 'No!' he said.

'You sent her a Valentine's card, didn't you?'

Petey's eyes shot wide.

'That was before she was going out with Shaun,' he stammered.

'And were you upset when she started going out with Shaun?'

'No!' said Petey, horrified. 'Shaun's my friend. So is Joe!'

'Did you ever ask her out?'

'No!' He stopped. 'I've never asked anyone out.' He blinked back tears.

'I'm going to get to the point here, Petey,' said Richie. 'Do you know anything about what happened the Friday night Katie went missing?'

'No,' said Petey. 'I told you. I was inside, like I was supposed to be.'

'Are you sure?' said Richie, forcefully.

'Yes,' said Petey. He started tapping his foot on the floor.

'Do you understand how important it is to tell us if you know anything?' said Richie. 'Another girl could die if we don't have all the information.' Petey looked shocked.

'Someone else could die?' he said. 'Oh my God.' The doorbell startled him.

'Stay where you are,' barked Richie. Petey was shaking.

Duke jumped up from the bench and put his ear to the thick round glass. He heard it again – a scratching sound, then churning, then scratching.

'Shit,' he said. The owner came over to him.

'You got a problem with the dryer?'

'Uh, yeah,' said Duke. 'Think I left a pin in my jeans.'

'Oh dear,' she said. 'Well, here.' She pushed a key into a slot at the side and turned it off. 'You should be able to open it now.'

He reached in and pulled out the warm, tangled jeans and jacket. On the bottom of the drum, a single euro coin was left. He picked it up, confused. It burned his palm.

'Money,' she said. 'Even better.' But Duke was panicked now, pulling out pockets, examining the denim, patting down the clothes he was wearing, emptying out his bag on the floor. His fingers ran over and through everything, until he was kneeling, panting, his heart pounding. He stood up and leaned heavily against the dryer, his head

bent. Beads of sweat had broken out on his forehead.

'Damn,' he roared, slamming his hands against
the machine, kicking it with his boot. 'Damn.'
Everyone was quiet around him. The owner didn't
move. Duke piled everything back into his bag
and walked out the door, past a woman holding
a pair of white trousers with a grass stain on the
knee.

'Molasses will get that out,' he snarled as he
walked by.

Joe stormed into the hall of the station, shouting,
'You better not have Petey Grant in here for your
sake,' even though he could see Petey sitting there
as pale as death, wringing his big hands.

'What's it to do with you?' asked Richie.

Joe said hi to Petey, then ushered Richie back
into the hall.

'What the hell is going on here?' said Joe. 'What
are you doing questioning Petey without a responsible adult present? Are you nuts? It's illegal.'

'No it's not. He's not under arrest. And it's none
of your business anyway,' said Richie.

'I'm making it my business,' said Joe.

'Make it your business all you like,' said Richie.
'I did nothing wrong, the guy wasn't being
arrested. I just wanted to have a little word with
him.'

'Why the hell didn't you do that at the school?

You're terrifying him,' said Joe. 'It's written all over his face. A guy like that. I've talked with him. He knows nothing about Katie.'

'Oh, well, the great American detective has spoken. We can all go home now, case closed.'

'What the hell is that supposed to mean? I'm just telling you you're going about this the wrong way.'

'And I'm telling you – stay the fuck out of things you don't understand, right?'

'Do you have a fucking clue what you're doing?' asked Joe, raising his voice. 'Petey Grant, for Christ's sake! The guy is harmless. I know Petey Grant, Richie—'

'We've all known Petey Grant a hell of a lot longer than you and—'

'And WHAT? What deep dark secret do you know about him that I don't?'

'He knows something. He's not all there, he—'

'Is that the term? A shitty twist of fate is why Petey's where he's at. You know what happened? Yeah, I'm not surprised you don't. The kid didn't get enough oxygen at birth.' He threw his hands up. 'That's it. *There's* your big secret.'

'So what? That doesn't mean he couldn't—'

'Oh, come on, Richie. You know damn well that Petey Grant wouldn't hurt a fly. I had to tell him what a hooker was for Christ's sake. You think a guy like that . . . you saw Katie. You honestly think Petey Grant—'

'Look, he fancied her—'

'You could lock up half the guys in Mountcannon for that,' said Joe. 'This is bullshit, this is total bullshit. There's probably some fucking psycho out there and who are you looking at? Petey! Have you ever worked a serious crime in your life?'

'You arrogant prick,' said Richie. He stopped himself inches from Joe.

'Don't even try it,' said Joe. Richie stood in front of him, fuming. His face was crimson. Veins pulsed at his temples. He had a few inches on Joe, but none of his composure. He was all rough edges and rage. Joe went back in to Petey.

'Right,' he said to Richie who had followed him in. 'Ask him your questions. If he's only helping you out, there's nothing to stop me being here. Isn't that right, Petey?'

'Actually, Mr Lucchesi, would you mind if I did this on my own?'

Joe opened his mouth, then stopped. 'Uh, sure, Petey. If you're sure you're OK. You're not under any pressure here, are you?'

'No. I'm fine.'

'OK. Well, I guess I'll leave you to it then.'

'Thanks,' said Richie. 'I appreciate it.'

Joe walked past him and out the door.

'OK. I'm going to ask you again,' said Richie. 'Do you know anything about all this?'

Petey took a deep breath. 'Sort of.'

Richie shifted in his seat.

Petey looked up. 'I met Katie on the Friday night.'

'What do you mean you met her?'

'I bumped into her,' said Petey. 'She was crying.' He looked down, then straight back at Richie. 'She said she had a fight with Shaun.'

Richie smiled.

EIGHTEEN

Stinger's Creek, North Central Texas, 1986

Ashley Ames stood at her bedroom mirror deciding whether or not she had finished her makeup. It was subtle on her pale skin; blush, mascara and a slick of frosted lipstick. She emptied her cosmetic bag and ran her fingers over the products. She found what she was looking for, a black eyeliner she barely knew how to use. She uncapped it and leaned in to the glass. Her nine-year-old sister Luanne lay behind her on the bed.

When she was finished, Ashley turned to her, holding a hairbrush up to her mouth: 'Today, Ashley Ames is modelling a hot-pink off-the-shoulder top with a butt-length grey sweatshirt-skirt, complemented by a pair of classic white Keds. Or today, Ashley Ames meets her man in a hot-pink off-the-shoulder shirt with a mid-thigh ruffle skirt worn with black high-heel ankle boots.'

Luanne continued. 'Could her hair be any higher, could her eyeliner be any heavier—'

'Shut up, Lu,' said Ashley. 'So, what am I wearing?'

'The ruffles,' said Luanne. 'But Daddy's gonna freak.'

'Why?'

'It's kinda slutty,' said Luanne.

'Like you'd know.' Ashley wriggled into the skirt, zipping it at her side. A small roll of flesh slipped over the band. She turned and patted herself on the butt.

'Bask in my glory, Lu, bask in my glory.'

She sat on the bed and zipped up her boots over her chubby calves, tilting her legs to the side. She grabbed her bag, threw in some makeup and walked tall to the door. As she walked into the living room, Westley Ames lowered his newspaper.

'I don't know, Ash, honey,' he said, shaking his head.

'You don't know what, Daddy?'

'If they're the right clothes for a young lady, if they're saying the right thing.'

'What do *you* think they're saying, Daddy?'

'Don't you challenge me like that, Ashley.'

'I'm sorry, Daddy. It's just everyone . . . I mean, it's not like I'm the only one, I like my clothes, they're not saying anything to anyone.'

'And what's all that black around your eyes?' he said.

'It's eyeliner, Daddy, no big deal.'

'And who is this young man, anyway?' said Westley.

'Donnie Riggs, Daddy. You know Donnie.'

'I know *of* Donnie, Ashley, I do not *know* Donnie and neither do you. We can only pray he's nothing like his father, because if I so much as catch a whiff of alcohol on your breath when you come home, you'll never see the outside world again. Do you hear me, Ashley?'

'It's the middle of the day, Daddy. And you know I'd never drink,' she said and turned to walk out of the room, smiling.

Donnie Riggs sat on the kerb between two cars, a block away from Ashley's house. He flicked his cigarette butt on the road and stood up, smoothing down his dirty jeans. His legs were shaky and his face was hot. He didn't want to look Westley Ames in the eye today.

He rang the doorbell and Mrs Ames answered, her right arm hooked around her narrow waist, a string of pearls lying flat against her chest.

'Hello, Donnie,' she said, giving him a weak smile.

'Hello, ma'am,' said Donnie. 'Ashley here?'

'Come on in.'

She turned her head and smiled when she saw her daughter walk from the living room. She was close to tears when she looked at Donnie.

'You look after her,' she said.

'Mom!' said Ashley.

'You don't mind me saying that, Donnie, do you?' said Mrs Ames.

'Of course not, ma'am,' he said. 'And don't worry, I'll take good care of her.' Ashley smiled, taking Donnie's arm.

The sun was high, sending ripples of silver light across the water. Duke sat in the darkness of the densely packed trees, his legs drawn to his chest. A flashlight lay on the grass beside him. After waiting quietly for half an hour, he heard footsteps along the path and a girl laughing. Then he heard Donnie's voice and the dull clink of beer bottles. The sounds drifted away as they moved towards the water's edge.

'Nah. I didn't do too well in that one,' said Donnie. 'Geography's not my thing. And I hate Baxter. He's a loser.'

'Yeah,' said Ashley.

Donnie fidgeted with a bottle cap, flicking it in the air with his thumb over and over.

'Earth to Donnie, earth to Donnie,' said Ashley. He turned to look at her as if he had forgotten she was there.

'Sorry,' he muttered. 'Want another beer?'

'Sure,' she said.

He reached behind them to grab a bottle and when he sat up his face was inches from hers.

She closed her eyes. He leaned in and kissed her on the lips, guiding her gently back onto the grass beside him.

'Above the waist,' she said, smiling, slapping Donnie's hand away.

A twig cracked. Duke had been standing over them, watching silently. Ashley bolted upright, fixing her top, staring at Duke. Donnie sat up, panic flashing across his face.

'Hi, Pu—, uh, hi Duke,' she said, confused.

'Keep goin', guys, don't worry 'bout me,' said Duke.

She looked at him, alarmed. Then she smiled.

'Sure,' she said, looking at Donnie, laughing. Donnie looked nervous. She looked back to Duke.

'Seriously,' he said, his voice ice cold. 'Keep. Going.'

Donnie put his arm around her waist, pulling her towards him. She pushed him away.

'What y'all talkin' about?' she said, getting up. 'Are you crazy?'

'Just do it,' said Duke, shoving her on top of Donnie. Ashley's eyes were wide. She knew these guys, she could identify them. Then her heart sank. She knew she never would.

'Get down to it,' said Duke. 'I'll sit back here and take it all in and maybe I'll get myself a bit of the action later.'

* * *

'Come on now, Ashley,' said Duke when it was all over. He shook out her handbag, then picked up her compact. 'Fix that face of yours. You've ruined your mascara. Go on, now.'

He pushed the mirror in front of her face. She saw the tears roll down her cheeks. He picked up her brush from the grass and began brushing the back of her hair. He pulled out the leaves and shook the dirt that clung to the matted brown mess. 'What would your daddy think? He would think his little girl was a whore, his little princess was out on her first date, givin' it up to a no-good like Donnie Riggs.' He laughed. Donnie stayed quiet beside him. Ashley took the brush from Duke and dragged it through her hair. 'Leave me alone,' she sobbed. 'I'm not going to tell anyone, I can't tell anyone. Just leave me alone. Please go.' Duke picked up the bloodied flashlight and walked away.

'Molasses takes out grass stains,' muttered Donnie as he turned to go.

Ashley looked into the tiny mirror and saw the mascara streaked down her face. When she wiped it all away and smeared on more makeup, she looked almost the same as when she had walked out her door. Except for her eyes. She picked herself up off the ground and walked slowly to the edge of the woods and out on to the road.

As she walked the final few metres to her house, Duke passed her by and nodded.

'It coulda been a lot worse, Ashley.' He waited
a beat. 'You should see what we do for our next
trick.'

NINETEEN

Richie stood by a black station wagon, scribbling a parking ticket. He folded it and slipped it under the windscreen wiper. Shaun walked out of the coffee shop and rolled his eyes.

'I wouldn't mind a quick word,' said Richie, jogging up behind him. 'I just want to clear something up.' He stopped and took out his notebook, tilting it to avoid the misty rain that had started to fall.

'Sure,' said Shaun. 'But I'm on my way back to school.' He pulled up the hood on his parka, casting a shadow over his eyes.

'Just remind me again,' said Richie. 'Where exactly did you say goodbye to Katie?'

Shaun took a breath. 'Over there, I guess, by the wall down to the harbour.'

'Did you hear the singing?' asked Richie.

Shaun froze. 'What?'

'You said you were down by the dry dock before then.'

'Yes.'

'So was a Spanish boat with twenty drunk sailors singing at the top of their lungs.'

Shaun said nothing.

'So where did you go when you left Katie's house? It doesn't look like you were at the harbour.'

Shaun's heart pounded. Cold sweat trickled down his side.

'We were at the harbour, but earlier . . .'

The owner of the station wagon came out of Tynan's and threw his hands up in the air.

'Ah, for Christ's sake, guard. I was two minutes. Look – a newspaper! How long do you think that took? I've just come down from Dublin for a couple of days—'

Richie shrugged and turned away.

One of the old barflies was walking past and leaned into the Dublin man. 'He won't listen to you, you know. "Double yellows" he'll tell you. And he'll point at them. He's a bollox.'

Richie ignored the muttering behind him and stared at Shaun.

'Then we went to . . . for a walk,' said Shaun.

'Now you're talking shite to me, Shaun. Where were you really?'

'I told you. For a walk.'

'Leave the young lad alone,' shouted the barfly as he disappeared into Danaher's. 'Y'bollox,' he muttered.

'Where did you go for a walk?' said Richie.

'Up through the village and—'

'Out of town, then all the way back here out of the way of her house to say goodbye?'

'No.'

'Through the village where? Up to your house, then back here out of the way to say goodbye?'

Shaun couldn't stand still.

'Was something wrong, Shaun? You can tell me. Did you have a fight?'

'No. Everything was fine. I've said all this before.'

'So you didn't have a row or anything.'

'No,' said Shaun.

Richie started writing. 'She wasn't upset.'

'No,' said Shaun.

'She wasn't crying. She didn't tell anyone she had a fight with you a few minutes before she disappeared.'

'No.' His voice caught.

'You'd swear to that.'

'I . . . don't know.'

Richie kept writing, then closed the notebook and nodded. 'Cheers,' he said.

Frank was standing in front of the bulletin board at the station checking the notices were still in date. He pulled out tacks and repositioned posters, throwing the old ones in the bin. He didn't hear Joe come in.

'Sorry to bother you, but there's something I think you need to know. It might have a bearing on your investigation.'

'What is it?' said Frank.

'About a year ago, I killed someone,' said Joe. 'On the job. A guy called Donald Riggs. He kidnapped an eight-year-old girl, collected the ransom, then blew her and her mother to pieces. I saw it all. I shot Riggs and he was lying on the ground, dead. I walked over to him and he had a pin in the shape of a hawk in his hand. That same pin is in an evidence bag somewhere in One Police Plaza in New York. So why did I find one outside Danaher's on Sunday?' He held out his palm.

Frank looked at the pin, then looked at Joe.

'I don't know,' he said.

'I think someone is after me and my family,' said Joe. 'The man's name, I think, is Duke Rawlins.'

'That could be any old pin and—'

'It's not any old pin,' said Joe. 'It's specific to an event,' he could barely say it, 'that happened back in the eighties when . . . look, I know it sounds nuts, I don't know who this guy is, but he's—'

'You've been through an awful lot,' said Frank.

'What?' said Joe.

'You're under a lot of pressure.'

'Of course I'm under a lot of pressure,' said Joe. 'But that's got nothing to do with this. I think he's come to Ireland.'

'Have you seen him?'

'No,' said Joe. 'But there's no other explanation for that pin being there. No-one here would know about it and no-one attached any significance to it at the time of the crime. It was just another personal effect of a dead perp. The only reason it means anything to *me* is the fact that it was the first thing I saw in the hand of the first – and hopefully the last – man I ever killed.'

'There's not a lot I can do with that information,' said Frank.

'It could be related to Katie in some way. He could have gone after—'

'We have no way of finding out if he's here.'

'What? Immigration! At the airport!'

'Joe, it doesn't work that way. If he's a criminal, he's not going to come here with an official work permit. And if someone travels here on a short holiday visa, we don't take a record.' He shrugged his shoulders. 'They can pretty much do what they like.'

Shaun walked in to the empty computer room at St Declan's and sat down at a PC. He clicked on Mail and typed in his password. There was one message in his inbox. The subject was blank and the sender was a string of letters that made no sense. He opened the message and a photo appeared. It was the lighthouse. Flames burned on the grass in front of it. It was from his mother's shoot. He jerked the mouse across the mat, clicked the file closed, then grabbed his bag from the floor beside him. He was still furious when he got home.

'I really think it's sick the way you all can get on with your lives,' he shouted at Anna as he walked in.

'I'm not getting into this with you again,' said Anna. 'I'm tired and yes, I have to work. There is nothing I can do about that. I know you're going through a tough time—'

'So why are you rubbing my face in it?'

'I'm not rubbing your face in it,' she said. She turned around and saw his expression. 'How am I doing that?'

'Your email.'

'What email?'

'Of the fucking shoot!'

'What is wrong with you? I will not have you using language like that to me, whatever has happened. Have some respect. What email are you talking about?'

'The email I got today. From you.'

Joe came into the kitchen and put the portable phone down on the counter.

'That was Frank Deegan,' he said, furious. 'Shaun, were you talking to Richie Bates today?'

'Yeah. Why?' said Shaun.

'Richie said you denied having an argument with Katie before she disappeared. But they have a witness who says you did.'

'What are you talking about?' said Shaun.

'I'm just telling you what I heard. Richie said he spoke to you in the village earlier.'

'He did, but I never said—'

'Apparently, you denied, under caution, having an argument with Katie. He thinks you lied and he has it all written down in his notebook.'

'What does "under caution" mean? Like "anything you say or do can be held against you"?'

'Something like that.'

'Well, then he didn't caution me. I swear to God, Dad. I don't get this. We were just talking.'

'Jesus Christ, I'm gonna look like an idiot—'

'Why?' said Shaun.

'Nothing. Come on, you and me are gonna have to go down to the station now to talk to them, clear up a few of these things. I'd like to know myself, Shaun, what the hell is going on.'

Ray walked backwards out of his apartment, pulling a black bag with him. He hauled it over his shoulder and walked to the metal bins lined up on the road at the end of the cul de sac. He flung the bag across the top and it landed with a stink onto the others. It was then he saw the tear across it.

'For fuck's sake, Ray,' said Richie striding up behind him.

Ray turned around.

'Look,' said Richie, pointing to the mess Ray had left along the road from his house.

'Well done, Garda Richie,' said Ray. 'You have successfully followed a trail. They'll make you a sergeant yet.'

'Shut your face, Carmody. And clean that up.'

'Why are you so interested in what comes out of my sack?' Ray smirked.

Richie grabbed Ray's arm between his thumb and middle finger and squeezed hard.

'Ow,' said Ray. 'You wanker.' He couldn't pull his arm free.

'If I come home to this shit tonight,' said Richie, looking back at the rubbish, 'I swear to fuck, I'll shove it in your letterbox.' He released his grip.

'I get it now,' said Ray. 'Cleaning up the streets of Mountcannon.'

'Do you even own your apartment?' said Richie.

'What the fuck is that supposed to mean?' said Ray.

'Do you own it?'

'I'm renting. But what's that got to do with you? Just because you and your boyfriend clubbed together and bought a little love nest.'

'I own the place. Oran rents from me.'

'Why are we having this conversation? Is it because you're a woman?'

Richie shoved Ray's shoulder.

'Whoa, keeper of the peace,' said Ray. 'You're in uniform now. What will the neighbours say?'

Richie looked around at the empty streets.

'Fucking watch yourself,' he said, shoving his face into Ray's.

'I do. And I like what I see,' said Ray. 'I could watch myself all day.'

Shaun was slumped in a chair at the station, his long legs stretched away from the desk. He hadn't said a word apart from a muttered hello to Frank.

'We just have to wait for Richie,' said Frank. After five minutes, Richie walked in, red-faced and sweaty. Frank stared at him, then turned to Shaun.

'Just tell us where you were that night,' asked Frank. 'Please. This has gone on too long.'

Joe sat by Shaun's side, looking around the room, focusing in the silence on the bulletin board mounted on the pale cream wall. A bad colour photocopy was pinned in the corner with a girl's face framed at the centre. Her eyes were small under thick eyebrows, her hair a mass of black frizz. Her pudgy cheeks pushed against the edges of the shot. MISSING was printed above her. Siobhán Fallon. Last seen in American Heroes,

Tipperary town on Friday, September 7th. Joe had never heard anything about her. One missing person can capture the media's attention, while another, less attractive victim, went no further than a homemade poster on a station wall.

'Seascapes,' said Shaun, suddenly.

Joe spun around. 'I goddamn knew it.'

'Seascapes. Holiday homes?' said Frank, ignoring him.

'Yes.'

Joe was shaking his head.

'What time was that?' asked Frank.

'Seven-thirty.'

'And what were you doing there? Working?'

'No,' said Shaun. He glanced at his father. 'Me and Katie . . . we went there to be alone.'

'Why did you need to be alone?' asked Frank.

Shaun flushed. 'We were . . .'

Joe held his breath.

'What?' asked Frank.

'We went there to have sex.'

Joe exhaled and closed his eyes.

'Did Katie know that's why you were there?' said Frank.

'What?'

'Is this something Katie expected to happen?'

'Yes, she did,' he said.

'And did it happen?' asked Frank.

'Kind of. I don't know,' he said.

'How do you not know? Did you or didn't you?'

'She was, you know, it was her first time. She was nervous.' He began to cry. The questions got more personal, almost medical. Every answer was dragged out of him. Then it was Richie's turn.

'So, basically, nothing was happening, she was too tense and this pissed you off?'

'No,' said Shaun. 'That wasn't the way it was. It did happen, but then it hurt so we stopped.'

'And you got angry because this wasn't all going the way it was supposed to!'

'No.'

'She didn't give up the goods, so you lost it.'

'No!'

'Maybe she didn't even know why she was there at all. Maybe this was all a big surprise to her. You'd get her a bit drunk, then in you go.'

'You asshole!' said Shaun. Then he couldn't stop. 'You fucking asshole. I loved Katie. This is all bullshit.' He cried harder, his mouth quivering. 'You,' he said, pointing at Richie, 'have no clue what happened, you weren't there. I put my arms around her and told her not to worry, that she could call it off any time she wanted. You don't know anything about me and Katie! Why am I even telling you this stuff?'

'You called me and asked us to come in here for an informal chat, Frank, not abuse,' said Joe. His face ached with every word he had to get out. He propped his elbow on the desk and leaned his head against his hand. He looked up. 'We're helping you out here. If you had anything more on Shaun, he would be arrested by now. But you don't. Apart from his alleged denial of having an argument while under alleged caution.' Richie's eyes narrowed. He opened his mouth to reply, but Frank was quick to put a steadying hand on his arm.

'So is it true that after this you had an argument?' said Frank gently.

'Yes,' said Shaun, wiping away his tears.

'Why didn't you tell anyone this earlier?'

'Because I thought she was going to come back,' he sobbed. 'I thought she was trying to freak me out. I didn't want to let everyone know what had happened. Her mother would have killed her.' When he heard what he said, he started to sob harder. Everyone waited until he had calmed down.

'What was the argument about?' asked Frank.

'It was stupid,' said Shaun. 'She asked me had this happened to me before, with anyone back home and I asked her did she want me to be honest. And she said yes, so I told her it had never happened to me, that before when I had been with someone, everything had worked out OK, but that I didn't mind that it didn't happen properly for us.' Richie sucked in a breath. Shaun ignored him and kept talking in desperate bursts.

'I thought she knew it wasn't my first time, but she had presumed it was. I don't know why she asked me what she did, but I guess she was feeling bad and, I don't know. Anyway, she got upset that I hadn't told her I had done it before. And I tried to reassure her that it didn't matter what had happened before, which it didn't, but she was too upset. She said some things and then she stormed off. I ran after her, but she pushed me away.'

'What did she say exactly?' said Frank.

Shaun began sobbing again. 'She said, "Leave me alone. I feel like a loser. You made me feel like a total loser."'

'And what did you say to that?'

'I said,' he looked up at the ceiling, 'I fucking said, "Fine. I'll leave you alone, then."' He went on, through his sobs, 'And I did. I left her alone. I went back to the house and washed the goddamn dishes. And now look.' His body shook. His tears flowed. Joe put his arm around him. Shaun was wailing now. He got up and ran for the bathroom.

Joe shook his head at Frank and Richie.

'He shouldn't have lied,' said Frank.

Joe's jaw was locked shut and his teeth were like spines in his mouth. He had been grinding them hard through the entire interview.

'I'll go and check on him,' said Frank.

'You know, you never have to look too far to find the killer,' said Richie, when Frank was gone. 'What is it again? Ninety percent of murders are committed by the husband, the boyfriend—'

Joe shook his head. He thought of the guys he

grew up around, the ones you couldn't reason
with because they were so stupid. It was too easy
to fight them.

'You're fairly quiet now, aren't you?' said
Richie. 'Shiting on with your stupid fucking
suggestions until your son gets pulled in. Then all
we get is a guilty man's silence.'

Joe's jaw spasmed.

Richie lowered his voice to a growl, 'I'm just
saying young Shaun here bangs the arse off his
girlfriend, they have a fight, she storms off and
her body turns up three weeks later in his back
garden. He doesn't say a thing about any of this
when we question him. What would that say to
you? Would you look into him if it was your case,
detective?' He spat the last word.

A narrow strip of grass ran along the centre of the
laneway up to the Lucchesis' door. Two vans were
parked by the trees and to their right, hidden
behind the trunk of an oak, Duke Rawlins was
studying the phone numbers on their side panels.
Mark Nash. Lawn Order SUV. 089 676746. Duke
closed his eyes and stored the number. Suddenly,
he heard an engine from the top of the lane. He
hunched down. The Jeep moved up the drive
towards the front door of the house. Duke waited
until it stopped before slipping back through the
trees.

* * *

Frank was about to call O'Connor when O'Connor called him.

'Frank, hello, it's Myles. I've been going through the statements and I think I've come up with something.'

Frank tried to stop him. O'Connor ploughed on. 'Here's what Robert Harrington says: "I was at the harbour from seven p.m., checking out some new computer equipment on one of the boats that had come in. I saw Katie and Shaun up on the walkway. Then they were kissing and hugging." That's fine – four different fishermen confirm this. But further down, Robert says that later on, Katie and Shaun, "must have been down by the lifeboat launch." Not "were", but "must have been". Kevin Raftery and Finn Banks did not see Katie or Shaun at all. They arrived to meet Robert at eight-thirty p.m. So all sightings of Katie and Shaun happened before eight o'clock that evening. And the person with the strongest emotional attachment to the missing girl and her boyfriend – Robert Harrington – is leading us to believe they were nearby, but hasn't claimed to have actually seen them.'

'You're not wrong,' said Frank.

Anna was sitting on a keg in the cellar, staring at the rows of wine bottles, the stone wall cold against her back. A shaft of light cut through and she looked up at the silhouette in the doorway above. Joe walked down the steps and stood in front of her. He saw the pronounced angles of her cheekbones and reached out. She held his hand against her face and started to cry. He pulled her to his chest, holding her tight, letting his breath out. The effort of not touching for days had been exhausting them both. His stomach felt hollowed out, his head cloudy from medication, his eyes dry.

'Say something,' said Anna. He didn't move. He didn't look at her.

'Please,' she said.

'I guess I'm pissed off that I thought everything was so perfect,' he said.

'It was,' said Anna. 'It is. It was years ago . . .'

'I know that,' he said. 'But when I look at the guy, I see a fat, drunken loser and I think: that's what I'm up against. That guy had my wife.'

'That sounds so dreadful. And you're not up against anyone. It was so stupid. What I did was stupid. I've always known that, but I love you . . .'

'You should have told me,' he said.

'You would have left me.'

He pushed her back gently and looked into her eyes.

'Yeah, I would have,' he said. 'So maybe it's a good thing you didn't tell me.' He gave her a sad smile. 'I've spent the last few days thinking about it. In the middle of everything. And all I've come up with is that in the big picture, I guess it doesn't matter. What happened to Katie, what's happening to Shaun . . . there's only so much energy I have. And for now, it should be going Shaun's way. We can't be like this. I just can't live separately, whatever you did. It feels too weird. I'm sorry about what I said to you. I didn't mean that. I was just so angry.' He took both her hands in his. 'Why,' he said, squeezing them, 'has everything turned to shit?' He hugged her close; she sobbed and he kissed her hair.

Martha Lawson was curled up on her sofa, wrapped in an oversized cardigan with the belt pulled tight around her waist. The doorbell woke her from a light sleep and she rushed to the door. She smiled weakly when she saw Richie.

'How are you keeping?' he asked.

'I don't know,' she said, letting him in. She pulled newspapers and magazines off the sofa and offered him a seat.

'Have you any news?' she asked, grabbing cups and mugs of old tea from the table, wiping with her finger at the rings they left behind.

'Don't worry about all that,' said Richie. 'Sit down. I have a bit of news, but really, it's between yourself and myself. I'm telling you this in confidence. As a friend more than anything.'

She looked at him, puzzled.

'It's about Shaun.'

*　*　*

The bedroom was in total darkness, the black-out blinds pulled tightly down to the window sill. The smell of sleep hung in the air. Joe put his hand on Anna's shoulder and turned her gently towards him.

'I'm going to Dublin,' he whispered. She frowned and looked at the clock.

'It's seven in the morning.'

'I know,' he said. 'I have something to do.'

'Now? Are you crazy? What about Shaun? I can't even send him to school today. What am I supposed to do? We've barely talked about what happened at the station.'

'I'm going because of Shaun,' he said. 'They've let him go for now, but who knows what way they'll pull the evidence together . . .'

'How is anything in Dublin going to help?' she asked. 'Couldn't you do whatever it is over the phone?'

'No,' he said. He kissed her on the cheek before she had a chance to fully turn her face away.

Joe drove north on the Waterford Road and took the turn for Passage East, joining the queue for the ferry to Ballyhack. He left the Jeep for the five-minute trip, climbing the narrow steps to the deck. Each time, a different view was waiting when he reached the top. He stood against the railing and leaned into the cool breeze.

From Ballyhack, he drove east, passing signs for Rosslare to the right and Wexford town to the

left. He took the left and drove until he hit the
N11, making his way to Dublin in just over two
hours. Then he crawled through a senseless
system of one-way streets in the city until he
finally found a space in a multi-storey car park in
Temple Bar. He took a right onto Westmoreland
Street and made his way past the curved
stonework of the Bank of Ireland where he crossed
the busy street to Trinity. He'd been to Dublin
before, but had never walked the cobbles under
the famous arch.

He suddenly felt old, surrounded by students,
some of them dressed for Armagnac with the
chaps, others looking starkly modern against the
eighteenth century architecture. He made his way
past the library and turned right, taking in the
action on the rugby pitch where – stripped of the
helmets and padding of the NFL – crazy men put
themselves through similar paces. He soon found
himself standing at the vast, monastic wooden
doors of the zoology department. The impressive
stone building was over one hundred years old,
with a sense of history that hit Joe as soon as he
pushed into the tiny hallway. On his right was
Neal Columb's office – white wooden panelling
and frosted glass. There was a scrawled note on
a barely sticky Post-it slapped onto the door: Back
two-thirty. Even the smallest action gave a clue
to who someone was. Joe was already imagining
Neal Columb as disorganised and brusque. So

when, at two-twenty, a neat, freshly showered man with a sandwich in his hand walked by, Joe didn't pay much attention. The man shook his head at the Post-it, pulled it off and put it in his pocket. He unlocked the door, walked into the office and came out immediately with a perfectly scripted note that he stuck carefully on the door. 'Back at two-thirty p.m. Thank you. Neal Columb.' He called out to a secretary in another room, 'Jane, I left you the note. You needn't have wasted one of your precious Post-its.' He was smiling. She laughed back at him. Joe quickly revised his appraisal of Neal Columb to well-organised and friendly. He was happy to give him his ten minutes for lunch, even though he felt like storming the office.

Finally, after checking his watch several times, he rapped on the glass.

'Come in,' said Neal. 'Joe, is it? Have a seat.'

'Ah. I saw you out running,' said Joe. 'Around the rugby pitch.'

'I'd rather run around it than have a reason to be on it,' said Neal. He was in his early forties, trim, fit and clearly not a man planning to throw himself into a scrum. Joe's eyes wandered around the office. It had a definite academic feel, but enough photos on the walls and odds and ends on the shelves to make it cosy.

'Let's go up to the lab and have a look at what you've brought,' he said.

They made their way up two short flights of stairs onto a small landing. An arrow for the lab pointed right, but Neal gestured left.

'Would you like to see our Rogues' Gallery first?'

Joe looked at him.

'The museum,' said Neal.

'That would be great,' said Joe.

They walked through the doorway into the musty chemical air of the small museum. Joe was sucked back in time. Antique mahogany cabinets ran the length of each wall and a heavy mahogany counter sat on top of more cabinets at the centre of the room. Behind each door were shelves of stuffed animals and creatures suspended in jars of murky formaldehyde.

'Take a guess,' said Neal, stopping at one of the displays and covering the plaque. Inside, was a large round, delicate-looking object the colour of ginger root, with a strange bulbous growth at one side. Around the back, a hollow was carved out revealing a centre lined with a gaping honey-combed effect.

'I have no clue,' said Joe.

'It's a camel's stomach. Those little pockets inside are where they store water.'

'Wow. That's not what I expected.'

Neal pointed to another jar in one of the cabinets. There was a long string of what looked like tagliatelle suspended in a greenish solution.

'Do you eat black pudding?' asked Neal.

'Aw, don't spoil that for me,' said Joe.

'Well, this guy is the reason you should always cook it thoroughly. Tapeworm. It's a big fan of pigs.'

'I'll be nuking it from now on.' Joe squinted into the jar. 'That's just way too long,' he said, shaking his head.

When he turned around, Neal was pulling out trays from a drawer that smelt of wood and naphthalene. Rows of preserved insects were secured onto a cream backing by straight pins. Neal talked through the different species, then stopped eventually to check his watch.

'OK. The lab,' he said. 'I've got a meeting to go to. Remind me again what can I help you with.'

Joe lied for a living, but he was feeling a strange compulsion to be honest with Neal Columb. However, he knew he couldn't. So his compromise was to start with the truth.

'There's a forest near my house. I found this empty pupal case there two nights ago. I guess I was just curious. I did a little entomology in college, back in the States, but I dropped out . . . I'm still fascinated by it, though, but not one hundred per cent clued in.'

Then he moved on to the lie.

'There was a dead animal nearby and I wondered if it had anything to do with that. Or if you could maybe pinpoint the species of the fly and how long it's been there, you know . . .'

'OK,' said Neal, reaching out for the small brown pill jar where Joe had put the pupal case. He slipped it under a dissecting microscope and peered in.

'You're absolutely right. It is, indeed, a fly pupal case. Now let's see if we can put a name on the little fellow.'

He pulled out taxonomic guides and looked back and forth between them and the pupal case. Every now and then, he would stop and point something out to Joe. Eventually, he went to a cupboard packed with bottled insect specimens and brought out a jar that held a pupal case and larva, suspended in a formaldehyde solution.

'Right,' he said after an hour. 'What you have is a *Calliphora*, which as I'm sure you know, is a bluebottle. Species-wise, I would have said *vicina* or *vomitoria*, but now I can say for definite that it's *vomitoria*, based on comparisons. That would also tie in with where you found it – it's much more likely to show up in rural areas, particularly forests. It's actually a great tool for estimating time of death in murder investigations.' He raised an eyebrow. 'But, of course, you know all this.'

Joe nodded. 'OK. And what would that mean in terms of life cycle . . .' He trailed off, hoping Neal would just give him a time frame, so he could find something out that would help Shaun.

'Well, bluebottles come to the body almost immediately. They have an extremely advanced radar for death. This, of course, won't happen during the night, but it will during the day. So if your little fox or whatever was killed in the evening, the blow fly would be there the next morning, busily laying anything up to 300 eggs in one go, heading straight for the orifices or wound sites.' He looked up at Joe. 'I'm doing it again, telling you things you already know. So I'll get down to it. Basically taking into account what you've told me, I'd say this would mean that your little creature died about twenty days before you found this.'

Joe hesitated. 'Thanks.' He tried to hide his disappointment. This put Katie's death back to the night of her disappearance when the last person to see her alive apart from her killer was poor Petey Grant and before that – Shaun. He threw the pupal case in the bin as he walked back through the campus. His anger he understood, but the emotion that came out of nowhere hitting him like a slap, was an unfamiliar sense of embarrassment.

'I meant to tell you,' said Frank, 'before Shaun was called in yesterday, Joe Lucchesi was here with some new information.'

'That's convenient,' said Richie.

'Come on now. Our job is to take it all in. Joe was concerned because he thinks someone from a previous case back in New York could be out to get him and went through Katie to do it. Joe shot someone dead last year – that's not common knowledge – and the man's friend has just got out of prison and could possibly have come over here.'

Frank watched how Richie's eyes would glaze over if the conversation stretched to more than a few sentences. His right eye would turn out slightly, then in again as he came back to reality.

'Why does Joe think that?' he said eventually.

'Well, in fairness to the man, he found some evidence outside Danaher's the other night that was a direct link to the original shooting.'

'Wow,' said Richie after thinking it through. 'That's weird. There could be something to this.'

Frank strained to find the sarcasm until he realised there was none. He could not understand Richie. One minute he was one way, the next minute he was another. He clung to each new development as if it was a single unit. Whoever was attached to that development was, by Richie's rationale, a suspect. Suspects walked in and out of his sights accordingly: Petey, Shaun, Joe, Duke Rawlins . . .

Frank was about to remark on this, give a weights and measures speech, but he was too tired for a head-on collision with the spiky young guard. Instead, he filled him in on more details and left.

Anna was sitting on the sofa with her glasses on, reading a book. Her legs were stretched out onto the low coffee table. Joe walked in and sat beside her. He grabbed the remote control, flicking channels on the muted TV.

'So you're not going to tell me anything,' Anna said. 'Our son has been lying to us, you've been keeping things from me . . .'

'Not this again.'

'Yes, this again. We don't just talk when it suits you, Joe. This is serious. He lied.'

'Shaun's sixteen. He was scared. The last thing you're gonna do is tell any grown-up that you were having sex, let alone your parents and a bunch of cops.'

She stared at him.

'What?' he said. 'You've never lied to your parents?'

'You were never arrested for murder,' she hissed. 'Are you crazy?'

He stood up. 'I'm going for a walk.'

Oran Butler and Keith Twomey sat in an unmarked squad car outside Healy's Carpet Warehouse. Two other guards were in a car at the entrance to the industrial estate.

'I can't believe this is happening again,' said Keith.

'We don't know that,' said Oran. 'They could show up yet.'

'It's two in the morning. We've been here four hours, Butler. Not a chance.' Oran leaned back against the headrest and closed his eyes. He dozed for an hour until the surveillance was called off and Keith drove them back to Waterford station.

Anna had forgotten to ask Shaun about the email he had received at school. She knocked lightly on his bedroom door and walked in. His thumbs were hammering on a Game Boy Advance, his blood-shot eyes focused on the bright screen.

'I just wanted to know what you were talking about the other day,' she said. 'Some email I was supposed to have sent you.'

'Supposed to,' snorted Shaun, fixed on the game. 'Who else would be sending me a photo of your stupid shoot?'

'But I haven't even seen those photos yet, Shaun. Brendan hasn't emailed them to me.'

'What?' He lost his last life and threw down the game. 'Damn!' He stared at her. 'But I saw it. In my school account.'

'Why would I do that? Why would I even use your school account? I'd use Hotmail if I was going to email you. Bring it home to me tomorrow.'

'I get my school mails forwarded to Hotmail. I can show it to you now.'

They went into the den and Shaun downloaded his mail. He clicked on the newest one. The image appeared on screen. Anna frowned. It was defin-itely the shoot.

'But look,' she said, pointing to the screen.

'There's Brendan. He's in it. He couldn't have taken this.'

Frank hated being in the station after hours. It was too quiet. He was reading and rereading every statement he had copied. Endless scenarios were running through his head. The phone on his desk rang and he was surprised to hear O'Connor at the other end.

'Frank? Myles. I've a bit of news for you on Katie's phone records.'

'Fire away.'

'The last person she called that night—'

'She called someone?'

'No. I should say "the last person she tried to call" . . .'

'Yes?'

'Was you, Frank.'

The house was quiet when Joe got back. He went into the den and closed the door quietly behind him. He took a deep breath, then dialled international directory enquiries for a number in a town that wasn't even a tiny dot on the world map.

'Officer Henson, Stinger's Creek.' The voice was slow, laconic.

'My name is Detective Joe Lucchesi, NYPD. I'd like to speak to someone about a local guy, a Duke Rawlins, got out of prison some months back, would have been sent away in the mid-nineties.'

'Duke Rawlins. Doesn't sound familiar, but I'm kinda new here. Why are you asking?'

Joe chose his words carefully.

'You think he might be involved in something? Well, you let me go check that for you,' said Henson. 'But I won't be able to get back to you for a day or two.'

'I just need—'

'We lost an officer, detective. Funeral's tomorrow.'

'Oh. I'm sorry,' said Joe. 'What happened?'

'Uh, self-inflicted gunshot wound. Tragedy. Former Police Chief, too. Ogden Parnum, a good man. Retired only recently.'

'I'm sorry to hear that,' said Joe.

'So were we,' said Henson. 'Give me your number. I'll call you as soon as I can.'

Joe turned on the computer and waited while it started up. He connected to the Internet and typed in three words: Stinger's Creek Parnum. He got several hits on what seemed to be the same story. He clicked on the first one, a short piece from the *Herald Democrat Online*.

Town in Mourning after Suicide Tragedy

Former Police Chief Ogden Parnum from the small Grayson County town of Stinger's Creek was found dead yesterday morning of a self-inflicted gunshot wound to the head. Chief Parnum first hit the

*headlines in the late eighties/early nineties for his
work on the Crosscut Killer Investigation when
nine young women were brutally raped and
murdered, their bodies left in wooded areas off the
I-35. To date, the case remains unsolved . . .*

'Jesus Christ,' said Joe.

TWENTY

Sherman, North Central Texas, 1987

'One of these days, someone's gonna snap you right in half, Alexis,' said Diner Dave, picking up her bony wrist and dropping it back on the counter.

'Skinny is in, or haven't you heard?' said Alexis, pushing her bright plastic bangles up to her elbow and letting them slide down again.

Suddenly, Dave reached out and squeezed her by both hands.

'You look after yourself out there, sweetheart. I mean that,' he said.

'Aw, Dave, you say that to me all the time,' she said, squeezing back. She stopped. 'You look so sad.'

'But I see how you come in sometimes,' he said.

'I know what I'm doin', but thanks for carin',' she said. 'Now, get me a basket of greasy chicken and fries.'

When she had finished eating, she slid off the red leather stool, leaving two hot sweat stains from the bare cheeks under her short satin skirt. She swayed out the door.

'Bye, Diner Dave!' she called as she swung the heavy door open. 'Until the next time,' she said in a deep superhero voiceover. Her words were drowned out by the meat, slapped and sizzling on the grill in front of Dave.

She walked to the corner, then crossed the street to a rundown brownstone. If she had taken one second longer to climb the stairs to her apartment, the phone would have stopped ringing and the caller would have moved on to the fourth business card he had found in the phone booth. But she made it, panting into the receiver as she grabbed it to her mouth.

'Sounds like we're off to a good start already,' said Donnie. Alexis laughed.

'I've been a busy girl,' she said, switching to business. 'All by myself.'

'Wanna tell me about it?' he said.

'Why don't you come over and see for yourself?' she said.

'Your card here says you're blond, 110 lbs. I'm not gonna arrive and find some big momma with a moustache now, am I?'

'No, sir,' said Alexis. 'You'll find the sweetest little pussy you've ever—'

'Lunchtime OK?' he said.

'Why, that's when I really get goin',' said Alexis.

Donnie put the phone down and ran to the truck where Duke was waiting.

When it was all over, Alexis sat on the edge of the bed.

'You look sad, sweetheart,' said Donnie. 'Is it because—'

'I love what I do,' she said. 'I make people happy. Men come to me because they want to be happy. I give them that, they walk away on a cloud.' She stopped. 'You look like you don't get it.'

'I get it,' said Donnie.

'You're a sweet guy,' she said.

'Let me take you for a drive.'

'Where?' said Alexis.

'You go to your prom?' he asked.

'What?' she said. 'No, I did not. Was long gone at prom time.'

'Well, why not come on a little prom date with me?' said Donnie.

She searched his eyes for danger and saw just honesty.

'In the afternoon? What the hell,' she said. 'It's never too late.'

One hour later, Alexis found herself naked from the waist up, her skirt blowing in the breeze.

'What's your real name?' roared Duke, grabbing her by the hair and shaking her. She screamed.

'I said, What's. Your. Real. Name.' He pulled her backwards and she twisted her body to take the weight off her hair. He shook her again.

'Janet,' she said.

'Janet WHAT?' he roared.

'Janet Bell,' she said, whimpering.

'Well, it's goodbye Janet Bell . . .' He stopped. 'In fact, it's goodbye Janet Bell, hello no-one! It's goodbye Janet Bell and it's goodbye Alexis, the trampy little whore with the dumb name. It's goodbye all of you!'

He released her hair, then turned her away from him, kicking her, sending her stumbling onto the hard earth. She was too weak to move, her head hanging listlessly.

'Run, little lady, run,' said Duke. 'Go on, Donnie, chase her down!'

Donnie ran, while Duke pulled a three-blade arrow from his pack, raising his bow to shoulder height, then squeezing shut his left eye.

Alexis turned to him, confused, then screamed when she saw what he was doing. She fell back, then pushed herself up from the ground, now desperate to stay alive, desperate to run. Donnie was right behind her. She staggered away from him until the first arrow hit, piercing her left kidney.

'Ten points,' shouted Duke, laughing at Donnie.

As she went down, the second arrow flew wide, missing her by an inch.

'Damn,' said Duke, running towards her. 'Damn.' He stood over her with Donnie, listening to her shallow breath.

'Make it go away,' she whispered through chattering teeth. 'Make it stop.' She looked towards Donnie. He was standing there, mesmerised.

'OK,' said Duke as he turned her on her stomach, slid the knife under her for the first cut and pressed down hard.

When he was finished, he got up and walked to the truck, pulling two shovels from under the tarpaulin, throwing one to Donnie. He went back to where Alexis lay, face down in the dirt. He kicked her bloodied ribs and smiled.

He walked over to a tree nearby and struck the hard earth with his shovel. 'Damn this! Donnie, get the hell over here.'

They dug until sweat soaked their shirts and a shallow grave opened up before them. Duke grabbed Alexis' wrists and slid her across the ground into the hole, pebbles hopping up around her. They covered her with earth, then branches and leaves. Donnie sat in the truck. Duke stood solemnly over the grave and clasped his hands.

'Goodbye, Alexis,' he said and walked away smiling, humming the theme tune to *Dynasty*. 'Goodbye, JR. G'night Mary Ellen . . . isn't that it?'

*   *   *

Donnie was sitting at the bar in the Amazon, his hands wrapped around his fifth bottle of Busch.

'Look at your eyes, boy, one playin' pool, the other keepin' the score,' said Jake, the barman.

'How can I look at my own eyes?' said Donnie.

'Such a shame your daddy didn't whip that smart mouth offa you,' said Jake, shaking his head.

'Nothin' wrong with my eyes, anyways,' said Donnie, nodding towards the girls twisted high and low around poles on the low platform in front of them.

One of the dancers strode across the floor, her eyes blazing.

'You wanna raise that goddamn stage, Jake,' she said, stabbing the air with her spiky finger. 'I can't work with those truckers pawin' me all night. I'm about three inches higher than 'em. How in the hell's that gonna stop their roamin' hands?'

'Wouldn't mind roamin' all over those titties of yours,' said Donnie, sitting up on the stool. His foot slipped off the metal bar and he swayed backwards, grabbing out at her to keep his balance. She batted his hand away.

'Go fuck yourself, Donnie Riggs, like I said before. She turned to Jake. 'Two things always to say to Donnie. Fuck and you.'

Jake laughed.

'They real?' asked Donnie, pointing at her breasts.

'When I'm naked,' she said slowly. 'And I'm looking in the mirror, touching them, they're very, very real. Soft, the way they should be. One hundred per cent all-American. But for you, honey, they'll never be real, they'll only ever be in your fucking dreams.' She tapped her nails on the bar to get Jake's attention.

'You can't make a man's dick hard like that, then leave him hangin',' said Donnie, throwing his hands up.

Jake ignored him and spoke to the girl. 'Stage stays the way it is, sugar. Maybe you should look into gettin' yourself some higher heels.'

She glared at him and walked away.

'You're hot for me,' Donnie yelled after her.

Without turning her head and with her dancer's grace, she raised her elbow into the air, followed by her middle finger.

'Man, she even makes that look sexy,' whined Donnie.

Jake started to sing, 'I learnt the truth at seventeen . . .'

Donnie threw a beer mat at him. 'I'm nearly eighteen,' he said.

'And whatcha gonna do then, boy?' laughed Jake, 'vote her up the ass?'

The door to the bar opened and Duke walked in, taking a seat beside Donnie.

'Two Buschs, Jake,' he said.

'Hey, Duke,' said Donnie. 'Jake here's been givin' me a hard time.'

'No surprises there.'

'I need to talk to you,' said Duke.

''Bout what?' said Donnie.

'Stuff,' said Duke. 'Drink that back and let's go.' He glanced over at the dancers and saw someone wave. He squinted into the spotlight and realised it was one of his mother's old friends. He slammed down his bottle and left.

Duke drove along the road to Donnie's house. ''Member what I was saying before?' said Duke. 'Donnie? Donnie?' he said, shaking him. 'You awake?'

'Let me sleep,' slurred Donnie. Duke punched him in the face.

Donnie sprang up.

'Jesus Christ, what the hell was that for?' he asked, his anger calmed only by the menace in Duke's eyes.

'I was talkin' to you,' growled Duke.

'Alright, alright. What?' said Donnie.

'I think that was too easy. Our plan. Today. You know? She was like a willin' accomplice, a girl like that.'

'She didn't look too willin' to me,' said Donnie.

'You don't think she was willin' back at her apartment when she knew there was fifty dollars waitin' for her at the other end?' spat Duke. 'You don't think a girl like that is *willing*? Let me tell you, she'd do worse things than what we done to her to get some money in her pocket, Donnie boy. Nothing comes between a whore and her money. And her drugs. Nothing. You flushed her out, didn't you? And was that hard? Or did she just walk out that door with a total stranger who had just left fifty dollars on her nightstand?'

'Yeah, well—,' said Donnie.

'Quit your whinin'.'

TWENTY-ONE

Joe sat at the kitchen window staring out to sea, following a white trail from a small fishing boat that furrowed the water halfway to the horizon. Anna's footsteps were light on the tiled floors.

Without saying a word, she handed Joe the email.

'What? Who's this from?'

'I don't know,' said Anna. 'It came to Shaun's school address. The "from" box is empty and when you click on it, it's just symbols and numbers. It's of the lighthouse, the night of Katie's funeral, when the shoot was happening. But it wasn't taken by Brendan. It's like it was taken by someone from across the road.'

She caught the tiniest flicker on Joe's face.

'What?' she said. 'What?'

'Nothing,' said Joe.

'If there is something you're not telling me—'

'There's nothing,' he said. *'Calmez vous.'* His

accent was bad. He smiled, but it didn't reach his eyes. And Anna exploded.

'You are a liar! You are lying! You think I'm stupid? Do you?' She grabbed his face in her hands and shook him. 'Do you think I'm stupid?'

'I can't do this right now,' said Joe.

'I don't give a damn!' she said. 'I'm sick of it. You're hiding stuff from me, sneaking around in the den, on the phone . . .'

'Oh, and you can talk about hiding things.'

'No, no, no,' she said, holding up her hand. 'We're not doing this all the time. You forgive me or you don't. Simple. You don't use things again to punish me.'

He shrugged. She hit him on the shoulder. '*Connard*!'

'Whoa, Betty.' She was Betty Blue when her temper flared and she slipped back into French to call him a bastard.

She smiled, but let it fade.

'There are lots of things I know about you, Joe. But they're mostly the things that everyone else knows about you. You're smart, funny, in control—' She stopped. 'You know, I'm not in the mood for complimenting you.'

Joe laughed. She ignored him and continued, 'Then there are a few extra things that I know about because I am your wife: your honesty, your love. You know, you're actually a sensitive guy. And then there's all the horrible stuff you hide, things I never get to see. But, you know? I still feel the effect of what's hiding there. I have no idea what's going on in your head right now.'

'Jesus, why do you want to know everything?'

'I don't want to know everything, but I don't want to be lied to. Everyone's lying to me.'

'No, they're not.'

'Oh, come on. My two boys are lying to me. I'm like a fool.'

'Well, you're a sexy fool,' he said, pulling her towards him. 'Very sexy when you're angry.'

'It's not funny.'

'Yes it is,' he said. But his expression told a different story as he held her to his chest and stroked her hair.

What Shaun and Anna hadn't seen was the doctored confidentiality note at the end of the email:

This email is intended for *the person responsible for Katie's murder* and may contain *the truth that you strangled her to death*.

The contents of this message represent the expressed view of the sender *and everyone else*. Storage, disclosure or copying of this information is *not* prohibited.

The phone made Anna jump, but she beat Joe to answer it. She listened, then narrowed her eyes at him.

'There's an officer Henson on the line for you.' She covered the mouthpiece. 'What's this about?'

'Work,' whispered Joe.

'*T'as raison,*' said Anna, handing him the receiver. Joe thought she had simply said, 'Right', but what she was saying was, 'Yeah, right.'

'I'm taking Shaun into the village,' she whispered, then left.

'Officer, hi,' said Joe.

'I got the file here you're looking for,' said Henson, 'but I think you'll find that someone's yanking your chain, buddy. Duke Rawlins is dead.'

Nora smoothed open the newspaper on the counter in the station. The headline ran across two pages. *Gone, But Not Forgotten.* On the right-hand side was a montage of photographs of smiling young girls and women who had disappeared or been murdered in Ireland over the previous ten years. The main shot was a beautiful, smiling, brown-haired girl. The caption underneath read *Katie Lawson (16), Mountcannon, Co. Waterford, murdered.* Frank got up from his desk and walked over.

'My God, there's another recent one,' she said, pointing to a pretty blonde. Frank leaned across as she read, '*Mary Casey (19) from Doon in Limerick, brutally raped and murdered outside her home.*'

'Apparently,' said Nora, 'she had left one of the gates in the field open and the father made her go out to close it. They're in bits over it. The parents had gone to bed. They didn't find her 'til the next morning.'

'God love them,' said Frank.

'That town is tiny. And they haven't got anyone for it. Awful. And there's the Tipperary girl from your poster.' She pointed to the bulletin board.

Frank shook his head. 'I can't read upside down. What are they saying about the investigation into Katie?'

'No leads, basically. And that "a young man has been brought in a second time to help with enquiries", as if no-one's going to know who that is. And, they're implying that you could be doing more.'

'Implying or saying straight out?' said Frank.

'Well, saying straight out.'

'It's always the same,' said Frank.

'I'll take this home,' she said, folding the paper. 'I don't want you having a stroke on me.' Frank smiled and went into his office. Nora walked into the hallway and was almost knocked over by Myles O'Connor. He barged into Frank's office, closing the door behind him, slamming a newspaper on the desk.

'What is this?'

Frank looked down. 'What?' he said, putting on his glasses.

'This interview.' He hammered his finger on the same spread Nora had started to read. 'You shouldn't have been talking to this guy. He should have been referred to Waterford. Especially if you're not used to speaking to journalists. Jesus Christ.'

Frank stared at the page. 'Oh. They were sniffing around. They must have been watching the station when the Lucchesis came in. I couldn't risk . . . I don't know, I—'

'Ah yes, the I-don't-knows,' said O'Connor. He grabbed a highlighter from the desk and in light strokes went through the text. There were eight sentences highlighted when he was finished. All of them said, 'I don't know.'

'It's a turn of phrase,' said Frank, taking off his glasses and looking up at O'Connor.

'Well, it's a stupid one when you're being interviewed on a murder case,' said O'Connor. 'We look like gobshites. "I don't know". What were you thinking?'

'I don't know. He seemed like a nice enough chap, I thought it wouldn't do any harm. He said he'd tidy up what I said.'

'We're doing a good job here, we don't need this shit,' said O'Connor. 'We're getting a bollocking for our perceived lack of progress in the investigation—'

'Well, where is the progress? We don't know a thing,' said Frank. 'We've got a couple of suspects and not a shred of evidence to tie them to anything. All we have is a few people helping us with our enquiries. Or *not* helping us . . .'

'Look, journalists have been ringing here and getting no answer or being diverted to Waterford and they're saying it's no wonder people are getting murdered if there are no guards in the village.'

'But it's the same—'

'Ah for God's sake, I know – it's the usual rubbish they come out with to sell papers.'

He fumed silently for a few seconds then snapped, 'Someone did this.' He hammered on the photo of Katie. 'And I'll be fucked if I'm letting them away with it.'

Anna was parking the Jeep outside the super-market when Shaun tapped her on the arm.

'Mom, it's Mrs Shanley, I'm just going to ask her about work.'

'Follow me into Tynan's,' she said.

Betty Shanley stood by her car outside the bakery, struggling to balance cake boxes and shopping bags. Shaun was at the other side of the street when he saw her. He jogged over to help.

'Hi, Mrs Shanley,' he said. 'Let me take that.' He reached out for the box. She held it tight.

'It's all right. I can manage it,' she said. He looked at her. Something shifted in her eyes. He blushed.

'Uh, I was wondering when you need me to come in . . . or is it quiet?'

'It's busy enough,' she said, looking past him. 'But I'm sorry. I won't be needing you any more. My sister's young lad is saving for a new car, a little Renault he's getting. So I said I'd give him the work. Barry.'

Black Hawk Down Barry with his shaved head. 'Oh, OK. He's in my year in school.' He couldn't think of anything else to say.

Joe's stomach was churning, waiting through the painful silence as Henson thumbed through pages of documents at the other end of the phone. Joe heard him swallow a mouthful of something before he spoke.

'Yeah, I got it here. Rawlins, William. Died in prison. Your dates were wrong too – he died in 1992, so he couldn't have gone to prison in '97. He was in for the murder of a Rachel Wade, 1988. Around the time of the Crosscut Killer, but they couldn't pin any of the rest of them on him. It was vicious what happened to all those women. In broad daylight.'

'It's Duke I was asking about. Duke Rawlins.'

'Duke's this guy's middle name.'

'How old was he when he died?'

'He would have been, let me see, fifty-four years old.'

'That's the wrong guy. This guy would be younger. Do you have any other Rawlins on file?'

'Don't think so. Let me go check. Can you hold the line?'

Joe thought his chest would explode waiting for Henson to organise himself.

'Oh, here we are,' he said, coming back. 'Rawlins, Duke, DOB 12/2/1970, knifed a trucker in a parking lot, 1997, sent to Ely, Nevada. You were right. My apologies. It's my filing system.'

'Is that it?' said Joe. 'Nothing else? No kidnap, nothing more violent?'

'Nope,' said Henson. 'What d'you think the guy's done?'

'I've no idea,' said Joe. 'But thanks for your help. Hey, could you fax me through his mug shot?'

'Sure thing.'

John Miller was stooped in the corner of Tynan's flicking through a car magazine.

'Not that I've got a licence or anything,' he said to Anna as she tried to slip past him. He leered at her and raised an eyebrow.

'Make up your mind, John. One minute you apologise, the next minute you're behaving like this . . . and what have you been saying to Joe?'

He looked like he was trying to remember.

Anna glared at him. 'I don't want to talk to you,' she said, jabbing a finger towards him.

'Ah, come on,' he said, reaching his arms out to her. His breath was ethanol. She jerked her hands away.

'Don't touch me!' she said.

'That's not what you used to say.'

'Jesus, John. Can you not get over it?' She was furious. 'I don't get it. What went wrong? I can't understand how you changed from a nice, normal guy into a drunken wife-beater!' She stopped as the full weight of what she had said hit them both. It was too late. She lowered her voice.

'Your mother,' she said. 'She told someone.'

A glimpse of clarity flashed across his eyes. He struggled to find a sober voice and steady his gaze. 'I never beat my wife,' he said, sadly. 'My mother was talking about herself. My father. She slips back and forth into the past. She's not well. Alzheimer's. It's not common knowledge.' Then, 'He used to kick the shit out of her.'

Joe went to the kitchen and made the call he'd put off the day before. Danny picked up straightaway.

'. . . whole tip went green and fell off. Hello?'

'One of these days, your mother's gonna call and you'll do that.'

'She already has. Told her it was a nasty case I was working on.'

'Danny, the police called Shaun in for an informal chat the other day that's got me worried. They say he was cautioned, he says he wasn't. Turns out he'd been lying to us anyway, so what's another lie? But I think I believe him about this. He's also admitted to having a fight with Katie the night she went missing. They know everything now, even that he and Katie were having sex before she disappeared and that they had an argument about it.'

'Poor kid. Jesus.'

'You know, I agree with you, but I really wanted to punch his lights out. It was the worst day of my life, watching him get grilled like that. You know, there I am, trying to help with the investigation—'

'—be one of those people we hate . . .'

'Pretty much. And my own son is lying his butt off.'

'He's young and scared. Makes people do shit they wouldn't normally do.'

'I know that, but now I'm worried a big huge finger is pointing in his direction and there's no reason for it to swing anywhere else. They don't seem to have anything and he's their number one suspect.'

'So am I just a therapy line or is there anything else I can do here?'

'Thought you'd never ask.'

'Do you want me to come over? Kick ass? Chat up a few colleens?'

'I couldn't put them through that. But, there is a helpful warden in Nevada who might let you talk to a certain cell mate.'

'Rawlins' cell mate.'

'You know, see what it throws up.'

Shaun was sitting in an armchair with his feet up beside the television.

'I know you're probably not in the mood for anything,' said Anna, 'but I thought this might cheer you up.'

'What?' said Shaun.

'Well, you know it's your father's fortieth on Friday. I thought maybe we could have something small to celebrate. I'm not talking about a big party or anything, obviously. Just the three of us.'

Shaun shrugged.

'Come on, I think we need something to lift things a little. It will just be a cake, candles, that sort of thing . . .'

'It's not like I'm in the mood for celebrating.'

'None of us are in the mood,' said Anna. 'But I think it would be nice. I think your father would appreciate it.'

'Do you need me to do anything?' said Shaun. Anna laughed.

'Say it like you mean it,' she said.

He smiled. 'I *do* mean it.'

'I'll order the cake in town. And get balloons delivered to the house when your father's out. But

the big surprise, he'll know about on the night.'
Shaun looked at her to find out more. She put a
finger to her lips when she saw Joe walk into the
room. He turned to her when Shaun left.

'I'm missing something,' he said. He looked at
his watch. 'You know, it's been exactly a month
since Katie went. I'm going out to walk that road
again and see if I don't think of something I didn't
the last time.'

'Before you do that – against my wishes,' said
Anna, 'I just want to tell you one thing, because
it's relevant to the investigation. I spoke to John
Miller . . .'

Frank walked along the harbour with his head
bowed and his hands in his pockets, obsessing
about his earlier embarrassment. He felt a sudden
flash of resentment at the Lucchesis that he could
only explain by drawing a line between before
they moved to Mountcannon and after. Because
he couldn't blame them for Katie's death. But
before they arrived, the village was what it was –
something he could take for granted because life
was good. Now he wanted to rewind and appreciate every day he investigated a stolen car because
it was the worst thing that could happen.

More rifts had appeared in the village in one
month than in its entire history. People fought
with neighbours over who suspected whom; they
cursed the guards, they defended the guards, they

got frustrated trying to fit theories to facts. Families were arguing over who left the back door unlocked when it had been that way for sixty years. The only thing that united them all was their desperate need for a killer to be found and locked away. It was a heavy collective power they wielded. Frank wasn't surprised that O'Connor's composure was starting to waver. He knew nothing about the man's home life, but part of him hoped he had a Nora waiting for him every night to ease the burden.

He didn't want to think about his own position. It broke his heart that his last year would be marked by tragedy. He only hoped it would have a resolution.

He sat on a battered bench by the edge of the water, closed his eyes and started to pray.

Joe followed the same route he knew Katie had taken. He wondered if he was also walking in the footsteps of her killer. She had been alone on an exposed stretch of road. It was quiet. He could hear his breath, the vinyl of his jacket, the gentle waves of the sea, even the rubber soles of his shoes. Katie would have heard footsteps. But it could all have happened too quickly; a door opening, one man driving, the other pushing her in, a van door sliding back, a group of men grabbing her. Or it could have been someone she knew, someone she trusted, someone who had walked her home or pulled up beside her and offered her a lift. But none of this felt right.

He took a left into the cemetery and stopped again at Matt Lawson's grave. He traced a path slowly back out and stood at the bend where the Lower Road met Manor Road. If he took a left at the end, he would be at Katie's house. He looked around and stopped when he saw a car up ahead, pulled in to the right-hand side of road. He walked towards it and saw Richie Bates inside, his stereo cranked up. Joe knocked on the passenger window. Richie jumped.

'What do you want?' he barked, rolling down the window.

'Nothing,' said Joe. 'Taking a walk. What about you? Stereo busted at home?'

Richie shouted over it.

'You've some nerve,' he said. 'I've an investigation to run, here.'

Joe snorted. 'I heard a D.I. from Waterford is doing that.'

'Fuck you,' said Richie. His right leg was out of control, jerking up and down.

'Doing this on your own time?' asked Joe, looking at Richie's jeans and sweater.

'Would you ever just get lost?' shouted Richie. 'I've a pain in my fucking arse with you.'

'Jesus, relax,' said Joe. Richie revved the engine and reversed to within inches of Joe, turning the

car towards the village. Joe walked back and took
the road for Katie's house.

D.I. O'Connor's eyes were on the untouched mug
of hot tea in front of him and the Danish beside
it. He rolled backwards in his chair, leaned down
and pulled open the bottom drawer of his desk.
There was a white lighter with the slanted green
and yellow logo of a soup company across it. He
remembered finding it in his pocket the morning
after a charity ball. He was about to reach for it
when his phone beeped. He hit speaker.

'Call for you on line one.'

He closed the drawer and picked up.

'Is that Detective Inspector O'Connor? Hi, it's
Alan Brophy from the Technical Bureau. The fragments from Katie Lawson's skull? It turns out
they're from a snail.'

'What?'

'I know. Here it is: the fragments come from a
thick-walled shell, dark with yellowish white
spirally things. It's been identified as the Sandhill
Snail or White Snail. You don't need the Latin,
right? If you do, it's *Theba pisana*, sounds like a
Spanish painter to me. Annnyway, it's found on
sand dunes, cliff faces, that kind of thing. It clings
to plants and stuff. So there you have it. The most
likely scenario is that she was struck with a rock,
snail attached, shell embedded in skull. Next thing
we know, she's in the forest. Maggots eat away

the snail – escargot, thank you very much – and leave the shell behind.'

'But there was no sand on the body—'

'No, but these little beauties are also found on waste ground near the sea, so that could explain the no sand. It could have happened on a grassy bit or near a stone wall or something.'

Mariner's Strand flashed into O'Connor's mind. 'OK, Alan. Thanks.'

'My pleasure.'

Joe walked back through the village and slipped into Danaher's for a last drink. Ray and Hugh were sitting at the bar.

'Welcome, sir,' said Hugh, dragging a stool out for him.

'Thanks,' said Joe. 'I've had a shit day, evening, night . . .'

'I've a shit life, if that makes you feel any better,' said Hugh, shrugging. Joe admired the two messers. They came to Katie's funeral in black suits, white shirts and black ties, both so respectable. Even Hugh's ponytail looked groomed. The men had tears in their eyes that day, but they never brought the subject up unless he wanted to talk about it. They knew their job was to keep things light.

'I had a run-in with Richie Bates tonight,' said Joe, knowing this would stir them.

'He used to be called Rich Tea Biscuits at school,' said Hugh pretend-fondly. Rich Tea Biscuits were an Irish tradition, plain, flat and round – made to dissolve in hot tea.

'Didn't anyone tell you you're supposed to shorten people's names?' said Joe.

'My name is Hugh. You can't shorten Hugh.'

'Wasn't there a guy called H in that pop band? That had to have been short for an H name,' said Ray.

'Gentlemen, my Richie Bates story? He was in his car tonight by the strand, the stereo blasting like a—'

'Goon,' said Ray. 'Gimp?'

'Asshole?' said Hugh.

'I was gonna say loser,' said Joe.

'We can apply all four,' said Hugh.

'. . . and I scare the shit out of him,' said Joe, 'and he loses it, shooting his mouth off like a psycho.'

'I've got a better one,' said Ray. 'He went loop the fucking loop the other day on the road outside the house. Because my garbage bag split. And I'm saying garbage for your benefit, Joe. I would normally be calling it rubbish.'

Joe laughed.

'I'm telling you. He lost it. Total—'

Joe vaguely heard Ray say something about Richie and road rage as he was distracted by a bony hand on his arm. He turned to see one of the local hard drinkers, his pinched face looming close. He pointed a finger at Joe.

'It's well you may knock back a pint and laugh, Mr Lucchesi, with everything that's gone on.' And as he was walking away, he muttered loud, 'Ya fuckin' blow-in.'

Joe finished his drink, grabbed his jacket and left Danaher's, irritated by the bitter old man. He was shocked at how the family had been welcomed to Mountcannon, then pitied after Katie's death and now suddenly rejected. He realised that frustration was never the right word when an innocent person found themselves a suspect. Frustration was harmless. This was overwhelming, suffocating, exhausting. It wasn't just Shaun they were doubting. It was Joe because of his experience with crime, it was Anna for possibly covering up for her son or her husband. They had been plunged into a situation they had no control over. Then he realised – this is exactly what someone might want.

Danny Markey walked in at the end of the lunch time rush when the crowd at Buttinsky Burger had thinned out. Wrappers and boxes littered the tables and floors. He waited until the last customer left the counter.

'Cheeseburger, regular fries, regular Coke,' he said. The large black man behind the counter pulled two cartons from a lukewarm shelf behind him and slid them onto a tray. 'And anything you'd like to tell me about Duke Rawlins.'

Abelard Kane looked up slowly, his huge brown eyes staring into Danny's.

Danny shrugged, 'I'm afraid I'm a buttinsky.'

'Couldn't you find someone else's life to butt into?'

'Yo' the man,' said Danny.

'Duke Rawlins.' Kane's broad face lit up. 'What's my fly guy done now?'

'Fly guy?' said Danny.

Kane picked up the cheeseburger carton and guided it through the air.

'The guy was obsessed.'

'With flying.'

'With birds.'

'What kind of birds?' said Danny.

'Whoa now,' said Kane. 'No introduction, nothin'. Who the hell are you and what's your business?'

'Detective Danny Markey, NYPD.'

'That's how you found me. But why you lookin'?'

'I can't tell you,' said Danny, 'but I just need to know a bit more about Rawlins, anything that might help us understand him better.'

Kane whistled. 'Good luck to you, detective.'

'Just tell me what he was like. You lived with him for five years.'

'N.U.T.S.'

'Anything more specific?'

'Yup. All capital letters.'

Danny looked at him.

'Like what specific?' said Kane.

'His temperament, what he was into, likes, dislikes – whatever, you know?'

'Dating Game stuff,' cried Kane. He put a hand on his hip, raised his pitch an octave and lisped. 'Hello, my name is Duke and I like shooting tin cans and sleeping with my cousins. My pastimes include—'

'All right, big guy. Cut to the chase. Help me out here.'

'Is this where I say no, but you slip me a few benjis across the counter?'

'And then I tell you I'm not a good cop, I'm a real bad cop and I'll break every bone in your body if you don't tell me what I need to know.'

Kane grinned.

'Tell me about the birds,' said Danny.

'Hawks. Harris' Hawks. Pictures all over the cell, books, bullshit about them, you name it. I coulda got a job in a bird place by the end of my time.'

'That's it? What about the kidnapping his friend had planned?'

'Loser got killed. Wouldn't want to be puttin' no faith in that man's plans. I'd be lookin' for someone else to get plans from, I was you. Man, you should have seen Pukey that day. That was his nickname, Pukey Dukey. The guy lost it. He started off upset, then angry, then real fucking angry, saying Donnie should have known better,

that he shouldn't have trapped himself in a corner.
Then he blew chunks.'

'Anything else?'

'He said the only thing Donnie got right was
killing those two people when that woman called
the cops. "You make good on your promises," he'd
say.'

'Honourable guy,' said Danny.

'Yeah,' said Kane.

'Did he say he had any plans himself, for when
he got out?'

'Sure. He showed me blueprints of bank vaults
and gave me times, dates and locations. Oh, and
Oswald was a patsy.'

'All right,' said Danny. 'All right. But nothing
else you can think of?'

Kane shook his head. 'Mystery to me,' he said.
'You know, you give them the best years of your
life . . .' He chuckled and turned back to the till,
putting his hand out. 'Burger, fries, coke. That'll
be six dollars ninety-nine.'

Danny tossed some one-dollar bills on the
counter. 'George Washington's the best I can do.'
He walked away.

'Hey, detective. One more thing,' said Kane.

Danny spun around.

'Your drink,' said Kane, shaking a Coke. 'What?
You think I was gonna solve your case?' His laugh
echoed off the stainless steel. Danny had to smile.

'You know? There *was* something,' said Kane.

'Do you know what was funny? Ha-ha, not pecu-
liar?'

'What?'

'Duke was beating himself up about the whole
kidnapping/shooting mess, because Donnie was
getting this money for him, but rumour has it,
there was a whole other person about to hit the
jackpot, someone who needed money so's *not* to
be around when Duke Rawlins got out.' He
laughed. 'No doubt about it, Dukey'd be seriously
pukey if he knew who that was. Techni-fuckin'-
colour pukey.'

Joe stopped the Jeep to let a group of children cross
the street to the harbour. He looked down at the
mug shot on the passenger seat. Duke Rawlins
stared back at him from a bad fax. Joe thought of
the Italian doctor in the eighteen hundreds who
studied criminals' faces and came to the conclusion that most of them had a long face, prominent
jaw and thick dark hair. Not Duke Rawlins. Joe
drove on, pulling up outside the station.

'Magnum's back,' Richie muttered to Frank
when he walked in.

'Look, there's something you should know
about Mae Miller,' said Joe.

They looked at him blankly.

'She's got Alzheimer's.'

'There is nothing wrong with Mae Miller's
mind,' said Frank, standing up. 'The woman is as

bright as a button.' He tapped his temple with two fingers. 'Why would you go around saying a thing like that?'

'I'm not saying it for the hell of it,' snapped Joe. 'John Miller told Anna. Uh, confidentially.'

'Well, it's absolute nonsense,' said Frank. 'She seems perfectly fine to me. It's John Miller's sanity I'd be worried about.'

'There was nothing you thought unusual about her when you two spoke that time?' said Joe.

'No,' said Frank. But his mind went back to the strange sexual embrace he had been pulled into by the respectable schoolteacher.

The phone rang and Richie picked up. 'OK,' he said. He turned to Frank, 'The Water Unit's here.'

'Water Unit?' said Joe. 'Why?'

Frank shook his head. 'Joe, I have to go.' He grabbed his keys and walked out the door. Joe followed him.

'Frank, look, before you go . . .'

'I'm on my way to the harbour. Can this wait?'

'No, no,' said Joe. 'I've got a mug shot for you to look at. Of the guy I was telling you about? Duke Rawlins. Just in case. I have some friends checking into him in the States.

'And this,' said Joe, handing him the email. 'Someone emailed this to Shaun the other day, no return address. Read the confidentiality note. This can't all be a coincidence. I've spent time on this. I know what I'm talking about.'

'OK, Joe. I'll report this all to Waterford in the morning. They can check this Rawlins man out through Interpol, but with all the red tape, I'd say your friends in the States will be able to get back to you quicker.'

'Thank you, Frank. I appreciate this.' He grabbed Frank's arm as he was trying to get into the car. 'You've found something new, haven't you? That's why the Water Unit's down at the harbour. What did you find?'

'You know I can't tell you that.'

'What does it mean for Shaun?'

'I think it's what it means for Katie that matters most.'

Frank got into the car and looked at the email again. He decided to make a detour on his way home that evening.

Anna filled two buckets with hot water, squirting liquid soap into one. She pulled a grey fleece hat low over her head and slipped on a pair of gardening gloves.

Shaun was slumped in the window seat.

'Want to help?' she asked cheerily.

'Yeah, right. Only moms think housework makes people feel better.'

She sighed. 'OK, OK. I was just asking.'

Anna tucked a bag of cloths under her arm and pushed her way out the back door. It was eleven-thirty a.m., but so overcast, it was almost dark.

She barely looked up as she crossed the grass, keeping her eyes on the water level in the buckets. She couldn't help but feel better when she arrived at the lighthouse. She unlocked the doors and went up to the gallery to start cleaning the lens. Within twenty minutes, she was in the workshop, pulling out as many buckets and cloths as she could find. She went back into the house to Shaun.

'Sorry, but you've got no choice. I can't keep going up and down those steps all day. You'll have to help me take some water up.'

Shaun glared at her. 'I can't believe you're making me do this right now. I've just lost everything in my life, even my shitty job, and you want me to—'

'Carry some buckets, Shaun. Nothing more dramatic than that. It will take half an hour. I'll make it up to you. Believe me, I would rather not be doing this myself, but unfortunately life goes on.'

'You sound so cold,' he said. In her face, he got the reaction he was hoping for.

When he was finished helping her, he went to his room and lay on the bed, reaching for the remote control. It switched on to the news. 'A team of Garda divers has arrived in Mountcannon, Co. Waterford, following the emergence of new evidence in the Katie Lawson murder inquiry . . .' The shot cut to the harbour. A reporter in a beige

coat and red check scarf raised her microphone.
Shaun jumped up and grabbed his jacket.

For four hours, Anna washed down the lens,
inside and out, then swept and scrubbed the floors.
Darts of pain ran across the small of her back. Her
shoulders ached and she was starving. She went
back into the kitchen and there was a sandwich
and a bottle of Coke on the counter from Shaun
with a note beside it – gone out. She ate quickly
and headed out again, rolling the top of a pair of
overalls down to her waist, tying the arms in a
knot. She pulled a blue sweatshirt over her T-shirt
and walked towards the lighthouse.

'Excuse me? Mrs Lucchesi?' She turned around
to see a man smiling down at her.

'Hi. I'm Gary. Mark from Lawn Order can't
make it today or tomorrow. Personal stuff. He
sometimes calls me to fill in.'

'Oh,' she said, puzzled. 'He didn't say anything
about that. It would have been OK for him not
to come in for a couple of days. There's no real
need for you to be here.'

He looked down at the pot he was carrying.
'Well, I've brought some things, so I may as well
just unload them.'

'That's very pretty,' she said, touching one of
the leaves. 'What is it?'

'Uh, that's a—' he looked at the label, 'Hosta.'

Anna studied his face. 'Well, you can put it

down there,' she said. 'Near the bottom of the steps. Are you sure that's it? That it's something personal, that's why Mark didn't come to work?'

He stopped. 'Sure,' he said. 'That's all it is.'

Anna watched as he walked away, then went back into the house and dialled Mark's number. It was diverted.

When Shaun got to the harbour, the first thing he saw was the crew from the TV station, the cameraman heaving off his equipment and swinging it through the open doors of a news van. The reporter stood a few feet away, pushing away the hair that blew across her face, then climbing into the passenger seat. Shaun watched as they drove up the slope, the driver nodding as he passed him. Small crowds had gathered to watch the activity by the dock. Shaun stood far enough away to go unnoticed.

Seven men in black drysuits stood on the harbour wall, looking into the water, a line of boats rocking back and forth against the concrete beneath them. One of them nodded and the first diver slid down the side into the water, holding a thick rope in his hand. His head stayed above the surface. Then three divers pulled on black masks and jumped in after him, each with white dual cylinder oxygen tanks mounted on their backs. They held on to the rope and moved under the boats.

Martha Lawson brought a tissue up to her nose

and looked away, as though they were immediately going to find a new horror for her to face. She linked her sister's arm. The divers continued for hours, moving around the harbour, then further out, working from a small boat.

Shaun was still there after most of the onlookers had gone home. Everything he saw depressed him. The boats that could have spent a month carrying evidence out to sea in tangled fishing nets, the churning tides crashing off the rocks, even the hungry seagulls that flew overhead. The secrets of the harbour today were not the same secrets as a month ago. Suddenly, he heard a shout from one of the divers in the boat. The three divers in the water surfaced. One of them held a pink sneaker in his right hand. Shaun watched as it was placed into a clear plastic evidence bag. He started to cry. He loved those sneakers. They were so Katie.

Victor Nicotero was sitting on his deck with a cardigan zipped up to his neck and a can of beer that was freezing his hand. Patti handed him the phone.

'Nic, when do I call you?'

'When you're looking for something, Joe.'

'I know, I know. And this time, it's for another alarm bell check. Because they are ringing loud, here. But honestly? I don't know if a part of me is wanting something to be this way or not . . .'

'Spell it out for me.'

'OK, if you heard what I'm about to tell you . . . what would *you* think? Two guys from the same small town, one a kidnapper/murderer, the other – done time for stabbing a guy. The big crime around the area before then is the rape of nine women who were then hunted down like animals and killed. Case goes unsolved. Years later, the first guy is shot dead. The second guy's out of prison and within two months, a new girl is found dead in the woods where he's at. Meanwhile, the Police Chief in their town, head of the original serial killer task force, commits suicide.'

'I gotta tell you, I'd be hearing a ringing too, Joe. Especially if it was my son's girlfriend . . .'

'You don't miss a trick.' They were quiet for a while. 'So, how'd you like a trip to Texas, Nic?'

'I'm old. I need heat. I say yes.'

'If you hiked those pants up to your armpits like you're supposed to—'

'You're right behind me, buddy. When's the big five oh?'

'Four days. And ten years.'

'Sure, Lucchesi. So, what's the plan?'

'I need you to go talk to the lonely widow of a man called Ogden Parnum. Find out what you can about why her Police Chief husband decided to blow his brains out. And anything you can about the Crosscut case he had been working on—'

'Crosscut? OK. I'm on it.'

*   *   *

Nora Deegan stood at the wall in front of her favourite painting, a simple watercolour that picked up the greens and purples in the living room. She was holding a paint card beside it, moving along rows of small squares, each with a different shade of white.

'I can't make up my mind,' she said. 'For the gallery.'

'Too many shades of white,' said Frank. He pointed to one. 'I like that.' Nora nodded.

'I need you to do something for me,' he said suddenly. 'On one of your little coffee mornings.'

'What do you mean little? They're huge, important affairs. Do you mind?'

'Of course they are,' said Frank, smiling. 'I just need you to, I don't know, settle things down around the place.'

'What?'

'The Lucchesis. It's all around the village about Shaun,' he said. 'But the lad's not involved. If he was, he'd be locked up by now. He's in bits. I've seen how people are reacting. And Anna and Joe. Joe has been a pain in the backside since this all happened, but you can't blame him. I think the poor man is driven mad. He's getting fierce paranoid. He got this email in and it was total nonsense and he was thinking the worst as usual. Anyway, enough of that, it's safe to say, the family is under a fair bit of pressure. Is there any chance you could, I don't know, say the right thing to the right people? I know you tell the golf ladies about my cases.'

She raised an eyebrow.

'You're the sergeant's wife, honey. They'll trust you.'

Lime-scented steam filled the bathroom. Joe walked in and stepped around a pile of Anna's clothes that lay crumpled on the floor.

'Don't go near them,' she shouted from the shower. 'Toxic.'

He tried to smile.

'I'm serious. I had to do everything today. Some of the workmen didn't show up and neither did Mark. I'm starting to get nervous.'

He made a face. He opened the mirrored door of the cabinet and started searching through it.

'Well, would you show up for work if you thought someone was being questioned in the house about a murder?' said Anna.

Joe kept searching, holding a finger up to let Anna know he couldn't speak. A flash of frustration crossed her face.

'But Shaun went in voluntarily,' he managed, 'no big deal.'

'That's not the way people's minds work. I think something funny's going on, Joe. With you trying to stick your nose in and Shaun being questioned, I think everyone's avoiding us.'

'Don't be silly, honey.'

'At least Mark had the decency to send a replacement. Even if he was a bit clueless. You know the way Mark strides around, knows every bit of the land. This guy seemed out of it. I sent him away, though. I'd rather wait.'

'Mark will be back and so will the others.'

'I'm the one who needs a rest,' said Anna. 'I'm exhausted.' She turned off the shower.

Joe reached for her bathrobe. She saw him wince when he turned his head.

'I got you some heat packs for your jaw. Like eye masks. They're in hot water.' She pointed to the sink and the round objects floating in it. Joe looked in and saw two gel-filled plastic faces. One was Homer Simpson, the other was Bart. He looked at her and raised his eyebrows. She smiled.

He took them out, dried them on a towel and put one up to each cheek.

'Hmm. Warm.'

Suddenly, they heard frantic pounding on the front door. They exchanged glances. Joe looked at his watch; it was almost midnight. He put the packs back in the sink. They both walked slowly downstairs into the hall, Joe holding his hand back to keep Anna behind him. She pushed it away.

'Uh-oh,' said Joe as he looked through the glass. He opened the door.

'What is wrong with your family?' said Martha hysterically. 'What is wrong with you all?' Her eyes were dark and sunken, her hair pulled back

into a thin ponytail. In one month, she had lost
thirty pounds from her slender frame.

She looked from Joe to Anna. 'Your son comes
over here, has . . . has sex with my daughter
. . . I didn't raise my daughter to be having sex
before marriage! Then he lies to the guards. What
did he do to her?' Anna almost cried at what she
was witnessing, more for the broken woman
before her than what she was saying about her
son.

'Martha . . .' Joe's jaw felt like it was being torn
apart.

'You're a murderer!' she shouted. 'Who are you
to comment on anything? Shooting someone
dead, I heard. And I came to you looking for help!
You, of all people. Was I mad? You . . . carried
her coffin!' She raised her hand, then lowered it,
clenching it into a fist in front of her. 'If I find out
that . . . he, that . . . I swear to God . . .' She
trailed off. Joe stared at her.

'Have you nothing at all to say for yourself?'
she shouted.

Anna finally spoke. 'Shaun really loved Katie.
You know in your heart, Martha, he would never
hurt her.'

'I know nothing,' she cried. 'Nothing about
anything! I don't know what to think! Why did
he leave her to walk home alone?' she said, her
voice strangled and desperate. Shaun had come
to the door. Tears were falling down his cheeks.

'I don't know why,' he sobbed. 'I don't know why either. It was a mistake.'

'Martha, I'm so sorry about Katie,' said Anna. 'We all are. But none of us knows why it happened.'

'Someone has to know!' said Martha. 'Someone has to know! What else do you know?' she pleaded with Shaun. 'What else haven't you told them?'

Shaun was wailing, his hands covering his face. 'Nothing, nothing, nothing. I've told them everything now. She's just gone. I can't believe any of it.'

'Lies, lies and more lies,' said Martha. 'You're a disgrace of a family.' She turned and staggered down the path. Shaun ran to his room.

Joe shook his head and looked at Anna.

'Jesus Christ,' he said through gritted teeth. 'This is a fucking nightmare.'

TWENTY-TWO

Denison, North Central Texas, 1988

The engine was running, a low hum in the darkened street. Donnie and Duke sat in the front seat of the pickup.

'Hello, Barbara,' said Donnie, putting out his hand.

'Why you shakin' her hand?' asked Duke. 'Do you shake her hand every time you meet her?'

'No,' said Donnie.

'Well, why the hell do it tonight?' said Duke. 'It won't look right.' He nodded for Donnie to try again.

'Hi, Barbara,' said Donnie. 'We're having a party for Rick and I was wondering if you'd like to help me work on a guest list.'

'That's more like it,' said Duke.

A car pulled into the driveway ahead and a man in a grey suit stepped out. He walked towards the front door.

'What the fuck is this?' hissed Duke. 'Who the fuck is this guy?'

Donnie closed his eyes.

'The husband,' he said.

'What time is it, Donnie?' said Duke.

Donnie looked at his watch, but he knew.

'Eleven-oh-five.'

'And what night is it?' said Duke, thumping the dashboard.

'Tuesday,' said Donnie.

'You stupid fuckin' son of a bitch,' said Duke. 'You dumb fuck. I talked you through this, Donnie. Visualise it, I said. Visualise everythin'. Imagine a big fuckin' clock with a big fuckin' Tuesday on it and a big fuckin' time printed in big black letters across the centre. Eleven. Oh. Five.'

Donnie leaned back against the seat and exhaled slowly.

'I'm sorry,' he said, looking over at Duke.

'I love you too, sweetheart,' whined Duke. 'I hate it when we fight.'

Silence hung in the air.

'You fuckin' loser,' boomed Duke, starting the engine. 'I've had it. Time to move on. I can't—'

'No!' cried Donnie. 'Listen, I know I messed up, but I won't do it again. I swear to God.'

'Messed up?' roared Duke. 'Messed up? Messed up is gettin' the time of a movie wrong or puttin' salt on your fuckin' Cheerios. Your brand of messin' up could have had us face down and handcuffed, bent over takin' it up the ass in some fuckin' prison shower. This,' he roared, stabbing the air with his finger, 'this was the biggest mistake of your life. And it's the last one you'll ever make.'

Donnie's heart pounded. A sharp pain seared through his chest. Duke reached across him and opened the door.

'Get out,' he said. 'Get the fuck out of my vehicle.'

Donnie stumbled from the pickup, closing the door behind him with a soft thud. Through a screech of brakes, he heard Duke push the door open again and slam it closed.

Rachel Wade wiped along the counter of Beeler's with a dirty towel that stank of stale beer and ash. She turned to polish the mounted bottles behind the bar, her thin, blonde hair swinging. She moved into the back bar to clear the last of the tables, gripping dirty glasses in her slender fingers. She flicked off the lights with her free hand on her way back into the bar. Suddenly, a man appeared behind her in the darkened lounge.

'Excuse me?' he said.

Rachel jumped. 'Holy shit!' she said, turning around, her hand to her chest. 'You scared the hell outta me. I thought I locked the door.' She squinted into the black, but all she could see was his eyes, magnetic and blue.

'Sorry, ma'am,' he said, smiling. 'Just wonderin'
if I was too late to order myself a beer.'

'Closin' at four,' she said. 'But you're the first
to come by since midnight.'

'Bottle of Busch, then,' he said.

She put down his beer, then came out from
behind the bar, picking up glasses, wiping down
surfaces, sticking darts back into the board. Duke
watched her slim hips as she moved between the
tables, watched the pink lace bra pushing against
her white shirt.

'Why don't you come join me for a drink?' he
asked.

'OK.' She grabbed a bottle of Jack Daniel's and
took the stool beside him. After an hour, she
locked the doors and after two, they were at the
end of the bottle. Rachel stood up to go to the
bathroom and rocked back on her heels.

'Whoa. You think you're doin' OK, 'til you're
on your feet,' she laughed.

Duke laughed with her and watched the denim
sway as she walked to the bathroom.

Rachel used the hand dryer, then looked at herself
in the mirror. Her eyes were red and she could
barely focus. She pulled a tube of gloss from her
pocket and slicked it across her lips. As she reached
out to pull open the door, it swung back in her
face. Duke pushed his way in, quickly moving his
right arm behind her back and pushing her up

against the cold tile wall. He kissed her roughly, pushing his tongue around her mouth, his teeth clashing with hers. Rachel held him back, taking in a sharp breath.

'Hey,' she said. 'Calm down. Let's go back into the bar.'

'Let's not,' said Duke, his hand shooting down, grabbing her roughly between the legs, his tongue out, ready to plunge into her mouth again.

'Ow,' she said. 'Relax.' She leaned her head back and looked, confused, into his eyes. They were black now, his pupils huge. She waved her hand in front of his face.

'Hello?' she said. 'This is no way to treat a lady.' She smiled at him, but the panic was rising in her chest. She started to think about the bar, the doors, the phone, the neighbours, the screams. She told herself she was being stupid. Then her eyes locked with his and she knew this was it. At the same time, her body went limp and she knew her arms, her fists, everything would be useless to her. Her legs had dissolved into shakes. She managed to shove her knee up, but it missed his groin, harmlessly connecting with his rigid thigh. He grabbed her throat now, pushing her head against the wall, kissing her again, clawing at her everywhere. With one final push, she freed herself, pulling at the door, running and staggering into the black of the lounge. The place she knew so well was suddenly foreign to her as she tripped over tables and stools, desperately trying to reach the bolted door. Duke was on her in seconds, pushing her effortlessly to the floor, her jaw smashing into the sticky blue carpet. The smell of smoke and beer filled her nostrils once more. She tried to wriggle free, but something inside her told her to lay still. She thought he might feel sorry for her, she was so small, he couldn't want to hurt her. She was crying out in pain now, but too weak from alcohol and fear to do anything about his weight bearing down on top of her.

She felt the fabric of her shirt being ripped up her back, the breeze freezing the cold sweat. Then she felt something sharp. He wasn't ripping her shirt, he was slicing through it with a knife.

'Please,' she sobbed.

'Shut your fuckin' mouth,' he said. His voice was utterly chilling, stripped of the earlier warmth.

'Please don't,' she tried again, her words mumbled through broken jaw and carpet.

'I. Said. Shut. The. Fuck. Up.'

She saw the knife. It was so small, curved and vicious in his hand. It was a carpet cutter. Oh God. She remembered how quickly she had seen one cut through the same carpet she was lying on now. She started to wail. He covered her mouth, using his free hand to reach for her jeans. Her whole body started to convulse. He got up and stood over her. Fear rooted her to the floor. Then a desperate surge of energy and panic made her scramble on her side and she crawled uselessly away from him in one last attempt to survive. He let her go, let her get to the door, her hand clawing up the wood to the bolt, but in three strides he was there, dragging her back face down again on the carpet. He undid his jeans, pulling at himself, then, enraged, he grabbed at a beer bottle nearby and knelt down in front of her. Her screams were piercing. He smashed the bottle into the fireplace and then everything was quiet. Pain coursed through her, but she still hoped this would be enough for him. She didn't care, he could leave her here, he could get away. Then she saw the knife again and she let out a scream that sent vibrations through his fingers. He reached into his pocket and pulled out a handkerchief, stuffing it into her mouth, holding it shut. He flipped her over, then slid the knife under her and used his weight on top to force it through the flesh beneath her ribs. He released it, then plunged it in again, making a second, then a third gaping wound. Then, as he was about to work on her left side, he heard a crunch. Outside.

'Rach? Rach, honey? You there?'

Duke looked down at her. 'Shit, shit, shit.' Her eyes were pleading. He reached for a stool.

Donnie flicked on the TV set and caught the closing minutes of the report.

'. . . not believed to be connected to the other killings, all of which appear to have been committed during daylight hours.' As he watched a body being taken from a bar on a stretcher covered in black, he heard someone pounding on the side door.

'Donnie, open up, open up – I'm sorry man, goddammit, Donnie.' His fists hammered on the wood until he heard the latch slide back and Donnie was in front of him.

'Jesus Christ,' said Donnie. Duke was covered in blood, his T-shirt soaked through, his jeans splattered, his fly half undone. He stumbled into the kitchen, his chest heaving. Donnie grabbed a cloth from the sink and started to clean the smears from the door.

'Why didn't you go to the creek like normal?' said Donnie.

'I lost it, man, I lost it,' said Duke. 'Someone showed up. I was nearly leavin' her alive in there.'

'The girl on the TV.'

'It was on TV already? Son of a bitch.'

'What if Geoff was here?'

'His car's outside the Amazon,' said Duke.

Donnie watched him stride towards the bathroom. 'So I'm good for somethin' then,' he called after him.

'You are, Donnie. I fucked up, before. I was mad. I ain't goin' it alone. That was crazy talk.'

TWENTY-THREE

'Update on Katie Lawson,' said O'Connor, standing in his familiar spot at the top of the conference room.

'As you've heard, evidence has come back from the post-mortem – fragments of a snail shell – to indicate that Katie was murdered elsewhere and her body transported to the forest. The place we're concentrating on is Mariner's Strand, where we've found other samples of the, uh . . . Sandhill Snail. The Water Unit searched the area yesterday, along with the harbour, where they found one of Katie's pink running shoes, which is being checked for fingerprints today. We think at this point that Katie paid a visit to her father's grave on Church Road – a white rose was left there – and she may have moved across the road to the Mariner's Strand area when she was attacked. She could have been lured there for some reason – whether this was an opportunistic crime or someone had been watching her movements, we don't know. We know that the last call she tried to make on her mobile phone was to Frank Deegan.' He nodded at Frank, who had a troubled expression on his face. 'This could mean that she was aware she was in danger or that maybe she was calling in another crime. The fact that she rang Frank and not 999 is an interesting one, although she does know the Deegan family quite well.

'Because of the three-week delay in finding the body, we don't expect any new evidence to come to light from our search of Mariner's Strand. Something to note is that Katie's possible movements on that night would directly conflict with the witness statement of Mae Miller, so that's something we'll have to explore. As to the body being left in the forest, that could be for any number of reasons, including its secluded nature, its familiarity to the killer, convenience or it could have some deeper significance we're as yet unaware of. The closest properties to the forest would obviously be the Lucchesis' house and Millers' Orchard. We need to keep thoroughly investigating the players involved here.'

The music thumped through the speakers, a tinny repeat melody over a booming bass. Duke looked up at the hairdresser. She wore low-rise jeans that pinched her extra pounds and pushed her pierced stomach over the waistband. Her black glitter halter top plunged low, revealing a chest with a bad reaction to fake tan. Her lips moved to the lyrics of the track. As she cut, the hair fell in wet clumps onto the open newspaper.

She reached down and wiped it onto the floor, leaving a police composite sketch exposed on the damp page.

'That was awful, wasn't it?' she said, pointing at it with her comb. 'That girl in Tipperary who disappeared.'

'Awful,' said Duke, looking down at a face meant to be his.

'Some young girl came forward after weeks and told the guards. She was in that American diner when the guy was there. Imagine, she didn't come forward because she thought she'd get in trouble at school. What a waste.'

She kept cutting. 'God knows at this stage, that girl could have forgotten what the man looked like.'

'Probably,' said Duke. 'But some faces stay with you for life, good or bad. I guess we'll know if they catch him.' The scissors moved close to his ears, snipping the hair tight to his head.

The den was quiet but for the slow hum of the fax machine. One after another, the pages slid out, floating to land in a pile on the floorboards below. Shaun walked over and stood confused, trying to focus on the smudged images from a stray upturned page. He bent down, taking it in his hand, bringing it closer. It was a woman, her face peacefully untouched, but her body, desecrated, black ink for blood. Crude hand-drawn arrows pointed to *'puncture wounds like claws'* to the torso, *'three symmetrical lacerations to the area beneath the ribs'*, *'partial disembowelling'*. An icy sensation pulsed through Shaun's head. He fell to his knees, clawing through the pages, finding layer upon layer of blurred but vivid images that highlighted in white a handbag or a sideways shoe to make these dead women strangers seem so real. He slumped to the floor.

'Oh, Jesus Christ,' shouted Joe as he ran into the room. 'Shaun, no.'

He stumbled to the ground, pulling his son towards him, prising his clenched fingers from the crumpled page.

'That was my fax, that was just for me,' he said uselessly.

'Is that what happened to her, Dad?' Shaun pleaded. 'Is that what happened to Katie? Because that is fucked up. That is the most fucked up thing I've ever seen. That is so fucked up. Did some guy do that? Did some guy do that shit?' He was choking, the words and sobs mangled horribly in his throat. Joe put his arms around him. He couldn't remember the last time they'd been so close. He felt no different to his father. He released his hold and started to gather up the pages. He knew now he'd have to take another trip to Dublin.

Mae Miller opened the door as wide as it would go. She was dressed in a long silver evening gown, with a string of purple beads knotted halfway and falling to her waist. She wore black velvet gloves to her elbows and a thick pearl bracelet on her wrist. She had swept her grey hair from her face and secured it in a chignon.

'Hello,' she said, smiling broadly.

'Oh, Mrs Miller,' said Richie. 'I didn't mean to catch you on your way out.' He looked at his watch. It was eleven-thirty a.m. and he'd just had breakfast.

'Not at all,' said Mae. 'I'm just enjoying the performance. I didn't know you were an opera buff.'

Richie looked away. 'Eh, I was wondering if I could have a word with John.'

'It's the interval. He's gone to the bar.'

'Danaher's?' said Richie.

'No. Here,' she said, pointing upstairs.

'Would you mind giving him a shout?'

'My pleasure,' said Mae, gliding away from him.

'John? John?' she called. 'Look who I bumped into.'

Richie had stepped into the hall and was standing by the door. John lumbered down the stairs and frowned when he saw his mother.

'Howiya, Richie,' he said, abruptly.

'Ah, John,' said Mae. 'Are you ready?' She turned toward the kitchen door and held out her arm as if she was waiting to be escorted. She looked back over her shoulder to Richie. 'We don't want to miss the second half.'

'That's fair enough, Mrs Miller,' said Richie, looking down at the floor.

Joe drove north through Dublin onto the Malahide Road. Before he hit the motorway to the airport, he took a left through the red iron gates of the Fire Training Centre, following a curved tree-lined drive. The sign to the mortuary guided him around a large field where half an aeroplane leant on its wing in the corner. When he saw the fake front of a nightclub painted onto a brick wall, it hit him – fire, training. He pulled up in front of four prefabs, the temporary home of the State Pathologist's office. He hoped Dr McClatchie was sitting at her desk. She wasn't. She was standing inside the door talking to her assistant.

'Dr McClatchie, hi – my name is Joe Lucchesi, I'm an NYPD detective and, uh, I was wondering if you'd have a minute.' He smiled.

She looked trapped, but she said, 'OK, come into my office.'

'It's about the murder of Katie Lawson,' he said.

'Ah,' she said, sitting down, gesturing for him

to do the same. 'NYPD? Why have you been drafted in?'

He weighed it up. 'Uh, we haven't,' he said finally. He pulled out the fax and placed it on the desk between them with one of the more graphic photos on top. The name Tonya Ramer was printed above. She was laid out in the morgue, her face ghostly, but almost serene. The body had clearly been found within days of her murder. Between her legs was a mess of tissue and sharp black shards of what he knew was timber. The only other visible injuries were uneven lacerations on her knees and three slashes of similar length under each side of her rib cage. Lara looked down, then back up quickly, but she was using her fingers to spread out the other pages as she stared at him.

'What are you playing at?' she asked, bemused more than annoyed.

'I wanted you to look at these photos and tell me if they are similar in any way to the injuries sustained to Katie Lawson.'

'Are you mad?' she asked in her clipped way, as if she was about to wave her hand and order someone to 'have this man beheaded.'

He inhaled sharply and said, 'Katie Lawson was my son's girlfriend.' She sat back and sighed. 'And I know,' he continued, 'that my son is the number one suspect. I think the man who committed *these* murders,' he pointed to the table, 'could be the same man who killed Katie.'

She looked down reflexively, her eyes sweeping over the photos.

'You know I couldn't possibly discuss this with you. I'm actually amazed that you came in.'

'You can't blame a guy for trying. Believe me, I have a very real appreciation for what you're trying to do over here – probably more than anyone else working on this case.'

'Ah, but you're *not* working on this case.'

'You got me,' he said. 'But I'm dyin', here.' He flashed a look out at the morgue door. He smiled and leaned across the desk to drag the photos back into a pile.

'I'm sorry for bothering you,' he said, locking eyes with her. 'But I hope my visit will go no further.'

'Pardon?' she said.

'I can't have the guards knowing I showed up here.'

She threw her eyes up to heaven. 'Well, I've told you nothing.'

Ah, but you've told me everything, thought Joe. He was trained on gut reactions and reactions to gut reactions: flickers, twitches, shakes, gulps – cartoonish words for things that helped him differentiate an honest man from a liar. Her reaction to the photos had spoken volumes to him – the wounds were not the same. The one thing he couldn't pinpoint, though, was the reason for the tiniest frown he caught on her face at the last second and her almost reluctant release of the photos.

'Here's my card if you need to get in contact with me.' She stared at him. He ignored her expression, crossed out his New York number and wrote in his Irish mobile. He stood up to leave, but the motion was too quick on an empty stomach and he staggered to the side, grabbing onto the desk for support.

'Are you OK?' said Lara, moving towards him. When he raised his head, tiny silver spots danced before his eyes.

'Sit down,' said Lara, pulling out the seat for him. 'Are you OK?'

He managed a nod. He put his hand to the back of his neck and started rubbing it.

'I just got a bit dizzy,' he said. 'I haven't eaten.' Suddenly he reached for her waste basket and retched violently, spitting saliva onto the crumpled papers and pencil parings inside. His face burned.

'I knew I shouldn't have bought wicker,' she said.

'Jesus, I'm sorry,' he said. 'I don't know . . .'

'Have you got a stomach bug?' she asked. 'You're terribly pale.'

'No. I just haven't eaten and I've taken some painkillers and other stuff. And coffee.'

'Do you mind me asking why you're on painkillers? Or do all cops follow that diet?'

He snorted a laugh. 'No to the first question

and yes to the second. But I get a lot of jaw pain and pressure in my head. It can hurt to eat, so I guess that's why I get light-headed . . .'

'Do you mind if I have a look?' she said, already reaching her hands out. He jerked his head back.

'You're wasting your time.'

'I'm the boss in my office,' she said, ignoring his reluctance, pressing cold thumbs down the side of his nose and across his cheeks, then above both eyebrows. He held his breath. They avoided eye contact.

'Sorry,' he said, pushing her hand away. 'I have to breathe.'

'I never asked you to stop breathing,' she said.

He flashed a glance at the wicker basket.

She laughed. 'You should smell my world.'

She sat back against the edge of her desk.

'Well, it's not your sinuses,' she said. 'You say it's sore to eat. Where?'

'Here,' he said, rubbing his fingers against the sharp ends of his sideburns. He shifted in his seat.

'OK,' she said and he took his hands down. She put two thumbs each side on the same spot.

'Open and close your mouth,' she said. 'Can you feel anything?'

'Like a crackle,' he said.

'Pain?'

'No, but I've taken a lot to kill that.'

'Oh, yes. Does your jaw ever lock? Do you ever hear it click?'

'Yes.'

'Do you get pain in your neck or your cheeks?'

'Yes.'

'Did you ever get diagnosed with toothache, earache or sinusitis?'

'Yes, look I appreciate this, but I really have to get a move on.'

'Have you ever suffered an injury to your face or jaw?'

Images of childhood fights flashed through his mind, a teenage car accident, a punch-up in a bar at his bachelor party, a door slammed against him in a raid, the explosion . . .

'Uh-huh,' he said.

She stepped back. 'Good news or bad?'

'Bad.'

She shook her head. 'Pessimist?'

'Worst Case Scenario Man.'

'First of all, I'm not your GP, so what I'm giving you here is an educated guess. It could be one of two things: some form of facial neuralgia or possibly, TMJ dysfunction. The TMJ bit stands for Temporo-Mandibular Joint, the all-important joint that helps you open and close your jaw. And you're American, you'll understand the dysfunction part.'

Nothing was beyond a comment with Lara McClatchie.

'I'm leaning towards TMJ dysfunction,' she said. 'I've seen it before. And my brother has it.'

She studied him for a moment. 'Why am I getting the impression you're just playing along?'

Joe said nothing.

'You know this already, don't you?'

'I guess so.'

'Why haven't you done anything about it?'

'I was too busy.'

'You really should find the time to get treated. Your brain spends a lot of energy looking after that joint. And the problem is worse if you're stressed, which, under the circumstances, I'd say you are.

'They'll probably just fit you with a splint – a mouth guard that you wear all the time or just at night. And there are other options as well – surgery . . .' She laughed when she saw his reaction. 'Ah,' she said. 'I've come to the root of the denial.'

He shrugged.

'It won't go away,' she said.

'Can't you give me anything for now?'

'You're forgetting. I see dead people.'

'Oh, yeah.' He smiled.

'Bet you haven't been doing a lot of that lately,' she said.

'No,' he said.

'Here,' she said, bending over the desk, scribbling on a notepad. 'Here's the name of a specialist in the Eye and Ear Hospital, Dr Morley. She should sort you out. We went to college together. She stole my boyfriend.'

'And what? Sending me in is your revenge?'

'Good point,' said Lara with a smirk. 'Give me that back.' She crossed out the name and wrote another one. 'Here. Go with this guy. He's not a big fan of surgery.' She smiled.

He thanked her and left. Lara walked out the door to her assistant.

'Gill?' she said. 'You know my forceps?'

Gill nodded.

'Well, if I could remove one thing with them right now, it would be the platinum band on the fourth digit of that man's left hand.'

'Platinum,' said Gill, 'says it all.'

'I can't believe I nearly sent him to that cow in the Eye and Ear.' She sighed. 'On a more serious note, I need you to get me a file.'

'But you *were* being serious about him.'

'True.'

John Miller was sitting at the bar holding a pint and playing with a shot glass of whisky. Ed stood watching him for a few minutes, then suddenly leaned across the counter and spoke firmly into his ear.

'I'm going to tell you something,' he said, 'and I hope you're listening.'

'What?' said John.

'You're not an alcoholic.'

John put his pint down gently.

'What I'm saying to you, Miller, is that your

body is not addicted to alcohol. You're just addicted to being out of your mind so you can forget. You could stop in the morning without help and I think you know that yourself. But in six months' time, it might be a different story.'

'Jesus, I just came in for a couple of drinks,' said John. Ed slammed his fist down on the bar. Then he turned around and grabbed one of the photos from the wall. It was the Munster rugby team, 1979. Ed slapped it down on the counter and pointed angrily to the back row where John Miller stood, young and healthy, with a wide, friendly smile.

'You were a winner!' said Ed.

'Ah, it's all a load of bollocks in the end,' said John.

Ed almost shouted at him, 'Stop being so bloody difficult, for the love of God! I have enough customers that one less isn't going to matter a flying fiddler's. I've listened to you shite on about your wife and kids every day for over a month now. What I'm telling you is stop your moaning and do something about it. If your wife didn't want the nice guy back, she definitely won't want the waster you've turned into.'

Victor Nicotero was about to make a call when he saw the flashing red light on his machine. He hit play.

'Hi, Nic, it's Joe. Texas trip's off. I'm not sure, I . . . What can I say? Everything and nothing's adding up. My head's all screwed up. But thanks anyway.'

Anna was tired and pale when she arrived at the supermarket. She moved quickly through the short aisles, trying to ignore the looks being directed her way. Her face was growing hot, her hands clammy. The basket almost slipped from her grip and when she bent to keep it under control she saw two fishermen's boots on the ground in front of her. She looked up.

'I'm not happy with what Shaun did,' said Mick Harrington. He had prepared for this, but he was clearly embarrassed.

'What do you mean?' said Anna.

'You know, he got Robert to cover his tracks. He got him to go to Seascapes and turn out the light after he was in the place with Katie. Robert could have been arrested.'

'I didn't know that Shaun had done that,' said Anna. 'But I know it wasn't right. I cannot say much to you, Mick. Shaun is very upset. I had no idea any of this was going on. I would have done something about it.'

'You and Joe seem to be in the dark a fair bit, don't you?' said Mick. 'Or is it denial you're in?'

Anna couldn't speak.

'Robert won't be around again,' said Mick.

Anna was alone in the aisle. She held back tears as she walked to the checkout. As she stood in

line, she heard someone call out her name. She
didn't want to look around.

'Anna,' came the voice again, this time with a
tap on the shoulder. 'How are you?'

She turned to face Nora Deegan who was
smiling warmly.

'It must be just awful what you're going
through. Awful.' Her voice was loud and firm.

She squeezed Anna's arm. The woman at the
till stared.

'Anyway, we won't dwell on that,' said Nora.
'I was wondering if you'd like to come over for
coffee this afternoon.'

'Sure,' said Anna. 'That would be great.'

Barry Shanley came to his front door, dabbing a
bloody spot on his shaved head. He took a deep
breath when he saw who was outside.

'Hello, Barry. Can I come in?' said Frank. He
glanced at Barry's combats and his black T-shirt
stamped with *Leave No Man Behind*.

'Yeah, sure.' Barry stepped back.

'Is your father here?'

Barry's father worked on the ferries out of
Rosslare. He was rarely home.

'Uh, yeah.'

'Is your mother?'

Barry nodded. 'Do you want me to get them?
I'm in the middle of my homework.' He grabbed
on to the banister.

'I need to speak with you too,' said Frank.

'Oh. OK.'

Mr and Mrs Shanley led Frank into the living room and sat on the sofa warily. Barry slouched by the door. Frank pulled out a piece of paper and unfolded the email, handing it to Mr Shanley.

'What's this?' he said.

'Well, in the old days, we'd call it a poison pen letter. But these days, you can do it by email. It was sent to Shaun Lucchesi and I believe it came from Barry.' His parents looked at him.

'I've never seen that before in my life,' he said. His parents nodded.

'Come on now, Barry,' said Frank. 'On my way home from work yesterday, I paid a visit to Mr Russell, the computer teacher at the school and he was able to trace it back to you.'

'There must be some kind of mistake,' said Mrs Shanley. 'This is terrible. An awful thing to send, no matter what Shaun Lucchesi has done.'

'What do you think Shaun Lucchesi has done?' said Frank.

Mrs Shanley blushed.

'Yes, it is an awful thing to send,' said Frank. 'And I'm afraid that Barry is the person who sent it.' He turned to him. 'Mr Russell is an expert and he would swear to it in court if he had to.'

Barry's eyes widened. 'I have to go to court?' He started to tremble.

'This is your fault,' said Mrs Shanley to her husband. Everyone turned to her.

'Well, it is,' she said. 'You're never here to discipline the child.'

Frank focused on Barry. 'No,' he said, 'you won't have to go to court. But I think you owe the Lucchesis an apology.'

Barry started to cry.

Danny Markey hung over the back of his sofa at six a.m. and grabbed the phone.

'You just do not know who's spitting into your hamburger these days,' he said.

'Danny. What's up? Why are *you* up?'

'It's another sofa night in the Markey household. I spoke with Kane. Flipping burgers right here in New York, so thanks for bringing the mountain to Mohammed. And I mean mountain. Huge guy, yet strangely cuddly. Bit of a comedian. Can't put him with his rap sheet though. Torture, mutilation . . . he gouged a guy's eye out – with a crutch – for whistling. Psycho motherfucker.'

'So, what about Rawlins?'

'Nothing major, I'm afraid. Here we go: nuts, Kane spelt that out for me too, like *he* can talk, obsessed with Harris' Hawks, which would back up the first claim, he lost it when Riggs got killed, but also thought he was right to blow up the mother and daughter, that you make good on your promises. That was pretty much it. You didn't get a mention, buddy.'

'I didn't think I would. I just, I don't know . . .' The words felt scrambled together in his head, climbing over each other to get out.

'You really need to chill about all this, Joe. You don't sound yourself. Is everything all right? What time is it over there? Have you been on the beer?'

'No,' said Joe. 'Just the pain.' Nothing was coming out right. He started to panic.

'Look,' said Danny, 'it'll all be over and some local whack job will be locked up for it.'

'I'm not so sure,' said Joe.

'Man, you sound like you need to get some sleep.'

Joe snorted. 'Sleep. Great.' He rubbed his eyes.

'Well, take a shower then. I'm the one calling in the middle of the night, remember.' He laughed. He got no response.

'Jesus, I'm forgetting to tell you the weirdest thing,' said Danny, 'what he said about the ransom money . . . I did a bit of checking and it looks like he's right. I'm gonna FedEx you over the Hayley Gray file.'

Anna had never been to the Deegans' house before. It was down a small side street in Mountcannon, but on the opposite side to the station, so it didn't have a sea view. It was beautifully painted, with a newly thatched roof and traditional green window frames and door. There was no bell, so Anna tapped gently with the brass knocker.

'Well, the sergeant's wife isn't going to invite the mother of a murderer into her home, now, is she?' said Nora as she let her in.

Nora's directness could be shocking, but Anna managed a laugh.

'Thank you,' she said. 'This is very kind.'

'My pleasure. Well, actually, it's also a bit selfish of me, really,' said Nora. 'I was hoping to pick your brain while you're here.'

'Sure. About what?'

'The gallery. The interior, more specifically. I want it to be perfect, but I haven't got the budget, you know.'

'I'd love to help,' said Anna. 'But are you sure? I don't want to make things difficult for you. I know what people are like.'

Nora rolled her eyes. 'I need an expert and that's that. Don't mind them and their nonsense.'

'I'm not really an expert,' said Anna. 'I'm new to this.'

'But you're working for one of the top interior mags in the world.'

'It was luck and contacts,' said Anna. 'They didn't come to me. I was only starting really, just four years a designer. I went to *them* . . . with a proposal I was hoping they couldn't say no to. My teacher at interior design school gave me good grades. When I told her my idea, she sent me to her friend in the magazine who likes to take risks.'

'Well, then you deserve it. This is an expensive risk. I mean to say, they wouldn't have given it to you if they didn't think you could handle it.'

'Joe would say I'm not very good with budgets.'

Shaun pulled his suitcase from the closet and laid it open on the bed. He was taking a pile of fresh clothes from the dresser when Joe walked down the stairs to his room.

'What's going on?' he said.

Shaun spun around. 'Couldn't you knock?'

'I did knock. You didn't answer. What are you doing?'

'Packing.'

'Come on, Shaun, less of the attitude. Where do you think you're going?'

'Home. Back to New York.'

'What?'

Shaun looked down. 'Granddad sent me a ticket.' He pointed to the desk. Joe snatched up a slim travel wallet.

'Yeah, well, we'll see about that,' he said, walking to the door. 'And you can put that suitcase away,' he called back. 'After I speak with your grandfather, I'm going for a walk, then I'm going to Danaher's. You better be here when I get back.'

'They probably won't serve you,' Shaun called after him. 'Everyone hates us.'

Nora slid a pile of books, magazines and papers off a desk in the corner and brought them over to the kitchen table. She flipped the books open to pages she had marked with index cards, showing Anna the artists whose paintings she was hoping to exhibit. She went through newspaper cuttings from cultural sections, magazine articles on art and faxes from contacts in other small galleries around the country.

'I think I might have something at home you might like to see,' said Anna. 'An idea I started working on before, but didn't get a chance to finish.'

'Brilliant,' said Nora, sorting through more documents.

'Who's this guy?' said Anna, pointing to the top half of a solemn face, hidden by the pages on top. 'An artist?'

Nora reached for the fax, flustered, but Anna had already pulled it free and knew that what she was staring at was a mug shot. She raised her hand to her mouth.

'That's Frank's,' said Nora. 'I must have taken it with my own stuff.'

Anna's face was pale. 'Oh my God,' she said. 'Who is he?' She turned to Nora.

'Who is he? Why does Frank have his photo?'

Her hand was shaking. Nora said nothing. Anna looked back at the page and noticed a scribble, five letters cut off at the edge of the page, 'chesi'. 'Does this have something to do with Joe?' she asked, her voice trembling.

'You'll have to ask him,' said Nora. 'I'm sorry. This is my fault.'

'No it's not,' said Anna. 'But I'm going to have to go. I have to talk to Joe.'

Joe punched the numbers into the phone and was pacing across the kitchen before Giulio even picked up.

'What the hell do you think you're doing?' said Joe.

'I presume you're talking about the plane tickets. I was helping my grandson out.'

'Playing the big shot. He doesn't need your help.'

'The kid's been through too much. He needs a break.'

'That's not up to you. Are you crazy? Coming in, trying to drag him back to New York? Do you think that'll look good to everyone around here?'

'He called me, looking for help. So I'm helping him.'

'To run away. I can't believe I'm even having this conversation. I can't believe Shaun even called you.'

'I don't think you fully appreciate what's been going on in his head,' said Giulio.

'What are you talking about?'

'He feels like a criminal. He's only sixteen—'

'And what the hell would you know about sixteen-year-olds?'

'And then there's you, running around trying to get involved, embarrassing the poor kid.'

Joe was taken aback. 'None of this is any of your business,' he snapped.

'It *is* my business if my grandson's unhappy.'

'But if your son's unhappy—'

'Get over it, Joe. Mommy and Daddy still love you, they just can't live together.' His voice was a cruel whine.

'You're a real cold guy, Giulio.'

'Shaun needs to get away, relax, where no-one is crossing the street to avoid him.'

'No-one's crossing the street to avoid him, for crying out loud.'

'He sees things differently. He needs to be accepted at this stage of his life. And that's not happening in your quaint little village over there. Get him the hell away before any permanent damage is done. He's at an important stage—'

'What? You making up for lost time now? Is that it? You're going to be there for him 'cos you weren't for me?'

'Well, look how you turned out, you can't stick with anything.'

'Jesus Christ Almighty, he's on to the college thing again. Let me spell it out for you – it was never gonna happen. I was not born to become anything you think makes you look good to your professor friends or whoever the hell you want to impress. Yeah, my son is a cop, yeah, yeah. I bet that doesn't come up in conversation too much at lunch with the dean. Dad? I would have made a shit entomologist, OK? I make a damn good cop.'

'Why are you not working now, then?'

Joe was apoplectic.

'You blew it, Joe, and you know it.'

The line hummed. Joe couldn't get any angrier, so he did the next best thing. He took some breaths, lowered his voice and spoke gently.

'You think I can't stick to anything, huh? Is that how you feel? What about Anna? What about the woman I love and promised to love with all my heart the day I married her? Seventeen years of marriage. So there you have it, there's something – I've stuck with my wife. Which I think we'll agree is a whole hell of a lot more honourable than walking out on a dying one.'

The Jeep was gone and the house was empty when Anna got back. Joe's mobile phone was on the kitchen counter. She was still trying to come to terms with the photo. She didn't want to think about what it meant. She remembered the project she wanted to show Nora and went to the filing cabinet in the den. She tried the top drawer, but it jammed. The one underneath was still open. She bent down and pulled it out. At the back, the corner of a page stuck out from a brown folder with no tab. Her hand hovered over it. This was Joe's drawer. But she reached in and slid the page free. It was a short letter, addressed to The Personnel Department, One Police Plaza. Her heart fell. Scanning down, she saw

'Joe Lucchesi...Shield Number..., would like to be re-instated, as soon as possible, consider my application...

Anna slammed the drawer shut with a swift kick.

The sky was grey over Mariner's Strand. Joe walked along the pebbled sand wishing he was one of the people there to enjoy the view. Instead, he was thinking about grief: his for the loss of a perfect marriage, Shaun's for a beautiful dead girlfriend. He saw Frank and Nora Deegan by the water and walked towards them. Frank nodded at his wife and she went on ahead.

'I don't know whether this is good news or bad for you, Joe, but I found out who sent Shaun that email. It was Barry Shanley, a fifth year student in St Declan's who was trying his hand at being the tough man.'

'Are you sure?' said Joe. 'But—'

'I've gone through everything in detail with the computer teacher at the school. There's absolutely no question about it and Barry admitted it himself. He was crying by the time I left him. You've been through a lot, Joe. It's understandable things like that would rattle you. Oh, and Richie went to see Mae Miller today and he said there's not a bother on her. We don't think she's suffering from Alzheimer's, Joe. John Miller can be a funny fish. Probably looking for some sort of sympathy vote.'

Anna walked around the house trying to decide what to do. She didn't want to waste her anger on a phone call Joe could hang up on. She wanted him to register every bit of hurt and disappointment she was feeling. She had been right – both her boys were lying to her. She had fought for them over and over and this was how they had paid her back.

'Screw you,' she said. She was going back over to the drawer when she heard the doorbell ring. She didn't move. It rang again. She stormed through the hall and jerked the door open. A man stood smiling in front of her. He wore brown hiking boots, skinny jeans, a check shirt and a cream-coloured vest. Anna's heart rate soared so sharply, she froze. He was reminding her that he was Gary, the replacement gardener. She found herself staring at the tendons in his arms. Then she realised he had stopped talking. She looked up. Their eyes met. His smile died. She started fumbling desperately for the door. She tried to jam her bare foot against it. Duke was already pushing her back, sliding her towards the wall. The rough wood scraped up her foot, dragging splinters through the torn skin. She cried out and jerked her foot away, slamming backwards into the wall. She dropped to her knees and scrambled past Duke. In one stride he was behind her. He wrapped his arm around her waist then wrenched it towards him, crushing her stomach and ribs. She tried to prise his arm away, but he held her rigid. Something inside her sank. As he carried her back through the door, she caught his strange, distorted reflection in the glass. The only thing she could make out were two dilated pupils that made her scream. Windows to the soul . . . and the soul was black.

Ray and Hugh were standing at the bar having one of their discussions when Joe joined them.

'To me, faces from those police sketches are like a whole separate species,' said Hugh. 'Like, that guy from that American Heroes place. That face doesn't exist in any reality. Only in a police file or in a newspaper. I mean, the face we see isn't actually anyone's face. It's like a mutant, pulled together from memory. I always picture these two-D faces floating around the place, with these evil eyes, sharp cheekbones and always the creepy, slitty little mouth. "Hi, I'm the sketch from the robbery? The bank job?" "Wow! You are so not like the guy they got for that!"' He looked from Ray to Joe. 'Know what I mean?' he added.

'Hugh's PC is in for repair,' said Ray. 'It's been very upsetting for him.' Hugh nodded sadly.

'I haven't seen the one you're talking about, but I think they're always shite,' said Ray. 'A couple of years ago, there was a rapist around Waterford and the police brought out some composite thing that was the image of me. I swear to God. It was in all the papers. I thought I'd be the only one to notice, but everyone started staring at me—'

'I'd say Richie Bates drew that just to piss you off,' said Hugh.

'I wouldn't put it past him,' said Ray.

'Well, after his road rage moment the other day . . .' said Joe.

'What has he done now?' said Ray.

'What do you mean? You're the one who was there.'

Ray stared at him.

'With the garbage on the road outside your house?'

Ray and Hugh exchanged glances. Ray snorted a laugh.

Three beers arrived in front of them and the conversation changed.

Robert Harrington climbed out his window onto the conservatory roof, straddling the glass panes, placing his feet carefully on the aluminium. He walked down slowly, then jumped into the garden, sprinting across it and out onto the road.

'Free gaff,' said Shaun, when he answered the door. 'Mom and Dad are out.'

'You and your Irish expressions,' said Robert. 'Shouldn't you be saying, like "home alone" or something? You look like shit, by the way.'

'Thanks. Come in. I'll tell you everything. My life is a mess. I think we should raid the drinks cabinet.'

'Any excuse,' said Robert. 'And I've called Ali. She's on her way.'

The kitchen table was covered with files. Frank sat, leaning on his elbows, studying an open folder. Nora stood in the doorway.

'I thought I'd tell you about what happened today—'

Frank raised his hand to stop her. Then he looked up with his magnified eyes.

'I'm sorry,' he said. 'I'm up to my neck trying to work it all out.' He pushed himself back from the table.

'I know you are, pet,' said Nora. 'You look pale. And your dark circles are huge,' she smiled. 'Are you all right?'

'My stomach is in bits.' He nodded towards the coffee pot.

'It's worth it sometimes,' she said, smiling. 'If you've got a lot on. To keep you going.'

'I just . . . it's driving me mad trying to work out why Katie picked me out of everyone to call. Why not 999 or the station or Shaun for that matter? Although, they were arguing, so I suppose . . .' He sighed. 'I just don't know.'

'Don't let O'Connor hear you say that.'

They laughed.

'Don't worry about the call. You'll find out soon enough what it was all about,' said Nora, walking over and squeezing his shoulders. She tilted the lamp beside him.

'That's better.'

'Thanks,' he said.

'I'll leave you to it.'

As Joe swung the Jeep into the drive, his head-lights hit the top of the lighthouse, where he saw a figure leaning dangerously over the balcony rail-ings. He reversed the car and the headlights picked up two other people underneath waving at the person above. He slammed his foot on the gas and drove halfway down the lane, cutting the engine and jumping out at the steps down to the light-house. A misty, drenching rain was falling and as he approached, he saw Ali rooted to the spot. Robert staggered around to face him.

'Mr Lucchesi,' he said, pointing up at the balcony. 'It's Shaun. He's hammered. He says he's going to jump.' Robert stank of beer, but had been shocked almost sober.

'Jesus Christ,' said Joe. 'What the hell's going on?'

'Ohmygod, ohmygod, ohmygod.' Ali was hysterical.

'We were drinking in the house,' said Robert. 'Then he wanted to come outside in the rain, so we said yeah and he said he wanted to show us the lighthouse and he ran ahead and he's been hanging over the railings for ages saying he wants to die. We didn't know what to do. We couldn't leave him.'

'Where's Anna?' said Joe.

'I don't know,' said Robert. 'Shaun said she's out.'

'Did he take anything?' said Joe.

'Like drugs? No. He just mixed his drinks.'

'Shit,' said Joe.

They both watched as Shaun vomited into the wind and it flew back against him.

'I want to die,' he moaned.

'Well, I want to kill you,' said Joe under his breath.

Robert smiled. 'I'm sorry, Mr Lucchesi. I had no idea—'

'It's not your fault,' said Joe. 'He's been having a rough time. It was inevitable.'

'You don't want to die, Shaun,' shouted Joe. 'Come on down, for God's sake. I'll get you a coffee.'

'My life is over,' shouted Shaun, holding onto

the railings, swaying backwards. 'Katie's gone and everyone thinks I killed her.'

'No, they don't,' shouted Robert.

'What would you know?' said Shaun. 'Your dad doesn't even want you near me.'

Robert shrugged his shoulders at Joe.

'Come on, son,' said Joe to Shaun. 'This is just the beer talking. I'm gonna come up to you and we're gonna come down together. Can you stay where you are?'

'Just fuck off and leave me alone,' roared Shaun, trying to raise his knee to climb up. He stumbled back, slumping against the wall, his stomach folded in two. He threw up again, wiping the vomit away with his sleeve.

'Aw, Jesus,' said Joe. 'I'm going up, guys. Wait here. He's not gonna jump. He wouldn't even be able to get his leg over that railing.'

Joe ran through the double doors and up the stairs into the lantern house, pushing through the open door onto the balcony. Shaun was weeping now, his hands rubbing at his eyes, his shoulders heaving. Joe sat down and pulled him towards him, smoothing his hair down, telling him it was all going to work out just fine. He called down to Robert and Ali to go home.

After half an hour, he managed to drag Shaun to his feet and guide him back down the stairs and out for a walk across the grass to the house. Shaun muttered random thoughts the whole way, swinging wildly from one emotion to the next.

'Anna,' called Joe when he arrived in.

'Mother,' shouted Shaun in an English accent. 'Oh, Mother.' Joe laughed.

'Did Mother tell you she was going out earlier?' asked Joe.

'No,' said Shaun. 'I don't remember. Maybe. But who really knows?' He sighed.

'Well, you're clearly no use to me. Bed. Now. Actually, shower first.'

Shaun slumped to the floor and curled into a ball, his face resting on a bristled mat, his eyes closed.

'Get up,' said Joe, hauling him off the carpet. He dragged him towards his room. 'You can do the rest.'

Joe looked into the kitchen, but it was dark and empty. He went upstairs and called Anna's name again. He got no answer.

TWENTY-FOUR

Stinger's Creek, North Central Texas, 1989

The wooden benches were empty and the sprinklers were on. An elderly gardener in a light plaid shirt reached back and pulled the cotton free from his sweaty back. Duke Rawlins stood at a huge sign that told him in fancy green writing that he was outside Pleasance Retirement Home.

In ripped jeans, a black T-shirt and black biker boots, Duke walked the long drive and wiped an arm across his forehead when he reached the cool entrance hall. A smiling nurse pointed him towards the elevator. He got out on the third floor and found the sixth door on the left. It was open. He knocked softly.

'Mrs Genzel? It's Duke. Duke Rawlins. From fifth grade?'

'Still?' said Mrs Genzel, turning her head briefly from the window. 'I'd have hoped you moved on.'

Duke smiled.

The room had lilac walls and smelled of perfume and roses. There was no medical equipment, no oxygen tanks, no drips, pills or syrups, no walkers or canes. The double bed at the centre was covered with bright quilted cushions. A string of purple flower-shaped lights were looped through the white iron frame.

Mrs Genzel sat on a straight-backed chair in the window. She hadn't changed her hairstyle, she hadn't put on a pound of weight since Duke last saw her, the year she retired, the year he finished fifth grade. She was dressed in grey pants and navy shoes, with a white blouse and a white cardigan with ribbon trims.

'Sit down,' she said. 'I get separation anxiety when I'm away from the window.'

'It sure is a nice view,' said Duke, pulling up a soft pink armchair beside her.

'Yes. Some of the others watch TV all day in there. When hell freezes over, I'll march right in and join them. I've got my regular books,' she pointed, 'and my audio books.' A CD player with oversized headphones lay on the bedside table. Duke looked over.

'I don't like those little hearing-aid headphones. They hurt my ears or they fall out . . .' She smiled at Duke.

'I thought you might not remember me,' he said.

'I remember you,' she said. 'It's nice of you to come visit.'

'I heard you were here. How do you like it?'

'I like it more than you think I'd like it.'

'Nah. It's homey. Nice homey.'

'Yes, it is. And I've made some good friends here I get to see every day. And we talk about whatever we want to talk about, books, movies, theatre, their families . . .'

'Regular stuff, I guess.'

She nodded.

'What about you, Duke? What have you been doing? Work-wise.'

'Aw, different things. You know. I worked in the diner for a while. And at the karting track. That was fun.'

'Do you still see your friend, Donald?'

'All the time. He's doin' great. Workin' in a store-room for some big stationery place.'

They spoke about everything they could speak about for two people who didn't really know each other. Then they sat in silence. Duke eventually leaned forward, rubbing his hands up and down his thighs.

'It was you, wasn't it?' he said suddenly. He spoke without looking at her.

'What was?' she said.

'Who called them that time. After Sparky died. Whatever authority it was . . . they came to our house, you know. They looked around. They spoke to Mama.' He squeezed his eyes shut. 'And they never came back.'

Mrs Genzel reached out and put a hand gently on his arm. 'I'm sorry. I'm so sorry.'

'Was it you?'

'An anonymous caller, I would say.' She patted his arm.

Duke studied her profile, then turned back to the window.

'Well, I best be gettin' along,' he said, standing up. He pushed his chair into the corner and went back to her.

'You look after yourself,' he said.

'You too, Duke.'

'Thank you,' he said from the doorway.

Mrs Genzel pulled her cardigan tightly around her. She took off her glasses and rubbed them with a small square cloth she kept folded in her pocket. She reached back and took a thick travel guide from her bedside table. She slid out the bookmark and tried to read. When that didn't work, she sat quietly, following the scenes in the gardens.

A young nurse walked through the open door.

'Well, Mrs Genzel, you *are* the dark horse of this establishment. Who was *he*?'

Mrs Genzel didn't turn around to answer. 'I wish I knew.' She shook her head sadly. 'But who can I call now?'

The nurse shook herself out of her daze. 'He was *cute.*'

The yellow tricycle sparkled, its rainbow-coloured streamers hanging limp from the handlebars in the dead heat. Cynthia Sloane opened the back door of her house wide. The sunlight shone through her dress, making silhouettes of her slender legs through the sheer fabric. She was tired and cranky. For three afternoons in a row, each time she tried to nap, she had woken up to the sound of a cat crying like a baby in her back yard. With two toddlers and a newborn, sleep was all she dreamed about and waking up to a whining animal was making her crazy. She held a broom in her right hand and waited. She finally heard the mewling and this time she was ready. She charged to the middle of the yard and stopped. She heard a rustle in the shaded corner that backed onto the lane. She moved quietly forward and pushed the broom into the brush. She drew back and pushed in again.

'Go on, git!' she said. 'Git, you little—' Suddenly a hand reached out and grabbed the broom, jerking her forward, then backwards onto the dirt. She cried out. Donnie bolted for her, pressing his hand over her mouth. She reached down, and picked up the broom, smashing it into the side of his face. He tightened his grip, dragging her out into the laneway where Duke was waiting, the car hidden in the shadows.

TWENTY-FIVE

Joe walked through every room in the house and ended up in the den.

'Aw, shit,' he said when he saw his application letter on the floor. He shook his head. 'Shit.' He felt the heavy weight of guilt in his chest. His first thought was to lie, to pretend the letter was a back-up plan; he could bat the guilt back into Anna's court by saying he wrote it when she had told him about John Miller. His next thought was that his wife was too smart for that. She wouldn't have left if she thought there was an explanation for the letter other than the obvious.

Then he felt a surge of annoyance. He fast forwarded to an argument with her and imagined himself shouting, 'Being a cop is my life, Anna. Why do I have to go along with whatever you want to do all the time?' Lame. It wasn't even true. He'd only done that once, when he came to Ireland. And he knew anything he said in an argument would be useless. He knew that there shouldn't be an argument if she was ever to forgive him. He wondered what he had been thinking writing the letter without telling her.

He went into the bedroom and pulled open her wardrobe to check if she had taken a suitcase. He let out a breath when he saw the number of bags crammed into the top shelf. He wouldn't have a clue if she'd taken one. The same went for her clothes, her underwear, her shoes. 'Shit,' he said. He sat down on the bed and rested his head on the pillow. He caught the faintest smell of her perfume – citrus and herbs. She never liked strong scents. Everything was subtle with Anna. He frowned. Walking out on him wasn't subtle. He pushed himself up off the bed and ran down to the phone. He dialled her mobile and heard a bright voice tell him, 'The person you are calling may have their unit powered off . . .' *or may be totally pissed with you*, thought Joe. He checked his watch. It was one a.m. Would she really be that angry not to leave a note or call him? He pressed his hand against his chest to soothe the pain that shot across it. He pulled back the curtain by the front door and looked out. It was like searching for keys on an empty table top.

He went into the living room with the portable phone and sat on the sofa. He switched on the lamp, picked up the remote control and sped through every channel. He stopped at the news, then moved on. He hit mute every time he heard a noise. Eventually, he gave up and sat in silence.

He dialled Anna's number again and got the same cheery message. He started to get angry. He didn't deserve this, whatever he'd done. He loved her, she knew that. He wasn't some asshole husband who treated her badly. But she'd had an affair and now she'd walked out. He must be doing something wrong. He tried her again. 'Come on, Anna.'

He grabbed the first book he found from the shelf under the coffee table and started skimming through pictures of luxury hotels . . . which made him think of Anna. He just wanted her to come home. He couldn't bear the thought of her leaving him. Their marriage used to be perfect. Every time she had gone away on business or to visit with her parents, he felt lost. Even though she wasn't the kind of wife who did everything for him, he always ended up eating TV dinners when she wasn't there. He felt sick at the thought of her walking out on him. All because of his job. He leaned his head against the back of the sofa and closed his eyes. Twenty minutes later, he jerked awake, his heart thudding. For a moment, he didn't know where he was.

He looked around him. 'Anna?' He called out. He got up and walked into the kitchen. It was dark. He checked the fridge again for a message. He checked the empty table top.

He found himself back on the sofa and this time he knew he was panicked. It was two-thirty. She couldn't be doing this to him. He tried her again and when she didn't answer, he went to the hall and grabbed the keys to the Jeep. He drove up the hill and felt a strange shiver when he passed the spot where Katie was found. He slowed as he passed John Miller's house, then sped up again. 'Come on, Anna,' he said. 'You're freaking me out here.' He tapped nervously on the steering wheel. It was cold and dark and his wife was gone and she hadn't told him where and his gut was saying something was wrong. But it was late and he didn't know if he could trust his gut when he hadn't slept and he was wracked with guilt. He tried to work out what he was afraid of: that something had happened to her or just that his shitty letter had happened to her. He didn't want to be alone. He imagined himself sitting in McDonald's with Shaun at weekends trying to be his buddy like all the other divorced fathers staring into those slack teenage faces.

Suddenly, he saw a shape in the centre of the road. He wrenched the steering wheel to the right and swerved into a shallow ditch. He looked back and saw a dead fox. It was clear that most other drivers hadn't been as quick to avoid it. He reversed back onto the road and kept driving.

Within minutes he had grabbed his mobile again and redialled. 'Dammit,' he yelled, throwing it back on the seat. He drove for hours, just to give her enough time to be home when he got back. His gut spasmed again. He headed home and pulled into the lane, studying the house for any sign that it had changed since he left. He walked in the door and knew it was the same. But he went up the stairs anyway and checked all the rooms. His head started to pound. His jaw felt nailed shut. When he opened his mouth, it was like he was pulling each tooth. He went to the kitchen where he had left his pills and he took too many. He sat on the bed in the spare room, with the portable phone and his mobile beside him. He could feel his head get heavy. If he slept, she could be there in the morning, angry probably, but OK.

He woke to the phone ringing. His heart leapt.

Nora never liked Frank's old armchair. It was brown velour and filled with limp kapok. The arms were bald and the covers were loose. It sat in the downstairs hallway waiting to be taken away for scrap. It was where she found Frank asleep at eight in the morning, his head back, his mouth open. A stack of files was fanned out on the floor in front of him. She knelt down and lay her hands gently on his.

'Sweetheart,' she said.

His eyes opened slowly and he struggled to focus on her.

'Oh,' he said. 'I must have fallen asleep. What time is it?'

'Eight,' she said. 'Is this some kind of protest? If I'd known you were going to have a sit-in, I never would have suggested giving the thing away.'

He smiled. 'I just sat down for a minute to rest my eyes . . .'

'What time were you up until?'

'About five,' he said.

'You poor divil. Anything new?'

He shook his head. 'Not really, no.'

'Come on,' she said, patting his hands and standing up. 'Brekkie.'

Joe's heart sank when the voice he heard was not his wife's.

'Have I caught you at a bad time?' said Dr McClatchie.

'No. I'm – no.'

'Did you get in contact with that specialist?'

'No.'

'I hate to ask, but the fax you brought me the other day . . . well, I was wondering if I could get another look at it.'

'No.'

'It's really quite important.'

Joe took a deep breath and spoke quickly to lessen the pain that had built overnight in his jaw. 'I was way out of line with that, doctor. I was in an emotional situation that shouldn't have compromised my judgment. And my theory was wrong—'

'I can barely hear you. Could you speak up?'

He repeated what he said, his gums throbbing, pain pressing against his temples.

'Well, there's a project it may help me with. I'm giving a talk to—'

'I'm sorry,' said Joe. 'I put it in the garbage once I knew it had nothing to do with Katie.'

'Oh. Did someone tell you that?'

'Not in so many words.'

He put down the phone and walked around the house again. He felt as if his veins were running hot and cold. He tried Anna's phone, he took more pills. He lay on the sofa until a pleasant numbness washed over him. But it was happening too quickly; he was sinking too deep. He blinked to keep his eyes focused.

Myles O'Connor was leaning two elbows on the roof of his car. He had his mobile in one hand and the cord of a handsfree set hanging from his ear. He pulled the small microphone towards his mouth.

'Look! Bottom line? I'm new. He's old. I'm on the way in, Frank Deegan's on the way out. Fresh blood versus retiree. Who do you *think* gives more of a damn about this case than me?'

Frank stood frozen behind the wall with his sandwich bag in his hand.

* * *

Shaun woke up sweating and unable to move. He stayed that way for five minutes until he finally managed to turn his head. There was a pint of water on his bedside table. He reached out and knocked it onto the floor. He tried to say, 'Shit', but he couldn't pull his tongue free. As soon as he sat up, he felt a rush to his head and he slumped back onto his pillow. His stomach flipped and he knew he wasn't going to make it to the bathroom. He leaned over the side of the bed and vomited yellow bile into the basin Joe had left there. He vomited again and it shot through his nose, his eyes bulging with the force. He hacked from the acid coating the back of his throat, then heaved until there was nothing left to throw up. He grabbed a T-shirt from the floor and wiped his mouth. He sank back onto the bed, his head swimming. Fragments from the previous night flooded in. He knew Robert and Ali would laugh, but he was not looking forward to facing his parents. Suddenly images of Katie were everywhere. He couldn't cope with the alcohol coursing through his system and addling his mind.

Joe knocked on the door and came down. Shaun opened his eyes slowly and thought his father looked drunk. His hair was unkempt and his eyes bloodshot.

Shaun groaned. 'I'm sorry, Dad.'

Joe tried to smile at him. 'It's OK, son.' He walked over to the bed and took the basin out of the way. He sat down.

'I've got something to tell you,' he said. 'I needed you to sleep this off . . .'

Shaun saw fear in his father's eyes for the first time in his life.

'When we got back last night, your mother was gone.' His words were slow, gently slurred.

'What?'

'She's . . . gone,' said Joe. He was blinking again, concentrating to hold his head up. He wanted to lie down on the bed and wake up when it was all over.

'What? What do you mean gone? Where?'

'I don't know,' said Joe. 'She's not here. She wasn't here when we came home.' His lids were heavy.

'Dad, Dad! Are you OK? You don't seem . . . are you . . . have you been drinking?' He shook Joe's arm and brought him back.

'No,' said Joe firmly. 'No, I haven't.'

'What are you saying about Mom?' said Shaun.

'Your mom is gone somewhere.'

'Where? Did she have plans or something?'

'Not that I know of.'

'No offence, but your memory sucks.'

'Look, she may have been . . . mad at me for something.'

'What?'

'That's between me and your mother.'

Shaun frowned. 'Well, she wasn't mad at me. She would have told me if she was going somewhere.'

'Maybe not.'

Shaun looked hurt. 'What will we do?'

'Nothing for now. I'll take care of it. You go to school. She'll be back by the time you're home.'

'I'd rather stay here . . . I could wait for her . . . I don't feel well.' He flopped his head onto the pillow.

Joe stood up and threw back the covers. Shaun moaned and curled into a foetal position.

Joe shook his head. 'You're a loser, you do know that.'

Frank sat at his desk, wondering what O'Connor really wanted that morning. He asked some questions about the progress in the case, but then he just stood with his hands in his pocket, staring out at the sea. The only thing Frank got from his visit was offended. He felt himself redden at the thought. He hoped O'Connor said what he said in anger or to impress someone, not because he thought it was true. Frank found out afterwards that the call had been to Superintendent Brady. And Brady didn't appreciate bad-mouthing. Maybe that's what O'Connor had been considering when he was staring out the window.

Frank unwrapped his sandwich and peeled back the bread. Ham and mustard. There was some comfort in that. But before he ate, he made a quick call to someone he knew would appreciate it.

'Dr McClatchie. Sergeant Frank Deegan here, Mountcannon.'

'Oh, hello.'

'Just a quick call; thought you might be interested to know what those fragments came back as . . . from Katie Lawson's skull. You know, after what you said about never finding anything out.'

'Absolutely.'

'It was shell. From a Sandhill Snail, would you believe. Probably under the rock you said was used.'

'Well, it's very decent of you to let me know, sergeant. So I guess the body was moved after all.'

'Yes, but we think it was immediately after the murder. And none of the other trace evidence brought up anything, so . . .'

'Well, that would make sense.'

'Right. So . . . well, I'll let you get back to it.'

'While I have you on, there's something quite curious I'd like you to hear. I had a visit the other day from Joe Lucchesi . . .'

'What?' said Frank.

Lara had to jerk the phone away from her ear. 'Well, *he's* clearly not in your good books,' she said. 'Anyway, he showed me some crime scene photos from the US, asking me if there were any similarities between them and Katie Lawson, which there weren't. And no, I didn't tell *him* that. However, the curious part is, the wounds were almost identical to a PM I carried out just over three weeks ago on that poor girl from Doon – Mary Casey, the one found dead in the field beside her house. I pulled out my file and I would swear that the crimes were committed by the same person. Hers seems more careless, but they're almost identical.'

'Jesus Christ Almighty,' said Frank.

'Yes. The odd thing is that when Joe came to my office, which was a bold move, you have to admit, he was very . . . I wouldn't like to say pushy, but he was certainly a man on a mission. But when I telephoned him this morning, he had no interest. I mean, I was half-lying to the man about why I was asking, maybe he picked up on that, but anyway, he said he'd thrown the fax away . . . which I found odd, considering the lengths he'd gone to in the first place. What do you think?'

The doorbell rang in three short bursts. Joe ran. He fumbled with the latch, then opened the door to a FedEx guy who reached out with a thick, rectangular package and a clipboard. Joe scrawled a signature and closed the door. The Gray file. Joe tore at the plastic and pulled it out. He stared at it – just a bunch of pages with words on them in a plain brown folder. The same kind of folder that could contain your medical notes, tax records, your personnel file . . . your divorce papers. Every day people got shat on by files. And this one meant more than Joe could bear thinking about. He looked down and saw a bright blue tab towards the back. He flipped it open and scanned a long list of names, one of which was circled. There it was. In black and white, just as Danny liked it. Black and white.

Oran Butler was bent over in a coughing fit, holding his throat and spraying specks of tomato sauce onto the kitchen floor. A ball of mozzarella and mushrooms shot out. He collapsed into a chair and tried to slow his breathing. Then he picked up the bare pizza slice in front of him and flung it into the sink.

Richie came in from the living room. 'Are you all right?' he said, glancing down at the mess.

Oran grunted. 'The whole topping came off in my mouth.'

'I'll clean that up, don't worry,' said Richie, pointing to the floor.

'Well, we know that,' said Oran.

Richie was already reaching for a mop.

'We'll be having a word or two from your pal, tomorrow, by the way,' said Oran.

'My pal who?'

'Why, D.I. O'Connor. The D.S. is off for the week, so O'Connor is lowering himself to get street with the Drug Squad.'

'Really?' said Richie. 'You'll enjoy that.'

'Not if I'm coming home every evening and you're here pining for him.'

* * *

Joe sped along the Waterford road, hyper-aware of the few cars that passed him. His mind was shocked out of its fog and raced with the adrenaline pounding through him. He went heavy on the accelerator, feeding the part of him that wanted to keep driving and driving until everything was behind him and Anna was home.

He parked the Jeep by the quays and went straight to Fingleton's bookstore, his hand gripping his mobile. From the busy cobbled street, Fingleton's looked like a regular sized store, but inside, it opened out and up three storeys. It was dark and quiet with a sunken area on the ground floor bordered by tall black shelves. Joe quickly scanned the natural history section and picked out the only book on Harris' Hawks. The cover shot was of two of them, poised and alert on the branch of a tree. He fumbled as he flicked through the pages, pausing at the photographs and sketches, stopping to skim random passages. The writer was a falconer in awe of his subject. Joe was intrigued by a bird that could capture the imagination of a falconer, a criminal and, now, a cop. He stood for several minutes, absorbed in the words, torn between reassurance and a desperate gnawing panic.

Duke Rawlins sat back in the white wooden chair, his face lit by the glow from Anna's mobile phone. He pushed rows of buttons, stumbling in and out of menus. His thumb hovered when a game he vaguely recognised opened up in front of him. He turned the phone around in his hand, held down a small red key and the screen went blank.

Anna lay curled on her side facing the bedroom wall. She knew the cottage was remote, because for hours she had been allowed to shout her throat raw, buck on the floor against the bindings on her wrists and ankles, wear herself out. But not enough that she was ever going to sleep in this man's company. She held her eyes closed to block out the absolute darkness; there were no houses nearby, no streetlights, no headlights to give her hope.

Shaun was waiting in the hallway as Joe walked in. His face was a mixture of hope, relief and anxiety. He looked down at the bag in Joe's hand.

'You were *shopping*?' he asked.

Joe folded the plastic tight around the book. 'Research.'

'Mom isn't back.' His voice was full of blame.

'I guessed that.'

'Don't you think it's a little strange? Mom has never in her life run out on us. Ever.'

'No I don't think it's strange. Right now? I'm thinking your mom was angry at me and she's looking for space. We'll just tell everyone that she's gone to Paris for a few days to see her folks. Do you think you can do that?'

'Yes. But I don't see why we have to.'

'Because it gives us all time. Your mom will be back and I'll buy her some flowers and take her out to dinner and everything will be fine.'

Shaun studied his face. 'You don't even believe that.'

'Yes, I do.' Joe eyed the phone and briefly thought about calling Frank.

'Stop treating me like some kind of idiot.'

'I'm not,' said Joe patiently. 'I just need to be calm here.'

'Detached, you mean.' Shaun snorted.

'Son, you're angry,' said Joe gently. 'I think this is about you looking for someone to lash out at . . .'

'Look at Katie! Look at her! What about that? Look how that turned out! That worked out all right. Didn't it? Didn't it?' His voice rose steadily the more hysterical he got. 'What if someone's taken Mom? We're here waiting like two losers . . .'

'No-one's taken your mom.'

'What if they have?' said Shaun. He looked up like he had just thought of something. 'Could this be to do with that weird email I got?'

'No, it's not,' said Joe patiently. 'Turns out it was from that commando wannabe from your school.'

'Barry Shanley?' said Shaun, stunned.

* * *

Frank called Richie into his office and asked him to close the door behind him.

'OK, I need to fill you in on something unusual that's come up.' He explained about Joe, Dr McClatchie and the fax.

'Wow,' said Richie. 'That's weird.' Frank could almost hear the workings of his mind. He was reminded of a game with an upright plastic panel where you had to rotate a series of cogs with slots to manoeuvre a small counter into a tray at the bottom. Downfall. That was the name. He wondered when Richie's counter would fall down.

'I called Limerick and spoke briefly to the Super there. I'll be meeting him tomorrow. He's on holidays up in some log cabin in the Ballyhoura mountains. They've no leads. They've checked out a couple of local men, but have ruled them out. So this news from Dr McClatchie is interesting. And look at this.' He turned a map around so Richie could see it. Richie's wandering right eye rolled back into place.

'No-one wants these crimes to be connected,' said Frank. 'But look.' He unfolded the map until he could see the southern half of the country. He drew a ring around Doon where Mary Casey had been found dead in the field, then Tipperary town where Siobhán Fallon had disappeared. Slowly, he did the same around Mountcannon. He looked at Richie. 'These towns are all along the same route.' He paused. 'I think Joe is a step ahead of us. And in fairness, after the whole snail business, it seems he was right about where Katie went that night, regardless of Mae Miller. We have to follow up on this. Remember, Joe bypassed us to go direct to the State Pathologist . . .' Richie nodded.

'. . . so there's something he's not telling us,' said Frank. He threw down his pen and sighed. 'Not that I blame the man.'

TWENTY-SIX

Stinger's Creek, North Central Texas, 1990

Donnie looked down at an imaginary clipboard. 'I'm lookin' for a Homemaker,' he called. 'A Miss Suzy Homemaker.'

'Very fuckin' funny.' Duke was standing in his front yard in grey track pants and a pair of yellow rubber gloves. He was wringing dirty water out of a dish cloth.

'Well, holy shit,' said Donnie. 'Your house was white all along.'

'He's on fire this mornin'.'

Donnie stepped around a pail of water to get closer to the clapboard house. The left hand side was a dull brownish grey and the right side had been washed down, leaving it as white as it was ever going to be. The paint was chipped and peeling and skinny rivers of dirty water had dried onto the surface.

'You need to blast this with a hose,' said Donnie.

'Yeah, after I do my little rain dance here in the yard,' said Duke.

Donnie made a move to sit on the step.

'Don't even think about it,' shouted Duke, throwing a wet sponge hard against his bare chest.

'Son of a bitch,' said Donnie. He picked up the sponge, slapped it into the pail beside him and threw it back, wide. Duke laughed, then ran after him, grabbing him from behind. Donnie wriggled against him. 'Aw, c'mon,' he said. Duke ground the filthy sponge into Donnie's face until he was weak from laughing.

Donnie pulled away, leaning over and spitting out grit. 'Point fuckin' blank,' he said, shaking his head. He went into the house, and stuck his head under the cold tap. 'Isn't it weird not havin' Wanda here?' he called. He got no reply. 'I said,' he shouted, sticking his head out the window, 'isn't it weird—'

'I heard you the first time,' said Duke.

Donnie came back out, grabbed the sponge from the pail and started washing down the wood.

Every few minutes, he stopped and said, 'I hate this shit.'

Duke ignored him.

'I really do,' said Donnie. 'I hate this shit.'

'That's it,' said Duke. 'Go over and pack some of that crap away. Do you think that's a job you can handle?'

'Hallelujah.' Donnie threw down his sponge and walked over to a big cardboard box marked with an X.

'Let me get this straight,' he said. 'Anythin' with an X we're gettin' rid of.'

'Yes,' said Duke. 'Like I said.'

Donnie looked around the yard and saw Xs everywhere.

'Didn't you leave anythin' inside?'

He bent down to one of the boxes.

'The mystery box from the closet. I recognise the Keep Out sticker. You know that was supposed to be for your bedroom door.'

He wrapped his arms around it and lifted it to waist height. But he squeezed too hard and the bottom fell through. He stared, open-mouthed.

'Where did you get all this shit?' he asked. He turned around to Duke for an answer, but Duke was staring into space. Donnie knelt down and started picking through the piles of toys, all unopened. Pristine action heroes behind clear plastic windows, tipper trucks, fighter planes, boxing gloves, a candy dispenser, a mechanic's tool kit. Bright primary colours shining in the sun.

'You had Space Invaders all along?' blurted Donnie, pointing to another box. 'Hey, look at this little guy,' he said, picking up a pale yellow teddy-bear with a tag that said Benton. 'How could you hide poor Benton here in a dark closet . . .' he picked up a tall black figure, '. . . with Darth Vader.

Unless he's . . .' he lowered his voice dramatically, '. . . his father.' He laughed nervously. He looked over at Duke. He waited in the silence, then stood up and started packing the toys into an empty box beside him, holding each one in his hand a fraction longer than he had to.

'Maybe . . . I mean, shouldn't these be goin' to some children's home or somethin'?'

'Are you fuckin' blind? There's an X on the side of that box. A big fuckin' black X.'

Duke carried a pot of red paint into his bedroom. The walls were grey and streaked with beige. Wanda had never finished the wallpaper job she started when they moved in.

'OK. What's next?' said Donnie, walking in behind him. He looked around the room, rubbing his bare belly with his hand. 'The dresser?'

'I'm thinkin' of doin' one wall red, one wall black,' said Duke, pointing. 'What do you reckon?'

'That's cool. Are we takin' the dresser?' he said, slapping the top of it.

'Yup,' said Duke.

They bent down and gripped each end, rocking it back to keep the drawers from sliding. Donnie slammed his shoulder into the door jamb on the way through.

'Goddammit,' he said. He dropped his end and reached around to feel the damage. 'There's a big flap of skin back here,' he said.

'I'll get you some ointment in a minute,' said Duke. 'Now, take a hold of this and get movin'.'

'In the pickup?' said Donnie, backing down the front steps.

'Yup,' said Duke.

They heaved it up and walked back towards the house.

'That's it, except for the bed,' said Donnie.

'I'll take care of that,' said Duke.

'Not on your own, you won't.'

'Go have a cigarette,' said Duke, taking the steps two at a time.

Donnie shrugged, pulled a pack of Marlboro from his jeans and walked into a shaded corner of the yard. He could see Duke silhouetted in the window, struggling to keep the mattress upright.

'I can come in, help you, when I finish this,' he shouted.

'I got it,' said Duke, letting the mattress spring back onto the bed. He disappeared, then showed up minutes later with a saw.

'Probably right,' said Donnie when he walked back into the room. He looked around at the chunks of wood and mattress. 'I don't think the whole thing would have fitted through the door.'

Duke threw down the saw.

'Ointment,' said Donnie.

'Oh yeah. In the bathroom.'

Duke opened the cabinet and pulled out a flattened tube curled up almost to the top. He squeezed some ointment onto his finger tip and turned Donnie by the shoulders towards the light. Donnie caught sight of himself in a mirror on the door and sucked in his gut.

'Have you done it yet?' he asked, trying to crane his neck around.

'I'm doin' it right now,' said Duke, smoothing the ointment in gentle strokes across the broken skin. He picked the tube up again and squeezed out more. Donnie shifted slightly on his feet.

Duke stepped back. His hand hovered, trembling, over the base of Donnie's spine.

TWENTY-SEVEN

Joe stepped out of the shower, focused, reeling from the fright he had given himself with the pills, shocked by the control he had felt slowly slip away from him. He wrapped a towel around his waist and looked at himself in the mirror. He looked tired, but his eyes were clear. He was shaken by his recklessness – leaving the house, leaving Shaun alone, driving with his head spinning. He barely remembered getting to Waterford. He went into the bedroom and grabbed a lime green LV8 from the dresser. He used it to knock back four hits of Fuel It. Then his mobile rang. Anna's number flashed across the screen. His knees buckled.

'Thank—'

'Rise and shine.'

Joe went rigid at the sound of the Texan drawl.

'Hello?' said Duke. 'Hello?'

'Do you have Anna . . . my wife?'

'I know who she is. And what do you think?'

Joe's heart thumped. Shards of pain exploded inside him.

'Please,' he said. 'Please don't hurt my wife.'

Duke laughed. 'Only if you promise not to shoot my partner dead.'

Joe hesitated.

'Let's talk about that some other time,' said Duke.

Joe jumped in. 'You need to know . . .' He thought of those two words from the Gray file and the battle began – should he tell Duke Rawlins what he knew or was it better to hold back? '. . . uh, that my wife . . .'

'What?' snapped Duke. 'Is a diabetic? Needs sugar, doesn't need sugar? Needs medication or she'll die? You know, like the movies?'

'No,' said Joe slowly. 'This is a very real situation. I know that. This is important for both of us. We both need something here and what I need is Anna, my wife, home safe.' A slight tremor shook his voice. 'What do *you* need . . . Mr Rawlins?' He stared up at the ceiling and waited.

He heard a rattle as Duke put the phone down and started to clap. After several seconds, he picked it back up.

'You know your shit. Mr Rawlins – I like that. But I wouldn't have taken your wife if I was just gonna bring her right back. Where's the sense in that?'

'Is Anna OK?' said Joe. 'Have you hurt her in any way? Let me talk to my wife. Please.'

'She said to say hi,' said Duke. 'Except no, she didn't.'

'Please tell me what you need and I'll get it for you,' said Joe. 'I can promise you that.'

'What I need? That's my business. What *you* need? Now that's a lot more interesting. That's my priority here, with all this.'

'I don't understand,' said Joe.

'When it's all over, it won't matter a good goddamn what you understand or don't understand, detective. It'll be over. A dead end. It doesn't matter how the hell you find yourself there when it's the end of the road.'

'Let me talk to my wife.'

'No.'

'Can I see her?'

Duke snorted. 'Come to the parkin' lot at that big high cliff by the harbour in five minutes. What are those things again? Oh yeah, lemmin's.'

The phone, slick with sweat, slid through Joe's palm and clattered onto the floor.

Frank Deegan was halfway down the path when Nora shouted after him.

'What I was trying to tell you the other night . . . I may have done something stupid.' She walked out to him. 'I let Anna Lucchesi see that picture that Joe gave you. The mugshot.'

'How did you manage that?'

'I'm sorry. It was an accident. It had slipped in

among my papers. She seemed a bit shaken by
the whole thing. I thought maybe she was angry
that Joe hadn't let her in on it, whatever it was.'
She paused. 'But now that I think about it, she
actually seemed quite nervous.'

'How do you mean nervous?'

'Well, I thought I saw the page shake when she
took it. Then she put her hand to her mouth. She
was sort of looking around, a bit panicky.'

Frank was familiar with that reaction. It usually
ended with, 'That's him. That's the man.'

Joe ran for the Jeep and pulled out of Shore's
Rock. He drove towards the village, his mind
racing, the caffeine high kicking in. He had taken
in the equivalent of eighteen spoons of coffee.

He thought about Hayley Gray. He remembered
her parents waiting, powerless, because they'd
called the police. Gordon Gray had sat on the sofa,
reading the newspaper. Joe thought he was cold
and detached. But then the man had bolted
upright, shouting, 'What do I do here? What am
I supposed to do? Do I watch TV, do I work, what
the hell do I do when this is going on? Someone
has taken my child!'

This powerful businessman had collapsed
against a police officer, sobbing, 'This is torture,
this is torture – why is this happening?' Then he
stopped suddenly. In the silence that followed, his
quiet words sounded roared.

'I did this.' His eyes were wide and blinking, his mouth open. 'Oh God, this is my fault. All of it.'

Joe stared ahead. He knew now exactly how Gordon Gray felt. This was *his* fault. This was payback for Donald Riggs. He might have been wrong about Katie, about the women in Texas, but he was right about one thing: a man called Duke Rawlins had him in his crosshairs.

He wondered what to do with the information from the file. The thought of making a call on it made the panic surge again. He clenched the steering wheel and floored the accelerator. He thought about calling Frank Deegan. He even reached out for his mobile. Then he was jolted back to the last seconds of Hayley Gray's life . . . and realised that Duke Rawlins could be safe in the knowledge that he was never going to call the police.

'Who do you love most, your husband or your son? If you had to choose,' Duke said suddenly.

'My son,' said Anna calmly.

Duke laughed. 'Just like that?' he said.

'Yes. I'm leaving my husband.'

'You bullshittin' me?' said Duke.

'No,' she said. 'It's over.' Her heart thumped. Duke studied her face.

'You better not be bullshittin' me.'

'I'm not. Please don't touch my son.'

Duke stared, then reached back and slapped her hard with the back of his hand. Her bottom lip split wide.

'Nice fuckin' try,' he said, brushing her hair from her face to look into her eyes. She was crying.

'Don't you dare fuckin' lie to me,' he said. 'You'd never be able to choose between them. It's written all over your skinny little French face.'

'Sorry,' she whispered. 'I'm sorry.'

Duke shrugged. 'Too late,' he said. 'Plan B, just for the holy hell of it.'

Barry Shanley was on his way to school punching a text message into his phone when he felt someone grab the back of his knapsack and wrench him to the ground. The phone spun out onto the road. Barry lay on his back on the path, struggling to find his feet. He managed to turn on his side, but Shaun pulled on his bag again, dragging him backwards. Barry's hands scraped across the stone.

'Fucking get off me,' said Barry, trying to stand up.

'Fuck you,' said Shaun. 'You sick fuck. Sending me emails like a fucking psycho.'

'Got you there, Lucky, didn't I?'

'Are you nuts? My mom was—' Shaun had to stop. He squeezed his eyes shut.

'Oh, your mom!' said Barry. 'You pussy.'

Barry let his bag slide off his shoulders and

dumped it on the ground. He started moving on the balls of his feet in front of Shaun, his arms raised. Shaun snorted.

'You're scaring me, Karate Kid.'

Barry reached out and tried to chop Shaun across the neck. Shaun grabbed Barry's wrist and twisted it behind his back, pulling it up until he cried out. He pushed him forward onto the ground.

'I'm not going to bother fighting you,' said Shaun. He bent down and picked up Barry's phone. He scrolled through the message on the screen. He read it out loud. '"Tape *Home and Away* for me. I'll be back at 7. Kiss Kiss." Now, who are you sending that to? Oh yeah, here we are: Mom. Fuck you, Shanley.'

Joe frowned. Up ahead, a woman was standing by the side of the road.

'What the?'

She was swaying back and forth like a drunk, trying to flag him down with heavy arms. He frowned and checked the clock. He had three minutes to get to the car park. He looked around, hoping someone else would drive by and help this woman. Then he saw the blood, dripping from her arm. He looked for signs of a crash or another person, but she was alone and the closer he got the more hysterical she became. She suddenly started flailing wildly.

'Shit,' he muttered, pulling in beside her. She grabbed at the handle, missing it several times before the door finally opened and she could heave herself up onto the passenger seat. Something about her made the hairs on the back of his neck stand up.

He watched her as she sat back in the seat. 'Thanks so much for stopping, sir, thank you,' she said. Her face was flushed and slick with sweat. Her breathing was heavy. She pushed back her hair and tried to smooth it down, catching a wiry strand in one of three tiny gold hoop earrings.

'What happened?' said Joe.

'Some maniac attacked me! I was going for a walk and he just came out of nowhere.' She stared at him with wide eyes. 'I think he was going to rape me,' she added. Joe took in her bulk. The seats of the Jeep were wide, but she was filling hers and almost spilling over. Only a very large man would try to tackle her down. Maybe that's why she'd got away.

'I need to get to a hospital. He stabbed me. With a knife.' She looked amazed. Then a strange flash of anger passed across her face as if she was about to finish with, 'The asshole.'

'Show me,' said Joe, nodding at her arm. She hesitated. 'I'm a police officer,' he said.

She pulled back the sweater wrapped around her arm and he saw a deep slash stretching diagonally across her fleshy forearm. It was a clean

slice, delivered – Joe imagined – with quick down-
ward force as she was raising her arm to deflect
it. He started the engine and turned to her.

'You're gonna be just fine,' he said. 'But I can't
take you to the hospital. I have a meeting—'

'A meeting? You're a policeman!' she said. 'You
can't just—'

'I'm off duty,' he said. 'I'm sorry. What I will
do is leave you at the garda station and the
sergeant in there, Frank Deegan or the guard,
Richie Bates, will take you to the hospital. Tell
them Joe Lucchesi left you off.' He glanced down
at the clock. He was already three minutes late as
he turned onto the main street and pulled up
outside Danaher's.

'It's over there,' he pointed. She didn't get out
of the car. He couldn't ask her to, so he climbed
out and ran around to her side, opening the door
and guiding her gently by her left arm.

'Everything's gonna be OK,' he said, squeezing
her hand. 'I'm sorry about what happened to you.
I'm sorry I have to leave you here.'

'Thank you,' she said. 'You're very . . . kind.'
She looked like she was going to cry. He hopped
back into the Jeep, did a swift U-turn and headed
for the cliff. Four minutes late. Adrenaline surged
through him. His hands started to shake. He
stepped out of the Jeep and looked at the empty
space around him.

* * *

D.I. O'Connor sat at his desk with a row of files open in front of him. Everything he read was irritating him. There were six members in the Drug Squad and it was clear that nothing they had done over the previous year had amounted to anything. He knew this already, but reading it now – in one sitting – for the first time in months made him wonder. Since he had left them, where did it all go wrong?

'Uh-ohhh,' said Duke. 'Who's showed up late for the party?' Joe's heart sank.

The call didn't sound like it was being made outdoors. Joe looked around, but the car park was empty – no cars, no people.

'You can't just—'

'I can do what I like, buddy,' said Duke. 'I'm the one with the little froggie here. She's cute too. Ribbit. Ribbit.'

Joe was at a loss. 'I . . . c'mon, man. I'll give you whatever you want.' He paced up and down in front of the car.

'I wanted you to be here at three-thirty.'

'It's just three-thirty-five.'

'Uh-huh, which is why I'm telling you YOU ARE LATE FOR THE PARTY. You shouldn't have stopped for the girl, you fuckin' sucker.' He hung up.

Joe tried hard to slow his breathing. He focused on the view. From high on the cliff above the harbour he could see just a small part of the village. And the road to Shore's Rock was invisible after the first curve it took out of town. Joe frowned. From where he stood, it was impossible to see the place where he had stopped for the girl. All Rawlins could have seen was Joe's car driving toward Danaher's, but he wouldn't have been able to make out a passenger. Unless Duke had never intended to bring Anna here and was watching him from an entirely different location. Joe jumped into the Jeep and drove out of the village, stopping at intervals along the route he had taken. He ran along the trees that bordered the road, looking for any sign that Duke Rawlins had been there. He didn't want to think that Anna could have been metres away from him all this time. But he couldn't see how. He took the turn into Shore's Rock and drove cautiously up the lane. When he got into the house, he dialled the station.

'Hi, Frank? It's Joe. I was just checking in with you, wondering if that young girl got to the hospital all right.'

Silence.

'Frank?'

'What girl?'

'The one I left outside Danaher's. With the stab wound. I told her to go into you. She, she needed an ambulance. I had to – Jesus, I hope she didn't collapse . . .'

'I don't know what you're talking about, Joe. I've been here all morning, no-one has been in and no-one has collapsed outside Danaher's. I think I'd have heard about it. Are you OK? Joe?'

Joe pictured the girl lying on the pavement bleeding out. Then he imagined Frank standing at the counter in the station thinking he was out of his mind. And then it hit him.

'Gotta go,' said Joe.

He ran to the den, grabbed the Harris' Hawk book, scanned the index, then flipped to the page he was looking for. His finger moved under the words as he read; *'hunt collaboratively'*, *'working in pairs'*, *'observing from a height'*, *'one flushing out, the other attacking'*. He picked up the phone and put another call into Frank.

'Sorry about earlier,' said Joe. 'Total confusion. Just wondering . . . you know your missing girl from Tipperary? She's on your bulletin board? Big girl?'

'Yes,' said Frank. 'Uh, Siobhán Fallon.'

'That's the one. Can you check the photo and give me the distinguishing features bit?'

'Well, we have large mole on left shoulder, pierced navel, three gold hoops in right ear.'

Joe felt a surge of heat to his face. Nausea swept over him. Then anger. Then rage.

He managed to thank Frank and hang up before he asked any questions.

Frank turned to Richie. 'I've just had the strangest phone call. Joe Lucchesi wanting to know the

distinguishing features on that Fallon girl.' He
pointed to the missing person poster. He frowned.
'Can you explain that?'

Shaun came home for lunch and didn't want to
go back to school. He was hoping Anna would be
there but the house was empty and cold. He sat
in the kitchen, too numb to fix something to eat.
He looked up when the doorbell rang. There was
no way he could answer it. He was under orders.
It rang again. Then someone knocked loudly on
the door.

'Mrs Lucchesi?' He spoke in a thick Dublin
accent and was pronouncing the name Le Chessy.
Shaun moved towards the voice, debating what
to do. He could see a man standing at the glass
by the front door. He was waving a clipboard and
pointing at it. Shaun almost laughed. There was
no way this chubby delivery man was anything
other than harmless.

Shaun slid open the door. 'I'm here with your
balloons,' said the man.

Shaun looked shocked.

'Jaysus,' said the man, looking at his clipboard.
'You're not the bloke the surprise is for, are you?'
He read his sheet. 'Oh no, you're not.' He glanced
at Shaun. 'You definitely don't look forty to me.'
He laughed.

'Uh yeah, it's my dad. They're for him.'

'I hope you're not going to look that miserable

when you're giving them to him.' The man laughed and Shaun thought again how strange it was that life for everyone else goes on, no matter what is happening in yours.

'Are these paid for?' he managed to ask.

'Luckily for you they are,' said the man, 'judging by the panic on your face there. Don't worry, your mother covered it.'

'Is she here?' asked Shaun, excited. He craned his neck around the porch to look down the lane.

The man frowned. 'Eh, no. It was by credit card, over the phone.'

'Today?' asked Shaun, his eyes wide.

'No,' said the man. 'Last week.'

'Oh,' said Shaun.

'You must be very close,' said the man, frowning. He nodded to the van. 'Where do you want them?'

Shaun looked around as if he'd find his answer in the trees.

'The lighthouse over there,' he pointed.

The man contemplated the walk. 'Eh, I think you can handle it yourself, bud. There aren't that many.' He went out to the van and grabbed three clear plastic covers, tied in a knot at the bottom, each one covering a bunch of five helium balloons. They were weighted down with a small navy balloon filled with sand. *Happy 40th* was written across them.

'Thanks,' said Shaun.

'Hey?' said the guy as he walked away. 'Cheer up!'

'Your wife lied to me,' said Duke. Joe could hear a loud slap down the phone line. 'So I taught her a lesson.' Slap. 'Your wife tried to tell me she was leaving you, so's I wouldn't hurt little Shaun.' Slap. 'Your wife insulted my intelligence.' A final slap.

Joe's tone plunged ice-cold. 'Enough about *my* wife, Rawlins. Let's talk about *your*s.'

TWENTY-EIGHT

Stinger's Creek, North Central Texas, 1991

'You look mighty pretty,' said Vincent Farraday. 'Let me take your hand.' Wanda Rawlins was wearing a lilac suit with a pencil skirt to her knee, white stockings and white court shoes. She bent low as she stepped out of the car, holding her lilac hat against the breeze.

She looked around at the small clapboard church and the arch of white roses at the entrance.

'It's so beautiful, Vince,' she said, patting the corners of her eyes with a lace handkerchief. 'It's like I'm seeing things I've never seen before.'

'Hush now, little lady,' said Vincent. 'You just enjoy this day. Forget about all the bad stuff.'

'I'll try,' she said.

Reverend Ellis stepped through the arch into the sun, shielding his eyes with a mass booklet. He waved it at Wanda and walked down towards her.

'Wanda Rawlins, it must be two years. Welcome home,' he said, gripping her hand. 'I am so glad to see you looking so well.' His smile was warm and sincere. 'I hope this isn't just a fleeting visit.'

''Fraid so, Reverend. We're livin' in Denison now.'

'This must be the lucky man,' he said, pumping Vince's hand.

'Yessir. Vincent Farraday's my name. Pleasure to make your acquaintance.'

'You're very welcome to Stinger's Creek. Now, please excuse me as I go find the groom.'

Duke sat hunched outside the back of the church, smoking a cigarette.

'Mr Rawlins, how're you doin' on this happy day?'

'Fine thank you, Reverend,' said Duke, standing up. 'My suit's a half-size too small,' he added, touching the tight navy velvet. He noticed flecks of ash on his ruffled shirt front and flicked them into the breeze.

'I'm sure Samantha won't notice,' said the Reverend.

'No-one'll be lookin' at me,' smiled Duke. 'This day is for Sammi.'

Reverend Ellis led Duke through the back door of the church and out onto the altar. Duke inhaled sharply when he saw his mother in the front pew. She gave him a small wave and a nervous smile. He walked over to her.

'Mama,' he said. 'How did you know?'

'Sammi's mama's sister's in my church in Denison . . .'

'You go to church?'

Wanda blushed.

'You live in Denison?' he said.

'This is my husband, Vincent,' said Wanda. 'He helped me through my, you know—'

Duke could see the guilt and fear in her eyes, the brittle smile on her filled-out face and wondered without drugs, how she could live every day knowing what she knew. He smiled and shook Vincent's hand. The man gave him a broad grin.

'Pleasure, son, happy to be here today.'

'Thank you,' said Duke and he took his place at the altar. He checked his watch and looked around. Reverend Ellis walked over to him. 'I'm afraid I just got a call from Donald,' he said. 'He's stuck behind an accident on the interstate. He won't be able to make it. He did say you had the rings, though, and to go ahead without him. He should make it to the reception.'

Duke shook his head. He looked around the church for a replacement. The guests were mainly from Sammi's side of the family. The only person he could ask was Vincent. He gestured him over.

Suddenly, the music started and the double doors at the back of the church opened. Sammi's father walked in with Sammi to his right, her small hand on his forearm. Her brown hair was permed and glossy, falling below her shoulders, swept high in front and held with a clip from her long veil. Her gown sparkled with tiny beads. Her father passed her over to Duke and shook his hand. His smile was tight.

When the service was over, the guests moved across the street to The Railroad Bar, a tongue-in-cheek name in a town that was bypassed by the railroad in the eighteen hundreds and hadn't recovered since.

The dance floor was small and couples pressed against each other to fit on the wooden circle. The women wore tight satin dresses edged in lace and stretched across full stomachs, their high heels tipping them to one side. The men were in narrow-legged suits or dressed-up cowboy shirts and starched denim. They drank beer, chased it with whisky and shouted at the band. Duke stood at the edge of the dance floor watching his new wife swaying her hips to the music, her head back, her eyes closed.

'You OK?' she said as she danced over to him, pinching his cheeks and kissing him on the lips.

'Course I am,' he said. 'I guess I'm just a little sad Uncle Bill isn't here today to see all this.'

'I know, sweetheart. He sounds like he was the nicest man. I wish I coulda met him.'

'I wish you coulda too,' said Duke. 'You know somethin', Sammi, you are the prettiest bride in the whole world. And I promise to be faithful to you for the rest of my life. I know I've made some mistakes, but one thing I know, if someone means somethin' to me as much as you do, loyalty's what I give. I'm sure of that.' His words were beginning to slur.

'Don't you get drunk on me tonight,' she said.

'No, ma'am,' said Duke.

'I want you standin' to attention.' She smiled and raised her eyebrows.

Duke frowned.

'Shut up, Sammi,' he said.

'Not today,' she said. 'Don't speak to me like that today. We had a deal.'

'OK,' he said. 'Just don't go on at me.'

'I won't, long as you don't get drunk. I'll be keepin' an eye on you and Donnie, whenever he shows up.'

Wanda leaned against the sink, her face tilted to the light above the mirror.

'That the kinda powder you're into these days?' came a voice beside her. Wanda said nothing.

'I'm talkin' to you!'

'I'm not interested, Darla,' said Wanda, putting her compact back in her bag.

'Think you're all respectable now in your fancy suit with your big husband?'

'I said I'm not interested,' said Wanda calmly.

'You white trash whore.'

Wanda spun around and grabbed Darla by the hair, pulling her up tall. Then she leaned back and spat in her startled face, watching the saliva drip from her eyelids.

'Don't,' said Wanda, pointing a finger at her. 'This is my son's wedding.' She threw Darla's head back against the door, washed her hands and left the bathroom.

'Like you give a good goddamn,' Darla shouted after her.

Donnie walked into the bar and raised his arms.

'Well, look who it is!' said Duke. 'You missed my big moment!' He smiled wide.

'Congratulations,' said Donnie, shaking Duke's hand and patting his back. 'Did I miss much?'

'Where in the hell did you get to?' hissed Duke, grabbing his elbow, leaning in close to his ear.

'Officially? In back of a line of cars,' said Donnie. 'Unofficially? Had that bit of business to take care of . . . you know, hide and seek in the woods.' He winked. 'Gave an extra little whoosh with the shovel too. Oh, I remember – Tally was her name.'

Duke looked at him like he didn't care.

Sammi came up and tapped him on the shoulder.

'Hey, Donnie,' she said.

'Little Mrs Rawlins,' he said, swinging her around. 'Married at nineteen, pregnant at twenty?'

'Don't even joke about that,' said Sammi, skipping over to her bridesmaids.

'Bring one back for me,' he called after her. She waved back. He went to the bar.

'I had to choose,' said Wanda, coming up behind Duke. 'And it broke my heart.'

Duke turned and stared at her.

'Choose between you and Vincent,' she explained. 'It was the hardest thing a mother's ever had to do. I guess I figured you'd be all growed up and you wouldn't need your mama no more.'

'You're right about that,' said Duke. 'But you're wrong about one thing. You didn't choose Vincent, Mama. All you ever chose was you.'

Donnie grabbed the bridesmaid's waist and swung her around him as he made his way back over to Duke.

'She wanted me,' he said.

'Sure,' said Duke. 'And thanks for lookin' after everythin'. I shouldn't have been mad . . .'

'Hey,' said Donnie. 'Who's that in the blue shirt and the cowboy hat? Ain't that Vincent Farraday, the singer? Who's the lady with him in the purple suit?'

'Pretty fuckin' Woman,' said Duke.

TWENTY-NINE

'Rumour has it that Sammi Rawlins has been having a few jobs done around the house . . .'

Joe let it hang there.

'What do you mean jobs?' said Duke.

'Oh you know, hand jobs, blow jobs . . .'

'If you're tryin' to tell me my wife's a ho, I know you're bullshittin' me.'

'Who said anything about ho? Your wife has been one hundred per cent faithful to one man since you've been in jail. It's just a shame it wasn't you.'

'You're talkin' shit.'

'Aw, I haven't even come to the best part yet,' said Joe. 'Don't you want to know who the guy is? Come on, I'd wanna know, if it was me. Have you seen your wife since you've been out?'

'She's at her mother's . . . look why am I talkin' to you? Why am I listenin' to you and your bullshit?'

'Face it, Rawlins. Your wife's been bending over for another man while you've been in prison, one hand on your—

'Are you fuckin' de-ranged?' Duke suddenly roared. 'You think I believe a single shit-drippin' word out of your mouth? You're a cop! And you're a cop who can shut the fuck up right now. One more word and I'll kill your wife. Are you nuts?'

Joe's heart pounded. All he had succeeded in doing was rattling this psycho off his hinges.

D.I. O'Connor stood in front of the room.

'I'm fed up,' he said. 'For some reason, these dealers are a step ahead of us. We show up, they don't. They don't show up, we do.' He looked around the room and saw a group of bored and tired guards.

'Wake fucking up!' he roared. Some of the men jumped. O'Connor shook his head.

'Jesus Christ, lads! What are you like?' The men shifted in their seats.

'What happens,' said O'Connor, 'when your plan doesn't work? What do people do? Owens?'

'Uh, change the plan?'

'Scrap the whole thing and come up with a new plan,' came a voice from the back.

'Or?' said O'Connor, smiling, 'just don't have a plan.' They looked at him blankly.

'I want you all to think for a minute about surprises. In the next ten minutes I want three places in town that each team is going to go to at some stage today in the hope of catching one of these scumbags at work. No major plan here, just the name of a place and two of you in a car outside it. Butler, you're with Twomey.' There was a clatter of chairs on tiles as the men got up and headed outside to their cars.

As he put down the phone to Duke Rawlins, Joe heard the rumble of voices downstairs.

'Hello? Who's down there?' he said, walking into the hall, leaning into the door of Shaun's bedroom.

He could hear Shaun jogging up the steps. He opened the door a crack.

'Me,' said Shaun, irritated. 'And Ali. Why?'

'I didn't tell you you could bring anyone home.'

'I haven't told her about Mom, if that's what you mean.'

'Send her home now.'

'What is wrong with you?'

'Just get her out of here,' hissed Joe.

Shaun gave a start. 'OK, OK.'

He ran back down the steps. Joe paced up and down the living room. He heard Ali walk through the hall.

'Hey, Mr Lucchesi,' she shouted in.

'Where are you going?' asked Joe.

Shaun stood behind Ali and stared at his dad as if he had lost his mind.

'She's going home?' he said.

'On your own?' said Joe, turning to Ali.

'Yeah,' she said. 'I'm a big girl now.' She smiled.

'Shaun, come here a minute,' said Joe.

'Hold on,' said Shaun, leaving Ali in the hall.

Joe grabbed Shaun's elbow, then felt him jerk hard from his grip. His voice was low and urgent as he handed Shaun the phone. 'You put her on this phone to her father and get him to pick her up right outside that door. And you wait until he does that.'

'What's going on?' said Shaun, panic creeping in to his voice.

'Just do it,' said Joe.

Ali made the call and stuck her head into the living room.

'Frank Deegan was on his way here,' she said. 'So Dad asked him to take me home. He'll be here any minute.'

Joe wanted to explode. The last thing he needed anyone to see outside his house was a garda car.

He stood up quickly. 'I'll give you a ride.'

'No, you're grand,' said Ali. 'I couldn't drag you out of your way. Honest to God, Frank's on his way. I'll be fine.'

'It's not a problem.'

'I want to play her one more track on my CD,' said Shaun, pulling her towards the basement.

Joe sat back down and put his head in his hands. He stayed that way until the doorbell rang.

'Hello, Joe,' said Frank. He handed him a card in a blue envelope. 'I met the postman on the way in.' Joe recognised Danny's writing.

'Could I come in for a chat?' said Frank.

'Uh, not really. I haven't got the time right now. I've got a lot on.' His eyes flicked around, past Frank into the trees.

'You don't really have much of a choice, Joe. It's about the fax you brought to Dr McClatchie.'

Joe felt a wave of anger at the betrayal.

'It's not a problem, the fact that you did that,' said Frank. 'I just need to see it. Dr McClatchie has some concerns.' Joe could see that Frank had a police sketch in his hand and the mug shot of Duke.

'I don't have it. It's in the garbage.'

'Sorry. I think you do. Can I come in?'

'All right,' snapped Joe, hustling Frank into the hall and closing the door quickly behind him.

'I don't have time for this.'

'Neither do I,' said Frank. 'I'm on my way to a meeting in Limerick and I need to see it. I've doubted you before about this Rawlins man. I'm letting you know now that I've changed my mind. I'm going out on a limb, here. I haven't run this by my superiors, because I need to make sure I've everything tied up before I do.'

Joe felt the urge to shake Frank by his shoulders and roar at him, 'It's too little, too late.' He went to the den and got the fax. He folded it up and put it in a brown envelope. He steadied himself on the desk as a sharp pain sliced a path between his temples. He pulled open the desk drawer and saw an empty bottle of Advil. He shut the drawer quickly. Even if there had been twenty tablets in there, he had promised himself that until this was over, he wouldn't take any medication . . . unless the pain was extreme.

He saw Danny's card on the desk and ripped it open in case it was important. It was a print of The Scream by Munch. Joe shook his head and tried to smile. Inside it said, 'Remind you of anyone? Happy fortieth, partner. Have a good one.' Joe wished he could.

'Here,' he said when he came down, handing Frank the fax. 'Put it in your inside pocket now.'

Frank frowned. 'OK,' he said. 'Why?'

'Doesn't matter. Is that everything?'

'No. I need to speak with Anna.'

'Oh. She's in Paris, sorry.'

Frank shook his head. 'Do you have a number where I could contact her?'

'No,' said Joe. 'Her parents don't have a phone.'

'Really? Well, I might as well tell you that she saw this mug shot. She was in the house with Nora the other day. She had a very bad reaction. It was as if—'

Joe's heart pounded. 'I hadn't told her I was checking things out,' he said quickly. 'She was annoyed with me for not telling her. That's why she's gone to Paris.'

'Tell me why you phoned me about Siobhán Fallon,' Frank said suddenly. 'Have you seen her?'

'No. But I thought I might have the other day.'

'Where?'

'In town. But it wasn't her. Frank, I really can't hang around talking.' He pressed his hand to his jaw. Frank turned around and opened the front door.

'I'll send Ali out to you.'

'Right, so. Thanks for the fax, Joe. I appreciate that.' He stepped outside, then looked back. 'What I don't appreciate is being lied to.'

Oran Butler and Keith Twomey sat in their Ford Mondeo in the car park of Tobin's Supermarket. It was a grim, red-brick building in a bad neighbourhood. Two fat butchers in bloodied aprons stood at a corner, gunning cigarettes. A group of long-haired boys in baggy pants and big sweatshirts skateboarded by them along the smooth concrete.

'How long have we been here?' asked Oran, picking toffee out of his teeth. A pile of empty wrappers were gathered between his legs.

'Two hours,' said Keith.

'Have you seen *one* of them actually complete a trick?'

'Nope,' said Keith as they watched another skateboarder try to jump onto a railing. He stumbled down the steps instead, his board smacking onto the tarmac.

'The fucking noise is going through me,' said Keith.

Oran swept the sweet wrappers onto the floor and started on a new pile. Keith glanced down.

'Of all the people to be sharing a place with Richie Bates, it's the messiest fucker around. I don't know which one of you to feel sorrier for.'

Another skateboarder flipped his board halfway over, then landed with his feet on the ground at either side.

The two men looked at each other and shook their heads. When they looked back, a man was walking past the boys towards the entrance. He moved jerkily, like his joints were popping in and out of their sockets with each step. He led with his chin, his narrow mouth downturned, his eyes like slits. He smoothed his greasy red Caesar forward onto his zitty forehead and slowed as he approached the eldest of the boys.

'I don't believe it,' said Keith, sitting up. 'Let's see what happens here. That's Marcus Canney, total scumbag.'

They watched as Canney spoke, then reached into his pocket, pulling something out, extending his arm towards the boy, giving him more than a handshake. Oran and Keith bolted and were on the pair in seconds.

Joe spoke before Duke could – as soon as he hit the green button to answer the call.

'Why are you doing this?'

'You know why,' said Duke.

'OK, yeah, I do. But you've got it all wrong, buddy. I need you to take in some new information, see if you still want to do what you came all this way to do.'

'This is not a dialogue situation.'

'But two people work better for you, Rawlins, don't they?'

'What the fuck are you talkin' about?'

'Two on one makes it a bit easier?'

He could hear Duke's breathing, slow and laboured.

'I notice things,' said Joe. 'I have eyes . . . like a hawk.'

Duke said nothing.

'I know what you were doing today,' said Joe, 'and I pity that girl you've found to shovel your shit. But, then you wouldn't be able to do it on your own . . .' He paused. 'You think you're a man? You're nothing but a piece of shit, a cowardly piece of shit.'

'Fuck you,' said Duke. 'You know nothin'.'

'You're wrong. Here's one thing I know for sure: Mrs Duke Rawlins is with the Stinger's Creek police department right now making some pretty serious allegations against you.'

Duke snorted. 'BullSHIT. Now I KNOW you're talkin' bullshit.'

'You might remember some murders a while

back,' said Joe, slipping into the same patterns of speech as Duke, using the same trick he used with junkies and hookers.

'Turns out,' said Joe, 'your wife's telling whoever's gonna listen that you're the guy they should be looking for. The Crosscut Killer. One guy. Just you. That she covered your ass for too long.'

Duke said nothing.

'Now, why would your wife suddenly want you locked up when you've just gotten out?' said Joe. 'Maybe so's you won't come after her and kill her for banging your friend.' He waited a beat. 'It was Donnie, Duke. Your wife was fucking Donnie.'

Duke laughed loud and hard.

'I've got proof,' said Joe quickly. When Duke didn't stop him, he continued, 'The name Rawlins was familiar to me because your wife was there the day Donnie died. She was a witness at the wrong side of a police cordon. She had to give her name. She was searched. She had a passport. Bet you didn't know your wife had a passport. She was there to help Donnie—'

'What proof?'

'The case file. Her name is on it. I have it here.'

'Show me a look at that,' said Duke.

'Show *me* a look at my wife.'

As soon as he put down the phone, Joe sensed something behind him in the room. He turned his head slowly. Shaun stood, shaken and pale, in the doorway.

Joe stared at him. 'How long . . .'

'How long what? Could you keep lying to me?'

'What did you hear?'

'Where's Mom? Who were you talking to?' He fought back tears.

'I'm taking care of this.'

'What? Who's got her? Who's taken her? Where is she?'

'You don't need to know the details.'

'Did you call the cops?'

Joe waited. 'No.'

'Please tell me you are kidding me,' said Shaun.

'Of course I'm not,' snapped Joe. 'I can't bring the police into this.'

'You're such a hypocrite,' said Shaun, his voice rising. 'What's that rule? If you don't find them in the first twenty-four hours, forty-eight hours, whatever, it's a recovery operation, not a rescue?'

Joe shook his head. 'For Christ's sake, Shaun.'

'You make people call the cops all the time.'

'Maybe that's not always for the best.'

'Yeah, if it's Detective Joe Lucchesi who shows up at your door.'

Joe didn't rise to it.

'I'm sorry, Dad.'

'I know you are.'

A stream of steady tears rolled down Shaun's cheeks.

'I'm tired of crying,' he said. 'I'm so tired. You pick up that phone, Dad. Pick it up. Pick it up!'

He lunged for it. Joe stepped forward, fighting him for it, holding it high in the air, trying to push him away.

Shaun stumbled back, horrified.

'I can't do it,' said Joe. 'I'm sorry. I cannot make that call.'

'How are we going to get her back? What's going to happen to her? Why Mom? What's Mom . . . ?'

Joe waited for what was next.

'Oh my God. This is because of you, isn't it?' said Shaun. 'Someone's taken her and it's because of you. No-one would be interested in a mom, but they'd be interested in a cop's wife, wouldn't they?' He stopped. 'Has this got something to do with Katie?' He grabbed at Joe's arm, jerking it back and forth.

'No, no,' said Joe. 'Please calm down, Shaun. Please. I still have things to find out. For now, we can't let anyone know anything about this, the cops or anyone else. Are you listening to me? It's very important that we say nothing.'

Marcus Canney sat with his knees pulled to his chest on the floor of the cell in Waterford garda station. His legs were skinny in a pair of black nylon track pants and his white trainers were caked in mud. A green bomber jacket hung from his shoulders.

'Mind yourself going into your bedroom,' said O'Connor, walking in to the cell holding a neat white package. Canney looked up at him, frowning.

'There seems to be a hole in your floorboard,' said O'Connor. 'Did you know you had,' he looked at the coke, 'about thirty grand stashed under there?'

Canney paled. 'Go fuck yourself,' he said.

'I'm too busy fucking you,' said O'Connor.

'I've never seen that before in my life.'

O'Connor rolled his eyes. 'Just tell me where you're getting it. And why you weren't sitting in here twelve months ago.'

Canney flashed him a look.

'Yeah, I know,' said O'Connor. 'That there's a very good reason why we haven't caught up with you until now. So that's what we'll be waiting for here this morning.'

Duke turned to Anna and laughed. 'Your husband thinks I'm some kinda retard.' He punched his home number into Anna's mobile. It clicked straight onto the machine and he was about to leave a message when he realised he was listening to a voice he didn't know. 'This number is no longer in service. Please contact . . .' Duke hung up, checked the number and dialled again. He got the same message. He patted his jacket pockets, then his jeans pockets. Then he looked around the room, settling on Anna.

'Now, where did I put my knife?'

* * *

Victor Nicotero walked up the path through the late Police Chief Ogden Parnum's tidy garden, shrugging his shoulders so his suit jacket would hang just right. An empty folder was lodged under his left arm, his free hand aimed for the doorbell. Before he could touch it, the door swung open and a striking blonde in her late forties stood before him.

'Who are you?'

'Delroy Finch,' he said, 'FOP, Fraternal Order of Police.'

'Oh,' she said, her eyes downcast. 'Come in, Mr Finch.'

'Thank you, ma'am.'

She led him into an old-fashioned living room, gestured to the sofa, then sat opposite him on a high-backed wicker chair.

'First of all, Mrs Parnum, I would like to express my condolences on the loss of your husband.'

'He wasn't lost, Mr Finch. He shot himself in the head with a high calibre rifle. There's no need to spare me from horrors I already know.'

'I apologise,' said Victor. 'Let me get straight to the point, here. The reason for my visit is to ask you in what way you would like the Fraternal Order of Police to commemorate your husband, Mrs Parnum. We can offer you a memorial plaque . . .'

'Allow me to stop you there, Mr Finch. My husband was a son of a bitch. He has left me quite a few reminders of his existence as it is and each and every one of them is a bad memory. I appreciate what you're trying to do and I know your organisation does fine work, but some of its finest work could be done by forgetting that Chief of Police Ogden Parnum ever existed.'

'Ma'am, again, I apologise if I've dredged up anything painful for you, but—'

'No, you absolutely have not, Mr Finch. You are not the guilty party here.'

'Tell me, Mrs Parnum. Why do you think your husband committed suicide?'

'Because he was miserable. Because he was depressed. Because he hated himself. Because his life was unbearable. Why does anyone commit suicide?'

Victor waited.

'There I go again,' said Mrs Parnum. 'Can't help myself.' She gave a short, nervous laugh. 'Specifically, I don't know why he committed suicide. He didn't leave a note if that's what you mean, but—' She stopped, then looked up abruptly. 'Why do you want to know?'

'It happens with the job sometimes and I'm always interested, you know, what can be done to stop it happening again, to save someone else.' He was groping. 'Sorry, what were you about to say? You said "but"?'

'But . . . that morning, a woman called to our house to speak with Ogden. I had never seen her before in my life. She was blonde, late thirties, tailored suit. And the strangest expression passed over her face when she saw me.' She paused. 'I guess it could best be described as pity.'

'Pity?'

'Well, that was the thing. Why would this stranger pity me? Hell, to the people who know me, I have a charmed life. But it was like this woman showed up on my doorstep and saw right through my soul.'

Victor nodded slowly.

'Ogden's face when he saw her. It turns out it was Marcy Winbaum, the DA. I hadn't recognised her. She used to work with Ogden years ago. She's changed a lot since then. And she definitely had a bee in her bonnet that day. Anyhow, she insisted on speaking to Ogden in private. He brought her out back to his study. Well, I was curious, so I put my ear to the door after they were in there quite a while and this woman's voice was raised, which kinda struck me as unusual. I heard her saying something about "burying" things and "live with yourself". She said she had found someone who would swear something in a court of law and that he had two choices. Then the timer went on my cooker and I had to go back into the kitchen to take out a pie.'

'Did you ask your husband afterwards what it was all about?'

'I didn't like to ask. And it seemed apparent to

me the next night that he'd created a third choice
for himself and that was to blow his brains out.'

'Can I ask you? Your husband worked on the
Crosscut case. Those murders remained unsolved
up until his death. Do you think that may have
affected him—'

'Those poor girls. Ogden took it real bad. But
it was quite some time ago.' She frowned. 'Isn't
your organisation supposed to gloss over the fail-
ings of a dead cop?' Victor frowned, then remembered his role.

'I guess I was asking out of personal curiosity,'
he said. 'Are you sure there isn't anything we could
do for you to commemorate your husband's life?'

'Let me tell you about Ogden Parnum,' she said,
suddenly. 'I would see scratches on his back, tiny
little scratches and little crescent moons from
hungry nails. And on his face. I would catch
glimpses of them, only glimpses, because I was
never in a position to do otherwise. And look at
me.' Her hand traced the curves to her slender hips.

'I am not a woman content to let herself go.'
She stopped. 'And what I don't understand is that
there is nothing I would not have done for him,
if you get my meaning. I've been around the block,
Mr Finch. He wasn't marrying a sweet and innocent young thing.' She looked up. 'What was
wrong with me?' she said, tears suddenly flowing
from her eyes. 'What was wrong with me?'

*   *   *

Marcus Canney bit and picked at his filthy nails.

'This isn't a rap on the knuckles in the District Court,' said O'Connor, pointing at him. 'You'll be standing in your cheap little shiny suit with your hair all flat like your mammy does it, that thick look on your face . . . and it won't matter a damn. Because it'll be Delaney.' He smiled. 'The judge with the grudge. And you'll be pissing in the wind.'

Canney twitched.

'I'll get no pleasure sending you down,' said O'Connor. 'But your suppliers . . .'

Silence.

'Come on, Canney. You're not playing Cowboys and Indians now. This is big time and you'll go down for five to seven. You're on your own then.'

Canney twitched.

'And where will the big players be? Busy training in the new guy. They might do a better job this time, though. And after that, they'll be wondering what's the best way to get you off the scene. Will they take care of it inside or will they wait 'til you're free and easy and thinking your whole life is ahead of you?'

Canney stared straight ahead.

'Look,' said O'Connor. 'You can walk out of here and they'll never have to know a thing. I can promise you that.'

'Yeah, right.'

'You're in it up to your neck, Canney. I don't know what other way I can say it to you. But you have a way out. We'll forget all about this. Off you go. No-one's any the wiser. And we're all happy.'

'There's no fucking way I'm going to fall for that.'

'Why do you think I'm sitting here and not in an interview room with the tapes rolling?'

Canney stared past him, frowning. 'Yeah, well . . .'

'Well, what? Tell me. Who's supplying you?'

'Look, I'm saying nothing. Are you fucking stupid?'

'Your call,' said O'Connor, standing up. 'I've done what I can. See you in the interview room.' He walked towards the door. 'Seven years, though. Even five. That's the absolute minimum with this guy. I don't think that's registering,' he said, tapping his forehead. He held the door handle longer than he needed to.

Canney finally spoke. 'What if I knew something about that Mountcannon girl that was murdered?'

O'Connor spun around. Canney was smiling, nodding his head slowly.

'You're the lowest of the low, Canney . . .'

'What if I'm serious?'

O'Connor turned back towards the door, shaking his head.

Canney shrugged. 'What if I was one of the last people to see her alive?'

* * *

Old Nic went into the Stinger's Creek diner and swapped twenty dollars for a handful of coins. He went outside to a payphone and dialled Joe's number.

'I can't talk right now,' said Joe quickly.

'Yeah, but you can listen. And I mean it. I know you called off my trip, but here I am, North Central Texas. My bells told me to come. I spoke to the widow and let me tell you, Mrs Parnum is one foxy lady. But she's a bitter one. Hated the husband, seems he was cheating on her, blah, blah—'

'Did she say anything about why he killed himself? Or anything about the case?'

'Just that he took it real bad. As to why her husband killed himself, she could care less, rattled off the standard reasons. Ice cold. But I think we have a very big reason why. You know who you might want to talk to? The last person who paid a visit to Ogden Parnum before he played Russian Roulette with a full chamber. Marcy Winbaum, the DA, used to work under Parnum, went back to college, yada yada, now she's ordered the case reopened in the "someone has stepped forward with new information" kinda way. No-one has told Dorothy Parnum yet, because it seems her late husband is – or was – in very deep shit. Marcy Winbaum's keeping her cards close to her chest, but rumour has it that's because she's about to throw down a killer hand.'

* * *

Anna had watched Duke Rawlins search the cottage and from a damp and filthy corner pull the sack that now covered her head. With every breath she took, the rank odour of wet cats and spoiled milk filled her nostrils. She had retched through the entire journey, curled helplessly on the cramped floor of the van. Now she was outside again, dimly aware of a freshness fighting through the stench.

'OK, here,' whispered Duke, jerking on her arm. Anna stopped. But she could hear the heaviest set of footsteps continue on ahead.

'Sheba,' hissed Duke. 'Sheba, back here, you fat—'

Siobhán Fallon spun around, her face unable to hide her hurt. She walked slowly back toward him as he tied Anna's legs at the ankles.

'Please stop calling me Sheba,' said Siobhán quietly. 'It's not that hard to say. Shiv-awn. It's easy.'

'Let me see,' said Duke. 'Sh . . . Sh . . . She. Bah. Right?' His smile was fixed.

'Why are you . . . what did I do?' She reached a hand to his cheek. He stopped it halfway, squeezing her wrist too tight.

'Oh, you did good work,' he said. 'You did. Think of your best burger order with fries on the side and a milkshake and a hold-the-mayo and a hold-the-pickle and an extra barbecue sauce, all written down in your little notebook, spelled right, times ten.'

She smiled nervously. Her pulse pumped under his grip. She tried to pull away. He moved closer.

'Take that big ol' sweater of yours off,' he said.

'Why?' she said, her voice catching.

'Because I have this.' He let go of her wrist and pulled a curved blade from his back pocket and held it up to her face. She froze. Duke stared through her. She slowly pulled her arm from the right sleeve, keeping her elbow close to her body. She did the same with her left arm until the sweater hung around her neck. The sleeves fell loose, barely covering her faded grey cotton bra. Goosebumps rose on her pale skin. She started to shiver. Duke leaned over and untied the rope around Anna's neck, lifting the hood free. Anna turned her head away. Duke grabbed her face, forcing her to look.

'You don't wanna miss this,' he said. He raised the knife to his mouth, biting down on the handle to keep his hands free.

'Now, let me see if I remember how to do this,' he said, reaching around Siobhán's back and unhooking her bra. Her broad, flat breasts fell to the rolls of flesh at her waist. A look of disgust flashed across Duke's face. Suddenly, Siobhán thrust out her hand, grabbing the handle of the knife, pulling it towards her sharply so the blade sliced through the side of Duke's mouth. She turned to run, but he was on her, quickly throwing her down, pinning her arms above her head.

'Son of a bitch,' he hissed, spitting onto the grass beside her. Then he held his face over hers, letting long, slow drops of blood fall onto her lips and run gently down her cheeks with her tears.

'Stand up. Get up! And take off your jeans—'

'Leave her alone,' spat Anna. 'Leave her.' Duke grabbed her face and shook it with a force that silenced her.

He turned back to Siobhán. 'Take them off, everything. You've seen what this knife can do,' he smiled, raising a hand to the gash in his face.

She did as he asked, desperately trying to cover her body with her hands. Anna's stomach was heaving. She hoped Siobhán would catch her eye and maybe she could let her know that everything would be OK, that she would never tell anyone what she had to go through. Then when she saw what Duke pulled out of his bag, she knew the girl was going to die. And nothing would matter.

'Don't look back, now.'

Siobhán got up, but she instinctively turned around. And screamed when she saw the bow.

'Run, rabbit, run!' he yelled, raising the bow to his shoulder. Siobhán ran from him, stumbling through the low gorse, her bare feet twisting over sharp rocks. She made it thirty metres when the first arrow hit.

Joe picked up the phone to Marcy Winbaum, the first person he had to tell the truth to since Anna had been taken. She spoke with the confidence of a woman who had worked hard to get where she was. Every word she said quickened his heart beat, weakened his body, but strengthened his resolve. He had never experienced this before – a raw panic that coursed through him, starting in his chest, moving downwards, throbbing simultaneously in his head. He tried hard to slow his breathing. Flashes of the fax came into his mind, the victims discarded like broken dolls. The images were replaced with the mug shot of Duke Rawlins, the dead body of Donald Riggs. And then Anna. Joe felt something rip inside. He had led his wife into the path of this maniac. His only hope was that now, he had a bargaining chip.

Victor Nicotero walked away from the phone booth, thinking about Dorothy Parnum, thinking about how people can be so strong, yet so weak at the same time. He liked that. He pulled out his phony FOP folder to write that down for his memoirs. He reached into his inside jacket pocket for his retirement pen. It wasn't there. He checked his folder. He patted his other pockets.

'Goddammit,' he said and turned around.

Duke knelt by the body of Siobhán Fallon, working on it with the curved blade. Anna, free from the bindings on her ankles, but bound to a narrow tree trunk, jerked forward and vomited between her legs. With the force, she felt the slightest slip of the knot that tied her wrists.

'Keep watchin',' Duke said to her, 'or I'll make you do something you might regret.' Anna looked up at him through watery eyes.

'Don't blame yourself,' said Duke. 'This is on account of you *and* your husband. Blame the both of you while you're at it.' He smiled and completed each step of his ritual, all the while looking back over his shoulder to Anna whose beautiful horrified face sent pleasant shivers down his spine. When he turned away again, she ran.

Frank Deegan fanned out the pages of the fax on the passenger seat, thinking he could glance at them on the drive. By the second page, he had to pull over. He studied the photos and read the detached descriptions of young skin and bones and hair and limbs and the hideous wounds that defiled them all. He never understood how men would want to shatter these delicate creatures.

He looked again at the photos. He could connect the dots between the American victims' injuries and those suffered by Mary Casey in Doon. But there was an extra dot, that bit further out that he couldn't quite draw a line to – Joe Lucchesi. Then another dot right beside it – the small, delicate Anna.

Dorothy Parnum was dabbing the corner of her eyes with a balled-up handkerchief when she answered the door. Her mascara had run and her frosted lipstick had disappeared, leaving an ugly pink trail of lip liner around her mouth.

'I forgot my pen,' he said, but she was already holding it out to him.

'Thanks,' he said.

'Thank you,' she said. 'I apologise for my behaviour earlier. I don't know why I was telling you all that.' Fresh tears welled in her eyes. 'But you look like the kindest man a grieving widow could hope to meet.' She squeezed his arm, but it only made her cry harder. Finally, she took in a deep breath and tried to smile.

'No more boo-hoos,' she said. 'That's what Ogden used to say to me. No more boo-hoos . . . but there were always more.'

THIRTY

Stinger's Creek, North Central Texas, 1992

Ogden Parnum closed the plastic folder and watched a hand print of sweat shrink and dry on the surface. He stared at the space between two photos on the wall ahead of him, then hung his head until his neck strained and blood pulsed at his temples. He ran trembling fingers over and over through his thin hair. Then he hit the intercom.

'Marcy, I think we need to call someone to the station. Come in to my office.'

'Sure, Chief.' Ogden Parnum had worked with five deputies over the years, but none was as bright and efficient as Marcy Winbaum. He knew now that she was the last person he needed on this case. And the suspect he was forced to call in was the last person he wanted to see.

'Isn't it exciting?' she smiled, pointing at the lab report.

'Take it easy there, Marcy. I think it's all a bit premature and there could be a whole 'nother explanation.'

'Well, I've got something else I'm excited about, if you're willing to listen, boss. I've been going through the rest of the Crosscut Killer file. And uh, then I cross-referenced it with the Janet Bell file, the body found in '88, the prostitute also went by the name of Alexis? I think she's one of them, sir.'

'She's a gunshot wound, Marcy.'

'OK, bear with me on this one, bear with me. The body of Mimi Bartillo shows up the same year, our "first victim", puncture wounds to the kidneys, six slashes to the ribs. The body is left out for us to find. Then eight months later, the body of Janet Bell, buried, badly decomposed, an *apparent* gunshot wound to the kidney. But, look at this.' She pointed to one of the crime scene photos. 'On her satin skirt. If you look closely, you can see a triangular tear in the fabric.' She looked at him. His face was blank. 'What if it wasn't a gunshot wound, but a wound from another weapon, an arrow? A three-blade arrow. Triangular. I've checked with the M.E. and he thinks it's a definite possibility. When a body has been hit by a projectile at high speed, a wound opens up and lets us know what happened – we can tell a stab wound from a gunshot wound, because of the type of damage done. But if the body decomposes over a time, well, it's harder to tell, it gets kind of . . . mushy or whatever.' She blushed. 'I guess the, uh, flesh around the wound would be . . . compromised.' She nodded. 'The triangle on the clothing here is the key.' She paused. 'I think Janet Bell was the first victim, sir. She was buried, but then the killer kinda liked the idea of leaving the bodies out, so that's what he started to do.'

'But Bell wasn't shot in the leg, so how's that her skirt would be cut?'

'OK. Imagine that I'm running in a satin skirt. Chances are the wind would catch it and it would blow up. Remember Marilyn Monroe over the vent? Well, what if Ms Bell was running away from her killer, the skirt blew up and whoosh, the arrow goes through the fabric, penetrating her back?'

'Jeez, Marcy,' said Parnum. 'That's a bit of a leap, don't you think?'

'I know you hate me interfering and all, but I really think I'm on to something here. So far, our guy has killed Mimi Bartillo, '88, Cynthia Sloane, '89, Tonya Ramer, '90, Tally Sanders, '91 and now our Jane Doe. And, I think Janet Bell, '87. That's six women, boss. And if the evidence today—'

'But didn't you think Rachel Wade, that barmaid, didn't you think she was one of the Crosscut Killer's too, when Bill Rawlins was locked up for that?' As soon as he mentioned the case, everything he had been working on over the last four years crystallised into one depressing reality.

He managed to keep talking. 'You're new to this, Marcy. Stay focused, all right? Let's not jump the gun.'

Her smile faded and as soon as she took the details from him, she walked out, back to the file open on her desk and the yellow pad beside it. Parnum followed her, flipped the file closed and pushed it under his arm.

The interview room of the Stinger's Creek Police Department was small and windowless. Light came from a dim bulb that hung loosely from the ceiling, barely covered by a dusty green lampshade. It cast grim shadows.

'Will you wait here to speak with the Chief?' said Marcy.

'I *will* speak to the Chief, ma'am, yes I will. But I'd like to speak to him alone.' Duke Rawlins sprawled himself on a metal chair with his back to the door, spreading his legs wide, tilting his pelvis upwards. Marcy Winbaum turned and left. Parnum stood in the doorway and stared at the man sitting in front of him. Beads of sweat sprang up across his brow. He wiped them away with a handkerchief pulled from his pants pocket.

'Remember me?' Duke turned around and leaned an elbow over the back of the chair. Parnum shut the door behind him, then pushed against it until he heard a click.

Duke raised his eyebrows and smiled. 'What am I again? Your little bitch, your little faggot, your baby boy, your tight-ass whore, your, oh yeah, your, oh yeah, your buckin' bronco?'

'I got a report from the lab an hour ago,' said Parnum, dropping his voice to a hiss, 'to say they've matched the paint on our Jane Doe's shoe to a Dodge Ram pickup. And Jesus Christ Almighty there's only one that I know of round here and it's sitting in your yard.'

Duke looked at him calmly.

Parnum slammed his fist onto the table. 'Don't you get it? Other people know. Marcy, the lab . . . we've found evidence!'

'Well, here's the thing,' said Duke, leaning on his palms, pushing himself close, 'you can damn well UNfuckingfind it.'

Parnum recoiled. 'Are you out of your mind? I can't, I . . .'

'Now let me think. What about Mrs Police Chief and the baby Chiefs? They like to know your secret? What about Reverend Ellis? What about the amazing grace of the First Baptist Church Choir?'

Parnum remained silent. Eventually he spoke. 'I'll see what I can do.'

'No – you'll DO what you can do.'

'You've murdered five women.'

'D'ya think?'

Parnum swallowed.

'Oh, don't you judge me – don't you dare judge me, you motherfuckin' son of a bitch.'

Waves of nausea swept over Parnum. He gripped the table edge.

'You were there Friday night—'

'If I was *there* Friday night, Chief, how could I have gone all-in against your poker of sevens?'

'I wouldn't play poker with a—'

'You wouldn't play *poker* with me?' He snorted. 'Anyway, wasn't just me. Donnie Riggs was there too. We wouldn't have had any beer if it wasn't for Donnie.'

'Sweet Jesus. Donnie Riggs. We never—'

'I guess your life's about flashin' before your eyes right now, big boy.'

'You sick son of a bitch.'

'Me?' Duke laughed loud.

'I know about Rachel Wade,' said Parnum. 'You let your uncle go to jail . . .'

Duke's eyes narrowed. 'What? Do I look like a judge to you? Do I look like twelve angry men to you? Or,' he stopped, 'maybe I look like the fat fuckin' donut boys who worked the case. You got the wrong guy. And then, all I could do was support him. I went to that trial every day—'

'Sat there and listened to the details of your—'

'Watch your mouth now. You watch what you're sayin' there. Wouldn't want to make any accusations you can't back up, now, would you?'

'Bill Rawlins was a good man,' said Parnum.

'Never said he wasn't.'

'His handkerchief was found in that girl's mouth . . .'

Parnum shook his head. 'You let him die.'

'I will say to you again. I let nothing happen. I wasn't there in that prison cell when he clutched his heart and fell to the floor. If I was, I would have been pumpin' his chest a lot quicker than the retards who found him.'

'You are one—'

'Shh, shh, shh, now.'

The room was silent. Outside, Marcy Winbaum banged a drawer shut. The phone rang.

The air conditioning hummed.

Duke spoke. 'Do you think you're a good man, Chief? Do you?'

'Uh, I, uh . . .'

'DO you?' boomed Duke. 'Do you?'

'Yes.'

'You know, I knew that. I knew that's what you thought. Which makes this all the more pleasurable.' Duke thrust his crotch out and grabbed it with his hand. 'This way, it's win-win for me. I get to keep on keepin' on. I get the goddamn purity of the pleasure that that brings. And for my bonus round, I know that every night when you lie in bed you will be thinkin' about me. And this time, you won't be gettin' no woody in your shorts. You'll be gettin' the cold sweat of fear soakin' into your sheets.'

Parnum was rigid. Duke eased himself up and bent low into his ashen face. He leaned in and kissed him hard on the cheek, trailing his tongue down his jaw. Parnum shuddered.

'My ass may have been yours at one time, Parnum . . . but now your ass is well and truly mine.' He kicked back his chair and walked out of the room.

'Nothin' to see here,' he said to the deputy as he stepped into the cool night air.

THIRTY-ONE

D.I. O'Connor wrenched open the door to the interview room and charged down the corridor. He grabbed the phone from the front desk and punched in the number for Mountcannon station. He was instantly diverted back to his own switchboard. He ran for his car. The siren rang out through the city as he sped onto the road to the small village.

Joe was bent over the drawer in the kitchen, dragging his hands frantically through blister packs and bottles of medicine that would do nothing to stop the pain building all over his skull. He filled a glass of water and tried to drink, but the cold ripped through his teeth and made his head spin. His mind ran through images like slides from a projector, flashing white corpses and black blood. He tried desperately not to imagine Anna among them, injured or dead or . . . he couldn't consider what else Duke Rawlins was capable of. Somewhere inside him, a shutter descended to preserve his sanity. He willed himself to think of every beautiful image he had of Anna – walking down the aisle, holding Shaun on her hip, painting their new apartment, standing in the hallway with her tousled hair when he was going to sleep in the spare room.

He wiped away tears and concentrated on the man he knew he would be forced to face. Duke Rawlins had gone to jail for a minor stabbing, but had got away with his vilest crimes. He had managed to get an alibi from a Police Chief that lasted him over ten years. Joe knew he was unlikely to ever find out why. What mattered now was that he had been sucked into the world of a psychopath. His actions on a sunny day in a New York park had brought this killer to his family and to the village they loved. Joe decided he deserved the pain he was feeling.

His one consolation was that he had already struck what he hoped was the final blow to Rawlins' plan. He had stripped it of its reason for being. He had told him that his wife and his best friend had betrayed him. Then he realised, with a desperate surge of panic, that he had just created a situation where Duke Rawlins had nothing to lose.

The phone rang.

'There is somebody waitin' for you at the end

of your garden,' said Duke. 'And I mean . . . Some. Body.'

Joe's stomach spasmed. He ran, grabbing a torch and sprinting from the house into the dusk. He slipped on the damp grass, breaking his fall with his hand, pushing himself up again and running until he came close enough to see the figure lying face down by a tangle of wild bushes. He moved the beam slowly across the grass towards it. His breath caught, then slipped out as a small, guilty sigh of relief. Siobhán Fallon had been trying to run away when two arrows from behind had pierced her flesh. Blood pooled out from under her, showing up black against the grass. Joe recognised the slash on her arm. He remembered the way she had looked at it, surprise replaced by anger. Now he understood. It was the first wound from a man who had promised her the world to join his game, then taken it all back when her part was played.

The phone rang in Joe's pocket. He pulled it out. After a silence that stretched for several seconds, Joe realised Duke was struggling to breathe he was laughing so hard.

'Aw, man!' he said, chuckling. 'Aw, man.' Then his voice dropped to a growl. 'Happy now? It's just you and me – one on one.'

Joe closed his eyes and spoke slowly through a mouth he could barely open.

'In some dark corner of your mind, you think

what you do is noble, that what you do when you hunt down and rape and murder is noble. You have your technique, your games, your bullshit. But when you strip away the technique, Rawlins, what's left? Vengeance. Plain old vengeance. A low motivation that makes you no different to the next pathetic piece of shit and the next and the next.'

'And if you got the chance,' said Duke, 'you wouldn't put a bullet through my heart for what I'm about to do?'

'What do you mean what you're about to do?' Then Joe pulled the phone away from his ear and shouted into it. 'You know what? I'm not playing anymore, you cowardly, fucked-up son of a bitch!' He threw the phone across the grass. His vocal cords were raw. Pain erupted across his face. He buried his head in his hands. Then he realised Duke Rawlins wouldn't be getting any pleasure from all this if he wasn't watching. So he stopped and looked around, focusing on the best vantage point he could see.

'Don't you want the file?' he roared into the dark. 'I've got the file.'

Suddenly a thick beam of light swept across him and out to sea.

'Ah, for God's sake,' said O'Connor, leaning to his left, trying to watch the road and punch Frank's number into the new mobile phone mounted by his radio. The tiny joystick in the centre was lost under his finger. 'You fiddley little shit,' he said, pulling into the side of the road. He took the phone in his hand and scrolled to Frank's number. He dialled and got his message minder.

'Where are you, you dozy . . .' He instantly felt bad. He liked Frank. But right now, he wanted to slap him, even though this was something everyone had missed. O'Connor swerved back onto the road and put his foot to the floor. What happened to Katie was so wrong. A wave of sadness swept over him as he thought of a girl he knew only from a photograph. With D.I. Myles O'Connor at the helm, they had all let her down. His name would always be associated with a travesty of an investigation. All he could do now was get there in time to bring it to the only close that would do Katie Lawson justice.

Richie Bates had parked the squad car carefully behind a row of bushes outside Shore's Rock. He was transfixed by Joe Lucchesi, cast in an eerie light from an upturned torch on his lawn, slamming something into the air and roaring. He saw him run for the lighthouse.

O'Connor screeched to a stop outside the station within an inch of the wall. He jumped out and ran for the door, about to slam the heel of his hand into the intercom. He stopped, took a deep

breath and pressed the button gently. He waited.
He rang again. He shouted for Frank. There was
no answer.

Anna was slipping in and out of consciousness,
slumped forward, folded over the rope that bound
her to the ladder, weak with the pressure that cut
through her stomach. Her knees had buckled, her
feet desperate to take the weight. Bound by thin
strips of wire, her wrists were curled tight behind
her. A thick piece of tape stretched across her
mouth.

'Jesus Christ!' said Joe, his voice cracking. Her
eyes were closed, her body limp. He slipped the
file into his jacket and pulled the tape from her
mouth. He reached around the back of the ladder
and pulled at the bloody rope. It quickly slipped
free and hung in loose folds around her thighs.
He tried to pull her close but his hand slid across
her lower back with a sensation that turned his
stomach. He drew his hand up slowly and, over
her shoulder, saw his hand and forearm dripping
with blood. He looked down. Her sweatshirt and
the top of her jeans were soaked.

Suddenly, he heard footsteps, then a roar
behind him. 'Mom! Mom!'

He spun around. Shaun stood and stared at his
parents, shocked into silence.

'I told you to stay in the house,' Joe yelled over
the noise. Upstairs, the wind howled around the

lantern house, slamming the door loudly back and forth.

Joe shouted at him, 'Close the door up there.'

Joe tried to ease Anna onto the floor in the tiny space and had to kick the loose rope out from under her . . . rope that had come free with the smallest of efforts. A chill swept over him with a buried memory. Too. Easy. Anna spasmed against him and she was awake. She shook her head violently from side to side. Her eyes were screaming.

Shaun pushed the door closed against the force of the wind. It smashed back against him, knocking him to the ground.

Joe looked up towards the noise and saw Duke Rawlins through the trap door, his face tight against Shaun's, the dried blood of his knife wound flaking onto the boy's skin.

'You just don't fuckin' learn, do you?' said Duke. 'Things just don't fall into your lap, detective.' He grabbed Shaun harder, jerking him back, pushing a curved blade against his throat.

'Oh,' he said, reaching down to Joe, handing him a string. Joe took it and looked up to see a silver helium balloon floating at the other end. Duke smiled. 'Happy birthday.'

As Frank Deegan drove away from the mountains, his mobile beeped back to life. It stayed in coverage long enough to tell him Myles O'Connor had tried him seven times. But not long enough that he could do anything about it.

Richie closed the car door gently behind him and stepped across the ditch and through a gap in the hedge. He crouched low and moved towards the lighthouse and the shadows dancing high in the tower.

'She tried to help that fat bitch,' said Duke, nodding towards Anna, her tiny body slumped against the wall. 'Sheba.'

'Siobhán,' muttered Anna. 'Her name was Siobhán.'

Duke snorted and made a face like he didn't care. He nodded at Anna again. 'She even got away from me . . . but just for a little while.' He smiled.

The lighthouse lens rotated above them, sending out a sound like a giant blowtorch. Joe looked at the brass vents that ran around the room at floor level and at six feet. He knew from Anna that either the north- or south-facing vents should have been open, depending on the direction of the wind. But they were closed and there was no way to suck out the fumes from the kerosene that were filling the cramped space.

'OK. This won't take long,' said Duke. 'It'll be one of those quick decisions, you know, like whether or not to shoot an unarmed man, for example. Yup, I know he was unarmed, detective, because all poor Donnie was holding was the pin. And that was for a reason. He was keeping that close to him for a reason that you will never understand. Loyalty . . .' He closed his eyes.

'A loyal man wouldn't sleep with your wife, Rawlins.'

'Well, that's just the thing.'

'The file,' said Joe, pulling it out, staining the cover with Anna's blood. 'It's here. Her name is in this. She was in New York the same day in the same park. Can you explain that? She has admitted to the Grayson County D.A. that Donald Riggs was getting that ransom money for them, not for you – for her and Riggs so that they could be as far enough away from you as possible when you became a free man.

'Donnie wanted to die holdin' that pin—'

'No, he did not,' said Joe calmly, setting the file gently on the floor between them. 'He wanted to throw it away.' He nodded down at the stack of photos, witness statements, autopsy findings, court reports, all held in their light cardboard folder. Duke flashed a glance at it, but he was shaking his head.

'No,' he said. 'No.'

They stood in silence like that for some time, Duke swaying gently as he stared into space. Joe held his breath as he watched him, unnerved by thoughts of what could explode out of the growing calm.

'You can leave now,' he said. 'You won't be caught. You won't have to spend the rest of your life in jail for all those murders.'

'What murders?' said Duke, shrugging. Then something snapped in him again and when he spoke, his voice was ice.

'Look, I'm not wastin' my time here, detective. I'm givin' you a chance. Real quick.' He clicked his fingers. 'You gotta be quick.'

Richie Bates could see now that Duke Rawlins had arrived . . . and had brought with him an opportunity that could change everything.

Shaun stood on the three-inch ledge that ran outside the railing to the balcony. Duke's arm was gripped around his chest.

'Shaun, hold tight,' shouted Joe through the noise of the lens above him and the wind rushing in from the balcony. The pain seared through his jaw and he jerked his hand to his right cheek reflexively.

'Somethin' hurtin' you?' said Duke, a smile breaking out across his face. He took a step towards him. Shaun rocked back and forth.

Joe's breath caught. He tried to shake his head.

'Somethin' like this?' said Duke, smashing his fist against Joe's fingers, driving the pressure deep into his skull. A sharp spasm tore through Joe's stomach. He doubled over. Water streamed from his eyes.

'Now, shut your mouth,' said Duke. He pulled out a mobile phone with his free hand and punched in a number with his thumb. He held it up for Joe to see: 999.

'I think your wife could use an ambulance,' said Duke. Joe turned around and looked at Anna. She was in a pool of blood, her face grey, her eyes closed.

'So here's your choice,' said Duke. 'I drop the phone or I drop your son. Which is it?'

Joe was rooted to the floor. He looked around the room for something, anything that could help his decision or help him kill the man standing in front of him. His eyes fell on the file again.

'Please,' he said. Blood seeped from the corner of his mouth.

Duke stepped forward, but instead of bending down, he kicked the file open with the toe of his boot. Then he kicked again and the wind caught the sheets and blew them into the air.

'No,' said Duke, kicking again. 'One more time: I drop the phone or I drop your son. Which is it?'

Joe looked again at Anna. For just a second, her eyes flickered open. She shook her head, a tiny movement that took all her energy. Joe stepped towards her.

'Get the fuck away from her,' said Duke as he hit SEND on the phone. 'Ambulance, ma'am,' he said. He locked eyes with Joe. 'OK. Time up, detective. Which do I drop – the phone or the boy?'

He stretched his arm out, the phone hovering over the balcony.

'The phone,' Joe said quietly.

'Can't hear you,' said Duke. 'What's that you said?'

'No, Dad, no!' roared Shaun. 'No!' He bucked against the railings.

'What'll it be, detective?'

'The phone,' roared Joe. 'Drop the fucking phone, you sick son of a bitch.'

'Ambulance, hello, can I help you?' The voice was tinny and distant as Duke leaned over the balcony and let the phone fall thirty feet onto the ground below, shattering on impact.

Shaun cried out as Duke released his grip on his chest, then jerked him back quickly towards him at the last second.

'Oh, I've cut the line from your house too,' said Duke. He spoke to Shaun, 'Hook your hands into the railing. Then you can come in and say hi to your dad. He's just killed your mom.'

Shaun climbed back over and as soon as he turned to walk back in, Duke put a foot in the small of his back and sent him forward, landing against Joe, who stumbled backwards with the weight. Shaun staggered away and Joe lunged for the door, but Duke was too quick, out onto the balcony and gone.

Joe turned to Shaun. 'Get help. Tell the police what's happened. She'll be OK.' He went outside, pushing against the wind. It whistled through his mouth, finding the gaps to create more agony, layering it on top of pain he had never before experienced. When he looked around, the balcony was empty and a lone rope swung in the wind. Joe turned to run back through the lighthouse when he was lit from behind by flashes of blue and white.

'It's the guards,' he shouted to Shaun. 'They'll send an ambulance. I have to go.' He looked down as someone climbed out of the car. 'Fuck,' he said. 'It's Richie.' The guy would never believe him.

O'Connor pulled out a cigarette and lit up. He closed his eyes and sucked in a deep breath. His mobile vibrated once, then rang at the highest volume he could have set.

'Myles, it's Frank Deegan.'

'Where have you been?' barked O'Connor. 'I've been trying to get through to you all afternoon.'

Frank hesitated. 'The Ballyhoura mountains, the coverage is up and down like a yo-yo. I'm nearly back now. I've a bit of news for you. I'll tell you when I see you.'

'No, you fucking won't,' snapped O'Connor.

Frank was stunned. 'Pardon?'

'You'll tell me now, Frank, what the hell is going on.'

'What do you mean? About what? I was finding out about that Mary Casey woman in Doon. That

Duke Rawlins man that Joe Lucchesi was talking about – I've seen what he's done to women back in the States. And it's exactly what happened to that woman in Limerick, except the Americans were arrow wounds, instead of knife wounds. But if all someone had was a knife . . . I've a feeling this crime was more about opportunity than anything else. The man's in the country. I've no doubt about it.' He couldn't hear O'Connor shouting over him to shut up and listen.

'That's Limerick's case,' boomed O'Connor when Frank stopped talking. 'If you kept your eye on the fucking ball here—'

Frank's face burned.

'Look,' said O'Connor, 'you've passed on the information and that's enough—'

'What?' said Frank. 'But what about Katie Lawson? I think he changed his M.O. to make us think that Shaun or Joe—'

'Something's come up with Katie Lawson,' snapped O'Connor. 'Just go straight to the Lucchesi house. Don't go in. I'll see you there.'

Joe ran towards Richie, ready with his explanation, but he didn't need it.

'What the fuck was that?' said Richie. 'Some psycho pulled open my door and smashed in my radio.'

'I need an ambulance for Anna,' said Joe. 'It was him. Rawlins. He's done something to Anna.' They both looked at the shattered radio, sharp shards of plastic sticking out, its wires hanging, useless.

'Where is she?'

'With Shaun in the lighthouse. But . . .' Panic flared in Joe's eyes.

'I know,' said Richie. 'You need to get the fucker. Get in. The ambulance won't take long. I'll use my mobile.'

Richie moved away from the car to find a signal. He spoke urgently, then ran back to the car, starting the engine and screeching across the grass and onto the road.

'He's in a white Ford Fiesta van. He only has about five minutes on us,' said Richie. 'He's gone up the hill. I won't use the lights or siren, he'll panic. Where do you think he's headed?'

'He knows he's screwed,' said Joe. 'He's wanted for too many crimes back home, he knows that now. He'll want to get the fuck out of Dodge, but he won't make it onto any plane.'

'But he could get to England or Wales,' said Richie.

'On the ferry.'

'From Rosslare? Would he know that?'

'The guy is not stupid. He would have planned every bit of this.' 'Do you think we should call Frank?'

Richie raised an eyebrow, 'And follow the rules?' He glanced over at Joe. 'This guy tried to kill your wife . . .'

He got his answer in Joe's silence. They rounded the next bend and sped past the right-hand turn into Manor Road that would have brought them past the church and up through the village. They both glanced right. Richie braked.

'Jesus Christ,' said Joe, slamming his fist onto the glove box. Richie reversed and the abandoned white van came into view. 'What the fuck is he doing in the village?'

Shaun cradled his mother's head on his lap, feeling strange to have her so close. Her eyes were shut, her face pale. He had been rubbing her forehead compulsively for the fifteen minutes since Joe had left. A chill wind was whipping rain around the lighthouse and his ears hurt. He stopped and put his hand over Anna's ear so she wouldn't feel it. His sweatshirt lay across her stomach. He pressed it against her wounds. But he knew there was blood everywhere and he couldn't look down.

Richie parked the car at an angle, its headlights trained on the battered van. Joe jumped out, quickly wrenching the back door open with a crowbar. Empty, the small space seemed huge. He ran back to Richie, squinting against the light.

'Go! Let's go! There's nothing there. He's gone.'

'Fuck,' said Richie, turning the car towards the village, flooring the accelerator.

He hit seventy as he took the next bend, his mind on the chase, not on his driving.

'Jesus Christ, look out!' said Joe.

Richie jammed on the brakes, stunned by the scene ahead. There was no way through. The road outside the church was filled with cars, most of them parked, some of them moving and one at a ninety degree angle, its driver frozen by the speeding squad car bearing down on it. Richie jerked the steering wheel to the left and they spun out of control, skidding across the wet surface, sending up a spray of muddy rainwater, finally shuddering to a stop inches from impact.

'This is fucked up,' said Joe.

Richie jumped out and slammed the door violently. The glove box popped open. An icy fear flooded Joe's body. He grabbed Richie's mobile from the dash and ran. All around him, people were rushing for their cars, struggling with umbrellas in the wind. Drivers flashed headlights and honked their horns. As he ran, Joe hit redial to find Frank's number. Rain splashed onto the screen. He wiped it away and read through the list of dialled calls. Then he bolted, past the church steps where the crowd was at its thickest, where people were beginning to notice something wasn't right. He kept running. A cigarette tip caught on his sleeve, shedding a spray of sparks. Someone cursed behind him. As the crowd thinned out, he caught up with Richie. He dived for his legs, tackling him to the wet tarmac. He turned him over and punched hard, splitting the skin under Richie's eye.

Shaun heard the wail of a siren. Tears started to stream down his face. Lights flashed again outside the lighthouse. He heard the engine cut and shouts in the distance, slowly getting closer.

Joe sped through everything he knew. Richie's anger, his road rage. Ray's puzzled face when he had mentioned it. Ray hadn't said road rage, he'd said 'roid rage. Steroids. Drugs. The edgy coke-fuelled arrogance. Jumpy Richie by Mariner's Strand a month after Katie's death. He was probably there a month before, and would be there the following month too . . . a regular meeting with a dealer he could tip off. An image of Katie standing alone in the dark flashed into his mind. She was holding her mobile and she was calling Frank Deegan because she knew he was the only person she could trust. But she never got the chance to finish the call because a drug-addled six-foot-three keeper of the fucking peace—

Richie punched him in the jaw, sending pain rocketing through him. He staggered backwards and landed hard. A reluctant crowd had started to gather and Richie gestured for them all to stay back. He walked over to where Joe was lying and crouched down beside him.

*   *   *

Frank Deegan took the steps, two at a time, up to the lantern house. He climbed the ladder and raised his head carefully through the trap door. The first thing he saw was blood. He had to put his hands in it to push himself up. He had to sit in it before he could stand. His voice cracked as he called down to O'Connor,

'Get an ambulance, for the love of God, Myles.'

'Shaun,' said Frank gently. 'Who was here?'

'The guy who did this,' he whispered, squeezing his mother. 'My dad's gone after him. He's with Richie.'

Frank looked down at O'Connor. Their eyes locked. O'Connor grabbed his radio.

Joe leaned up into Richie's face. 'I saw your cell phone.'

'Give me that fucking phone,' said Richie, slamming his elbow onto Joe's wrist, releasing his grip.

'You didn't even call Anna her ambulance, you evil son of a bitch. They've found prints on Katie's sneaker from the harbour. Frank told me they'd ruled Shaun out. And you were hoping you could pin this on Duke Rawlins, get me to take care of that—'

'Oh, I think I could pin it on you after this,' he said, nodding towards the people who were starting to move up around them.

Joe snorted. 'They've got no respect for you.'

'Says the loose cannon murdering cop? I'm the

one in uniform here, remember,' Richie hissed. 'You haven't a fucking hope. There are no prints, Joe. And you're covered in blood, for fuck's sake. You're in a strange country. And we look after our own here. No-one's going to believe you. Watch this.' He looked back over his shoulder. 'Someone help me out here,' he shouted, his voice full of authority. 'This guy's a maniac.' Joe looked up at him, amazed. Anger flared inside him. He heaved Richie off him and struggled to his feet. Two stocky men stepped forward to face him, but were blocked by Petey Grant. Petey leaned forward awkwardly, his big hand holding the lapels of his coat tight under his chin. Rain streamed down his pale face.

'You didn't help your friend,' he said, pointing at Richie.

'Joe's not my friend,' said Richie, standing up slowly.

'You didn't help him.'

Richie ignored him and turned back to Joe, his fists clenched.

'You didn't help him!' shouted Petey. 'Your friend! Justin Dwyer. In the sea. I saw you. You stood there. He died.'

'What are you talking about?' said Richie.

'He was crying and you didn't help him—' A gust of wind caught his coat and it swung open, rain soaking quickly through his white shirt.

'It was an accident—', said Richie.

'I know, but you didn't help him. You can swim. Why didn't you help? Why? You were watching him drown. I saw you. I was there. Hide and seek . . .' Petey started crying.

'Shut up, you idiot,' said Richie. 'Just shut the fuck up.'

'No,' sobbed Petey. 'I can't. No.'

For seconds, the only other sound was the falling rain. The crowd stood suspended in confusion, thrown by the violence in Richie's tone, unsure of who the victim was in all the chaos. Mrs Grant stepped forward and reached for Petey's shaking hand. Before she had time to pull him back, he locked eyes with Joe, his face pleading and uncertain. Joe reached out and gripped Petey's shoulder, nodding to him proudly. Then he turned to Richie. 'You son of a bitch,' he said, charging him to the ground. He looked back at the crowd. 'Don't even *think* of trying to stop me. Your guard here . . .' He wanted to roar what Richie had done, but he could see Martha Lawson clinging, terrified, to her sister's arm and he knew he didn't want her to find out this way. Richie got back up quickly. Joe's hand shot out and clamped around his neck.

'You better let me after that bastard or . . .'

'Or what?' smiled Richie, looking over Joe's shoulder. The two men rushed past Petey and grabbed Joe, yanking his arms behind his back.

*   *   *

Anna was rushed from the ambulance into the resuscitation area of Waterford Regional Hospital. Shaun tried to follow, but a nurse laid a gentle hand on his arm and guided him down the corridor to wait in the relatives' room.

Richie was quick with the handcuffs. Joe struggled wildly, pleading with the other men. 'Don't fucking do this to me. Please don't do this to me. My wife is dying. Anna is dying, you fuckers.' He was roaring.

'That's what happens when you attack your own wife,' said Richie. He nodded at the others. 'This is a sick man we're dealing with here.'

'You son of a bitch! At least call an ambulance,' said Joe to the men. 'Someone call an ambulance to Shore's Rock.'

'Don't worry, guys,' said Richie. 'I can take care of that on the radio.'

'He's broken his radio,' shouted Joe hysterically. 'He broke his own radio with his torch. It's in the glove box. There are pieces everywhere.' But Richie was shouting louder, telling the men Joe was unstable, gesturing them away from the car, slamming the door shut, putting his foot to the floor.

The nurse slipped quietly into the relatives' room. She faltered when she saw the blood soaked into Shaun's T-shirt. He made a move to stand up.

'Stay where you are,' she said, sitting down beside him. 'Your mother is very sick. She's critical.'

Shaun thought he was going to cry again. What he didn't realise was that since he got into the ambulance he hadn't stopped.

Joe was paralysed by anger and frustration. He had to get to Anna. His mind sped through options he didn't have.

'Finally,' said Richie.

Joe looked up, but Richie was speaking into his mobile: 'I've been trying you all fucking day.'

Joe remembered the mobile and the fifteen dialled calls to someone called MC.

'Where the hell are you now?' Richie was saying. 'Yeah? Well you stay right fucking there. I'm on my way.'

Shaun rushed into the corridor as soon as he heard the knock on the door.

'What's going on?' he said.

'Is your father here yet?' said the nurse.

'No.'

'I'm sure he'll be here any minute, don't you worry.'

'I hope so.'

'OK, with the type of injuries your mother has suffered, we need to take her to theatre now.'

'What do you mean, the type of injuries?' said Shaun.

'A wound that could seem quite small on the surface, may have caused some internal damage. Maybe not, but it's something we have to look out for.'

'But all that blood . . .' He pointed at his T-shirt.

'Yes, she has lost a lot of blood, but she's also been given six units.' She paused. 'Come on, if you're quick, you can see her before she's brought up.'

Richie drove the car carefully around the deserted square at the centre of the rundown council estate. Weeds pushed up through cracks in the concrete, litter was strewn everywhere and in the corner, Marcus Canney leaned against the last garage in a row of five. Richie made the turn and slowed, pulling to a stop and jumping out of the car. He walked over to Marcus.

'What's the story?'

'No story,' said Richie.

'What have you been up to?'

Richie looked at him. 'Just give me the fuckin' gear.'

'Hold on a minute.'

Marcus stepped sideways, the garage door shot open and four guards burst out, honoured to make this one of Richie Bates' most memorable arrests.

Shaun could barely get past the shock of tubes and wires that connected Anna to monitors he didn't understand. He didn't know where he could touch her. He eventually reached out and put a hand on her forehead. He could sense the urgency of the staff. He didn't want her to go anywhere. She was alive now. He wanted her to stay that way. Surgery might make it worse. People died in surgery.

The tears still fell, but he wiped the last of them away and let out a shaky breath. He knew his words to his mother wouldn't be eloquent and if they were the last words she'd ever have to hear, he knew she wouldn't expect them to be.

He reached down and gently squeezed her finger tips. 'You'll be OK. I promise.' He hesitated. 'You will, Mom. I know you will. You're Lucky too.'

Joe burst through the hospital doors. He was covered in blood – his, Anna's, Richie's.

'I'm so sorry,' said Frank, rushing up to him. 'Rawlins got away, but every guard in the country has been alerted. Anna's just gone to theatre. Shaun's in the relatives' room.' He looked down. 'We had no idea about Richie . . .'

'I know,' said Joe.

He kept walking. He took a left through the door Frank had pointed to. Panic hit him in waves. He rounded a corner. Further down, an elderly woman was leaning against the wall, her body twisted in grief. A young man was trying to support her. Joe's heart lurched. He looked at the row of doors. He knocked on the first one and it was empty. He tried three before he heard a muffled yes. He walked in. Shaun raised his head, then rushed towards him.

'What?' said Joe. 'What?' Shaun clung to his shoulders, sobbing.

Richie Bates was led through the doors of Waterford Garda Station with his hands cuffed behind his back. His jacket gaped where the buttons had been pulled loose and his skin was split from temple to jaw. An old classmate stood by the front desk, slowly shaking his head.

Shaun spoke in anguished bursts, each breath quick and shallow.

'She was messed up real bad. They worked on her in the ambulance . . . and here . . . and now she's in theatre.'

Joe watched Shaun trying to be a grown up. It almost broke his heart. He wondered where he had found the strength after everything he had been through.

'Come here,' he said, pulling Shaun close. 'Come here. You shouldn't have had to deal with this on your own.'

'I'm OK,' said Shaun.

Joe wanted to cry at the simplicity of it. 'That's good,' he said. 'You did good.'

They sat down together and Joe put an arm

around him. He remembered going to the hospital with his mother when he was fourteen and showing none of this strength. She was distraught because she knew she was about to be told she had cancer. And all he was thinking about was himself. He was worried he'd meet the doctor who used to patch him up at the back door whenever he got into a fight.

'I can't do this – just sit here, waiting,' said Joe. 'I'll be back. I need to . . .' He ran for the emergency department. He looked around, panicked. A nurse rushed past him and before he realised it, his hand shot out and he grabbed her arm. 'Please,' he croaked. 'My wife. Anna Lucchesi. Is she . . . tell me is she going to be OK?' He took his hand away. 'I'm sorry, I'm . . .'

'Hold on,' said the nurse, gently. She disappeared behind one of the curtains and brought back the nurse that had spoken with Shaun.

'I don't even know what happened to her . . .' said Joe.

'As soon as she's out of surgery, the doctor will come and talk to you, Mr Lucchesi. We know where to find you. What I can tell you is your wife is critical and we're doing everything we can.' She looked at him with kind eyes. 'You're soaking wet,' she said. 'Let me get you some towels, you can dry off.' She paused. 'Is there anyone you think you might need to call?'

*   *   *

Frank Deegan stood with O'Connor in the waiting area, his head bowed. 'And I was stupid enough to think he wanted to be a guard to save people, to give himself a second chance. But watching that Dwyer boy drown . . . well, some part of him must have got a kick out of it.' He shook his head.

'It was a power thing with Richie,' said O'Connor.

'And this was the only job he thought would give him that? Jesus Christ.'

'How he came to that conclusion . . .'

'Did he feel he had to fight against something?' said Frank. 'But, you know, there was always a fight in him. You could see it there, waiting for a reason to—'

'There's no point,' said O'Connor. 'You didn't know. I didn't know . . .'

'Has the whole world gone mad?' said Frank, his voice cracking. He pulled a white handkerchief out of his pocket and pressed it against his eyes. 'This is it for me,' he said. 'You were right, what you said. I'm on my way out.' He shrugged his shoulders. 'And this is it.'

Joe couldn't bring himself to call Anna's parents. He would wait until he had good news, until she came out of theatre. He sat with Shaun and they tried desperately to fill the growing silences and keep their imaginations from making up the wrong endings. They talked about sport and school and New York and movies and books.

'We could talk about Mom,' said Shaun.

'I can't,' said Joe. 'I just can't.'

The red Renault Clio stood in a quiet corner of a reserved parking lot at Rosslare ferry terminal. Duke Rawlins sat low in the cramped passenger seat. He sensed the presence at the window, then grabbed his bag from the floor and got out.

'Come on,' said Barry Shanley. He was dressed in black combats and a green parka. Underneath he wore a grey T-shirt with a black Apache helicopter and *You Can Run But You Can't Hide* stamped across it. He led Duke along a darkened passageway through a thick wooden door and up a short flight of concrete steps.

'It's through here.' He checked his watch. 'We're going to have to wait a minute.' He leaned back against the wall. The strip light above him shone on his shaved head.

After two hours, a young surgeon knocked on the door. Joe stood up, his heart pounding and nodded for Shaun to stay where he was. He guided the surgeon into the corridor.

'How is she?'

'The surgery went well.'

'What happened to her? I haven't been told.'

'She was hit from behind with an arrow that

pierced her left kidney. It caused some damage to the kidney itself but, more importantly, to the main artery to the kidney. She also suffered a deep cut to her abdomen, but we didn't find any obvious damage to the bowel.'

'Was she assaulted in any other . . .'

'No. That was her only injury.'

'Will there be any long term . . .'

'She will have scars and she may have pain for quite some time, but it should be minimal. She's on her way to ICU. We'll see how the next few hours go. You can see her when she's settled.'

'Thank you,' said Joe. 'Thank you.'

The surgeon nodded, then walked away, leaving Joe standing, shaken, in the empty corridor. He took a deep breath and turned around as Shaun was pulling open the door.

'Your mom is one hell of a toughie,' he said, 'for a short-ass.' And he got the smile he wanted, not the tears.

Duke put a hand firmly on Barry Shanley's arm. 'You're sure this is all good,' he said.

'We always come this way because of my old man,' said Barry. 'Employee privileges.'

Duke stared at him.

'Look, it's cool, OK? Dad's friend will let us on. It's no problem. You're my friend, you're coming with me, we're going to Fishguard. Then I'll get off after you're on board.'

'The guy's gonna say somethin''—'

Barry smiled. 'This guy says nothing to no-one.' He looked through the small frosted glass panel in the door. 'This is all so easy for you, anyway,' he said, glancing back over his shoulder. 'Fucking Delta. Unreal. How can you walk around all normal after fast-roping down from a fucking Black Hawk into the middle of a shitstorm like that? Unreal.'

Duke shrugged. 'You do what you have to do.' *You fuckin' sucker*.

Barry looked back through the glass, then pulled the door open.

'OK. Go, go, go,' he said. And Duke Rawlins went.

EPILOGUE

Joe sat on the cream and gold sofa, staring at the coffee table. A glossy magazine wrapped in plastic lay on top. It was addressed to Pam Lucchesi. Joe slid it towards him and stuck his thumb into a puckered corner, tearing it slowly open, pulling until it came free. *Vogue Living. Rustic Revolution: Alight on the Coast of Ireland*. The cover shot was stunning: the stark white of the lighthouse against a bare platinum sky. He skipped the contents page and flicked through, suspending the moment when the full impact of his former life hit him. His breath caught when the spread finally appeared, the opening two pages of twelve. The house was pristine, warm whites and minimalism. Angles he had never seen the rooms from, perfect candles, unworn shoes and robes.

The kitchen was too empty, no chili sauce on the counter, no boots by the door, no Anna. Until he lifted his hand. Underneath, was the thinnest of shadows, stretching twisted and long-legged across the grass outside the sliding door. She usually refused to be photographed for a feature, but here she was, caught and kept forever in one shot, in shadow. Joe pressed his fingers to his eyes, but there were no tears. Everything he felt was held under pressure in his chest. The last photo in the spread was the lighthouse as it had stood, tragic and shabby and untouched. This was the photo he was still looking at an hour later when Giulio walked in.

'How is she?' he asked.

Joe blinked. 'We haven't spoken in a while. I guess she's doing OK.'

'You know you can go over there any time and I'll look after things here.'

'I'm only just back on the job. They're not gonna to let me take off.'

'I think under the circumstances—'

'Look, honestly? I don't think she's ready to see me yet,' said Joe. 'I'm responsible for the fuck-up that is our lives. And now I'm back catching psychos . . . oh, yeah, minus one pretty important one. You think that'll have her rushing back? Do you think that's something that makes her feel safe?'

'She'll come around. Your job is part of who you are . . . and you do it well.'

Joe raised his eyebrows.

'If I did it so well, Duke Rawlins would never

have gotten out of Ireland. But, no – he's got more freedom than we do, for Christ's sake.'

'Is there any hope of tracking him down?'

'Depends on your definition of hope. I get every shitty update on the investigation, hoping it'll be the one, but . . .' He shrugged. 'And I'm doing what I can. But I don't know. He's smart. He's been getting away with this shit half his life. Who's to say things aren't going to stay that way for the next half?'

'The authorities will find him.'

Joe stared at him. 'I don't want the *authorities* to find him.'

Silence stretched between them.

Joe took a deep breath. 'I think Anna needs to stay with her parents for now.'

'Maybe,' said Giulio. 'For now.'

'I just don't know how to help her. In the middle of the night, she's crying, I can't tell her it was only a nightmare and it's not real and it's never going to happen. What the hell use is that?' He exhaled slowly. 'And then there's her blaming me, which I know she can do nothing about right now. He said he'd kill her and Shaun. Not me. She knows that. He wanted a world of pain for me, but he didn't want to see me dead. No, I had to live through it all, like he did with whatever fucked-up life he had.'

He paused. 'And you know what? I have my own nightmares.'

'Time will take care of that.'

'Anna's not even forty and she's already hovered on a flatline. She's in pain, she's got scars she can't bear to look at. She keeps calling, wanting to know where Shaun is, who he's with, what he's doing. I'm not gonna tell her he's been drinking and out late. You've seen him. You've seen how hard it is to stop him. What do I do? Do I take the chance he'll come out the other end in better shape? I don't know what the hell I'm doing here. When Shaun talks to her on the phone, he's so patient. They have this weird bond. And I'm just this person watching. It's like they're afraid of me.'

As Giulio reached down to put a hand on Joe's shoulder, he saw the magazine. He picked it up and brought it close.

'Her work is very impressive.'

Joe nodded. 'Here, listen to this.' He took the magazine and read out the small type at the end of the page. '"*Anna Lucchesi is on vacation. For more details on this feature, please contact Chloe Da Silva.*"'

Joe laughed. 'Vacation? Jesus Christ. I wish.'

He leaned back and looked out the window to where Shaun sat on a low wooden bench in his oversized parka. He was bent forward, his legs crossed at the ankle, his mobile phone pressed to his ear. His breath was misting the cold air.

He snapped the phone shut and jogged towards the window. He was smiling, then mouthing something Joe couldn't make out. He gestured for him to open the latch.

'It's Mom,' he said. 'She's leaving Paris tonight. She's coming home, Dad.'

ACKNOWLEDGMENTS

I thank my agent, Darley Anderson, for his belief, enthusiasm and kindness. And for all their hard work, I thank everyone at The Darley Anderson Literary Agency.

Thanks to my publisher, Lynne Drew, for her insight and guidance.

Thanks to Amanda Ridout for her vision and thanks to everyone on the brilliant team at HarperCollins.

For outstanding achievement in editing and entertaining, thanks to my gifted editor, Wayne Brookes.

For their constant and gracious support, thanks to Moira Reilly and Fiona McIntosh.

For their expertise and their generosity in sharing it with a rookie, thanks to Ron Campbell, Dr Stuart Carr MRCSEd (A&E), Professor Marie Cassidy, Gerry Charlton Barrister-at-Law, Joan Deitch, Dick Driscoll, Jim Fuxa, Colin Hennessy, Martyn Linnie, Brett McHale, Tony O'Shea. They do the facts, I do the fiction; any mistakes are mine.

For their faith, love and laughter, I owe so much to my beloved family.

For their encouragement and the perfect environment for work and play, thanks to Sue Booth-Forbes, Maureen and Donal O'Sullivan and family, Anna Phillips, Una Brankin, Mary Maddison, Maggie Deas and Matthew Higgins.

Thanks to all my wonderful friends.

Special thanks to Brian and Dee for grabbing on, taking the leap and never ever letting go.

Coming soon

THE CALLER
by
Alex Barclay